SWEET SEDUCTION

"Carson?" Aurelia called softly. "Will you come here and . . . and kiss me?"

He stepped toward her, then hesitated.

"Please?" she asked.

He took another step, knelt on one knee, and bent to place a quick, chaste kiss on her lips.

Before he could rise, she reached around his neck and pulled his face to hers. As their lips met, excitement coursed down her spine. She opened her lips to his passion and felt his shoulders quiver beneath her fingers.

Her body came to life beneath his exploring lips and hands. She trembled in his arms, pulled him closer, held him tighter. Tonight would be all they'd ever have together, and she never wanted to let him go. . . .

VIVIAN VAUGHAN

Silver Surrender

ZEBRA BOOKS
KENSINGTON PUBLISHING CORP.

ZEBRA BOOKS

are published by

Kensington Publishing Corp.
850 Third Avenue
New York. NY 10022

Second Printing: August 1996

Printed in the United States of America

To Raul and Blanca Macias
Fellow travelers in search of Catorce

Chapter One

Real de Catorce, Mexico
September 1878

Aurelia Mazón took the stairs leading to the third floor of the Leal mansion two at a time. When she burst through the ornate double doors of the ballroom, the babble of a dozen girls ceased.

"Aurelia, you're late," Pia Leal admonished.

"I can explain." Aurelia caught her breath, feeling guilty. Anytime Pia used her baptismal name, Aurelia knew her best friend's patience had worn thin.

Señora Velez, the dressmaker, shoved a bundle of yellow satin and lace into Aurelia's arms. *"Andale, niña.* Hurry and get into your gown. Stand on that stool so we can finish the fittings before Vespers."

Around the room the other girls struggled into masses of lace in every shade of the rainbow. Most already stood on footstools, patiently awaiting the attention of the seamstresses Señora Velez had hired to help her put together the grandest wedding Catorce had ever seen. The ballroom of the Leal mansion had been converted to a sewing room for the purpose.

Pia stood in the center of the room, wearing a white satin chemise onto which three women pinned tiers of intricate Spanish lace.

Aurelia hurried to follow the señora's instructions, tugging and pulling her own clothing over her head. "Oh, Pia, you'll be the most beautiful bride in the whole world."

"And you will be the most beautiful maid of honor, Relie," Pia grinned, "if we get your gown fitted."

Fortunately, Pia's aggravation never lasted long. Together with Zita Tapis, they had been best friends all their lives. Aurelia moved her footstool to a position between the two girls.

"What have you been up to, Relie?" Zita whispered.

"Nothing."

"Your black eyes are dancing," Pia accused.

"With the devil," Zita added. "We're in for trouble."

Aurelia discarded her dress in a heap on the floor behind her, then wriggled into the yellow sheath and took her place on the stool. "Papá was home from the mine." She smiled broadly. "So I waited to hear his plans."

On either side of her, Pia and Zita inhaled deep breaths, to the consternation of the seamstresses who pinned their gowns.

"Stand still," one commanded.

"You don't want to walk down the aisle with a crooked ruffle," another admonished.

"Don't worry," Aurelia assured her friends. "Everything will be fine, like I told you."

"Like *I* feared." Zita moved a quarter turn away at the seamstress's instructions.

8

"Don't worry," Aurelia repeated. She lifted her chin, stretching her spine to her full height. Even without the footstool, she stood half a head taller than Zita and a full head above the petite Pia. Her additional inches always calmed her friends, instilling confidence in them. Nevertheless, when she spoke she purposefully avoided their eyes, concentrating instead on the seamstress who adjusted and pinned a ruffle of yellow lace around the scooped neckline of her yellow chemise.

"Papá is the one who is worried. He assured us if it happens one more time, he will send Mamá and me to Guanajuato to live with Tía Guadalupe and Tío Luís until the danger is past."

Turning at the seamstress's instructions, she ignored the silence that greeted her pronouncement.

"No," Zita mouthed.

"My wedding is in less than two months, Relie," Pia implored.

"I will return for your wedding, silly. Do you think I would miss the wedding of my best friend to my own brother?"

"What if my parents decide to do the same thing?" Zita asked. "What if—?"

"Don't worry," Aurelia insisted again. "Everything will work out." She heard additional intakes of breath from either side.

"Like always," Zita hissed. "You forget that I don't want to move away from Real de Catorce. Only you are determined to escape."

That was true, of course. Even the mention of her determination to escape this high-mountain prison—her term for their opulent but isolated home in the

9

eastern Sierra Madres—renewed Aurelia's resolve to do so.

But it would not do to upset the girls until she could get them alone and explain her plan. Adeptly, she changed the subject.

"Santos is coming tonight, Pia. Papá sent for him to discuss ways of stopping the difficulties at the mine. Mamá expects him by Vespers."

Zita sighed. "At least we will have a quiet night. You wouldn't dare drag us out when Pia wants to be with her betrothed."

"Will Lucinda accompany you to Vespers?" Pia asked.

Aurelia tilted her chin at a jaunty angle. "Sí. I have made arrangements for us to ride together. Mamá can tell Santos where we are."

The fittings completed, Pia's dozen bridesmaids drifted out of the converted ballroom. Under Aurelia's watchful eye, each girl hugged Pia's petite figure, reminding Aurelia of Pia's own problem. Tonight she must deal with that, too. A girl could not go to her wedding night filled with the kind of fears Pia had expressed. Especially not when the solution was so simple.

Would that the solution to her own problem were as easily accomplished! In two months her best friend would wed her brother, and he, traitor that he was, would spirit his new bride away from Real de Catorce to live at Rancho Mazón in the low country.

"You will visit us," Pia had assured Aurelia time and again. "Why, you can marry one of Santos's charro compadres—Rodrigo Fraga, perhaps—and we will both live happily ever after."

10

Happily ever after? Aurelia had thought. Happily ever after did not mean isolating herself on a ranch in the low country any more than it meant remaining here in Real de Catorce, a virtual prisoner of her parents.

Not that they were deprived in this town of over seven thousand inhabitants and five plazas. They had a cathedral and convent school and as much social life as could be fitted into a year with only three hundred sixty-five days.

Local silver mines financed a luxurious lifestyle for the owners, while the miners' families provided an ample service pool. Incoming trains brought necessities, luxuries, and catalogues and periodicals from around the world, which described more luxuries to be sent away for.

"We have everything right here in Catorce a girl could ever dream of wanting," her father, Don Domingo Mazón, always replied when she begged him to let her move to Guanajuato and live with Tía Guadalupe, her mother's sister, and Tío Luís, who was being spoken of as the next governor of the state of San Luís Potosí.

"My dreams have wings," Aurelia would retort. "My dreams cannot be bound by the walls of a high-mountain prison."

To which her father, miner and businessman, always assured her she would outgrow such foolishness. Then he established the Casa de Moneda Mazón—a duly sanctioned mint, establishing Real de Catorce as a financial center of some repute.

Afterwards, his position became as implacable as if his brain were carved from the hard rock of the mountain itself.

11

Her mother was no help, either, even though it had been the life of the young Bella Lopez that had influenced Aurelia's dreams. Doña Isabella Mazón de Lopez, now a mother and middle-aged, apparently had forgotten her early years at the Court of Maximilian in the City of Mexico, years Aurelia learned about from Tía Guadalupe, who told wonderful stories of the Lopez girls and their troops of virile young suitors and of the lavish parties they attended. These stories had inspired Aurelia's most romantic dreams and ambitions. Doña Bella Mazón might have forgotten the details of her romantic youth, but Tía Guadalupe kept them alive for Aurelia.

If anything, her mother's lack of romanticism made Aurelia even more determined to escape. She would not end up like her mother, she vowed, no matter how easy Isabella's life was with servants and silks and charities to attend to.

Everyone in Real de Catorce, especially the poor people from the miners' villages, considered Doña Bella the incarnation of their own personal guardian angel. From the ten children of Nuncio Quiroz, superintendent of the Mazón mine, to the family of the lowliest miner, she appeared at precisely the right time to birth their babies, to dress their dead, and to perform countless other ministrations in between. Which was well and good. Everyone should have such a benefactress. But Aurelia herself did not intend to become one — certainly not at the tender age of twenty-two.

Doña Bella, as always, had her own plans for Aurelia. "Don't rock the boat, Relie. Marry Enrique and Papá will build you a villa on the hill next to ours."

Enrique Villasur complicated the problem. Hired

12

by her father as the dashing young president of Casa de Moneda Mazón, he had become a regular dinner guest at the Mazón mansion. Aurelia suspected her father's intentions in hiring Enrique went beyond the man's position at the mint, well beyond, extending to that of intended son-in-law to the mint owner.

That, she knew, was preposterous. Nothing was more important to Don Domingo than his mint, unless it was his mine. No, she had no illusions about her father promoting Enrique as a candidate for her husband with anything more in mind than keeping control of the mint in the family — and silencing her pleas to leave Catorce.

Her father was right about Real de Catorce containing everything a girl could wish for. Aurelia didn't lack one single thing — except freedom. Freedom to live her own life, freedom to see the world around her. Why, she could grow up, grow old, and die right here without ever seeing the outside world. And she would if her parents had their way.

"Freedom?" her mother had inquired the one time Aurelia voiced that word. "You are free to breathe, Relie. You are free to live in the world our Lord God provided, but you are not free to complain about it in my house. You have visited the miners' shacks. You have seen their women, old and worn out before their time. I will hear no more complaints from a girl who has everything her heart *should* desire."

Aurelia had known then she would be forced to take matters into her own hands. Hers and those of her two inseparable friends, Pia and Zita.

Her method of escape had not been difficult to arrive at. Her father himself had provided the answer.

13

She could not count the number of times she had heard him say, "Hit a man where he is most vulnerable, he will go down every time. Like in the *colear* at the *charriada*—grab the bull by the tail. That will show him who is boss."

She didn't have to think twice to determine Don Domingo Mazón's most vulnerable spot—his business. If she could find a way to put his business in jeopardy—or to make him think his business was in jeopardy—she could show him who was boss.

Nor did it take long for her to decide how to accomplish such a feat.

"Not again, Relie," Pia implored. "My wedding is so close."

The carriage bounced along the bricked streets, carrying the two girls toward Zita's house, from where they would go to Vespers. Aurelia had insisted on picking up Pia before Zita, even though Zita lived much closer.

She had also persuaded Lucinda, her dueña, to ride on the box with the driver. It didn't take much to persuade Lucinda of such things, since the chatter of three girls did nothing to soothe one's thoughts in preparation for Vespers. Lucinda had learned from experience that stopping the chatter of these three girls was impossible short of separating them.

"We will talk about my plan after we pick up Zita," Aurelia told Pia. "First, we must discuss your problem."

Pia raised her eyebrows.

"Your wedding night," Aurelia reminded her. "When

14

you see Santos at the cathedral, you must tell him."

Pia's face glowed in the early evening dusk. "I don't want to talk about this, Relie."

"We must. Your fears will ruin the romance of your wedding night. Santos is a giant and you . . . well, you are no bigger than a honeybee. You have to do it."

"I can't." Pia crossed her arms protectively over her bosom, as if that were the part of her anatomy under discussion.

"Yes, you can. Santos will understand. And I'm sure he will be willing. All you have to do is tell him. Tonight. He is meeting us at Vespers."

"Relie, please. Let's not talk about it."

"You don't have much time, Pia. Santos won't be back in town often before the wedding. Just tell him, plain and simple, that you want to try it out before the wedding."

"Try it out?" Pia whispered.

Aurelia shrugged, exasperated with her friend's modesty. The carriage rocked to a stop. "Zita is coming, Pia. Now listen to me, quick. Your wedding night is supposed to be romantic. It can't be if you are afraid of the size of his—"

"Relie!"

Aurelia reached across the aisle and patted Pia's knee in a motherly fashion. "If you can't bring yourself to tell Santos you want to make love to him before the wedding, I'll tell him for you."

"Aurelia Mazón, you do that and I will never speak to you again."

Zita reached the carriage before Pia finished speaking. "What are you two arguing about?"

"Nothing," Pia whispered.

15

"Now about our next mission," Aurelia began after the carriage had pulled into the street. "Papá said they will ship another load of coins tomorrow night. I'll make sure Lucinda is properly worried about Señora Garcia's dying child to stay at the cathedral for a novena. That will give us more than enough time to slip away and be back before she misses us."

"Find another way, Relie," Pia pleaded.

"There isn't another way. This will be the last time, I promise."

Zita laughed, a high-pitched, nervous twitter. "If I had a centavo for every time you said that about one of your schemes, I would have as much money as your father has in his mint."

"*Our* schemes," Aurelia corrected, undaunted.

"The *our* part was when we were young," Pia reminded her.

"We are still young."

"We aren't children dressing up in disguise to play tricks on people," Zita admonished. "Robbing a train is not a trick."

"I know," Aurelia told them. "This is serious. But it's the only way. I sent María with a message for Kino and Joaquín. They will meet us at Vespers so we can work out the details. Last time went so well, we shouldn't have any trouble."

When Pia spoke, her voice trembled. "I don't see how this is going to help you, Relie. And my wedding—"

"Didn't you hear me this afternoon? Papá said if there is one more train robbery, he will send Mamá and me to Guanajuato." She hugged herself with excitement. "Once I get there, he can't make me come

16

home." The carriage stopped before the Cathedral of San Francisco. She winked at Pia. "Or were you too busy thinking about what you and Santos are going to do tonight to listen to my plans?"

"Relie!"

Inside, the church was dark. The music had just begun. Leaving Lucinda in the Mazón family pew, the girls headed for the vestry to don choir robes. The dueña's admonishment rang in their ears.

"Behave yourselves now. I can see everything that goes on in the choir loft from this pew."

"Don't worry, Lucinda. I won't embarrass the family."

It was the most ingenious arrangement Aurelia had ever devised, and she continually reminded herself of its usefulness. Since their mothers preferred to attend morning services, they were only too happy to send the girls to Vespers accompanied by one or the other's dueña. Lucinda was Aurelia's favorite. Not that she was dim-witted or anything.

The service of Vespers began in a darkened cathedral, and even after the office candles were lighted, the church remained dimly lit. Once the girls were encased in voluminous black choir robes with heavy cowls, their own mothers would not have been able to identify them from the family pews in the nave. Three bodies in the choir belonged to Aurelia, Pia, and Zita — or did they? Even other choir members, nuns from the convent mostly, remained unaware of the girls' subterfuge. After all, each and every person present was supposed to be engrossed in his or her own prayers.

All they needed were stand-ins. And stand-ins were

easily obtained with a little gold. Kino and Joaquín from El Astillero, an Indian village in the foothills, had always been agreeable to Aurelia's schemes. Not only did her intrigues relieve the monotony of daily life in the hills—she had yet to come up with something that didn't involve a measure of danger—but the boys could use the coins for serious things such as food, clothing, and medicines for their families.

Tonight María, a sister to Kino and Joaquín who was employed as Aurelia's personal maid, and two of their other sisters waited in the vestry, robed in choir vestments. From the chancel, Padre Antonio Bucareli could be heard beginning the service.

"The Lord Almighty grant us a peaceful night and a perfect end. Amen."

The organist's prelude resonated through the cavernous cathedral.

Quickly, the girls grabbed robes.

"Not you, Pia," Aurelia whispered. "Santos is waiting by the sacristy door."

Pia frowned. "He's already here?"

"I told him to meet you—"

"Aurelia Mazón, that had better be all you told him."

Aurelia hugged her friend. *"Suerte."* She and Zita turned toward the hallway and their clandestine meeting with Kino and Joaquín. "Good luck," she called to Pia again.

Behind her Pia watched the two of them sneak down the hall leading from the vestry, while the three village girls crept into the three empty places in the choir loft and knelt to pray. She turned, a prayer of a different sort whispering from her lips.

Santos Mazón loomed as a giant shadow in the sacristy doorway. The moment Pia saw him, her anxieties fled in anticipation of being alone with him. Without a word, he reached for her and gently pulled her through the door where, leaning back against the wall of the cathedral, he enfolded her in his massive arms and kissed her fervently.

"I've missed you, little one," he whispered.

"Yo también." She snuggled into his embrace. "I missed you, too, but in less than two months we will be married."

He held her close, reclaiming her lips, stroking them, feeling his need for her build. Finally, he caught up her hand and led her away from the cathedral. In the near dusk with the nuns at Vespers, he felt free to hold her hand. Above them the sky was turning dark, leaving only the surrounding hilltops illuminated by brilliant sprays of golden light from the sun, which had already set behind them. The same way his body was illuminated by fiery streaks of passion every time he was anywhere near Pia, he thought.

He guided her to a secluded part of the churchyard, where the nuns had planted a flower garden overlooking a precipice. One of the padres had built an elaborate little park with a fountain and a shrine to San Francisco, flanked by a couple of iron benches. Santos sat on the bench furthest from the cathedral and drew Pia onto his lap.

"Tell me what you've been doing."

She laughed, completely mesmerized by his presence, by his arms around her, by the moonlight on his loving face. "Attending to wedding preparations, of course. Today we had fittings. Señora Velez may never

19

forgive me for having twelve bridesmaids."

"Which reminds me," he said. "You can stop worrying about my attendants. They have all accepted. Eleven charros and my friend Jarrett, the Texas Ranger. He agreed to serve as best man. You're going to like him, Pia."

"Jarrett?" she asked. "He has only one name?"

He laughed. "The Jarrett clan includes so many brothers, everyone gets their names confused. To keep from stumbling, we call them all Jarrett."

"Padre Bucareli needs his complete name," she told him. "Since he isn't Catholic, the padre must petition the bishop for permission before he can serve in the wedding."

"Carson," Santos supplied. "Carson Jarrett's the one coming. You're going to like him."

Resting her elbows on his shoulders, she played her fingers through his thick black hair. "I don't have to like him, I *love* you."

"Not like I love you." He pulled her close, covering her lips with his own, smiling at her timid passion. She always returned his kisses eagerly but stiffened if his tongue touched her lips. She allowed him to hold her breasts through layers of clothing, but if he began to fondle them, she moved discreetly away. And she was always careful not to press the lower part of her body to his.

Not that he minded. He knew she loved him. He could wait for the rest. In less than two months she would be his wife; then he would teach her all the ways to please her man — and all the ways her man could please her.

Swaying against the sensual strokes of his lips, Pia

nestled herself into his lap, feeling quite suddenly the firm evidence of his passion. It wasn't the first time she had felt this, of course. Usually, she maneuvered herself a modest inch or so away, but tonight this physical reminder of what lay ahead brought Aurelia's instructions to mind. Pia tensed.

"What is it, little one?" Santos held her face so that their lips brushed when he talked. "Am I going too fast?"

For a moment she could do no more than stare at him, recalling Aurelia's instructions, Aurelia's threat — her own problem. As usual, Aurelia's outrageous solution was the only one that made any sense.

But she couldn't *tell* him. How could she *say* such a thing? Suddenly, she began kissing him hungrily. At the same time, she wound her arms more tightly about his shoulders, pulling his chest to hers.

Once she began, he responded. Soon she realized all she had to do was reverse the tricks she had learned to avert his rising passion during these last few months of courtship.

Remembering his response when she had inadvertently touched one of his ears during an earlier tryst, Pia now ran a finger lightly around its outer rim, then behind it. The moan this elicited brought to mind another tactic she had used.

Recalling his tongue pressed against her closed lips, she opened her mouth and was delighted with the response. His subsequent exploration sent shivers down the back of her neck and caused her to wriggle with a far different intent on his lap.

Although she knew her face must glow at her boldness, his ardent reaction fueled an increasingly urgent demand inside her. This time when he reached to cup one of her breasts, instead of holding rigid, she pressed into him, inviting him to continue.

In the end, however, he shifted her to the bench beside him with a throaty apology. "I'm getting carried away."

She pulled his face back to hers. "I am, too."

He stared at her a minute, tempted, oh so tempted. "No." He sighed. "We can wait. I can wait. It isn't fair to you."

"But? . . ." *Now what was she supposed to do?* "What if. . . . I mean, what if I want you to continue?"

After a long pause, he clasped her to his chest. She heard his heart thump through his heavy shirt. "You are too good to me, little one. Still, it would be taking advantage of you."

"It isn't taking advantage if I . . . I mean, I want it to be good for you, Santos."

His hands were so large he could cradle her head in the two of them. He did so now, looking into her face, loving her with his eyes. Then, slowly, he kissed her — her lips, her eyes, her chin. "It will be, Pia. Believe me, our wedding night will be the best night of my life — and of yours. Except for all the wonderful nights that will come after it. I may look like nothing but a big old clumsy lunk, but I know a little about romance. A park bench isn't romantic enough for our first time."

"Oh, Santos." She hugged him tightly, rejoicing that she had found such a man. And since she had, she certainly couldn't hurt his feelings by telling him she was afraid of him. Besides, knowing her fears would probably make him more determined to wait until they were married. Embarrassed over the boldness she had already shown, she sat back and shyly kissed his lips. "Relie said—"

Santos frowned. "Relie? What outrageous scheme is my sister cooking up this time?"

"Nothing. I mean, nothing about . . ." Pia hedged. "Santos, you must persuade your father to send her to Guanajuato. She wants so desperately to go."

"I know she does. But there is nothing I can do. When Papá makes up his mind, the Lord above can't change it."

"We have to find her a husband then."

"Enrique—"

"She doesn't want to marry Enrique. She wants to live someplace else. She wants to live like your Tía Guadalupe. She wants a life full of glamour and parties. If she can't go to Guanajuato, we must find her something else. What about your Texas Ranger friend?"

"Jarrett?" Santos hee-hawed. "Jarrett provide a life of glamour and parties?" He shook his head. "No, Pia, we will have to look elsewhere for a beau for Relie."

Chapter Two

The following evening after Vespers, the same three Indian girls waited in the dark wings of a side chapel to replace a confident Aurelia and a reluctant Pia and Zita. Not only had Aurelia persuaded the pious Lucinda to observe a novena for Señora Garcia's dying child, but she had convinced the dueña to spend the entire nine hours of prayer in the cathedral, five of which had elapsed by the time Vespers was over. The four more required for the novena would give the girls ample time to carry out their scheme and return undetected.

"What if she becomes suspicious and investigates?" Zita questioned after the three girls had left the cathedral. They scurried up a side street, clad now in dark trousers and light shirts, with serapes over their shoulders and wide-brimmed sombreros on their heads.

"She didn't last time." Aurelia led her two companions toward the tunnel at the far end of town, by way of back roads and alleys. Darkness had begun to set in, and a few stars had come out.

"Things don't always work *like last time*," Pia reminded her. "I can read it now: *The wedding of Pia Leal*

24

and Santos Mazón was canceled after the bride robbed the groom's father's train. She will spend the rest of her life in prison."

Aurelia laughed. Her spirits were never so high as at the beginning of one of their adventures.

"Nothing can go wrong," she assured them. "Kino and Joaquín have the difficult part. We will wait inside the chapel until the guards get off the train . . ."

"What if they don't?" Zita hissed.

"Zita, you know as well as I do that when Nuncio Quiroz is on board, the train always stops at the chapel. Why do you think they call him padre instead of superintendent?"

"They don't mean it like that?" Zita replied.

"He never passes up a chance to pray in the tunnel chapel," Pia recited, adding, "except one day he might."

"Some say he does more than pray in that chapel. What if he is meeting a—?"

"The plan is perfect," Aurelia assured them. "Don't worry."

"I tell you, they won't fall for the same thing twice," Zita continued.

Aurelia cocked her head, tilting her chin at a jaunty angle—a gesture that either enchanted her companions or aggravated them, depending on the occasion. "Kino and Joaquín promised to think of something different."

When her friends sighed, she laughed. "Come on, you sillies. We only have an hour until the extra guards arrive at the tunnel."

"I'm not walking through that tunnel," Pia insisted.

"We aren't going through the tunnel," Aurelia supplied. "We will go over the top like before."

"I wish I had your nerve, Relie," Pia sighed.

"I'm glad you don't," Zita told her. "If two of us were crazy, none of us would have reached the age of twenty-two."

Carved into the mountain in the middle of the tunnel, Santa Bárbara Chapel was dedicated to the patron saint of miners. Her image was found on almost all the many tunnels in the area, but this was the only place where a duly consecrated chapel had been carved into the mountain itself.

Since this tunnel wound through the mountain, making it impossible to see from one end to the other, most engineers and any of their crew who had traveled the line into Real de Catorce more than a few times made the obligatory stop at the chapel. Their lives were in the hands of Santa Bárbara, whom they hoped would protect them against being hit head-on by a train traveling in the opposite direction.

The chapel had a second little known entrance on top of the mountain. No more than a set of steps dug into the mountain straight down to the floor of the chapel, it was entered by a small door to the right of the altar. Most people figured the door concealed a sacristy where the priest could change into his vestments. The ladies of the church made it known that neither valuables nor communion wine were left there between services. No sense tempting an otherwise honest person to fall into sin by stealing from Santa Bárbara.

The girls found the opening behind a rock shrine surrounded by *mizquitl* trees and cacti. Lighting a lantern, Aurelia led her friends down the steep, dusty passageway into the earth itself. She had taken a key from the ring her mother kept in a drawer, and although it had worked last time, she exhaled a long-held breath when the door creaked open on rusty hinges. After they stepped into the chapel, the other girls exhaled.

"It looks empty," Zita whispered.

"It's too dark to tell," Pia objected.

Aurelia held her tongue. She never expressed concern to her friends, usually because the situations they found themselves in were of her own doing and she could hardly admit trepidation.

"We can't see a thing," Pia whispered. "What if someone is here?"

"Whoever is here tonight," Aurelia assured them, "is sleeping off a drunk and won't run tell our parents."

"Or having a tryst," Zita added, calling to mind the romantic stories that circled school about girls from the miners' camp meeting their beaus in the chapel for a rendezvous. Nuncio Quiroz was rumored to meet girls from El Astillero here. Aurelia had always intended to ask María about that, but she had yet to remember. Reports varied concerning exactly what went on at such a time.

While they talked, Aurelia set the lantern on the altar, then searched for her tin of matches in the pocket of her breeches. Finally, she removed her serape and tossed it to the front pew, then withdrew the small tin she had brought from the Mazón kitchen.

"That reminds me of Santos," she said. "Did you talk to him last night, Pia?" She struck a match and began lighting the candles that stood in permanently affixed iron holders on the altar.

"Of course, I talked to him," Pia retorted. With a great deal of emphasis, she added, "We never left the

27

garden, Relie. What else could we do but talk for a whole hour while our stand-ins sang Vespers and you plotted our criminal future?"

Zita giggled, a high-pitched, nervous laugh. "Kiss, of course." She turned to Aurelia. "What are you doing? We don't need the candles lighted."

"Or *more*," Aurelia suggested to Pia. With the altar candles lit, she removed the globe from a wall lantern by the side of their escape door, touching a match to the wick. "And yes, we do need the candles lighted."

Pia favored her friend with a stern look. "Why?"

"Why *more?*" Aurelia teased.

"Why do we need light?"

"You will see." Aurelia studied the bare altar. "I should have brought a chalice and cruets and a missal and—"

"A chalice? . . . What are you doing?" Zita demanded.

"Kino and Joaquín have an ingenious plan. I should have thought of it myself. Like you suggested, another accident so soon after the last would be too obvious. They decided to hang a lantern on the bracket outside the door. You know, the signal that Mass is being read. The engineer will be obliged to stop for a service, in case Nuncio Quiroz passes up a chance to pray."

"I suppose you intend to play the part of the priest," Zita accused.

"We won't need a priest."

"When the crew finds no priest, Relie," Pia argued, "they will return to the train."

"Not until they have waited a while."

"A while?" Zita's voice quivered.

"Long enough," Aurelia assured them.

At that moment the outer door of the chapel creaked open to admit two figures, one of whom carried a lantern.

"Kino," Aurelia called. "Is everything in place?"

"*Sí*. As soon as we hear the whistle, I will hang the lantern. Joaquín and I will wait on the other side of the tunnel in that hollow made by the wreck of the Victoria Express."

Joaquín studied the girls. "And yourselves?"

"We will kneel in one of the back pews," Aurelia told him. "After the crew enters the chapel, we'll come help you unload the coins. In the dark we should pass for members of the crew, don't you think?"

The boys nodded.

"In case we are rushed afterwards, remember to bury the empty crates in a canyon where they can never be found," Aurelia instructed them.

"*Sí*," the boys replied.

"And this time," Pia worried, "the money must be taken further away than Ciudad Victoria. At least to Monterrey. The Federales will certainly be out combing the hills for the money."

"Papá will see to that," Aurelia agreed.

At the sound of the train whistle, they all jumped. "*¡Andale!*" Kino called. "We must hurry and hang the lantern. Be ready to work quickly."

The lantern stopped the train as the boys had predicted, only this time the crew was leery. Instead of everyone disembarking to pray in the chapel, Nuncio Quiroz left a guard with the crates of minted coins.

Fortunately, Kino and Joaquín were positioned on the opposite side of the train. When the girls sneaked out of the chapel and climbed on board, the guard challenged them.

Aurelia had no more than cleared her throat, hoping her voice would pass for a boy's, when Joaquín swung a club from behind, felling the guard.

Pia gasped. "Did you kill him?"

"Of course not," Aurelia hissed. "*¡Andale!*" She rushed toward the crates.

While Joaquín dragged the guard into the hollow where he and Kino had waited, Kino produced the same clippers he had used the time before and began cutting the cables that bound the crates of coins to the side of the car.

"*¡Andale!*" Pia whispered.

"How many crates do you want?" Kino questioned.

"Only a few," Aurelia told him. "Just enough to make my father feel vulnerable."

In the end they took five crates of minted coins. The boys lugged them into the hollow behind a stack of rocks. Since the powerful beam of the train's headlamp pointed straight ahead, it was unlikely the hollow would be noticed in the darkness.

According to plan, the three girls blended into the darkness, then merged with the men who exited the chapel grumbling about the priest not showing up.

Excitement erupted the moment the engineer stepped into the car and found the crates and the guard missing. The girls worked their way back inside the now-empty chapel, to the sound of pebbles flying against the rails as the crew dashed ahead toward the far end of the tunnel. The whistle blew.

Surreptitiously, the girls tiptoed through the chapel, extinguished the candles on the altar and the lantern beside the door, then headed for the passageway beside it.

Not until she had locked the door behind her did Aurelia recall her serape, which lay forgotten on the front pew. Although she doubted it could be used to identify her, she dared not take the chance.

"Wait for me at the shrine," she called to the girls, who were already halfway up the steps.

Quickly, she darted back into the chapel, rushed to the pew, and felt for the forgotten clothing.

An arm grabbed hers.

"So, I catch a thief." The words echoed menacingly through the pitch-dark chapel. "Where were you hiding?"

"Hiding?" she whispered.

"And the coins?"

"Coins?"

The arm jerked her around. She fell against a taut, muscled body. "You are no thief."

"Thief?" Aurelia felt weak. Her heart pounded so hard it hurt, or was that her fear? She had heard of fear causing a person's heart to stop. Was her heart stopping here in this dark chapel?

"You are nothing but a damned woman." As if to be certain, he jerked both her arms, throwing her chest against his own.

Aurelia froze. The dismay in her assailant's voice did nothing to conceal its familiarity. She knew this man.

Nuncio Quiroz.

She struggled to free herself, fearful now to speak lest he recognize her voice as well.

Nuncio Quiroz, her father's mine superintendent.

He gripped her arms tightly, hurting her. "Where is your lover, *puta?* Or were you waiting here for me?"

Desperately, she kicked at his shins with her booted feet. The word *puta,* whore, rang like a funeral dirge inside her head. Nuncio Quiroz had molested her with his eyes every time she'd gone into the miners' camp with her mother, until at length she had stopped going.

"Your lover cannot meet you tonight, *puta,*" Quiroz gloated, maneuvering her flailing arms behind her. "My men are chasing him down the tracks even now. And we are alone. Your lover stole my load of coins. How 'bout I steal his piece of fun?"

Aurelia felt like a caged animal, frightened, panicked. Her fear of Nuncio Quiroz had nothing to do with the robbery now, nor even with the fact that he worked for her father. Her fear of this man stemmed from the way he always made her flesh crawl by the very lust in his eyes.

Now he held her in his hands, and she struggled to free herself.

"Have you no voice, my little thief? No matter." His shaggy hair touched her face in the darkness and she jerked her head away, wrenching her neck in the process.

"Hold still now." His greater strength overpowered her and his lips slid across her face, wetting her cheek, while his hands worked behind her, transferring both her flailing arms to one of his large, work-strengthened hands.

She had heard it said that the double-jack hammer created muscles out of the weakest flesh. Nuncio Quiroz was known as one of the best double-jack men in the territory.

Struggle as she did, his one free hand was so strong he soon overpowered her. Gripping the back of her head, he forced her mouth to his and pushed her lips apart with his tongue, entering, violating, sickening her.

Her heart pumped painfully. She had never experienced anything as terrifying, until his hand left her head and began to fumble at the neck of her shirt.

She struggled; he persisted, jerking her arms so violently she began to fear he would wrench them from their sockets.

"You're a hellcat for sure," he mumbled. She felt his hand rip her shirt, try again, then rip her chemise.

His hand touched her flesh. She flinched.

"Come now, *puta*. You came here for a little fun. That is what I will give you. Where do you want it? Behind the altar where you were hiding?"

His words brought to mind the door. Pia and Zita.

His hand gripped her bare breast. She screamed, but the sound was muffled by his mouth as he closed his lips over hers again.

What if Pia and Zita returned? What if they called her name? She struggled, trying to kick him, trying to free herself.

She would be ruined forever if this monster discovered who she was.

She would be ruined forever anyway if he had his way.

Roughly, he kneaded her breast in his hamlike fist. "So ripe and firm. No sagging old mother, you. Who are you, anyhow? An Indian wench from El Astillero?"

With a great heave, he lifted Aurelia off her feet, bending her backward across his forearm with such force she expected to hear her spine crack. Her feet thrashed in a feeble attempt to inflict injury on this demon.

Suddenly, she felt something wet on her breast, a suckling sensation, teeth. A shudder convulsed through her body at the vileness of his touch. Then his hand moved downward, between their bodies. She felt him fumble with the band on her breeches. If he weren't the strongest man she had ever seen . . .

"Quiroz? You in here? Find anything?"

"Nada." Nuncio Quiroz grunted. "Nothing except . . ." He gave her breast one last suckle. "I'm coming." He shoved her away. "Next time, *puta,* I'll get them breeches off you."

"We must tell your parents."

"No, Pia. We can't."

"You can't stay in bed crying forever, Relie. We have to tell them."

For one brief moment this morning after María, her maid, awakened her with a glass of orange juice, Aurelia had felt fine, as though today were an ordinary autumn day. Then María had drawn back the heavy damask draperies, letting in the sunlight, and Aurelia uttered one word.

"Don't." An innocent word intended merely to alert the maid that she wished to sleep a while longer. An innocent word that brought vividly to mind the disaster of the evening before.

An innocent word, calling forth the geyser of tears that had kept her in bed the entire day.

She had not cried last night, at least, she couldn't

34

recall crying. After escaping the chapel, the three girls had run until their hearts struggled to pump, reaching the cathedral in time to relieve their stand-ins for the last half hour of the novena.

She had not told the others what had happened in the chapel; at least, she didn't think she had. The only thing she could recall of the trip home was the overwhelming need she felt to cleanse herself.

Time after time she had stopped and spat onto the ground in a furious attempt to purge all traces of Nuncio Quiroz from her body. Arriving home, she had drunk glass after glass of water, swishing the liquid around in her mouth, spitting out the residue.

Then before retiring, she repeatedly bathed the breast that monster had violated, rubbing it with oil of roses. Finally, she gave up cleansing herself and went to bed, finding a measure of security in the massive carved walnut four-poster with its damask and lace canopy. Snuggling into the feather mattress, she protected her body with a mound of fluffy pillows and closed her eyes.

Only then had she realized how badly her body trembled.

It had been her mother who summoned Pia, after María summoned her. Although Doña Bella was adept at dealing with the most appalling problems brought to her by the miners' wives, she had never had much luck with her own daughter.

"Relie is your daughter, not mine," Doña Bella was fond of telling her husband after an especially trying bout with a young, unmanageable Aurelia.

Which to Aurelia's mind was one more piece of evidence that her mother had completely forgotten her own youth. For in Aurelia's heart, she knew she resembled down to the most minute detail the youthful Bella Lopez at the Court of Maximilian.

The only thing she lacked was a chance to prove it.

Now that no longer mattered. Now she never wanted to leave the safety of her own bedchamber again in her entire life.

"Relie," Pia implored, "we must get you some help."

"Help? What kind of help? If I told my parents what happened in the chapel, I would have to tell them why I was there. You and Zita would be exposed, too."

"We will take our chances," Zita told her.

Although Pia arrived at mid-morning, having been summoned by Doña Bella, Zita didn't come until after siesta, bearing news of the town's uproar over the latest train robbery.

"I won't let you do that," Aurelia replied. "The whole thing was my fault." She stuffed a lacy pillow over her face and let it absorb a new rush of tears. "I refuse to ruin your reputations, which is the only thing that would come from telling them."

"Your father would fire Nuncio Quiroz," Pia retorted. "Or hang him."

Aurelia shook her head. "Nuncio Quiroz is a vile man. He would deny anything ever happened. And what proof do I have? My word?"

"And ours."

Aurelia sighed. "No one would believe us. Not after all the pranks we have pulled through the years. Papá would think I made it up to escape Catorce."

"No, he wouldn't," Zita objected. "The whole town is upset over this second robbery. That guard reported seeing three, maybe four bandits. And Nuncio Quiroz said he suspects one of them to be a woman."

"Suspects!" Aurelia shuddered, recalling the events of the evening before. "He knows."

"You are certain he didn't recognize you?" Pia asked.

Aurelia nodded, twisting a corner of her sheet in nervous fingers.

"If he had," Zita added, "you would be in a peck of trouble. He would also know you could get him fired."

"He called me an Indian *puta.*" Her tears returned. "I hate him."

Pia sat on the bed. Taking Aurelia's hands, she pulled them away from her swollen eyes. "It's you I'm worried about. What are we going to do?"

Aurelia threw her arms around Pia's neck. "Stop playing foolish games, that's what," she said between sobs. "I'm sorry, truly I am. I never knew how stupid my ideas were. I never thought of . . . of the consequences."

The girls jumped like the conspirators they were when the door burst open and Doña Bella bustled in.

"Relie, dear, the doctor is on his way. I cannot imagine what disease you must have picked up. Why, you haven't stayed in bed a full day since you learned to crawl about on your own."

"Doctor Perez?" Aurelia envisioned him looking into her mouth. Could he detect signs of the horrid ordeal she had experienced the evening before?

Or worse. What if he insisted on examining her body? She crossed her arms over her breasts in a protective fashion. "No. I will not see the doctor."

"Yes, you will, dear. No daughter of mine is going to lie abed with a possibly deadly disease without me doing my best to cure it."

"Doña Bella," Pia began, "the doctor isn't necessary."

Doña Bella frowned at her future daughter-in-law. "*¿Qué dice?*"

"I said . . ." Pia looked quickly to Aurelia, who noted the trepidation in her eyes. Soft-spoken Pia came from a family of quiet people; her mother probably never raised her voice to so much as scold her children.

Sitting up in bed, Aurelia inhaled a deep breath for courage. "Pia is right, Mamá. I was just saying how I must be up in time for dinner. I'm . . . I am famished. It was a passing thing, something in the air at Vespers last night."

Doña Bella scrutinized her daughter. Then she turned a sharp eye to each of the friends. Although the girls had exasperated most of the populace of Real de Catorce during their childhood, Doña Bella prided herself on being possibly the only person in town to stay ahead of them and their little schemes. "*¿Es verdad?*"

The girls nodded, solemn.

"It is true, Doña Bella," Zita assured her quickly. "I was not well this morning myself."

"Nor I," Pia interjected.

"And we are perfectly well now, Mamá. All of us. Perhaps we can invite the girls to dinner."

Long past feeling a social compunction to keep the three girls together twenty-four hours a day, Doña Bella shook her head. "Another time, my dear. Papá is bringing Enrique home for dinner. Get dressed now."

She dismissed the girls. "You may call tomorrow."

After hugging Aurelia, Pia and Zita followed the

señora from the room. Aurelia called Pia back.

"Help me find something to wear," she suggested. Then when her mother's footsteps echoed down the hall, she buried her face in the pillow again. "Enrique! If they had their way, I would be married to him even before your own wedding."

Pia was already going through Aurelia's wardrobe. She held up a peach-colored gown with a deep décolletage. "How about this?"

Aurelia's eyes riveted on the low-cut neckline. Tears gushed from her eyes. She crushed a wad of twisted sheets to her face to stem the flow.

Pia threw the gown to the bed and hugged her friend. "What is it, Relie? What have you not told us? That vile man kissed you, yes? What else? Did he? . . . I mean, he *didn't?* . . ."

"No, he didn't. But he . . . Oh, Pia, did you talk to Santos? I mean about—?"

Pia shook her head. "I couldn't work up the courage. And when I tried to show him, he misunderstood."

"Praise Saint Cecilia! Don't ever take my advice again. Not ever. I was so wrong. Being with a man . . . like *that* . . . is disgusting."

"You said he didn't—"

"He didn't, but he did more than I said. And I don't ever want a man to touch me again. It's disgusting. Sickening." She grabbed the gown Pia had taken from the wardrobe and threw it across the room. "I will never wear anything to expose my . . . my . . ." Suddenly, she crossed her arms over her breasts to control her shaking. "I will marry Enrique. He doesn't look like the sort who would try to touch me."

"What did that man do, Relie? Do you want to talk about it?"

Aurelia lifted her eyes to her friend's. "He put his tongue inside my mouth!" She shuddered. "I tried to bite him, but he held my jaws so tight I'm surprised I don't have bruises."

At the thought, she lifted her chin and turned it from side to side for Pia to inspect. "I don't, do I?"

Pia shook her head, her eyes sad, thoughtful.

"And then he . . . he ripped open my shirt, and he . . . he grabbed me . . . *here*." She covered the offended breast with her hand. "He hurt me, Pia, but that isn't the worst of it. He put his . . ." She stopped, took a deep breath for courage, then continued. "He put his mouth over me . . . *here*." She continued with a face so screwed with disgust that her words were barely audible. "He suckled like a babe, except that he bit me and he hurt. . . ."

"Stop, Relie. Stop." Pia embraced her friend, holding her head tight. "That's enough. Don't talk about it anymore." She smoothed Aurelia's hair against her head. "It's over. He won't ever touch you again."

"No one will."

Pia tightened her hold on her friend. "Don't say that, Relie. Someday you will fall in love. When you do, you will feel differently about things. I am not sure, but I don't think it was so much *what* he did as *how* he did it. And who he was. When you fall in love, things will be different."

"No, Pia, you were right to be frightened. Even if you do love your husband, it is something to be endured, not enjoyed, as I thought. There is nothing romantic about it."

Tears streamed down her face. "There is nothing romantic about life. I was foolish to believe so."

Dinner was a trial to be suffered, beginning as she had known it would when she descended the stairs.

"Relie, dear, whatever were you thinking, wearing that old gray morning gown?"

Aurelia glanced at the expanse of skin showing above her mother's properly low-cut dinner gown.

Doña Bella's frown deepened. "You have no time to change now. Yolanda has already called us to dinner. Did you not hear the first bell?"

Aurelia followed her mother into the drawing room, where Enrique and her father waited.

Enrique took her arm to escort her to the comedor behind her parents. "I'm sorry you are not feeling well, señorita."

She tried to smile, but most of her energy was engaged in keeping herself from flinching at his touch. Fortunately, her arms were covered, preventing the contact of his skin on hers.

At the table Don Domingo launched immediately into a discourse about the latest robbery and the efforts to catch the perpetrators.

Enrique's enthusiasm echoed her father's. "The Federales will apprehend those men before sunup."

"That is what Don Domingo told us at breakfast," Doña Bella agreed. "Except he predicted the culprits would be incarcerated by lunchtime."

Don Domingo cleared his throat. "Some things are unpredictable, my dear."

"Quite so. The robberies, however, appear not to be

41

among them. They are becoming all too predictable."

"Which is precisely why I am sending you and Relie to Guanajuato first thing in the morning."

Aurelia raised stricken eyes from her plate of carne asada. "There is no need, Papá. The outlaws have not shown themselves a threat to anyone in town."

She felt her parents' eyes rivet on her from either end of the table. Could they see how she felt? Could they read her mind? How would she explain such an outlandish thing as never wanting to leave the walls of this house again?

"Your mother is right. You are ill, *hija*," Don Domingo addressed his daughter. "When did you change your tune about going to Guanajuato?"

Aurelia picked at her food. "It doesn't seem necessary."

"I agree," Enrique interjected. "Begging your pardon, Don Domingo, but so far as we know, the robbers have never set foot inside Real de Catorce." He stared across the table at Aurelia with an impassioned gaze that set her hands to trembling.

Quickly, she set her fork down and clasped them in her lap. Guanajuato and Enrique Villasur be damned. She had enough worries just keeping her wits.

The look in his eyes caused her to wonder whether all men were not after exactly the same thing Nuncio Quiroz had attempted to take from her in the chapel.

The sight of Enrique's lips brought on a quaking she was unable to control. The thought of those lips on hers . . .

The sensation of them on her breast . . .

"Daughter, are you ill?"

Serphino, the table servant, caught her shoulders

just as she swayed from the chair. Across the table she saw Enrique jump to his feet. The last thought she entertained before she swooned was one of thanksgiving. Praise Saint Cecilia it was old Serphino who caught her in his arms, not Enrique Villasur.

Two days later a jubilant Don Domingo Mazón arrived home at midday with his familiar shadow, Enrique Villasur, following on his coattails. He shouted uncharacteristically up the stairs for his wife.

"Doña Bella! Doña Bella! Where the devil are you! I bring great news!"

Aurelia followed her mother down the broad staircase to the marble-floored foyer, where Don Domingo and Enrique awaited with beaming faces. She could not recall ever seeing such a smile on her father's face, except at the opening of the Casa de Moneda Mazón.

"We have caught the train robber!" he exclaimed. "He is incarcerated even as we speak."

"The Federales brought him in an hour ago," Enrique added. "No one has been allowed to question him yet."

43

Chapter Three

Only by exercising the greatest degree of discipline did Aurelia manage to sit through lunch with her parents and Enrique. She must, she cautioned herself, learn everything possible about the situation before deciding how to proceed.

Whichever of the two had been caught, Kino or Joaquín, she could not let him pay for a scheme she had hatched herself.

True, the boys had gained a great deal from the thefts—money to feed their families through the coming winter. Money that was badly needed in villages such as theirs.

And it wasn't as though they had not discussed this eventuality. They had. And both boys had agreed the rewards were worth the risk.

"The Federales are guarding him in our jail?" Doña Bella inquired. Often referred to as the "Free State of Catorce," this high-mountain town did not brook outside interference, especially not from the central government. Stories abounded of instances when the citizens had stood up against usurpers.

"*Sí,*" Enrique replied.

"Not for long, señora," Don Domingo assured his wife. "The Federales will be replaced as soon as the alcalde posts the necessary guards at the jail."

"Necessary?" Aurelia cleared her throat to cover the quiver in her voice. "How many guards does the mayor think necessary?"

"Enough to prevent the man's compadres from breaking him out," her father said. "We are not dealing with just any culprits."

"Breaking him out?" Aurelia echoed.

"These are rough characters, Relie."

"Even though one of them is a woman," Enrique added.

Aurelia glared at him. During the last two days her aversion to his touch had changed from a physical disgust to something more integral. Fair or not, she now disliked Enrique Villasur's looks—his fine black hair combed straight back from a widow's peak, his arched black eyebrows, his thin but neatly trimmed mustache that peaked beneath his nostrils and arched down to the outer edge of each lip. She disliked his proper dress—she had never seen him without waistcoat and tie—and his cultured, precise way of speaking, even his choice of words.

Especially his choice of words. "You do not credit a woman with sense enough to plan a train robbery?" she questioned.

He frowned from what had become his regular place opposite her at the Mazón dining table. "Why would a woman want to rob a train, señorita?"

To escape a lifetime with a fool like you, she thought, enraged by his condescending manner.

45

"The town is already in an uproar," Enrique continued. "Talk of lynching is heard on every corner. If you ask me, hanging's too good for the fool."

"I agree," said her father, "but I cannot allow a hanging here in the middle of town. I must find some way to contain the situation. Let the authorities see justice served."

"Still, for the misery those robbers have caused, hanging's too good for them," Enrique repeated.

Hanging's too good for them. The words reverberated through Aurelia's brain later while she rounded up Pia and Zita. The girls gathered beside the fountain on Careaga Street, a deserted part of town.

"We must do something." Aurelia sat between her two accomplices on the edge of the fountain.

"What?" Zita asked. "Anything we do will bring the Federales down on us."

"We cannot allow a man to hang for us, Zita."

"For *you*." Zita corrected. "I mean, what's the use of us all hanging?"

"We won't hang, silly."

"No," Pia agreed. "But we will be in serious trouble."

"We *are* in serious trouble," Aurelia reminded them. "And so is Kino or Joaquín, whichever one is in jail."

"How do we know it's either of them?" Zita questioned.

Aurelia tilted her chin. "Who else could it be?"

The girls remained silent for a moment. Thoughtful.

"Even if it weren't," Aurelia argued, "we couldn't stand by and let an innocent person hang."

Again the girls remained silent.

"What are we going to do?" Zita whispered.

"Whatever are we going to do?" Pia echoed.

Aurelia sighed. "The first thing is to get into that jail."

The girls gasped.

"Send María," Pia suggested. "She's their sister."

Aurelia shook her head.

"Yes," Zita encouraged.

"No. We cannot draw attention to whichever one is still free."

"You said yourself the Federales aren't allowing anyone to see the prisoner," Pia reminded Aurelia.

"So how do you propose we go about it?" Zita demanded.

Aurelia glanced up in time to see her friends exchange exasperated glances. "Don't bother yourselves! I got us into this mess. I will get us out of it."

"Relie," Pia cautioned, "don't go getting angry. When you get angry you usually do things you regret."

"Things we all regret," Zita corrected. But her voice was tender, and she hugged her arm around Aurelia's waist.

"First I must get inside that jail," Aurelia mused.

"Perhaps we will know one of the guards when the alcalde posts them," Pia suggested. "We could ask him to let you speak to the prisoner."

Aurelia shook her head. "We can't ask anyone. That would draw attention."

"I suppose you have a plan for getting inside the jail without drawing attention?" Zita demanded.

"I mean attention to the three of us," Aurelia said. "Since it was Papá's train he robbed—"

"*We* robbed," Pia corrected.

47

"It might not seem strange," Aurelia continued, "for me to try to see the prisoner."

Zita twittered nervously. "Not if you bring a handgun to shoot him with."

"Mamá is always taking meals and medical supplies to needy people," Aurelia plotted aloud. "It would be fitting for a Mazón to take food to the prisoner. To assure he is well treated, regardless of the misery he caused us."

"We should send for Santos," Pia suggested. "He would know what to do."

"Santos would side with Papá."

"Santos would not let an innocent man hang," Pia defended.

"He couldn't stop them. If the townsfolk don't lynch the prisoner, the Federales will hang him."

That idea left the girls even more despondent. Would the hanging take place here in Real de Catorce?

In the main plaza by the lovely fountain?

Which they passed every day?

Around which they held the San Francisco de Asís fireworks?

"We would never free ourselves of such an image," Zita wailed.

"Even on my wedding day the memory would still be fresh," Pia sighed.

Aurelia straightened her back, lifted her chin, and jumped to her feet. "That does it. I must do something."

She started down the hill. Pia and Zita followed, catching up. They linked arms, and for the next hour the three girls strolled around the central part of town, their faces long, their hearts heavy.

48

In contrast to everyone they passed. On the whole the townsfolk were elated by the capture. The words the girls heard most frequently were "Lynch him!"

"Lynching's too good for the scoundrel."

"We're civilized folk here in Catorce. Can't do more than lynch."

Across the bricked street from the jail, Aurelia stopped. Her friends halted beside her.

"I must get inside."

"You can't," Pia whispered.

But Aurelia only nodded, and neither friend said more. Once Aurelia Mazón made up her mind, Saint Cecilia herself could not change it.

"I cannot let a man hang on my account."

And they knew she was right.

Only thing, Aurelia's solutions often left them in more trouble than they had been in to begin with.

The girls, staunch friends to the end, returned to their homes, bided their time, and expected the worst. By the time Aurelia reached the Mazón mansion, she had decided three things.

First, she could not expose her friends to the danger she would be bringing on herself.

Second, she could not disgrace her family by allowing the town to gossip about her visiting a common criminal.

And third, whatever she did, she must do quickly. This fact became clearer as she passed knot after knot of citizens who were up in arms about the crime that had been committed against their town. They did not want outsiders to receive credit for hanging one of their own thieves. They did not want the Federales invading their territory.

49

They wanted to hang the criminal in the central plaza in plain sight of God and all Catorceans.

Fortunately, this was her mother's day at the mining camp, so Aurelia hurried to complete her mission before Doña Bella's return. Dressing in a black cotton shirtwaist a couple of sizes too large, she padded it with a piece of flannel toweling. In her mother's wardrobe she found a black bonnet with a mourning veil attached. Perfect. A widow helping the underprivileged. A pair of knitted black gloves would hide her youthful hands from view of the guards.

Stuffing both bonnet and gloves into a tapestry satchel, she hurried to the kitchen fifty meters or so behind the mansion, steering clear of the quarters where the Mazón servants were taking siesta. Grabbing the first basket she found, she stuffed it with food — leftover beefsteak wrapped in tortillas, tins of herring and salmon, a hunk of goat cheese. For good measure, she added an extra hunk of goat cheese, a whole loaf of sourdough bread, and a jar of agarita berry jelly.

Curiously, she began to wonder what foods the boys liked, then stopped herself. When a man was in jail, probably the only thing he wanted was out. Besides, this food was not for the physical nourishment of whichever one of her accomplices the prisoner turned out to be. She was making contact. Possibly he — Kino or Joaquín — already had a plan. She would serve as his messenger.

That thought greatly relieved her. Hopefully, she would be required to do nothing more than relay a message.

Delivering a message would be simple. A message to

someone who could vouch for his whereabouts, thereby clearing him of any involvement.

Unless he had been caught with the coins. The thought came like a blow from a double-jack hammer. Had the boys hidden the coins before the capture?

Since they hadn't both been captured, whichever one was still free probably had the coins. She hoped.

She prayed. *Por Santa Cecilia,* she prayed.

Why hadn't she asked her father about the coins? Neither he nor Enrique had mentioned them. Surely Enrique, eager as he had been to discredit the woman involved, would have gloated over recovering the coins.

"Hold up, señora. What've you got there?"

Aurelia came to an abrupt halt. The guard barring the door of the jail lifted the cloth to peer inside her basket.

"No one is allowed inside the building today, señora."

Her heart stopped. "I must enter." She spoke from deep in her throat, hoping to sound a few years older than she was.

"Who is this food for?"

She cleared her throat. "The prisoner."

"What prisoner?"

"The train robber, of course."

"That good-for-nothing varmint? He certainly don't deserve food from a widow like yourself."

"Everyone deserves food," Aurelia told him. "Let me pass."

The guard was adamant. "No one is allowed to see the prisoner. Strict orders of the captain. I will take the food."

Aurelia clung to the basket. "I must take it myself."

51

"Can't allow it," the guard insisted.

"Listen to me, young man. I am a poor widow woman, and it is my duty to serve the underprivileged, including prisoners. I made a vow to our Lord to provide for the worst of His creations. You know what He said: 'Judge not, lest you be judged.' If you do not let me see the prisoner, my vow will be broken and I will burn in hell. And you, señor, will meet the same fate."

For a moment the guard stood his ground. Then he turned away. "I will speak with my captain."

After an unsettling length of time, during which Aurelia felt the eyes of the entire town upon her, knowing any moment one pair could belong to her father or one pair to her mother or, at the very least, one pair to Enrique Villasur, the guard returned. He searched the basket item by item.

"You may hand him the basket. Nothing more."

Again her heart skipped. "I must pray with the prisoner. Food for the soul, that was my vow, along with sustenance for the body."

Through the black gauze of her veil, she watched the guard speak to the captain again, watched the captain at long last nod his head.

"Five minutes," the guard barked. "Follow the captain."

Aurelia's knees felt like the jelly she had packed inside the basket for her accomplice, but she managed to follow the captain to the second floor, where he pointed her toward a cell.

"Last cell on the left." Through her veil and from the distance, the cell looked empty.

As the guard had earlier, the captain examined the contents of her basket. "Five minutes. Not a second longer."

"*Gracias.*" After two steps, she glanced back to where he stood his ground. "I will pray with the prisoner alone," she demanded, her voice no more than a hiss.

"It's your time you're wasting, señora," the captain responded with an exasperated shrug. But he turned and trudged down the stairs.

Aurelia hurried to the last cell, lifting her veil as she went. She had expected them to limit her time with the prisoner, so she had ordered her thoughts on the way to town.

But the words she had carefully prepared died on her lips when she looked into the cell and saw neither Kino nor Joaquín, but a stranger. A total stranger.

A gringo, no less!

"Who are you?" she whispered.

"I would ask the same thing"—He rose from a cot in the far corner of the cell, taking a moment to limber first one knee joint, then another, all the while his brown eyes dancing across the distance to her—"but I never look a gift horse in the mouth."

He was in jolly form for a man in jail, she thought. Even though his clothing was dirty and one sleeve had a large tear in it, she could tell he was no ordinary tramp. His shoulders were broad enough to belong to a miner, and his muscles bespoke a man who knew hard work and practiced it. With movements she could hear Santos call *stove-up*, the prisoner crossed the cell, slipped a hand through the bars, and lifted the cloth from her basket.

She slapped his hand away. "This is for the train robber." She scanned the other cells—two across the way and one next to the stranger's.

All were empty.

"I'm the train robber," he announced in an amused tone of voice.

She jerked her attention back to him. "You are not."

His wide eyes mimicked her own expression. Aurelia knew that the moment she realized he was staring at her." *Laughing* at her was more like it.

"But I thought—?"

". . . you were my lover who has come to set me free," he sang. Again he reached through the bars and lifted the cloth, this time withdrawing a rolled tortilla filled with beefsteak, from which he took a large bite, continuing to sing around his mouthful of food. "Set me free. Set me free. I thought you were my lover who has come to set me free."

"You're mad!" Her mind reeled with the shock of finding a total stranger in jail for the crime she had so carefully planned and executed.

"Wouldn't you be," he questioned, "if you were set upon by Federales and thrown in jail for a crime you didn't commit?"

She nodded, thinking. Thinking. Voices reached them through the open window at the end of the room. Angry voices.

"From the sound of the crowd out there, I'm the most popular feller in town."

"They intend to wipe that smile off your face," she agreed, "unless I discover a way to get you out of here."

"You?"

She rose to her full height, lifting her chin in a manner that defied him to dispute her.

"Why you?" He scanned her clothing, taking in the mittens, the black costume, the gauze veil she had thrown back from her face. His warm brown gaze lingered on hers. "You are definitely an angel, regardless of the widow's weeds."

"It's a disguise," she insisted.

"A disguise?"

"Prayin' time's over."

She listened in horror to the captain's boots stomping up the stairs behind his booming voice.

"Praying time?" The stranger lifted an eyebrow, mocking her.

"I told him I had taken a vow to feed and pray with prisoners."

He laughed.

He must be mad, she thought.

She pushed the basket through the bars. He reached out and pulled her veil over her face.

"Can't have anyone else looking upon the countenance of my guardian angel."

She gritted her teeth. What to do? What to do?

"Don't suppose there's a gun under all this food?"

She shook her head. "Do you have any friends around here? Anyone I can send to help you?"

The captain took her by the arm. "Time's up, señora."

"Only you," the stranger called after her. "Your lovely countenance will travel with me on my dismal journey to . . ." His words faded beneath the angry shouts of the mob outside.

Leaving the jail, Aurelia headed for the fountain where Pia and Zita had agreed to wait for her, stripping off the bonnet and veil and the mittens as she went. At each corner knots of townsfolk discussed the prisoner. The word *lynch* resounded from the walls of the elaborately designed buildings—the civilized buildings of civilized Catorce.

Inside her brain the image of the prisoner remained imprinted as by the sure hand of God Himself.

Pia and Zita took the news in stunned silence, their faces showing the shock of finding a stranger—a gringo—in jail for an offense they had committed.

"How did you understand him?" Pia asked.

"He speaks our language," Aurelia told them, adding, "except for the crazy song he sang. It was in English."

"How do you know it was crazy if he sang it in English?" Zita questioned.

"The way his eyes danced," she said. "He's handsome all right. Handsome, but definitely mad."

"How did they catch him?" Pia asked.

Aurelia shrugged, silent. Thinking.

"He must be guilty of something or he wouldn't be in jail," Zita reasoned.

"He said the Federales arrested him for a crime he didn't commit. That's all we had time for."

"We already knew that much," Zita said.

The girls stared at one another, their eyes telling the sad truth. The truth that an innocent man was in jail and in danger of losing his life because of their folly.

"Now we must tell your father," Zita said at last.

They sat on the edge of the fountain, trailing their fingers absently in the water.

"Listen to that crowd," Pia said. "They sound like a pack of wolves on the scent of blood."

Aurelia agreed. "Even if we told Papá, he couldn't convince that crowd. They want a victim." She recalled Enrique's statement at lunch. "They would never believe three *girls* could plot and carry through such a plan."

"Whatever we do, we don't have much time," Zita said.

"We have to break him out."

Pia and Zita stared at Aurelia, their mouths agape.

"You're crazy," Zita whispered.

"She's serious," Pia said.

After assuring them she would do nothing without consulting them, Aurelia hurried home to change clothes. Before any decisions were made, she had to learn her father's plans. At lunch he had said he would prevent a lynching. If he had made plans, she must discover what they were. Surely she had a little time in which to plan an escape.

Even an execution took time to arrange, unless the townsfolk broke into the jail and hung the prisoner themselves. And that possibility was too dastardly to even consider.

Quickly changing her widow's weeds for a mint-green afternoon dress with matching parasol and pinning her hair into curls that tickled her shoulders, she called for Serphino to drive her to the Casa de Moneda Mazón to visit her father.

Enrique, as she had expected, was beside himself with pleasure at the sight of her. Her father, as she had also known, was at the mine.

"My dear, you have at length come to life." Enrique took her fingers and twirled her in a circle, admiring her gown. "Enchanting. Exactly the type of gown you should wear for the position you will have."

She walked in front of him down the long aisle to the rear of the room. "What are you talking about, Enri-

57

que? What position could I possibly aspire to that I do not already possess?"

He was taken aback, as always, by her jesting, but he managed to hold on to the tips of her fingers.

"Wife of the president of Casa de Moneda Mazón," he announced, bringing her fingers to his lips as he spoke.

"Oh? You have spoken to Papá?"

"Many times, my dear. He and I agree quite fully on that score. It is his daughter we seek to convince."

Over my dead body. Immediately, she retracted that thought. It was in the cause of a dead body — or rather for the preservation of a live one — that she allowed herself to be handled by this snobbish man.

"I suspected you two of conniving against me," she murmured.

"Never against you, my dear."

She stood in the doorway to Enrique's private office. The ornate furniture had been built in Mexico City especially for the president of the Casa de Moneda, and it was too large in both bulk and height for the slender frame of Enrique Villasur. "Then against Tío Luís," she corrected. "He was the intended president of Casa de Moneda."

Enrique coughed. "Until he decided to run for Governor of Potosí."

"Until Papá found you . . ." she purred. She heard nothing but silence from Enrique, who stood close behind her. Coming from outside the building, however, echoes of the unruly crowd reminded her of the seriousness of her mission.

". . . especially for me."

Turning her attention back to the front room, Aurelia walked beside the glass cases, trailing her fingers along the counter, examining the coins on display. She ignored the confused face of Enrique Villasur. "Fascinating," she mused. "Are these the same denomination as the coins taken in the robbery?"

At her elbow Enrique cleared his throat. "From the same lot, actually."

"How much did you lose, Enrique?"

He sputtered at her use of his Christian name. "Why . . . ah over twenty thousand dollars worth, señorita."

"Aurelia," she offered.

His mouth fell open. He closed it quickly. "Aurelia," he murmured, as though she had given him a handful of golden coins. "Twenty thousand dollars worth, Aurelia."

"Ah, and were they all found on the prisoner?"

"We have recovered none of them as yet. But never fear. We shall find every last one. That culprit will show us where he stashed our coins."

His inflection on the word *our* gave her pause, but she continued. "That might be a difficult thing to do, Enrique, if the townsfolk hang him."

"Hang him?"

"Like you said at lunch: The town is talking of nothing else. Of nothing but lynching. Why, on every street corner a mob is gathering."

"They will not accomplish such a thing," he stated definitively. "Even though the fellow deserves it."

She frowned. "How can you be so certain?"

"Of what, Aurelia?"

"How do the Federales know they caught the right man?"

He stared at her, aghast. "The right man? Why would they have arrested him otherwise?"

"But they found no coins?"

He shrugged.

"Not even the crates the coins were shipped in?"

He shrugged again. "In time, Aurelia . . . dear."

She stifled her disgust at his endearment. "They found nothing to connect him with the stolen coins?"

"I explained. The Federales intend to force the man to show them the exact spot before they. . . ah . . . before the trial. They have ways of extracting the truth, my dear Aurelia."

Even without the endearment, his last statement would have sent a shiver up her neck. "I thought the Federales left town."

"They did, but—" He stopped speaking abruptly.

"But what?"

"It isn't . . . ah . . ."

"What, Enrique? It isn't what?"

"I really can't say. It is to be kept secret. Afterwards, Aurelia, perhaps—"

"Relie," she whispered.

"Relie." He seized the name as he would have a prize given at the fair. The fire in his eyes brought a tremble to her limbs. Had Nuncio Quiroz's eyes glowed with such hunger that night in the chapel?

Her mouth was so dry she had trouble speaking. "Tell me, Enrique. I love a surprise. And I am very good at keeping secrets. You will see."

"Well, your father has . . . ah, we have laid plans to secrete the prisoner to Matehuala on a fake shipment of silver. The Federales will escort him from there to San Luís Potosí for safekeeping until the trial."

"Really? And until he can lead you to the coins?"

"Exactly, Relie. Exactly."

Her face fell. "Oh, dear. I hope it will be soon. The crowd is growing ever more belligerent. I fear—"

Enrique had taken her hands while she spoke. He brought them to his lips. "Do not fret, Relie dear. I know you worry as much for your father and myself as for the prisoner, but all will be well. The train leaves at midnight, and by tomorrow the prisoner will be safely incarcerated in San Luís Potosí."

Aurelia pressed her lips together to keep from smiling. "Midnight?" she whispered at last. "But . . . but what if? . . . I mean, his accomplices have not been caught. There were three of them or more, were there not? What? . . ."

"You worry too much, Relie. Nuncio Quiroz himself has volunteered to guard the prisoner."

A chill like an icy mountain stream raced through Aurelia's blood. It was what she had hoped to hear but also what she had feared.

"Well, Enrique, I have taken too much of your time. I must be on my way. I don't want to become a bother."

He lifted her trembling fingers to his lips. "My dear, dear Relie. You a bother? Never."

At the door she turned and favored him with what she hoped was a radiant smile. "What about the woman, Enrique? Do you suppose she would try to rescue her lover?" She cast her gaze toward the floor, then lifted her chin to stare into his startled eyes. "No, of course not. A woman would never think of such a thing."

"You do remember your promise, Relie?"

"Promise?"

"To tell no one of our secret. Only three people know the truth of it: your father, myself, and Quiroz."

She stilled the tremor that started in the pit of her stomach. "Four, but don't count me. You have my promise. Woman's honor."

Chapter Four

No one liked Aurelia's plan, she least of all. But she did not tell them that. Pia and Zita were hard enough to persuade without learning how much she feared another encounter with Nuncio Quiroz.

Zita's reaction was typically irate. "You have lost your mind, Relie."

As usual, Pia cloaked her anger in concern. "Aurelia! You cannot mean such a thing. Why, only two days ago you lay in bed crying your heart out over that man."

Aurelia shrugged. "This time I am forewarned."

"Forewarned means nothing. That man is an animal."

"Can you think of another solution?"

Neither girl replied.

"Well, I can't either. Nothing else would persuade him to stop the train. He certainly won't stop again for a lantern at the chapel."

Pia chewed her lip. "He won't stop for a rendezvous with you, either, Relie. His prisoner is too valuable."

"He'll stop." Aurelia recalled the vigor with which Nuncio Quiroz had pursued her. She suppressed a shudder. "He will stop," she repeated. "Enrique assured me they are posting two extra guards and securing the prisoner with a cable."

"It won't work," Pia argued. "You are risking your virginity for nothing."

Zita's eyes flew open. "Her vir—?"

Aurelia gritted her teeth. "I am not. Nothing of the sort is going to happen."

The girls looked unconvinced.

"Can you come up with a better way to save an innocent man's life?" She glared from one friend to the other. "Even if . . . even if it did . . . come to that, I would still be alive. A man's life is worth . . . worth something. *Por Santa Cecilia,* I put the noose around his neck. I must remove it. I don't want his death on my conscience."

The afternoon was spent in a flurry of activity. Kino and Joaquín had to be notified and the message sent.

Pia and Zita hovered over Aurelia while she struggled to compose the right sort of message to insure Nuncio Quiroz would stop at the chapel in the tunnel.

"Offer him a kiss," Zita suggested.

"He already had a kiss," Pia retorted.

Aurelia's fingers gripped the pencil. "I will make it vague. Say I want a second chance to please him . . . a man of such passions . . ." Her fingers flew to keep up with her lips. "That his runaway passions released my own . . . that I cannot bear . . ." Her fingers paused when her body rebelled.

"Don't get carried away, Relie," Pia cautioned.

"Where did you get those clothes?" Zita asked later

while the girls helped Aurelia dress for her rendezvous with the mine superintendent.

The message had been dispatched by a boy from the village, along with a gold coin and the promise of another when the answer was returned. The girls had nervously awaited Quiroz's reply.

To insure the boy not learn their identities, Zita had met the child near the deserted fountain and instructed him to return the answer to the same place after dark.

Since Zita's parents were the earliest to retire and since Aurelia knew her own father would pace the night away in his study awaiting word that the prisoner had been delivered safely, she and Pia arranged to spend the night at Zita's house.

As soon as the Tapis family retired, Aurelia pulled the clothing from her tapestry satchel: a faded black skirt and several colorful but shabby petticoats, a low-cut white blouse, daring but dingy, and a threadbare woolen cloak to cover it all.

"From the clothesline," Aurelia answered Zita's question, tightening the laces of her corset. "They belong to Sophía, our new second-floor maid. I will hide them in the servant's wash when I return." Before stepping into the first of four petticoats, she jerked the corset strings one last time, then tied them in a double knot.

"You aren't going to a dance," Pia admonished.

"You can't squeeze down the steps to the chapel in four petticoats," Zita argued.

"I must keep him occupied long enough for you to do your jobs." She slipped the blouse over her head.

"You don't need to make it easy for him," Pia chided.

"I'm not. My bloomers and these layers of petticoats

will slow him down." She threw the cloak over her shoulders, slipped her arms through the slits, and buttoned the multitude of black buttons that began at her throat and ended near her ankles. "He won't have time to get through all these buttons."

Checking the satchel for the supplies she brought for the prisoner once he was freed, Aurelia snapped it closed. "Let's go."

"You are too confident," Zita sighed.

Confident? Inside she shook like a poplar leaf in a chill wind. *Confident?* Her heart fluttered in such an erratic rhythm she could only pray she would not swoon. She struggled to keep her brain occupied with the task confronting them — with the roles each of them would play.

After stopping at the fountain for the message from Nuncio Quiroz, the three girls made their way to the shrine. Once there, Aurelia took out matches and, by the light of the shrine's candle, read the scrawled reply.

"It worked." She choked back her fears, trying to hide them from her friends. But they had been friends for too long.

"He didn't suspect us being involved with the robbers?"

Aurelia laughed. *"Nuncio Quiroz es un bufón."* She read the smudged message. *"Do not think to trick me tonight, puta. My men will guard the prisoner on the threat of death if he escapes, and you will pleasure me under the same terms."*

"Quiroz is a fool, yes, but so are we," Zita said. "We can't go through with this."

"Call it off, Relie," Pia pleaded. "Get in touch with Santos. He said there are more difficulties at the mine than the robberies. He would know what to do. I'm

66

sure he could get the gringo released. Why, he even knows authorities in Texas. He could wire the Rangers to come for the prisoner."

Aurelia rolled her eyes. "Be reasonable, Pia. The Federales are not going to release so valuable a prisoner to a foreign country, especially not to barbarians like the Texas Rangers."

"Even so, we must call this off."

"No. A man's life is in danger because of me. I will save him."

The message from Nuncio Quiroz held one heart-rending surprise: The time schedule had been moved up an hour.

"Eleven o'clock," Aurelia read. "Let's hurry."

"What if Kino and Joaquín don't come in time?"

"They will. I told them an hour early, like before."

"They had better be on time," Zita said.

"They can't be late," Pia murmured.

They weren't. The boys awaited them in the darkened chapel, where no sooner had the girls arrived than the rails began to clatter. No whistle tonight to alert the bandits.

"Bring the prisoner back here," she told Kino and Joaquín. "We will escape together by the staircase. And remember: Two guards will be in the compartment with the prisoner. Do you have cable cutters? And rifles?"

"*Sí,*" Kino mumbled as he dashed across the tracks behind Joaquín, just ahead of the beam of light from the engine.

Aurelia closed the chapel door and leaned against it. Her heart thrashed wildly. Her friends clung to her on either side.

"Move away from me," she warned. "He must think I am alone. Hide in the corners by the door, like we planned. When Kino and Joaquín come with the prisoner, lead them to the staircase." She groped her way up the aisle, praying the train would stop, praying it would not.

Iron wheels screeched. Aurelia clasped her hands over her ears to close out the sounds, to close out what lay ahead.

Footsteps echoed down the aisle. "Where are you, *puta*?" The footsteps scrunched to a halt on the rock surface of the floor. "I have no time for games. Where the hell are you?"

"Here." Her voice squeaked. The words broke in two, reminding her of her body broken over Nuncio Quiroz's arm here in this very chapel. She wanted to run. She wanted to scream.

Rough hands gripped her shoulders. "Had a change of mind?" He jerked her around and began to fumble with her clothing. "What the hell? . . . You're dressed up like for a snowstorm." She felt him tense. "What are you holding on to?" He tried to jerk the satchel from her hand, but Aurelia gripped the handle until at length he relented.

His mouth found hers.

She stiffened, started to pull away, but his arms bound her to him while his hands groped with the back of her dress.

Suddenly, he stopped. She felt him glance behind him. "Are you tricking me?"

She panicked. Throwing her arms around his neck, she buried her face in his foul-smelling chest. Her stomach flipped.

68

He relaxed. "What have I got hold of? Not a virgin?"

This time when his lips closed over hers she endured the repulsive kiss, while his hands fumbled with her garments. Aurelia could tell he was becoming angry, but she could not bring herself to stand still.

"You have enough clothes on to outfit my entire crew," he fussed. "Why are you jumping around like a frog? Can't wait, huh? Like me."

Then his hands found their mark. She felt them on her thighs. Only her bloomers separated her skin from his hand. Perhaps he did not know about . . .

The door of the chapel banged open. Footsteps shuffled down the aisle. The prisoner? Was it almost over?

But he did know about the opening in the crotch of women's bloomers. She would have laughed at her ignorance had she not been so terrified. A man like Nuncio Quiroz not knowing how to get inside a woman's bloomers?

Footsteps stumbled past them, but Quiroz paid no attention. More footsteps. She tried to count them, but her attention was diverted by her struggle. A minute longer, she prayed. A minute. She wiggled herself away from Quiroz's groping hand.

Too late.

"Ah, there it is." His hand stroked her in an intimate, sickening fashion, touching her body as no one had ever done before. Then suddenly he let go. She struggled.

"Hold still. I won't be a minute."

Before she realized he had done so, he had unsheathed himself. She felt something fleshy and hot and very hard against her bloomers.

His hand groped and shoved.

She flinched. He found the opening in her bloomers again, pressed himself through it. He felt hot, vile, large. Flesh touched flesh. Hot and wet.

"Aurelia, come on!"

He froze.

She pulled back, stumbling to find her footing.

"Aurelia?" he rasped. "Mazón?" The word was whispered on his foul breath.

She pulled away.

He slapped her. "Bitch!" He slapped her again. "Bitch. You thought to trick me?"

Suddenly, someone jerked her arm, pulling her backward, away from Quiroz.

"Bitch!" he roared. "I will kill you for this." His hands grazed her neck, scratching, reaching.

Then she was gone. Her feet left the floor. She felt a strong arm around her waist, carrying her past the altar, depositing her inside the narrow stairway. The door closed; she heard the lock turn.

The arm supported her, holding her close, guiding her up the narrow staircase.

"Who? . . ." Her voice rasped. Her brain felt frozen inside her head.

Strong hands gripped her about the waist, lifting her upward from step to step.

"Couldn't leave my guardian angel behind, could I?"

The air above ground hit her face, bringing a sense of life and urgency. Her legs buckled when she tried to hurry to the shrine where Pia and Zita awaited.

The prisoner steadied her. "I sent your friends ahead. Those two boys said they would see them safely home."

"They left me?"

70

"I told them I would get you home."

"They wouldn't leave me alone with a train robber."

He chuckled. "You must have convinced them I'm not a train robber." Sounds of boots scrambling up the hillside alerted them. "But those fellers don't know it. Let's get down off this mountain. Which way?"

Aurelia glanced toward town. "That—" Suddenly, a group of men cleared the ridge of the hill, running straight toward them.

"I think not." His hand grabbed Aurelia's. "We had best hightail it."

Her brain didn't start working again until the prisoner had dragged her down the opposite side of the mountain from Real de Catorce, led her into a deep ravine, pulled her in and out among the heavy growth of mesquite and cactus, over rocks and boulders, across the ravine and up the other side, then over it and down onto a stretch of open land at the foot of the hills.

He stopped, dropped her hand, and peered into the blackness around them. "Where are we?"

She groaned. "On the other side of the mountain from my home."

"Think you can pinpoint it a bit more than that?" His sarcastic question was voiced in a jocular tone of voice.

Was this man mad? Throwing back her head, Aurelia stared into the black sky. They said the sky was always blackest just before sunrise.

As though following her thoughts, he spoke. "Won't be long till daylight. The Federales will use us for target practice unless we find a place to hide."

"I have to get to the other side of the mountain."

"Why?"

"There's a . . . a place I know over there. I'll be safe."

He grunted. "Safe? From that madman you tricked back there? If you think he's fixin' to let you get away with breaking his train robber out of jail, you're crazy."

"For your information, that is not why he was angry."

"Oh? A lover's spat?"

Aurelia inhaled. "Look. You go your way, I will go mine. I merely saved your life, I didn't take you on to raise."

He laughed. "Seems we're even then, ma'am. I saved your life, too, case you didn't notice."

"If it hadn't been for you, my life would not be in jeopardy."

"I still owe you? Is that what you're saying?"

"You owe me nothing." She got her bearings and started north.

He followed. She stopped.

"Where are you going?" she demanded.

"North." He shrugged. "There's one place in this whole cotton-pickin' country where I might have a friend. Can I help it if it happens to be north of here?"

"If you have a friend in this *cotton-pickin'* country," she accused, "why didn't you let *him* get you out of jail, instead of involving me in your . . . in your criminal activities?"

He studied her with a suddenly grave expression. "I gave my word not to mention his name."

"Your word?"

"My word," he repeated. "My honor. Surely you understand. . . ."

"I understand honor, gringo. I also understand *danger*."

He held up a rifle and fingered the bandoleers slung across his chest. "Which is why you shouldn't object to me being along. I appear to be the only one of us who is armed." He screwed his neck around to gaze at her skirts. "Unless you carry a dagger in your garter—or in that satchel you're holding on to for dear life."

"Oh!"

"That's what I thought. You forgot to arm yourself."

"I didn't plan to shoot anyone," she retorted. "But I suppose you do."

"Only if they shoot at me first, ma'am. Or at you. Way I figure it, we haven't either one finished the jobs we set out to do tonight."

"What jobs?"

"Saving each other's lives."

She stomped off, and he fell in step.

"Where is the nearest Federales Station?" he asked.

"Matehuala."

"That close?" She heard concern in his voice.

"Now do you understand why I want to get to the other side of this damned mountain?" she demanded.

He was silent for a while. When he spoke, it was to jest again. "Can't figure you out. You dress like a widow, cuss like a—"

"I did not invite you to come with me." Did this man take nothing seriously? No wonder he ended up in jail.

"Sorry," he mumbled, but his tone didn't sound the least bit contrite. "Guess I'm naturally the curious sort."

"You certainly are that."

"Your voice, on the other hand," he continued, "is

73

cultured, sort of pleasing."

"Save your breath, gringo. If you're coming with me, you are going to need it. Don't expect me to wait for you to catch up."

He chuckled.

Strange, she thought. Although she was furious with him and with herself, his jesting calmed her. She hadn't had time to think back on the ordeal in the chapel. Once the thought came, however, she shuddered, then stumbled.

He caught her shoulders, holding her steady for a moment.

When she regained her balance and continued up the trail, her legs had stopped trembling. But he had felt her tremors, she knew he had, even though he hadn't mentioned it. In fact, he didn't speak again for several minutes.

It wasn't so bad having him along, she decided. The idea of being out here all alone was chilling. She began to think about arriving at Rancho Mazón. What if the stranger insisted on following her all the way to the ranch? How would she explain him to Santos? How would she explain any of this to Santos? Not only the breakout, but the robberies. Her robberies.

And Nuncio Quiroz. Nuncio Quiroz, she would never explain to anyone. Not until . . . Forcibly, she turned her thoughts to other things.

The fact that she had brought this desperate ordeal on herself disconcerted her further. A scheme to escape Real de Catorce. She had certainly succeeded in that.

At a widening in the trail, the stranger came up beside her. "Figure we have no more than an hour's worth of darkness left. Come morning, this country will be crawling with Federales."

She did not acknowledge his statement. What was the use? They both knew it to be true.

And what would the Federales do? Shoot first and ask questions later? Or would Nuncio Quiroz get to her first?

The country was broken and rugged. They stumbled up one ravine and down another, with first Aurelia leading, then the stranger, heading north, following the Star, climbing ever higher and higher.

Daylight found them on a precipice overlooking a gorge, with a fast-running stream a good five hundred meters below.

The stranger glanced to their backtrail. "How far are we from Real de Catorce?"

"Ten kilometers or so."

He groaned. "Behind us, I hope."

She nodded, scanning the landscape across the gorge. "And I need to go a good hundred kilometers that way, west."

He whistled. Hastily searching the area north and west, he turned and looked behind them. "Not today, we don't. Today we find a place to hole up." He studied the cliff across the river. "Are those caves?"

"Sí. There are many caves in these mountains. People live in some of them."

"People? Who?"

"Indians. But not close by. Mostly the Indians are west."

"Beyond where we're headed?"

"Between here and the . . . ah . . . between here and there."

75

He led her along a narrow trail that wound down to the river. "You failed to say where we're headed."

"Someplace safe, I hope," she responded.

Turning, he studied her. In the pale light of approaching day, she watched his brown eyes turn serious. She recalled how he had looked at her when she visited him in the jail.

"I hope so, too," he said. And she knew he wasn't teasing as before.

They drank at the river. She pulled a clay *olla* from the tapestry satchel and filled it with clear, cold water, while he studied the caves again. "These are too obvious. They'll search up and down here."

Aurelia inhaled a deep breath. What had she gotten them into? She had set out to save him, but instead she had put both their lives in jeopardy. Their stumbling trip surrounded by darkness had given her ample time to consider the situation. She had only herself to blame. No one else.

Pia and Zita had tried to talk sense into her. Ever since they were kids, Pia and Zita had been the sensible ones, she the *bufón*. Every time she came up with a foolish scheme, they would try to talk her out of it, but she always won them over. She could not recall a single time in all their lives when they had been able to keep her under control.

And out of trouble.

Why had she been born with such a hard head?

"What do you have in that war bag besides a water jug?" The stranger indicated her tapestry satchel.

Delving into it, Aurelia withdrew a cloth in which she had wrapped two tortillas rolled around slices of beefsteak. She handed him one, which he ate with relish.

"Just what my stomach's been asking for," he told her around bites. "You're a fine cook, ma'am."

His observation startled her and she looked quickly to the stream, reluctant to admit that she had never cooked a meal in her life. "It doesn't take much skill to roll up a tortilla," she finally managed.

But his attention had returned to the cliff that loomed in silhouette beyond them. "Up there," he said. "We'll head upstream and find a cave high on that cliff. One with a covering of brush." He started out and she followed.

Her feet ached. She was glad she had thought to wear boots beneath her skirts. She had worn them to climb the hill to the shrine, never dreaming morning would not find her asleep in her own bed.

A bit worked over by Nuncio Quiroz, perhaps, but . . .

"What's wrong?"

She looked up to see the stranger staring at her. For a moment she could but stare back, her thoughts in the chapel, on that horrible ordeal.

"Can't stop yet," the stranger encouraged.

She shook her head to clear the unwanted thoughts. "I'm coming."

The trail he found headed practically straight up from the river where they had drunk. She stumbled along behind him, trying to take her mind off her feet.

And off Nuncio Quiroz. Would he really kill her? Probably, she decided. He would have to kill her before she told Papá that he had raped her. The word

77

settled like a heavy black cloud over her heart. An indelible black cloud.

When Papá found out, Nuncio Quiros would stand to lose more than his job. Papá would kill him.

Exactly how she would tell her father and what she would say perplexed her. Perhaps she would tell Santos instead. When she got to the ranch, she would tell Santos the whole sordid story. He would tell Papá for her.

By the time they reached the top of the cliff, she was perspiring heavily. Working with the buttons on her cloak, she finally managed to tug it off, tossing it into the brush beside the trail.

The stranger turned at the sound. He stopped, staring first at the cloak, then at her. "Pick it up."

"I'm getting hot."

"Pick it up."

"It's heavy."

"Do you want to lead them straight to us?"

She bent to pick up the cloak. "I didn't think of that."

"Don't tell me you are smart enough to plan and execute my escape, but you don't know not to leave a trail for our pursuers."

She glared at him. "Obviously not, señor. If I had been the least bit smart, I would not have gotten myself involved in this mess in the first place."

His eyes softened. "I wondered when you would decide that."

An hour later, he found what he was looking for. "This should hide us well enough unless . . ." He peered into the dark mouth of the cave, then looked back at her, his eyes serious. "Do the Federales use dogs?"

"Dogs?" Her mouth went dry when his meaning became clear. "Dogs? No, I don't think so."

He smiled, a wry grin, but soothing nonetheless. "We'll hope not." With a flourish then, he pushed aside the branches of a bushy huisache tree. "Welcome to my home away from home."

"Is it? . . ." She peered into the darkness, hesitant.

"Inhabited? No varmints, best I could tell." After Aurelia stepped inside, he walked around the mouth of the cave, going back down the trail a good hundred meters or so, checking the ground, the branches, leaves.

When he returned, he sat on one side of the small cave and began tugging at his boots. "Ahhh," he moaned, wriggling his toes. "That feels good." He looked up to where she still stood, clutching the cloak to her chest. "Never was much on walking. What we need is Sunfisher. Pity you couldn't have helped him escape, too."

"Sunfisher?"

"My horse."

"Your horse?"

"An animal," he explained with care. "Four-legged critter. The kind you ride."

"We will get horses."

"Oh?"

"As soon as we reach . . . our destination. There are plenty of horses there. You can use one to continue to your friend's home."

"Bet you don't have a horse like Sunfisher," he said. "I raised him from a colt. Taught him everything he knows."

She stared at him.

"Not that I'm complaining, mind you," he added. "Don't guess I thought to mention how grateful I am for your help."

She nodded, still standing, numbed from their hours of walking through the wilderness as much as from the ordeal that had preceded it.

"You might as well lay yourself down and get some shut-eye," he suggested. "We aren't going anywhere till nightfall."

A small bit of morning light sifted through the lacy leaves of the huisache. "Could we . . . ah . . . light a fire?"

"You cold? Put on that cloak."

"No. I . . . I would like to look around."

"What for?"

"Snakes? . . ."

He stared at her.

"Spiders?"

"For a woman who believed in my innocence enough to risk her neck, you don't trust me very much, ma'am."

"It isn't that. I just don't like . . . places like this."

He laughed softly, not mocking now. "Neither do I. But I don't figure we have much chance of remaining alive and free if we run around this country in broad open daylight."

She sat down.

"If you're not going to wear it, roll that cloak up and use it for a pillow. Get some sleep. We'll be up all night." He studied her. "Or at least until we get to . . . wherever we're headed."

Although his tone remained light, Aurelia could tell he was serious about wanting to know their destina-

tion. Well, she wasn't going to tell him. The less anyone learned about her the better. When she got to the
ranch, Santos would decide how to help her out of this
fix. *If* she got to the ranch. "What if they come while
we're asleep."

"They won't find this place for a while, if at all. I'll
sleep a spell, then I'll keep watch."

She eyed him, skeptical.

He grinned. "Don't worry, ma'am. You're safe with
me. I would never attack a woman who saved my life."

She gasped.

His voice immediately softened. "I'm sorry. I didn't
mean to call that to mind."

She felt her face flush. "You saw?"

"Enough to know he wasn't acting like a gentleman
. . . and that you didn't cotton to him."

Her face must surely glow. Obeying him, she hastily
rolled the cloak into a ball and lay down. Her back
tensed at touching the rocks on the floor, but when
nothing crawled beneath her, she relaxed.

"Why don't you take your boots off . . . Aurelia?
Isn't that what your friend called you?"

She lay still a moment longer, letting his kindness
wash over her. Then she sat up and began tugging at
her boots.

"Yes, Aurelia," she admitted.

"What?"

"What . . . what?"

"Aurelia what?"

Her first name he already knew. If she could be
grateful for anything that had happened during the
past night, she supposed it would be that Nuncio
Quiroz had whispered her name. This stranger had

not heard it. God willing, he would never learn it, although she saw little hope of not dragging her father's good name through the mud in the long run. She couldn't expect to keep everything that had happened a secret. Even if Nuncio Quiroz's attack never became known, spending the night in a cave with a stranger — a wanted man, justly or not — would be enough to ruin her name forever. Her father would never forgive her.

She would be stuck in Real de Catorce, where she should have stayed in the first place. Only now it would be as a ruined woman.

"No last name?"

"No."

Her boots off, she lay back down.

"Feel better, Aurelia?" His voice was quiet, soft, gently soothing.

"Yes."

She closed her eyes.

"You know, Aurelia," he continued as though they were friends, "I've been thinking about you. Wondering why a pretty girl such as yourself would involve herself — at such risk — for a perfect stranger."

She raised her head, curious, resting on an elbow.

"You aren't a widow like you pretended at the jail?"

"No, I am not a widow."

"You are either married or you have a lover, and—"

"How dare you!"

"Not married," he decided aloud. "No lover?"

"Certainly not."

He sighed audibly. "Maybe I should have said sweetheart?"

"No." She thought of Enrique. "Except maybe a betrothed."

"*Maybe* a betrothed?"

"If my parents had their way."

"I thought it was either 'Yes, I am betrothed,' or 'No, I am not.' I wasn't aware there could be a maybe. But then, I'm not up on all your customs."

"Like keeping your mouth shut," she retorted.

He chuckled. "I may be breaking certain rules of conduct, but after all we've been through together, I figure propriety doesn't count for much between us."

"Then you are mistaken, señor. I may have risked my neck and my . . . ah . . . I may have risked my life to help you escape, but we are not bound by anything."

"That's the way I figured it."

"Good."

"It's your sweetheart who's the train robber. He wouldn't come forward when they arrested an innocent man, so you did, feeling guilty that I, the innocent man, would hang in your sweetheart's place. Am I warm?"

"You are not within a thousand *varas* of the truth. And Enrique is not my sweetheart. He . . . well, he is nothing to me. And he certainly didn't rob a train." The thought of it was too much. She laughed. Then once started, her emotions caught up with her and she laughed some more. Soon they were both laughing. Tears ran down her face. "If you knew him," she said between laughs, "you would know how ridiculous it is to picture him a train robber."

"Then who? Your father?"

Again she burst into laughter. "Of course not. My father is —" Her laughter stopped abruptly, along with her words. "My father is not a train robber," she finished, sobered by the fact that she had almost revealed her father's name and position. If this gringo had been in the country even a short time, he would have heard the Mazón name. Likely, if he knew he was harboring the daughter of the owner of the Mazón mine and of Casa de Moneda, he would tear out of here, leaving her to face the Federales alone.

Or else he would hold her for ransom.

"No, my father is completely innocent of any crime. As is his dear Enrique."

"Then I'm stumped," the stranger said. "If someone close to you wasn't involved in the robbery, how could you be so certain of my innocence? Certain enough to risk . . . all you did?"

For a long moment she remained deathly still. Thoughts of that chapel quickened her heart and dried her mouth. She reached for the *olla*, found it, and took a deep swig of cool water. Recorking it, she set it on the ground. In the near darkness, she watched him pick it up, remove the cork, and lift the jug to his lips without wiping off the mouth.

She studied him, drawing strength from his quietness, comfort from his lighthearted jesting.

"Because I am the train robber," she said.

He sputtered at her words, spewing water over both of them in the close confines of the cave. "You?"

She wiped drops of water from her face. "Do you doubt I could rob a train?"

Their gazes held for a long, long time. She watched the shock in his eyes turn to amazement, then to wonder. He wiped his mouth with the back of his hand and set the *olla* aside, still staring at her.

"No, Aurelia," he said at length, "I do not doubt you could rob a train."

She lay back down, closed her eyes, and relaxed. She was glad to be here, glad not to be in her own bed crying over Nuncio Quiroz, glad to be with someone who consoled her even amidst the turmoil surrounding them.

"What do I call you?" she asked into the growing daylight.

For a while he didn't answer. Finally, he said, "Since we are on a first-name basis, how about Carson?"

Chapter Five

The heat awakened her—midday was always hot in the Sierra Madres in September—the heat and the rocks. Rolling over, she tried to scrape rocks from beneath her. She felt like a trussed-up bird in her corset stays. Then she remembered where she was.

The evening before came back in a rush of anxiety. She looked around the dim cave. Nothing creepy-crawly. No stranger, either.

His name? Carson, that was it. Sunlight streamed through the lacy huisache leaves at the mouth of the cave. She listened but heard no sounds from outside.

Rising, she pushed aside the branches and peered out. Nothing. She studied the river down below, the far hillside. Nothing. She listened intently for sounds—of horses, of men. Still nothing.

Back inside she found where he had left the *olla* and beside it one of the two cartridge belts.

Her breath caught. She recalled telling him about the train robbery. Had he left, thinking her mad? Or worse, believing her tale, had he decided he would be safer alone?

Again she looked outside the cave. The sun was well past noon. And she was alone.

She studied the far hillside once more. Were the Federales chasing them even now? Had they come this way?

Had they captured Carson?

She sank to the cave floor and drank from the *olla*. The water felt cool, refreshing. Then from the depths of her consciousness came the memory of Nuncio Quiroz, of his mouth on hers. She wiped her lips furiously with the back of her hand. Recorking the jug, she lay back, her head on the cloak, tears forming in her eyes.

She was alone.

Alone with those dreadful memories.

After the first attack, Pia and Zita had been there to comfort her. Where were they now? What had happened to them? What had they told her parents? Were they looking for her?

Or chasing her?

In the dim interior of the cave, her memories danced to life. She recalled Nuncio Quiroz's mouth on hers again, his mouth on her throat, on her breast.

She shivered. Tears streamed from her eyes. She sobbed.

She recalled how his hands had felt fumbling with her skirts, felt again his hand inside her bloomers, felt his awful body on hers. The heat, the wetness.

Her sobs intensified, only ceasing when she drifted off to sleep. The next time she awakened it was to sounds outside the cave.

Stopping short of calling for Carson, she scarcely dared to breathe lest the sound give her away to the Federales.

Or to Nuncio Quiroz.

He had vowed to kill her. But she knew what he would do first.

"Aurelia? Are you hungry?"

Relief washed over her, suffocating her for a moment, bringing a return of her tears. Quickly, she dried her face on her skirt and forced the memories of Nuncio Quiroz aside.

Carson was here. Carson would make her laugh.

He had killed a squirrel.

"You risked a shot?"

He cocked an eyebrow. "You don't give me credit for enough sense to get myself out of the rain."

"Yes, I do. You found us a cave to hide in."

"I used this." He held up a piece of leather, as proud as a child with a piñata, she thought.

"A slingshot?" She studied the contraption — a leather strap no larger than the span of her hand with two leather cords, one attached to each end. "Where did you get it?"

"Made it." He showed her the remnants of the second bandoleer and a knife with an enormous blade, the kind Santos used for skinning deer at the ranch. She winced.

He laughed. "Courtesy of my guards."

She took the slingshot from his hands and turned it over. "Nice work."

"Thank you, ma'am."

Holding it by the cords, she whirled it over her head, then glanced at the squirrel. "You are *that* good with this little thing?"

He grinned. "I doubt I would be able to slay a giant like the young shepherd-king David did, but I may be able to keep us from starving altogether. You ready for dinner? I take it you could eat a bear."

She patted her stomach. "At least."

"Good. I don't like to travel with finicky women."

"You travel this way often?"

He laughed. "Actually, this is the first time I've taken a woman . . . a lady on the trail." He paused, rubbing his scruffy beard. "As you can see, I'm not prepared for the niceties of fancy living."

She spread her faded, now hopelessly wrinkled skirt. "We are one of a kind, señor."

His eyes danced. "Robbers of trains."

His reminder brought her out of playacting and back to reality, a reality she had created with her own foolhardiness. "I wish I weren't."

Watching her come to grips, his eyes softened. "Hey, we're partners." He held up the slingshot. "I'm still the armed and dangerous one."

He had cooked the squirrel over a fire a league or so away, he said, not wishing to draw their hunters to them. "What do you have in that war bag to go with this?"

She brought out the last of the tortillas and some goat cheese. The squirrel was tough and greasy and delicious. Aurelia could have eaten two whole ones, and she knew he could have, too.

"As soon as we reach . . . ah . . . our destination, we can fill our bellies."

He laughed. "Good. Mine's anxious to see what else you can cook up. Not that the tortillas and beef didn't hit the spot while they lasted."

She caught herself short of admitting her lack of culinary skills. "Thank you."

What would he think to learn she had never cooked a dish in her life? A woman raised with a houseful of ser-

89

vants out robbing trains? He would probably run as fast as his sore feet could carry him.

At his insistence, they spent the afternoon in the cave. "Best get some shut-eye while we can. Before you nod off, you might say a prayer for a few stars to guide us through the dark hours ahead."

"I'm afraid He won't listen to me anymore after all I've done."

He smiled at her, a wry, soft smile that warmed his brown eyes. "It can't as bad as all that."

His tenderness brought tears to her eyes. "You don't know."

She slept then, and when she awakened it was near dusk. Soft noises drifted to her from outside the cave. She smiled, hearing him sing in a hoarse, whispery sort of voice.

"Set me free. Set me free. I thought you were my lover who has come to set me free."

She found him sitting with a gourd full of water, holding the edge of that wicked blade to his face.

"What are you doing?"

He jumped at her voice, then eyed her fiercely. "Don't you know better than to scare a man while he's shaving?"

"Shaving?"

"Shaving." He swished the blade in the water and began to scrape his jaw.

"You'll cut yourself."

"I'm not in the habit of it."

"You are probably not in the habit of shaving without a looking glass, either." She glanced around. "Or soap."

He shrugged, sheepish.

She crossed to kneel in front of him, inspecting the blade, then the reddened streak down his jaw. "You don't have to shave for me."

"For you?" He grinned. "I'm shaving for myself."

She frowned, disbelieving.

"I am." He ran a hand under his grizzled jaw. "Can't stand the scratching on my neck."

"Then let me do it, so you won't cut your throat."

"You? Shave me?"

She reached for the knife, but he drew his hand away.

She persisted. "If you thought my cloak would lead the Federales to us, what about your blood?"

"Oh?" He appeared to consider her observation. "I forgot, you're the expert on escapes."

"I suspect you are much better at it than I am, since you surely have had more experience."

He frowned. "How's that?"

She liked the way he frowned, bringing his eyebrows together in the center so that they slanted down at angles almost touching the laugh-creases on his cheeks. He laughed more than any man she had ever known besides Santos.

"Like Zita said," she answered him, "you were probably up to no good, or you wouldn't have been in the wrong place at the right time to get yourself caught."

He stared at her a moment, his frown deepening. "I suppose it could look that way," he admitted. "For your information, I had never been in jail before."

She shrugged. "Like I said, you are probably experienced at escaping — if not jail, then apprehension." While he was distracted, she took the knife and scooted closer to him, inspecting his jaw. "Look up at the sky."

"You're crazy."

She inhaled. "Maybe, but that has nothing to do with shaving. Look up."

91

He caught her hand. "I'm not disputing your ability to shave a man, Aurelia. But I don't have a hankerin' to get my throat cut way up on the mountain like this. You could never carry me down to bury me."

"Why would I cut the throat of the man I lost my virginity to save from hanging?" The words tumbled out before she could stop them. Afterwards, she caught her lip between her teeth and closed her eyes to keep from staring into his startled face.

His hand tightened on her wrist. He held her steady, unmoving for what seemed like an eternity. When he spoke, his voice was soft, tired. "Look at me, Aurelia."

Reluctantly, she complied.

"Did he? . . ."

She glared at him, angry with herself for blurting out such a thing. "Yes, if you must know. Yes." Tears escaped the corners of her eyes and rolled down her dry cheeks, burning a trail as they went.

"My God, angel, I'm sorry. So sorry."

She looked into his eyes and saw the pools of agony through her own tears. He released her wrist and wiped the tears from her cheeks with his thumbs, cupping her face in his hands. She turned her lips into his palm and felt its warmth.

Gradually, a measure of peace like he had given her earlier seeped into her pain. She felt his other hand stroke her hair. Heard him mumble her name again and again, calling her angel.

She looked into his eyes. "I'm no angel. Ask anyone in town."

"To me you are," he whispered. "You are my guardian angel, and I didn't take very good care of you."

Their lips met by accident. Their heads had moved

closer and closer, as if to rein in their sorrow, their need. She drew back at the touch; he looked startled.

Then he eased her face toward his and their lips made contact again. For one brief moment thoughts of that other, despicable mouth flitted through her brain, only to be chased away by a rush of glorious heat.

At first he kissed her gently, his lips tender, caressing. As excitement built inside her, she dropped the knife to the ground and wrapped her arms about his neck. He drew her closer, stroking his hands up and down her back, stroking her lips with his own.

Before she knew what she had done, she had opened her lips and received him with as much awe as a child brings to the sacrament. Shafts of light soared through her brain, invigorating her, renewing her senses, reviving her spirits.

She twined her fingers in his hair and marveled at the softness of it. He shifted her onto his lap and she felt comforted. His strong arms around her brought solace.

At length he drew her face back to look into her eyes. She returned his stare with one of wonderment. When she caught her breath, she whispered, "Thank you. That was very good."

A wry smile creased his handsome face. Carefully, he smoothed the dingy ruffle about her shoulders. Then he favored her with a glint in his eye. "I'm glad you liked it, angel. I didn't find it half bad myself."

"I guess they're right," she mused. "About climbing back on a horse that throws you."

His brown eyes widened. He drew her to his chest and knew he didn't like being compared to a madman who raped women. He stroked her back, aggravated by her comparison. He thought about this beautiful but strange creature who had flown into his life as surely as though she were indeed his guardian angel. And if she had flown too close to danger for his sake and gotten her wings singed by some evil man then he must help her recover.

He held her close, felt her soft breasts nestle enticingly into his chest, her heart beat furiously against his. He grinned. She might think his kiss no more than an elixir, but her wildly thrashing heart said otherwise. She had liked it for what it was: a warm and sensual experience between a man and a woman. A man and a woman fate had thrown together.

He grinned again. Hell of a way to run into an angel.

Two days after the train holdup and Aurelia's kidnapping, Santos Mazón rode into Real de Catorce in response to an emotional message from Pia:

Relie is in trouble. Come quick.

"Why the devil didn't you talk some sense into her?" he demanded of Pia when they were finally alone.

No sooner had he arrived in town than Pia sent him to console his mother, who had taken to her bed over Aurelia's kidnapping by the train robber.

"Come back after you have seen your parents," Pia told him. "I will tell you everything. But first you must visit your mother."

So he had visited his mother, conferred with his father, and confronted Nuncio Quiroz, who had been entrusted with getting the prisoner safely to the Federales Station in Matehuala, from whence the man was to have been transferred to San Luís Potosí, the state capital.

When Santos returned to the Leal mansion, Pia had

94

suggested they ride to the hillside beyond the cathedral.

"Will you accompany us, Señora Leal?" Santos had dutifully inquired of Pia's mother, since Pia's old dueña was indisposed.

"No, no. Today you may take Pia out alone. Perhaps you can raise her spirits. I trust you to remain in full view of the townsfolk and ride with the carriage top down and on opposite sides."

"*Sí, señora,*" Santos replied.

They walked now through the garden they had come to think of as their own special place, reaching the precipice that overlooked a great rugged canyon. It was a beautiful vista, which always filled Santos with the love of his native land. Today it evoked no such emotions. Today he could see only Relie, his little sister, who was somewhere out there in his beloved Sierra Madres, prisoner to an escaped train robber.

Pia clutched his hand in an improper fashion. "I must tell you how it really happened. I'm afraid it will . . ." She paused, sighed, then continued. "It is certain to shock you, Santos dear. You will surely be angry with me."

Her voice faltered, and he struggled to grasp her meaning. "How it *really* happened?"

She led him out of sight of the cathedral, to the bench they had shared the night she'd tried unsuccessfully to seduce him.

At Relie's suggestion. Once more Relie's schemes had gotten them into a peck of trouble.

Santos stood, one foot propped on the bench beside where Pia sat, staring down at her. "My sister has done outrageous things for twenty-two years, Pia. I doubt anything you say will shock me."

"This will. You see, we were not out for a midnight stroll like Zita and I claimed. . . ."

His black eyes silently commanded her to continue.

She knew his parents had told him the story that was circulating Real de Catorce. At daybreak following the escape and kidnapping, she and Zita had confided to their own parents, who had rushed to the Mazón mansion bearing the dreadful news that the three of them had been out for a midnight stroll when the train robber overpowered his guards and escaped, taking Relie hostage.

It was the best story they could come up with without Relie's imagination to guide them. Actually, it was Relie's imagination that had gotten them into this mess, but the fear they had lived with since that night had stilled their tongues and kept them indoors. Pia had lived for one thing: Santos's arrival. Santos could right the wrong and save Relie from the prisoner. She knew he could. Yet now she trembled at telling him the truth.

"We freed the prisoner."

Santos's mouth dropped open. He wiped a large hand over his face, blinked his eyes, then challenged his petite fiancée to repeat her last statement. *"Despacio, por favor."*

She repeated her statement slowly, word by word, more from lack of breath than because he had directed her to do so. "We set out to free the prisoner. And we did."

Santos tossed his chin up, inhaling. He always reminded Pia of Relie when he did that, and moisture brimmed in her eyes.

With great care he settled himself on the bench beside her, turned her to face him, and commanded in gentle tones, "I'm sure you—that is to say, my sister—had the best of reasons for freeing the train robber. Do you mind telling me what they were?"

Pia gripped her emotions. "You see, Santos dear, that man was not the train robber, but the townsfolk were up in arms and the Federales were bent on hanging him. We couldn't let him hang for something we knew he did not do."

The big man's eyes widened. He sat deathly still while she spoke, staring at her. Finally, he loosened his grip on her shoulders and turned, burying his face in his hands, resting his elbows on his knees.

Pia sat quietly beside him. After a while he lifted two fingers and peered at her through the opening.

"*We?*" he questioned. "You are taking responsibility for this scheme, too?"

Pia sighed. "It's true Relie planned it. But there was no other way. Zita and I agreed. It had to be done."

"It had to be done?" Dropping his hands, he raised his shoulders, facing her again. "Let me get this straight: You helped the prisoner escape because he — the man the town wanted to lynch — was not really the train robber?"

She smiled, relieved that he understood. "Yes, dear Santos."

"Would you mind filling in the blanks, Pia? How the devil did the three of you know he wasn't the train robber? Who is he?"

Beside him, Pia tensed. "We don't know who he is . . . I mean, maybe Relie does . . . now."

He watched her clutch her hands in her lap, twisting her violet voile gown; he saw white knuckles sprout across her brown hands.

He lowered his voice. "If you didn't know who he was,

97

how did you know he wasn't the train robber?"

"I . . . ah . . . I don't think I should tell you that."

Gently, he tipped her chin with a single finger. "The worst is over, little one. You stopped a train—Lord knows how—and helped a prisoner escape . . . a vicious criminal who has taken Relie hostage. That's the worst. Now tell me how you knew he wasn't the train robber."

A tear slid from one of her eyes. "Because . . . because we . . . we were the train robbers."

For a long moment he held her chin as if they were both set in stone. "Say that again."

"It's true. We—Relie, Zita, and I—we robbed the train. Both times."

Santos dropped his hand and rose to his feet. Walking as though asleep, he crossed to the precipice and stared out, thumbs tucked in his waistband.

"My train? You robbed my train?" His words rasped from his throat. "I'm afraid to ask how . . . or why."

Pia came up behind him. Defying propriety, she reached her arms about his waist, as far as they would stretch around his enormous girth, and laid her cheek on his back. "I told you how miserable she was here. Did you not understand? Did your parents not understand? Relie was determined to escape Real de Catorce. You know yourself, Santos, she isn't one to stand by and meekly accept life on other people's terms."

Turning himself in her arms, he drew her close, consoling, consoled.

"You're right about that. Relie has a mind of her own. What a mind! I always accused her of scheming even in her sleep. But what did she hope to gain by robbing our own train? She had everything money could buy."

"Money can't buy freedom, Santos."

"Freedom?"

"Don't you see? Relie thought she could persuade Don Domingo to let her leave Catorce by 'hitting him where he was vulnerable,' as she said."

"That crazy girl."

Pia shook her head. "It was working — until an innocent man got himself arrested for the robberies. After the first holdup, your father had promised to send Relie and your mother to Guanajuato if there was one more."

"So you obliged him?"

She nodded meekly. "He intended to send them to live with your aunt and uncle the next day, except . . . except we couldn't let that man hang for our offenses."

"And now the madman has taken her hostage. I hope she lives long enough to learn —"

"She learned," Pia told him. "At the last holdup, she learned."

Santos tensed at the change in Pia's voice. "What do you mean?"

"We hid in the tunnel chapel and . . . ah . . . someone accosted her in the dark."

Santos's black eyes turned hard as flintstone. "Who? What did he do?"

"Tore her clothing . . . kissed her. She stayed in bed the next day, weeping, distraught. She vowed to give up her foolishness. She swore she would never let a man touch her again."

Santos's eyes held Pia's. Images of their own love engulfed them. He raised a hand to stroke her face. "You crazy, crazy girls. I will never understand either of you." His voice broke. "But I love you both." Gently, he kissed her lips, her eyes. "I may never let you out of my arms again, little one. I can't bear to think someone might hurt you."

They stood on the precipice, wrapped in an embrace that would have shamed them both had anyone seen, oblivious to it, uncaring at the moment, striving only to gain strength from each other, from their love.

Finally, Pia led Santos back to the bench, where they talked quietly. She told him how the scheme had worked, about the boys helping, even naming them when he asked, in hopes that Kino and Joaquín could help him locate Relie.

Gradually, the strength that had been sapped from him at Pia's unexpected revelations returned, and with it the urgency to save his sister.

"And now she is hostage to a madman."

"Not exactly hostage," Pia replied.

"He took her from the scene of the crime, didn't he?"

Pia nodded. "For her own protection. I think."

Again Santos stared at his fiancée, startled by this new piece of information. "Explain that, Pia. And include everything you have left out. I'm too addled to ask any more questions."

"The man who accosted her the first time was there."

"Again?"

Pia sighed. "That's how we arranged for the train to stop. We knew they wouldn't stop for any other reason."

"And?" he prompted when she drifted off.

"Relie sent the man a message, saying it was from the Indian girl he met in the chapel — that's who he thought she was the first time — asking him to stop for a rendezvous."

"Damnation! Does she not have any sense? Don't any of you?"

"There was no other way, Santos."

"You sound like Relie."

"There wasn't," she insisted.

Santos heaved a heavy sigh. "Tell me the rest."

"Well, the man wouldn't . . . I mean, she had trouble getting away from him, and we were already in the stairwell behind the altar, and I—" Stopping, Pia brought her hands to her face, covering her distraught features. When she spoke, her words were muffled by her hands. "I called to her . . . called her Aurelia."

She dropped her hands and stared at Santos, communicating all the horror in her small body. "I called out her name and he realized who she was, and he . . . he threatened to kill her. The prisoner heard, too. He sent Kino and Joaquín to escort Zita and me home."

"The prisoner did?"

She nodded. "He went back for Relie. He said he would see her home, but—"

"Damnation!"

"We were so frightened, Santos, and he sounded sincere. He went back for her at great danger to himself. That man in the chapel threatened to kill Relie, and—"

"Who?" Santos demanded, his breath short. "Who was the bastard in the chapel?"

"Your father's superintendent."

Santos's face tightened as the words registered in his brain. *"Padre* Quiroz?"

She nodded.

He lunged to his feet, rage growing inside him, building, escalating, exploding. He grabbed the thing closest to him, a wrought iron table, and threw it across the garden.

Pia ran to him, clinging to him.

"I'll kill the bastard. I'll kill him."

101

She held him with all her might.

"Let me go, Pia. I'll kill him."

Later she wondered how one so small as she could have held back a raging bull like Santos. He had always reminded her of the magnificent fighting bulls his family raised at Rancho Mazón, but she had never seen him angry before. She clung to him, desperate to keep him from charging from the garden to find Nuncio Quiroz.

She used no words, only her two small arms and her face, which she pressed to his chest. He was so large her head barely reached his heart. She felt it pound against her temple.

When it was over, she knew it had been neither her strength nor her body that held him in the garden, but rather her love. Like a spider's web, her love had surrounded him, snared him, held him, until at last he calmed enough so tears could flow from his eyes, releasing the rage that stemmed from his fear.

Fear that grew to hatred.

And when at length he returned her embrace, holding her close, he hid his face in the top of her head and cried until she felt his tears, hot and wet, on her scalp. She knew then she had won.

She drew him down beside her on the bench, and he pulled out a handkerchief and wiped his eyes and blew his nose.

"Quiroz will have to wait," he said finally, his voice weak, listless. "I can't go after him right away."

She lifted his hand to her lips.

"Quiroz may be involved in the difficulties at the mine that I told you about," he continued. "We don't know for sure, but—Anyway, he isn't a threat to Relie at the moment; the prisoner is."

102

Pia fought back tears.

"I'll find her, Pia. And when I do, that man will wish he had been a train robber. A lynch mob will look good to him. He will wish he had never heard of Real de Catorce."

She pressed his hand to her lips. He caught her shoulder and turned her to face him, kissing her gently. "Did you recognize him? Was he from around here?"

She shook her head. "It was dark in the chapel and stairwell, but when we came out on top of the hillside, I saw him in the moonlight. He looked dark for a gringo, but it might have been the darkness around us. He was tall, not as tall as you, but . . ." She paused, thinking. "He would probably come up to your nose. Relie said he had muscles like he worked hard, and that he was handsome."

"Relie said? When did she tell you this?"

"After she saw him in the jailhouse."

"Great God, Pia. I'm not sure I can take any more of this tale."

"The rest isn't so bad." Pia filled him in on Relie's visit to the jail. "She said he had brown hair and warm brown eyes, very warm, teasing. That for a man who faced hanging for a crime he didn't commit, he joked a lot and sang. He spoke our language, but the song he sang was in English. She said it was a crazy song; she could tell that by the way his eyes danced when he sang."

Suddenly, Santos listened closer. "A handsome gringo, about so high"— he held his hand up to his nose—"with brown hair and eyes . . . joked a lot and sang, even in jail?"

Pia nodded.

"What was he wearing?"

103

"I couldn't see, not with the bandoleers of shells across his chest. He had a rifle, too, now that I think of it. He must have stolen them from the guards."

Santos smiled for the first time since she began her strange tale. "He was a gringo? You are sure?"

"Relie said he was. And he looked like it . . . I guess. I don't think I've ever seen a gringo."

"Did he give a name?"

"No. He even refused to tell the jailers his name," she answered.

Santos pulled her closer. "I know a man who fits that description. Worked with him in Texas. He's a Ranger. First thing he would have done is grab a rifle and ammunition. The next thing would be to save a lady's life."

"We're a long way from Texas."

"Carson Jarrett isn't in Texas," Santos told her. "He's on his way to Real de Catorce to be best man at our wedding, remember?"

"He wouldn't come this early."

"I will tell you something, but you can't mention it to anyone, not even to Zita. My parents don't even know."

She waited expectantly.

"I asked Jarrett to come early to look into the difficulties at the mine. He was not to tell anyone who he was, why he was here, or that he knew me."

"But if he were thrown in jail for a crime he didn't commit, surely he would give his name — or send for you."

Santos shook his head. "He gave me his word that he wouldn't reveal himself to anyone until we clear up the mine difficulties. A Ranger's word is good as gold, Pia."

"Is it possible that he's the prisoner?"

Santos kissed her. "I *hope* it's possible. He was in the

vicinity. It sounds like him, too. Jarrett would never leave a lady in distress." He kissed her again, more soundly this time. She put her arms around his neck and held him close, returning his kiss impatiently.

Later, he vowed he didn't know what took hold of him. His lips stroked her lips, and when she opened to his passion, he accepted, urgently exploring the inner reaches of her mouth, delving, probing, exciting her timid passions.

When his hands roamed to her breasts, she nuzzled into his palms, and before either of them realized it, he had unbuttoned her bodice and clasped a warm, firm breast in his hand.

She gasped as her nipple reacted, sending a hot sensation of urgency down her body. When she moved her legs toward him, he reached around her, grasping her buttocks through layers of clothing. His broad hand spanned her with ease. She sighed into his mouth, snuggling to bring herself nearer to him.

Then suddenly he drew back, his face flushed. He retreated to a more acceptable distance. "I'm sorry, little one. I don't know how I could have gotten so carried away."

She kissed him without shame. "I do. I feel the same way."

"You're distraught. When you think about it later, you will fault me."

"No."

He nodded. "I caught you off guard. You are worried about Relie — we both are — and here I go taking advantage . . ."

Her laughter stopped him.

When he questioned, she kissed him again, openly.

"Relie would be pleased." She felt her face flush but continued anyway. "She suggested I persuade you to . . . ah . . . to make love to me before the wedding."

Although she thought she had shocked him as much as she ever could with the story of their train robberies, she learned now how wrong she had been. His mouth dropped open; his eyes flared.

Then he laughed and hugged her. "I believe it. That outrageous sister of mine!"

"She knew I was worried," Pia explained in her friend's defense.

"Worried?"

"About . . . ah . . ." She ducked her head. "Relie thought if we tried it out before, it wouldn't ruin our wedding night."

With the gentleness of a much smaller man, Santos lifted Pia's face and kissed her lips. "Let's talk about this again after we find Relie." He glanced around the garden, then winked at her. "I will keep my eye out for a better place."

She fell against his chest, weak from the multitude of emotions that assailed her. "You really think she is all right?"

"I hope she is, but I'm hitting the trail to make sure. If she's with Carson Jarrett, I know she's safe. He will protect her with his life — both her life and her honor. Especially when he finds out she's my sister. I have never had a better friend." He tugged Pia to her feet. "Except you."

They returned to the carriage, walking a discreet distance apart. "Santos," she worried, "what if Relie doesn't tell him she is your sister?"

"Why wouldn't she?"

"I doubt she will. She's determined not to drag the

106

family name into this mess any more than necessary."

"You said you called her by name. If it's Jarrett, he will recognize Relie Mazón. I told him all about Relie and her schemes."

"I didn't call her either Relie or Mazón," Pia wailed. "I only said Aurelia."

"Don't worry, little one." Santos squeezed her hand as he helped her into the carriage. "Carson Jarrett would never take advantage of a woman . . . no matter who he thought she was."

The following morning David Carson and Aurelia returned often, and found shelter during the day. They drew close were still expending the hours. That night, in the glow from their bivouac fire might deep, she saw water turn to ice in the elements . . . or perhaps, there said the light from campfires.

When Carson was so caught within the dream would be broken, and it all happened against would be I could Aurelia saw at the certainly dream would come from that certainty.

Aurelia had started long to let it pass long by, where in her response at any time. Merry long ago.

Suppose, you must be all of that and have twenty years.

"Twenty-two?" She answered Carson person's a question. May defiantly determination to force maturity to avoid trying up pursuing. She wondered whether his curiosity was simple than, or could he have been so affected by their one passionate kiss as she.

Aurelia had outright her intention, and this because she rejoiced that his lips had so carefully traced the trace of those other than still came. But there the world may even should he try to kiss her again.

107

Chapter Six

For the next three days Carson and Aurelia traveled by night and found shelter during the day. The Federales were out searching for them. That much they knew. From their hideouts during the day, they saw search parties in the distance. At night, they saw the light from campfires.

When Carson questioned whether the fires could be Indians and if so whether the Indians would be hostile, Aurelia assured him their only threat would come from the Federales.

"Apache raids stopped long before I was born."

To which he had cocked an eyebrow. "Long, long ago, I suppose. You must be all of an ancient twenty years."

"Twenty-two." She answered further personal questions vaguely, determined not to give away her family's name or position. She wondered whether his curiosity was merely that, or could he have been as affected by their one passionate kiss as she?

Aurelia had thought of little else, and on occasion she rejoiced that his lips had so successfully erased the memory of those other dastardly ones. She knew she would not resist should he try to kiss her again.

He didn't, but that didn't keep her from thinking about it — and about other things. Since his kiss had so easily quelled her fear of kissing a man, would a more intimate experience with him erase the chills that gripped her every time she recalled the lengths to which Nuncio Quiroz had gone in the chapel?

If so, it was certainly worth a try.

Pry as she did, she could learn nothing about her traveling companion other than that he was skilled at providing them with food and water in this dry desert country — at least with enough to keep them from starving or from dying of thirst in the heat of the day.

He was a strange man. Mysterious. Without a doubt he was an outlaw of some sort. How else would he have instinctively known to steal the guards' weapons?

Nothing seemed to worry him. He remained calm even when they sat in their hideout watching the Federales in the distance.

"What if they find us?" she asked more than once.

"They won't." His confidence was quiet. She hoped it was justified.

On one occasion she even asked him point-blank, "What were you doing when the Federales caught you?"

"Minding my own business."

She ignored the suggestion implied in his tone and continued her probing. "If you had been minding your own business, they wouldn't have arrested you."

He favored her with his wry grin. "They were looking for a train robber, remember?"

"But you weren't a train robber."

"We know that. They didn't. For that matter, they still don't."

"You must have looked suspicious," she retorted.

"They would not have arrested an innocent man."

He merely shrugged. "They did."

Nearing daylight of the third day, they crossed one of the rare streams in the area, this one near a high, narrow waterfall. While she filled their *olla,* he studied the flow of water and the deep pool in the center. Glancing to the top, he motioned.

"We'll find a campsite up there. How does fish sound for supper?"

"I suppose you intend to spear it with that knife?"

He shrugged. "Could. Then again, I might lose the knife. How 'bout loanin' me a couple of hairpins?"

She laughed, removing them from her hair. "That's about how many I have left."

Fascinated, she watched him straighten the two pins, twine them together — for strength, he explained — then fashion a perfect hook. Afterwards, he whittled a pole from a nearby branch and lashed the hook to it with a ribbon from one of her petticoats. She watched him tie a small pebble to the line for a weight.

"Don't know how the fish'll take to red," he teased. "Then again, maybe we'll get the biggest daddy of 'em all."

He leaped suddenly into a stand of grass near the bank, and when he came up, he offered her a clenched fist. "Hold this grasshopper while I catch some more."

She scrunched up her nose.

"You aren't afraid of grasshoppers, are you?"

She grimaced. "Give it to me." Taking the wriggling thing in her hand, she tore off a strip of petticoat and made a sack for it. By the time he finished, she held four plump grasshoppers neatly tied in blue cloth.

With the sky brightening overhead, Aurelia sat beside

him on the bank. He dipped the baited hook into the water. The waterfall made pleasant splashing sounds off to the north. From its perch high in a huisache tree, a mockingbird serenaded the coming morning.

"Tell me again," he suggested, returning to the topic they had discussed most of the past night: her role as a robber of trains. "You thought to convince this hardheaded father of yours to send you off to the city by robbing a train?"

She pulled her knees up to her chin, arranged her now frayed skirts, and lay her head on top of them. "You needn't sound so skeptical. It was working."

"Until I got caught in your trap."

"It wasn't my trap."

"It was your scheme."

She sighed.

"I take it you are good at scheming."

"And you're good at asking questions," she retorted. Throughout the night, she had avoided supplying any details that might identify her family. But he persisted in asking so many questions about Real de Catorce and the mine that she began to fear he worked for the railroad or something.

"Never hurts to try," he laughed. "Although you don't answer very many."

"You aren't a fountain of information yourself."

"Shh, we have a bite." While she watched, relaxed, contented, he jerked a fish from the water and threw it with force to the bank.

"It's huge."

He chuckled. "Not big enough to keep the two of us from going hungry today." He struck the fish with the shank of his knife, then strung it on another ribbon she obligingly tore from her petticoat and rebaited his hook.

"Good thing you wore so much clothing to stop that train," he quipped, tossing the hook into the water.

"It was my armor," she said, again resting her face on her knees.

"Armor?" He looked over at her. "Oh? From . . . him."

She nodded. "I figured he wouldn't have time to get through four petticoats, a corset, a corset cover, bloomers —" She jerked her head up, her eyes wide. "What am I saying? To you? . . ."

He laughed. "Don't mind me. I'm your companion-in-arms."

She lay her head back and watched him resume his fishing. He was right, of course. That was the reason she wasn't embarrassed to discuss such things with him: They had been through a lot the last few days and nights. She felt secure and comfortable with Carson, as though she had known him a long time, when in fact she knew nothing about him except the obvious: He was silent, but he had a good sense of humor; he avoided the Federales with an adeptness surely learned on the outlaw trail, yet he was gentle, even compassionate when he spoke of the sacrifice she had made to save him from hanging for her crime.

And he was passionate. His one kiss had lighted a fire inside her, a fire she saw burning in his own eyes when she caught him looking at her unawares.

"Do you think they will come today?" she asked.

"The Federales? You can count on it."

She glanced toward the horizon, where the sun was making a spectacle of rising.

"Don't worry. We'll find a place to hide." He nodded toward the waterfall. "Behind there, maybe."

Sure enough, high up the cliff behind the widest part of the waterfall he located a good-sized cave.

"It's perfect. They will never find us here." She surveyed the cave. Misty and damp from the falling water, it was even cleaner than the cave they had used the day before. "You certainly know how to spot a hideout."

Ignoring her statement, he studied the area, then began piling sticks together in a dry spot near one corner. "While I cook the fish, I want you to draw a map."

"Draw?"

"On the floor. Use a stick, scrape into the rock. It'll work."

"A map of what?"

He held her attention. "No matter what reasons you have for keeping our destination secret, I need to know approximately where we're headed in relation to where the Federales are searching for us."

She thought a minute. "I don't know where we are."

He raised his eyebrows, holding her gaze. "I think you do. You have been leading us west for some time now, whether you care to admit it or not."

She sighed.

"We headed north out of Catorce, turned west," he told her. "We crossed one stream not five kilometers from town. This cave is near the top of a cliff behind a waterfall. There can't be many waterfalls in this neck of the woods."

She squatted on the floor, a stick in hand.

"Start with Catorce, then work around it. Put in all the Federales Stations you know about. The one where they were taking me — Matehuala, you said. The central station they were going to transfer me to. Add any place you think they might look for us."

113

After he roasted the fish, they sat together near the map, and while they ate, he studied it.

"We'll save the other two fish for nightfall," he told her when they had eaten one fish each. "Have any idea when we will arrive at this mysterious destination — wherever I, with my trusting nature, am letting you lead me?"

She grimaced. "You have put your life in my hands," she whispered. "Without objecting."

He grinned. "Figured I'd be better off with you than with those fellers bent on stretching my neck. You're the one broke me out of . . ." His words drifted off. Their eyes held.

She knew he was thinking about the sacrifice she had made for his freedom. She had thought of little else through the long night's walk.

Reaching toward her, he cupped her face in his palm, then leaned over and planted a chaste kiss on her lips. "I trust you, angel. And don't think I don't appreciate your . . . all you've done for me."

She ran her tongue absently over her lips, savoring the warmth he left there. "I'm taking you to my home."

His eyes widened. "Back to Catorce?"

"No," she said quickly. "The place where we're going is . . . ah . . . the home of my relatives . . . my grandparents."

He studied the map, silent.

"I wouldn't take you into danger, Carson. Not after —"

Without warning, his hand shot out and covered her mouth. After a tense moment, he exhaled. "Fair enough." He turned back to the map she had drawn on the floor. "Provided your grandfather won't shoot me on sight."

A pang of guilt gnawed at her near-empty stomach.

114

"He won't be there." Suddenly, all her years of disguises and deceptions overwhelmed her. She was tired of play-acting. A warning issued by a distraught Sister Inéz, when as a young student Aurelia had been caught in one of her few unsuccessful deceptions, came to mind.

"Someday you will be sorry for your scheming mind, Aurelia Mazón. Some day you will wish you had learned to tell the truth."

Carson tapped an index finger to the map. "Show me."

She pointed to where she thought the ranch would be.

"Is there a Federales Station there?"

"At my home?"

"In the town?"

She held his gaze a moment, then shook her head. She dared not admit it was a ranch instead of a town. If her plan worked, this stranger would never know who she was, would never know her family name. As soon as they arrived at the ranch, Santos would arrange for him to escape. Whoever Carson was, wherever he came from, he would never be able to tell that the daughter of Don Domingo Mazón robbed trains. That was one fact she must conceal at all costs.

"It isn't really a town," she added. "More like a . . . a community. But we have horses. You will have no more reason to complain about walking."

At the suggestion, he began tugging at his boots. "It's plain and simple, angel. I don't like walking. Never have, never will. My feet don't care for it, either. When do you think we'll arrive at this . . . ah . . . home of your grand-parents?"

For a brief moment she considered the fact that he might not believe her. That he might know the truth. "One more night should get us there. I think."

Stacking his boots behind him, he lay down and used them as a pillow. "It's daybreak. Better get some shut-eye."

She watched him, wanting desperately to make a peace offering. Finally, she offered her cloak.

He raised himself on an elbow, staring at her. "I would never take a lady's pillow out from under her head."

"Go ahead," she insisted. "I can use one of my petticoats."

"I would never undress a lady, either. I mean . . . ah . . ."

His words faltered, and she laughed. "I would never let you. I can remove my own petticoat, thank you."

He stared at her a moment longer, then settled back on his boots and placed his hat over his face. "Wouldn't hear of such a thing, angel."

They settled down. Her body began to relax from the taxing night of travel. But her mind would not be still.

"Carson?"

"Hmm?"

"You said you had never been in jail before."

"That's right."

"But you didn't say you had never killed a man."

She waited for an answer that did not come. Finally, she asked another question.

"You said this is the first time you have taken a lady on the trail."

"Hmm," he agreed.

"It isn't the first time you have been on the run, though. Is it?"

Again he didn't answer for a while. When he did, it was with a joke. "On the run? Where did you pick up a technical term like that? Oh, I forgot, you are a robber of trains."

"I learned it the same place you learned to speak Spanish," she retorted.

"You've been to Texas?" he asked.

Texas, she thought. A clue. Not nearly enough to piece together the story of this man, but a beginning.

"No, I have never been to Texas, but we're discussing your sordid past, not mine."

"What makes you so sure I have one?"

"I can tell."

He laughed. "In Texas we do a lot of running — from Indians and the like."

They didn't talk after that. He went to sleep soon, leaving her awake to marvel that he could sleep so soundly yet so quietly, as though he was preserving all his energy for the tasks ahead.

She thought about that. The tasks ahead of them. The difficulties behind them. Strange, she thought, but the Federales didn't worry her, even though she knew they were all around and were not likely to give up their search.

Somehow she knew Carson would keep her safe, out of harm's way. How she knew this, she couldn't decide. But she did, and the resulting security lulled her into a state of near sleep where her brain began to work, the state where her best schemes were hatched.

Her most imaginative ones, anyway.

At last she slept, a pleased smile on her face.

By the time she awakened near dusk, her plan was laid. Aurelia lay still in the dim cave, pondering it. The plan wasn't exactly laid. The fact that she would persuade Carson to make love to her was the only certain part of it.

How to proceed left her in a quandary. It should be precipitated casually, almost by accident, like when she had interrupted his shaving and he'd kissed her. But how?

The only thing she had managed, past making the decision, was to remove most of her armor. While the day before she had merely loosened her stays to sleep, this time after Carson went to sleep, she removed her corset, then her bloomers and petticoats, so that now she lay clad in only her low-cut blouse and ragged black skirt.

Once the thought flitted through her mind that she should not force a seduction. Quickly, she stifled it. Since Carson's kiss had erased a good measure of her distress over the ordeal with Nuncio Quiroz, she knew making love to him would set her right.

It wasn't as if she had anything to lose by it, she reasoned. That bastard Quiroz had already taken her virginity. Now she had only bad dreams to erase.

And Carson could do that. She knew he could.

They had slept far back in the cave to escape the moisture from the waterfall. Peering now toward the light at the mouth of the cave, Aurelia could barely make out his form where he stood perched on his heels, staring past the water. Finally, he tossed something aside and stood up.

She inhaled and held her breath. Should she call to him?

When he turned toward the back of the cave, she quickly rolled to her side and closed her eyes.

"Aurelia," he called softly.

She lay still. He came closer, yet stopped at a distance.

118

"Wake up," he called again. "It's getting on to dark. Time to hit the trail."

Suddenly, she knew if she was going to do it, she must act now. "Carson?" She sat up, facing him.

"Hmm?"

"Will you come here . . . and kiss me?"

She watched him stiffen.

"Please?"

He took another step, hesitating. "Get on up, now," he told her, his voice husky.

She sat still, wondering what she would do if he refused. "Please."

He took another step, knelt on one knee, and bent to place a quick, chaste kiss on her lips.

Before he could rise, Aurelia reached around his neck and pulled his face to hers. As their lips met, he tumbled off balance, caught a hand on the other side of her shoulders, and groaned.

His lips covered hers. When she responded, her own lips trembled. Excitement coursed down her spine. Her arms tightened around his neck. His lips stroked hers.

Then he drew back. "We'd best get—"

She pulled him forward. "Please."

This time he led the way, his hands positioned about her face, his thumbs stroking her temples, his lips caressing hers. She opened her lips to his passion, felt his shoulders quiver beneath her fingers. She pulled him closer.

"Angel?" His voice objected, but his body settled into a more secure position. He drew her closer. Separated only by the thin cotton blouse and his shirt, her breasts nestled seductively into his chest. She could tell by the way his hands hesitated on her back that he was startled by her missing corset.

Her body came to life beneath his exploring lips and tongue and hands. She clutched at his back, her hands grasping great chunks of his shirt. She felt his muscles bunch at her touch.

Suddenly, his hands were inside her blouse, massaging her back with fiery strokes. They moved around her body and tugged her blouse over her arms. Before she knew it, the garment was crumpled about her waist, her breasts exposed. With exquisite gentleness, his hand cupped a bare breast, caressing it, sending sublime pleasure rippling down her body. His lips left hers, his tongue trailing down her cheek. He kissed her neck, nuzzling his face into it, then ran his tongue around her ear.

She trembled in his arms, pulling him closer, holding him tighter.

Then as suddenly as he had begun, he stopped. He pulled their faces apart, trying to lift her blouse to cover her nakedness.

"No," she whimpered into his lips, feeling herself weak, abandoned.

"We must stop now, angel, before I can't."

"Don't stop. Please."

With a heavy sigh, he pulled her to his chest. His rough shirt teased her sensitive nipples. She clung to him.

"Don't you want to make love to me?" she whispered.

His arms tightened. "Wanting has nothing to do with it."

"Yes, it does. I want it, too."

She felt him shake his head against her hair. "If I gave in, it would be taking advantage of you."

"It would not," she urged. "I want you to . . . I mean, I

want to make love to you." Her hands caressed his shoulders.

"Angel, you don't know what you're saying. Folks don't think straight when they're facing trouble. If I let myself take advantage of the situation, you would never forgive me."

She pulled her head back. Staring into his eyes, she almost swooned. The fire she saw there, the want, combined with the heat of his hands on her bare back, idly running up and down her spine, his fingers dipping beneath the waistband of her skirt, sent waves of desire pulsating through her. "Don't you understand anything?" she whispered. "There won't be a *never*. Right now is all we have." Anxiety gripped her.

"Don't you understand?" she repeated. "By morning we will arrive . . . we will be with my family. One of them will take you to safety. I will never see you again."

The words raced from her throat, whispered from her lips. "This is our only chance. Don't you want to make love to me?"

"Want to? I've wanted to for days, but . . ."

"Then do it. Please." Her lips covered his, and within moments she had kissed away his apprehensions, rekindled the flame of passion. "Please," she mumbled into his mouth.

Within moments his lips were on her breast, tugging, teasing, exciting, while he unbuttoned her skirt and pulled it over her legs.

He grinned at her nakedness. "Have I been set up, ma'am?"

She laughed, hugging his face to her chest. "Do you mind?"

"Do I mind?" He stroked her body, her belly, her thighs, her innermost secrets. At times his touch was so gentle she felt as if she were being kissed by the clouds. His caressing hands lifted her spirits higher, ever higher, until she seemed to soar above her troubles, like an eagle in flight, sweeping near the sun, dipping to the mountaintops, rising and falling as though riding the waves on a sea of fire.

"Do I mind?" he whispered into her lips. His hand left her to remove his own clothing, then he stretched closer, body to body. Taking one of her hands in his, he guided her downward, clutching her fingers around him.

"Mind?" He eased himself between her legs. He was firm and hot and she was moist and eager, and he thrust once deeply, joining them as with a shaft of the very sun itself.

Searing pain flashed through her lower body. She arched her back, tensed, tightening in an attempt to drive the pain from her body.

"Angel?" His voice, full of fear, accused. "You told me? . . ."

Clenching her teeth, she fought the pain that slashed through her.

"You said he . . . that man in the chapel . . . you said he raped? . . ."

"He did."

His face touched hers, his lips brushed her cheek. Slowly, he shook his head. "No, he didn't. No . . ." His voice faltered. "No one entered your body before me."

He kissed her lips tenderly. "I'm the first."

"But I . . ."

"If he had, he would have broken the barrier. I broke it. That's what hurt. If I had known, I would have gone slow . . . gentle."

His words made no sense. She had felt the horrid body of that man against hers. Now, though, with Carson embedded deeply within her, she knew she had never expe-

122

rienced this before. The pain began to subside, and in its place she felt a swelling of awe. Or pride. Or something truly wonderful. Exciting.

Exhilarating.

It had worked. Exactly as she had known it would. When Carson spoke, she barely heard his words, and when he began to move inside her, she lifted her hips, answering his thrusts with thrusts of her own.

Seeking. Answering.

Searching. Finding.

She felt as though she were standing on a precipice watching the sun rise . . . gradually . . . until at last it burst in all its glory over the horizon, showering the world with light.

Glorious light.

"Oh, Carson," she cried. He covered her lips before she could say more.

Finally, he rolled over and pulled her on top of him. "I'm sorry it hurt, angel. It won't ever hurt again. Next time —"

"There won't be a next time." Her throat tightened over the words.

Propping himself on one elbow, he kissed her lips, then tugged at a strand of her hair. "Want to bet?"

They dressed, ate the remaining fish, and at dark moved out following the North Star, as they had the previous nights.

But unlike previous nights, he held her hand in his, walking close, occasionally stopping to place a tender kiss on her lips. She was filled with happiness. More happiness than she had ever experienced.

Her experiment had worked. Although she had expected it would, given the success of that first kiss, Aurelia was filled with wonder at the exhilarating feelings the experience had left her with. *Por Santa Cecilia,* she sighed. That dreadful ordeal with Nuncio Quiroz was over.

When she said as much to Carson, he stooped to peer into her face in the moonlight.

"What?"

"It worked exactly as I knew it would," she explained. "The first time you kissed me erased the memory of his lips as though by magic. I knew if you made love to me, it would do the same to that other dreadful memory."

"You mean to say" — he jerked his head back toward the cave — "that was an experiment?"

"What's the matter? It worked, didn't it?"

Abruptly, he dropped her hand and started off up the trail. The rest of the night they traveled in morose silence. When she tried to start a conversation, Carson ignored her, not replying with so much as a grunt.

The country was broken, rising ever higher and higher. They wound around, taking animal trails. By the way he kept searching right and left and behind them, she knew he had not forgotten the Federales.

As he had forgotten her. Whatever had brought on his attitude, she didn't like it. It left her feeling guilty about something, but she wasn't sure what. Rarely had she experienced guilt, even when a scheme failed. A fact that made his reaction even more confusing. Her scheme had worked beautifully. And he had enjoyed it, too. He couldn't deny that.

When she asked him, he stared hard at her, then continued on his way. As though she were not even along, she thought.

Near daylight they approached one of the rare villages they had seen on the trip. This one was near the ranch.

She headed for the main street, but he stopped her.

"We'd best go around. Which way?"

"No one here is a threat," she told him.

"You can't be sure. If you go through that town, you're apt to get yourself caught. And if you get caught, they'll catch me, too. I don't hanker to hang for one of your schemes."

"Don't worry," she retorted. "I won't let you hang. We are almost . . . there."

A few leagues north of the village, she peered through the brush. "We should see the house from that hill over there."

He held her back, the first time he had intentionally touched her during the long night. "Is this a place the Federales would know to search for you?"

She considered his question, then nodded with a heavy sigh. Why hadn't she thought of such a thing? What if the ranch was encircled by Federales? "Nuncio Quiroz, too."

"Who?"

She stared at him through the growing light. "The man in the chapel."

She saw his jaws clench. Suddenly, she was very sorry she had aggravated him. No matter what else he was, he had been gentle and kind to her. He made her feel good . . . wonderful . . . in a way no one ever had before.

Lifting a hand, she touched his cheek and felt his jaw clench again beneath her touch. His eyes searched hers. Serious, demanding. What were they saying? What were they asking of her?

"Please, laugh," she whispered. "I love it when you laugh."

For the longest time they stood gazing at each other.

125

He didn't laugh, but finally that wry grin creased his lips. Reaching up, he took her hand in his.

"Come on. You say the house is over that rise?"

A hundred meters farther, he suddenly pulled her to her knees. "Don't go outlining yourself against the sky. Get down."

Below them the compound of Rancho Mazón stretched in all directions — the bighouse in the center, surrounded by outbuildings of first one nature then another.

"Which one is your house?"

Aurelia frowned, then realized he thought they were looking at a village. "The center."

From his sharp intake of breath, she gathered he had figured things out.

"How many guards?"

"One back. One front. Usually." She pointed to the north. "We can go in there, behind the hot springs."

"Nobody down there is going to string me up to the nearest tree?"

"I promise."

At length, he crawled off to the side and stood up under cover of a stand of mesquites. "I didn't see any sign of Federales, but we had best keep to cover. Don't talk."

She trailed behind him, step by step, his hand still holding hers. When they reached the guest buildings beside the springs, she relaxed. "We're safe now."

Without warning, he pulled her behind the building, framing her with his arms on either side of her head, her back to the building, and kissed her, deep, hard, passionately.

Lifting his lips a fraction, he whispered into her enraptured face, "Thank you for rescuing me, angel. I owe you my life, I know that." He kissed her again, tenderly this time, lighting fires, stirring passions. "But I don't owe you my body. That I give freely or not at all. The next time we make love, it will be just that — making love, not conducting an experiment. Do you understand?"

"But I told you — "

"To hell with what you told me. Now, let's get this over with so we can get back to business — our business."

Aurelia did not for a minute believe he meant what he said. Actually, she didn't know what he meant. But he filled her with a sense of goodness she wanted to savor forever . . . to savor and to share. Was this the feeling Pia talked about?

"Come on. I'll wake my brother, Santos. He will know how to help us."

Carson stopped dead in his tracks. "Your brother Santos?" He stared around the enormous compound. His eyes widened in a wild expression of disbelief.

She pulled on his hand. "Come on."

"Santos Mazón?" His voice echoed his incredulity.

She stared at him, wondering what he was saying, how he knew.

A door slammed at the bighouse. Bootsteps stomped toward them.

"Santos!" Aurelia ran to her brother. He swept her off her feet, gathering her to his chest in one arm without breaking stride.

Stopping in front of Carson, he thrust out his free hand.

"Carson Jarrett, you old leather pounder! How the hell did you get yourself snared in one of Relie's schemes?"

Chapter Seven

Carson Jarrett prided himself on his ability to retain control of any given situation, whether he faced bandits along the Texas and Mexico border, Indians on the western frontier, or the antics of his passel of brothers back in Tennessee.

Those who knew him credited him with having the coolest hand to grip a six-shooter, the steadiest nerves when facing an outlaw, and the most composure of any Ranger on the force in quelling a riot — all the while retaining his wry wit about him.

He tended to agree with them. Or had. Until he crossed the border, his Ranger badge hidden inside the lining of his vest, to search for the root of the trouble facing his longtime friend, Santos Mazón, at his mine in Real de Catorce.

Reflecting on it, Carson realized things had begun to fall apart back in August, soon after he decided to embark on this mission of goodwill. Before leaving Austin, he had received word from his sister-in-law, Ellie, that his brother Benjamin was missing; Ellie needed help. His promise to Santos having been made months back, along with his acceptance to serve in Santos's wedding, Carson dispatched a wire to another brother, Kale, asking him to look in on Ellie and Benjamin.

That settled, he had packed his gear and commenced to head out of town, only to be stopped by the captain, who wanted him to mop up a renegade outlaw down past Laredo.

"Some hotshot left over from that Juan Cortinas war a couple of years back," the captain had said. "Since you're headed for the border, anyhow."

He wasn't really headed for the border, he had considered telling the captain. His destination was the interior of Mexico, sans badge and Ranger credentials.

But he had not said as much, of course. And that little detour had taken the best part of six weeks, leaving him barely enough time to look into Santos's troubles before the wedding.

A week later he had located Catorce and made camp back in the foothills of the Sierra Madres. Patiently awaiting daylight, at which time he intended to implement his rather hazy plan, he had been set upon by a group of hungry Federales who claimed he had robbed a train.

Robbed a train! Fortunately, his years riding herd on the Texas-Mexico border had perfected his Spanish to the point that he understood what the ruckus was about. His readiness with their language, however, fueled the suspicions of the Federales.

A gringo who spoke fluent Spanish. Instead of aiding his defense, that fact only added to his captors' conviction that they had caught their train robber.

From there his life had taken a definite turn for the worse, although at the time he still figured he could pull off the double trick of locating Santos's trouble and keeping himself alive. Especially after they locked him up in the Catorce jail.

Then they started talking about a lynch mob. *Hollering* was more like it. The shouts and threats that filtered through his cell window were hot enough to singe the hair off a horned toad.

Things had looked up briefly with the arrival of his one and only visitor. A lovely creature posing as a widow, bringing food and reassurances that, though he had trouble believing them, raised his spirits nonetheless.

Then had come the breakout, the threats of bodily harm against his benefactress, his guardian angel.

Some guardian angel. Dressed for seduction in peasant garb, his angel Aurelia turned out to be an outrageously passionate and passionately outrageous female whom, up until the time of their first kiss, he had thought of in terms of . . . *cute*. Her pixie face with those dancing black eyes and a mouth that stretched from ear to ear when she laughed, reminding him of a Comanche bow drawn for battle, would have made a big brother proud, not to mention her undaunted courage and sassy spirit.

After that kiss, however, *cute* did not come close to fitting his description for her. By the time she invited him to her bed, such as it was, in the cave behind the waterfall, he had known that if he didn't get away from her posthaste, he would be one Ranger lost to the wiles of Mexico's hidden treasures.

Although in that skimpy blouse and those rustling skirts, her treasures had been far from hidden, even before their encounter behind the waterfall.

Afterwards, he figured the worst was over. She had won. Hands down. He had never given thought to set-

130

tling down, and he certainly would not have believed anyone had they claimed that when he did it would be with a cute little filly from south of the border.

But that morning in the cave changed everything. His outlook on life. His future plans.

Himself.

He tried to tell himself, as he told her, that the danger they were in, the difficulties they faced, kept them from thinking straight. Both of them.

He tried to convince himself it was the nights they had spent tramping through the mountains, the days he spent watching her sleep, so near yet so far away, that had fueled their fires of passion.

He tried to persuade himself to hold on to his senses, not to let himself be taken in by this outrageous female who had rescued him from the hangman's noose, only to snare him in her angel wings.

But her kiss had carried him too close to heaven. Much too close. Her olive skin felt like silken clouds, her curly black hair like angel tresses. And when he claimed her innocence in that one fateful thrust, he made her his. His in body and soul. His forever.

Not that she was the first virgin he had ever bedded. She wasn't. But she was different, and that one single act somehow made her his. As though it had been so from the beginning of time, that act confirmed the fact, tied her to him as with one of her petticoat ribbons.

As with a cord fashioned from frayed angel wings, they were tethered single-harness in his mind. She belonged to him. They belonged together.

Then she had revealed the next startling fact — that she had used their lovemaking as an experiment to drive away ghosts of the past.

Never mind that those ghosts were created in her service to him. Never mind she had not professed a desire for an attachment beyond helping each other escape those who pursued them.

Never mind the fact that she belonged to him; she didn't know it. She didn't want it. Numbed by this betrayal, he had finally rejected it.

He had seen through it, even if she hadn't. Experiment, she might call it. Experiment it was not.

To hell with her experiment. To hell with her idea of shipping him back to Texas.

He had told her so, only to be hit with the most confounding revelation of all.

"Your sister, Relie?" Carson stared from the relieved eyes of his friend to the startled expression on the face of his angel.

"Relie?" He rolled the name off his tongue. "Why didn't you tell me your name was Relie?"

"My name is Aurelia. Relie is a nickname."

"Relie is a name I would have recognized," he mumbled. "At least enough to question."

As the exchange progressed, Santos hugged his sister, then dragged them both inside the house, where he inspected her thoroughly.

"You're safe. Thank God for that. I prayed you were with Jarrett."

At Santos's intense perusal, Aurelia was suddenly very glad she had followed Carson's advice to wear her corset and petticoats.

"Carson Jarrett," she mused. "I should have questioned *Carson*. Santos has spoken of you often enough, except—"

Santos continued to talk, slapping his friend on the

back, while Aurelia and Carson stared at each other, shaking their heads in amazement.

"Thank God for a friend like Carson Jarr—" Santos stopped in mid sentence. "Hey, don't you two care that half of Mexico is out looking for you?"

Carson's attention immediately transferred to his friend. "Fill us in. We laid up days, traveled nights to avoid the Federales."

Santos slapped Carson on the back. "Then you are both ready for a good soft bed."

Aurelia's head jerked up. She caught Carson's eye.

He cleared his throat. "Aurelia, lead the way." He ran a hand through his unruly hair. "I should have suspected, her sticking to practically the same directions you gave me."

"No matter." Santos drew them inside the adobe mansion through a tiled foyer and into an indoor patio, with a burbling fountain and more colorful, flowering plants than Carson had ever seen in one place before. A maid brought orange juice and coffee at the clap of Santos's hands.

"Hola, señorita," she greeted Aurelia.

"Hello, Ana. This is Señor Jarrett." She laughed into Carson's face. "Señor Carson Jarrett." The name trilled from her lips. She turned back to the maid. *"Desayuno para los todos,"* she ordered for all of them, then turned again to Carson. "You are ready for breakfast, aren't you?"

He rubbed his stomach. "I could eat a bear."

"Or a squirrel?" she teased. "You should see him in the field, Santos. For one meal he killed a squirrel with a slingshot he made himself. Another time he used my hairpins to make a fishhook, and we had a wonderful fish dinner."

133

Santos laughed. "I've ridden a few trails with this hombre, Relie. He even saved my bacon a couple of times."

"And you mine," Carson answered in an absentminded fashion. He drained the glass of orange juice, then leaned back in his chair, still studying Aurelia with a look of wonderment.

Aurelia absorbed the truth gradually, accompanied by the warmth of Carson's attention, which he showered over her. Suddenly, she turned to Santos with a laugh. "Fortunately I saved him, *sí?* The best man for your wedding."

Sí," her brother agreed. "Fortunately you saved each other. Although you are both in more trouble than any ten people could handle."

"I should have known," Carson repeated, as though he had not heard Santos's prediction of doom. He grinned at his friend. "I even told her so." His eyes found Aurelia's again. "Remember? I said I had only known one other person in my life as crazy as you? Well, it's him." He nodded toward Santos. "Your brother. Damn!"

"I'm not crazy," she protested. "My scheme worked, didn't it? I got you away from the Federales."

Santos ruffled the mussed, dirty hair of his sister. "No, Jarrett, she isn't crazy. Just an incurable romantic who keeps this family tied in knots."

At the word *romantic,* they both blanched. Carson raised an eyebrow, as though to touch his hat for a point won. Aurelia felt her hand tremble, so she sat her coffee cup back in its saucer with a clatter.

Santos cleared his throat. Ana materialized carrying three platters of steaming huevos rancheros, which she set before them.

Aurelia stared at her plate, picked up a fork, and took a

134

bite of the eggs smothered in tomatoes and chiles.

A heavy silence engulfed them as they began to eat, Aurelia with relish, Carson more slowly, confining his attention to the plate Ana set before him.

After they started on second helpings, Santos cleared his throat again. "Now that your stomachs are full, think you two can concentrate on the Federales?"

Carson glanced up. "Shoot."

"They've been around," Santos said. "Every day a troop rides in, inspects the area, then leaves. They'll be back sometime today. You can count on it."

"What about Quiroz?" Carson questioned.

Santos studied Aurelia, then looked back to Carson. His eyes held a warning Aurelia had difficulty interpreting. She finally decided it was concern. She noted the worry lines around his eyes. He had always been a wonderfully protective brother. Her spirits fell with the realization that she had caused him so much concern.

"I want him, too, damn it," Santos was saying. "But we can't go after him right now."

"Why the hell not?" Carson turned to Aurelia. "Sorry, ang . . . ah . . . Aurelia."

She smiled, absorbing the warmth in his eyes. "I got us all in a lot of trouble, didn't I? I'm sorry."

Santos shook his head. "There's more to it than your scheme to escape Catorce."

"You mean more than the train robberies?" Carson questioned.

"A lot more," Santos acknowledged. "Accidents have been happening at a higher rate than usual."

"Such as?"

"The usual sort," Santos admitted. "Cave-ins, holes opening up, explosions . . . more than normal, though."

135

"Didn't you say you started using dynamite a few months back?"

Santos nodded.

"The men aren't accustomed to it yet," Carson suggested.

"It's more than that. More than carelessness. We are losing silver between the mine and the mint."

"How far apart are they?"

"About a league, maybe two," Aurelia supplied. "That's the reason Papá was able to obtain permission to establish a mint. I thought it solved everything."

Santos shook his head. "No, things have not improved at all. If anything, they are worse."

"How?" Carson questioned. "And what does Quiroz have to do with it?"

Santos shrugged. "The thefts are being implemented by someone inside. Someone with knowledge of when and how we ship silver bars to the mint. That's why we put Quiroz in charge of that shipment of coins. Even though we had never lost coins, we figured if he was the one with his hand in the till, he wouldn't be able to resist minted coins and we could nail him." He glanced toward Aurelia.

"I know, don't say it. I messed up everything." She turned to Carson with a shrug. Would he think her a complete fool?

Carson held her gaze, steady, serious, no hint of jesting. "No, you didn't."

Santos cleared his throat.

"I mean," Carson corrected, "you may have called his hand. Sent him packing."

"Quiroz hasn't missed a day at the mine."

Both Aurelia and Carson stared at Santos, aghast.

"Even after? . . ." Her question died on her lips.

"After what he did to Aurelia?" Carson demanded. "He dared show his face after that?"

"After what?" Santos asked. "From what Pia said, the chapel was so dark it would be his word against yours, Relie."

"His reply to my message should prove something."

"That you are a schemer, which everyone already knows. No one would believe *Padre* Quiroz, the mine superintendent with ten children to feed, would attack the mine owner's daughter. And Quiroz would know the mine owner's daughter would not risk ruining her reputation by reporting such an attack. He isn't stupid."

"That is definitely a matter of opinion," Carson retorted.

Santos stared hard at his guest. Finally, Carson broke the gaze. "So, what do we do now?"

Santos started to rise. "First you two need to get some sleep. Then . . ."

Aurelia felt her cheeks flush. She knew Carson was looking at her—and Santos. She studied her brother, tilting her chin in challenge.

Santos settled back down. "Get some rest. We'll leave for Catorce in the morning."

"Catorce isn't safe for Carson," she objected.

"We'll rig up a disguise."

Carson chuckled. "Shouldn't be hard. We have the mistress of disguises right here in the family."

Aurelia perked up. "*Sí*, I can—"

"Leave the disguise to me." Staring from one to the other, Santos's eyes settled on Carson. "How 'bout we outfit you as a monk for the duration of your stay?"

"Not a monk," Aurelia argued. "I can—"

137

Without taking his attention from Carson, Santos dismissed her with a curt, "Relie, run, see to your bath."

She bristled. How dare he treat her like a child? She smiled at Carson. "I'll have Ana prepare you a guest room."

"Let me take care of Jarrett," Santos countered, still holding Carson's eye. "As you said, he's *my* best man. Run along, Relie."

Aurelia glared from one to the other. Carson shrugged. Santos remained stoic. Finally she rose, threw her napkin in her plate, and turned to the stairs. When her foot touched the bottom rung, she heard Santos growl at Carson.

"If you took advantage of my little sister, I'll kill you. Compadre or not."

Turning her head, she started to protest but caught Carson's eye.

"Go ahead, angel."

"Angel?" Santos fumed when they were alone.

"I didn't know her name for a while," Carson told him. "Wouldn't you look on the woman who saved you from death by hanging as a guardian angel?"

"She isn't a woman who saved you, damnit. She's *my* sister and I am your friend. You had better not have—"

"Calm down, partner. I'm on *your* side. Your sister is . . ." He sighed. "Aurelia is special to me, too."

"What do you mean by that?"

Carson thought before he answered. "You said it. She's your sister."

"A fact you had better not forget, damn you."

For the remainder of the morning, Santos stuck to Carson's side as though they grew together. If it hadn't been so serious, he would have joked about it, Carson

138

thought. But here in Mexico folks looked on a maiden's virtue with even more sanctity than they did in the States. Santos had a right to be concerned; Aurelia was his sister.

And Carson had heard stories about her from the time he first met Santos Mazón on the Texas frontier. That Santos set store by his little sister had been obvious from the indulgent manner in which the big man had always talked about her. Laughing at her schemes, appreciating her wit and inventiveness. His little sister, Relie.

Carson had pictured Relie as just that: a little girl. Younger, she might be. But unbeknownst to Santos Mazón, his little sister had grown up. And his best friend was fast on the road to falling in love with her.

Carson considered how best to inform his friend of this fact while he followed Santos around the compound. First Santos installed him in a room in the bunkhouse — separated by a good hundred meters from the bighouse. Santos did not, however, leave him alone to get some of the rest he had suggested earlier.

Instead, he escorted him to the kitchen, where he left Carson in the hands of the cook, an elderly woman they called Tita, with instructions to cut not only Carson's hair but to shave off his mustache as well.

When he protested losing the mustache, Santos glared at the offending hair. "Every policeman on the Catorce force would recognize you the minute we set foot in town."

Santos left, only to return to the kitchen bearing a suit of clothing, which he carried along as he escorted Carson to an adobe bathhouse built over the hot springs.

"This puts a whole new meaning on bathing in the river," Carson quipped, letting the heated water ease tensions he had not known he felt.

He had lived so long on the trail that the aches and pains associated with the outdoors had become second nature to him. He rarely noticed them, except of a brisk morning when his knees creaked or in damp weather when his joints ached. Or as now when his feet hurt.

Instead of leaving his friend to bathe, Santos took a seat near the pool. Carson watched him fidget, scuffing his boot heels along the tiled surface, refusing to meet his Texan friend's eye.

Carson tried again at conversation. "Beats the old San Saba River by a long shot."

Santos grunted. "Yeah."

After a good scrubbing, Carson dried off and put on the clothes Santos had brought. They fit to a tee, even though Santos was a hefty two or three sizes larger than his Texas friend.

"Must have belonged to some Mexican dandy," Carson mused, buttoning the tight brown breeches that flared at the bottom to accommodate his boot tops—*calzoneras,* Santos called them.

"Some charro left them," Santos replied. "People are always running off and leaving things around here." He led the way from the bathhouse, even as Carson finished buttoning the fancy white shirt.

Aurelia remained upstairs for lunch, but Santos's disposition did not improve with her absence. If anything, he became more irritated as the meal wound down.

They discussed the mine, the problems, the possible folks involved. Still, Santos's spirits did not lift.

Finally, when Santos suggested siesta, Carson spoke up. "Silence doesn't become you, partner. How 'bout if we step behind the barn and settle this?"

140

Santos glared at him, startled.

Carson shrugged. "As I recall, you always preferred to settle disputes with your fists."

"What dispute?"

Carson studied him frankly. "Your notion that I took advantage of your sister; my contention that I did not."

"There's nothing to settle. You stay away from her, I'll be satisfied."

Carson laughed. "And tired. Both of us. You'll get fed up with shadowing me, me with being shadowed. You think I'm fool enough to search her out in this big mansion of a house and—?"

"That's enough." Santos scraped back his chair.

"Wait up," Carson called.

Santos turned, glaring at him.

Carson crossed the room. "I'm not much on siesta. I'll sleep tonight—in the bunkhouse. Why don't you show me those horses Aurelia bragged on every time I complained about my feet hurting?"

Santos held his gaze a minute, then seemed to relax. "Why not?"

By the time they reached the stables, Santos had eased up a bit. "Maybe I am overreacting," he agreed. "But, damnit, I've been worried sick ever since Pia told me about that good-for-nothing mine superintendent taking advantage of her."

Carson scanned the lavish adobe stables, outfitted with the finest equipment, spit and polished to the last bridle and bit. "And now a good-for-nothing Texas Ranger?"

"You know better than that."

"Do I?"

"I didn't know it was you out there. I mean, I hoped.

141

Great God, I hoped. After Pia described the prisoner, I hoped it was you, but I couldn't be certain. You didn't give your name."

"You warned me not to."

They stood at the corral rail watching several Andalusian horses. "You up to a ride?" Santos asked.

Carson laughed. "I'm always up to a ride. It's the walking does me in."

"Same ol' compadre," Santos mused.

"Yeah," Carson agreed. "And she's your same little sister. Only she's grown up."

Santos glared at him, then turned back to the horses, changing the subject. "Figure since it's to be a charro wedding, I'd better show you a few of the tricks."

"You show me tricks on a horse?"

"Watch me." Santos mounted a dappled gray stallion. Carson stepped into the ornately tooled saddle of the bay gelding the stable hand had saddled for him. They rode into the arena, the horses high-stepping as if on parade.

Again Carson surveyed the compound—the big adobe house looming behind a grove of silver-leafed poplar trees, outbuildings of undetermined use on either side of it.

"Beats the hell out of the San Saba River country," he mused.

Santos grunted. "The first event at the *charriada* is called a *cala de caballo*. That's where you ride hell-bent-for-leather, as you say in Texas, the length of the arena and draw your mount around on a coin."

Carson grinned. "I suppose you use a peso. How 'bout we try it with a centavo?"

"Brag now. Later you will be crawling."

For the next hour they raced up and down the arena,

142

spurring their mounts, wheeling their mounts, taking turns at the various events Santos described as part of a Mexican rodeo.

By the time they dismounted for water and to let the horses catch their breath, Santos seemed to have ridden his anxieties out.

"This wasn't how I figured you'd be spending your wedding night," Carson teased.

The joke fell on deaf ears. Santos glared in return. Suddenly, Carson was struck with the true nature of the problem. Santos was not merely being overprotective of a younger sister; he was protecting her *from* an undesirable match.

Carson's gaze once again swept the opulent compound. "I'm not a fit suitor for her, huh?"

"Suitor? What the hell are you talking about?"

"Me, my past, my future. I'm not a desirable candidate for your sister's hand."

Santos's jaws went slack. "Hand? As in marriage?"

"I told you she's special."

"You also told me you hadn't . . ."

"I didn't take advantage of her, Santos. Believe me. But I may have fallen in love with her. There's a hell of a big difference between the two."

"There is no difference at all." The big man swung and hit his friend on the chin, dropping him to the corral dirt. "A man doesn't fall in love in four days. That's called lust — and lust generally leads to assault."

Carson lay there, rubbing his chin. "I ought to get up and fight you for that, but you'd whip my butt. Never could beat you, not even when we were just partners. Now that we're going to be brother —"

"Don't say it, Jarrett. Don't even think it." Santos

143

reached a hand to pull Carson to his feet. "And it has nothing to do with who or what you are."

"It can't have anything to do with what you think I did," Carson objected, "because I did not assault her. That's what we're both after Quiroz for doing."

"Yeah," Santos admitted.

Carson cocked an eyebrow. "What does it have to do with?"

"She isn't your type, Jarrett. That's what I told Pia. You are sane and silent; Relie is . . ." His words softened and drifted off.

"Aurelia is a romantic." Carson supplied Santos's own word.

"She wants a life of high society, filled with balls and tea parties," Santos explained.

Carson slapped him on the back. "She may think that's what she wants, but she doesn't. You should have seen the way she took to life on the trail. Why, she went hungry and thirsty a lot of the time, walked all night, stumbling through brush, for the most part. Never complained. I was the one who complained." He chuckled, remembering. "She stayed after me about it, too."

"You're sure you didn't — ?"

"I'll swear it on any man's Bible. I did not take advantage of Aurelia."

The incident cleared the air. Santos calmed down, returning to the partner Carson had ridden many a trail beside, drinking from the same gyp-water streams and belly-rotting bottles of redeye, chasing the same cattle, even a few of the same women.

Then Aurelia approached the corral, giving Carson cause to wonder whether he would ever be able to pull off the disguise of a virtuous beau.

144

Although her womanly charms had driven him to the point of madness on the trail, displayed as they were now in tight-fitting leather pants and silk shirt, he felt his body flush with desire at the first glance.

Turning away, he found Santos glaring a warning that would not have escaped a man of the cloth. "You have my permission to pursue a courtship with her, Jarrett, but it must be conducted according to our customs. Which means getting the approval of her father," he grinned, "and a few dozen other things, like dueñas and—"

"I wouldn't have it any other way, partner." Carson extended his hand, sealing his agreement with the man he considered his best friend.

But when Aurelia drew nearer, he knew there was definitely another way he preferred to conduct the business of courting this passionate woman.

"So you decked him out like a charro?" she commented, perusing Carson in a provocative manner.

Carson studied his toes, deciding it best not to see how Santos took that.

"He'll pass," Santos said.

She laughed. "Until they see him ride."

"What do you mean, see me ride?" Carson questioned. "What did I do wrong?"

"Well," she hedged, grinning. "You could use some work on your turns."

"I'm rusty from all that walking we did," he retorted.

"And your hair is a lot shorter. It looks—"

"Don't say it," he rejoined.

"It'll pass," Santos told them, obviously trying to divert their attention. "The police in Catorce are looking for a gringo with long hair and a shaggy mustache."

Carson jumped when Aurelia's fingers touched his

145

now-nude upper lip.

"I liked it," she protested.

He jerked away from her touch. "Angel," he admonished, then bit his offending tongue.

"I warned you, Jarrett," Santos growled.

The clang of Tita's dinner bell saved Carson from further confrontation at the moment. Aurelia fell into stride between the two of them as they gave their reins to a stable hand and headed for the house.

Before they stepped through the back gate, Santos touched Carson's arm, drawing his attention. When Aurelia moved ahead a couple of paces, he growled at his guest.

"I don't trust you nearly as far as I can throw you, Jarrett. Cross me on this, and I promise I will toss your carcass back across the Río Bravo."

Chapter Eight

Aurelia awoke before dawn the next morning, overcome by anxiety. She had suddenly lost command of her life, and for the first time she could remember, she didn't have the slightest notion how to regain it. The evening before had merely compounded the problem.

At Tita's first call to dinner, she had left the corral and dashed upstairs to dress, returning to find Santos and Carson in the parlor sipping brandies.

Carson offered her one. Santos objected. She poured her own, then nearly choked on the fiery liquid at Carson's unabashed perusal of her gown.

"I take it you approve of my metamorphosis."

He bowed gallantly. "Most assuredly, ma'am. Yellow becomes you."

She had worn a yellow silk dress with a light woolen rebozo to cover her shoulders. The mention of yellow reminded her of Pia's wedding, of the yellow lace gown she would wear as Pia's maid of honor.

Her head still reeled from discovering Carson to be the friend whom Santos had spoken of at such lengths. The friend who would stand beside her at her brother's wedding.

Picturing Carson before the altar in the cathedral at Catorce gave her a queasy feeling. She supposed because she could not imagine him fitting in with eleven charros.

Yet he would, she thought, delighting in the way the trim *calzoneras* clung to his muscled thighs, at the expanse of his broad shoulders beneath the cropped jacket. He would look like one of them, and more. He would be the most handsome charro present.

It was her own desperate need to keep him from becoming one that confused her, that had led her to lash out at him at the corral, belittling his riding ability.

He rode superbly.

And he knew it. Her remark had not threatened his composure one whit; it had only heightened her own uneasiness at his transformation from cowboy to charro.

A transformation that threatened her in ways she could not interpret. Threatened, and at the same time exhilarated her.

Dinner progressed in a pleasant if awkward fashion. Santos escorted her to the comedor. Carson seated her, under her brother's watchful eye.

Talk turned mostly to the situation at Catorce — settling the problem Aurelia and Carson faced with the Federales while not endangering the ongoing investigation at the mine.

When she learned Santos had been to Catorce, she asked about her parents, then was bitterly embarrassed at his reply.

"Mamá took to her bed over your kidnapping."

"Kidnapping?"

He related Pia and Zita's story, which embarrassed her

148

even further. Hearing all this, Carson would think her the child Santos made her out to be. No one but a child would pull such a stupid prank.

"It wasn't stupid," Carson replied to her contention. "You saved my life, remember?"

She sighed. "There was surely another way."

He shook his head. His warm eyes held hers, bringing the now-familiar sensations of comfort and strength combined with a deep sensual yearning. Carson opened his mouth, but after a glance at Santos, he closed it without speaking.

Santos cleared his throat and changed the subject. "We will leave for Catorce in the morning, but I have to return here in time to drive bulls to the feria at Guanajuato."

For the remainder of the meal they talked bulls . . . raising them, fighting them. Aurelia listened and began to relax, enjoying the camaraderie between the two friends. As different as they appeared physically, the bond of friendship between them was evident.

But she had been lulled into a false feeling of easiness, she realized, for as soon as they left the comedor, Santos shooed her off to bed.

Aurelia turned on him with a ready lecture. "I am not a child, Santos Mazón, and I will not be dealt with like one." She lifted her chin in defiance, but when she spoke, her voice trembled. "You have never treated me this way before."

Santos eyed Carson, then took his sister by the arm. "Perhaps I have never had reason to — before. I'm sorry, Relie, but Jarrett and I have things to talk over, and you've had a rough few days. Say good night."

Aurelia jerked her arm from his grasp, feeling her face flush.

Carson had held himself back, but at the hurt in her voice, he stepped forward, extending a bent elbow. "May I escort you, señorita?"

Gathering her skirts in both hands, she stomped off. "Both of you can go to hell."

Carson caught up with her, taking her arm. When she turned to protest, her eyes found his. They were the same warm brown she had grown accustomed to. They perused her with the same hungry look.

"I can't very well escort you home," he said, "since you are already here. How about to the staircase?"

Hesitating, she felt a heavy tension grow around her. Finally, she took his arm and let him walk her across the wide tiled foyer. Santos's bootsteps echoed behind them.

"What is the matter with you two?" she hissed under her breath. "You are acting crazy, both of you."

"I know, angel," he whispered. "We'll work it out."

She stopped at the staircase and faced him with a smile. His lips looked strange, different without the covering of hair. She wanted to touch them, but she dared not. Not with Santos only a few steps away, one boot propped on the edge of the fountain.

"You had better work it out," she said. "I don't intend to ride all the way to Catorce with the two of you goading each other the whole time. It's a wonder you are friends."

When she took a step to ascend the stairs, Santos crossed the foyer. "Wait up, Relie." She heard him dismiss Carson, who retreated to the parlor, where he leaned against the arched doorway and watched them.

"Whether you know it or not," Santos told her quietly, "you're playing a dangerous game."

"What do you want me to do?" she snapped. "Turn myself in to the Federales? In case you have already forgotten, I apologized."

"Not that game," Santos said. "The one you and Jarrett are playing. He's my friend, Relie, and—"

"Carson and I are not playing games. We tease each other—like you and I used to tease each other until you decided to take on the role of substitute *father*."

"You don't understand, Relie."

"You're right, I don't understand. It's you and Carson who are playing some sort of vicious game. I don't understand why you are at each other's throats. No," she corrected, "why *you* are at *his* throat."

He sighed. "You're leading him on, Relie, and I won't have it. Dressing like that, showing off more than the law allows."

She stood on the second step up, he on the foyer floor, and they glared at each other eye to eye. At his words, she reached down and hiked up the neckline of her dress an inch or two. "Better?" As she spoke, however, her gaze strayed over Santos's shoulder. She caught Carson's eye.

He winked.

She stared, wide-eyed. He held her gaze.

"I didn't mean to," she whispered to Santos.

"I know, Relie. But the poor fellow thinks he's falling in love with you, and I don't want to see him hurt."

Her mouth went dry. Her eyes held Carson's. Santos's words echoed inside her head. "Love?"

She caught her bottom lip with her teeth.

"Love," Santos repeated. "He asked for permission to court you."

"Court?"

"Great God, Relie, don't you understand anything? He wants to marry you."

"Marry . . . me?"

151

Carson's gaze held her mesmerized across the distance. Santos's words struck a chord deep inside her.

"But I . . ."

"I know, Relie. You aren't ready for marriage. You want to go to Guanajuato. You want to go to balls and parties and have lots of beaus."

"Marry? . . ." Her breath came short. She jerked her arms from her brother's hold and turned to race up the stairs. He pulled her back.

"He's my friend, Relie. Don't come between us."

She looked into Santos's pleading eyes. Santos, her brother, whom she loved like no one else on earth. "I won't, Santos. I won't."

"Then tell him."

"Tell him what?"

"That you aren't ready. Tell him your plans."

She stared at him, gripped in a nightmare she had not envisioned, but one she instinctively knew had been born in her own scheming mind. "How?"

He shook his head. "I don't know. But you have to do it. He won't take it from me. I tried. You have to tell him."

"How can I?" she retorted, knowing as the words formed and left her mouth that she was reacting like the child he thought she was, like the child he wanted to keep her. "How can I tell him something of that nature with you always at his side?"

Santos shrugged his shoulders. "I'll give you a chance . . ." His words drifted off in thought. "In the morning before we leave, I'll be sure you get a chance to talk to him in private." His hand tightened about her arm. His eyes bore into hers. "Do it, Relie. And go easy on him. He's my very best friend."

Lying abed now waiting for the sun to rise, for Tita to

ring the first bell for breakfast, she recalled Santos's astonishing words. At first she had rejected them as the fantasy of an overprotective brother.

But thinking about it — which she had done off and on the entire night — she decided he was right. He was right, for in the end it was Carson's words that sang in her head, Carson's words about making love to her, his determination that they would be together again.

Is that what he meant when he talked about getting back to their business? That he was falling in love with her?

That he wanted to marry her?

Jumping from bed, she strode to the window and stared out at the corral, envisioning him as she had seen him the day before, riding that bay horse every bit as good as any charro she had ever seen.

She tried to picture him in Guanajuato. At the lavish new theater, wearing a black silk suit and top hat. At the governor's ball, twirling her around a room sparkling with chandeliers and ladies' jewels.

But the images would not come. Instead she saw him before the altar at Saint Francis Cathedral. Standing before the altar with her beside him, wearing her yellow lace dress.

At Pia and Santos's wedding.

Yes, she must tell him. She must not come between her brother and his best friend. Certainly not with the wedding so close at hand.

She found him standing beside the corral, and she pictured him in Guanajuato, riding the bay in the *charriada*.

"So you think I need work on my turns?"

"Have you ever been to Guanajuato?"

He shook his head.

153

"Would you like to come?"

"Are you going?"

She tilted her chin, thinking. She would face a giant hurdle convincing Papá to allow her to make the trip, even if she promised to return to Catorce after the feria. Perhaps if she promised to do penance of some sort when she returned . . .

"Yes," she replied.

"Then I'll be there, angel."

She looked up at him, her heart pounding with what she had to tell him. His appellation sang in her ears. "Carson, I . . ."

She never got to finish, because he lowered his lips, touching hers, igniting her with a fiery urgency that left her breathless. She threw her arms around his neck, drawing him near, eagerly returning his kiss.

As though she were starving for his touch, for his lips. His arms encircled her, bringing her closer to his body. Her body . . . craving his . . . starving for his body.

Finally, she tried again. Drawing her lips from his, she gazed into his eyes. His loving eyes. "Carson, I . . ."

"I missed you, angel. It feels like we've been apart a year already."

Her heart skipped a beat. "I know."

Once again their lips met, desperately seeking relief from the yearning that gnawed inside them.

Again she pulled away before she wanted to. She had promised Santos, after all. But how to begin?

Staring into Carson's eyes, Aurelia felt weak, vulnerable, lost. Yet a wonderful feeling, full of excitement and anxiety and something soft and sensual, also simmered inside her.

"I must talk to you," she hurried to say.

He cocked an eyebrow, his wry grin tipping the corners of his nude lips. She reached to stroke his upper lip, recalling how she had wanted to do so the evening before.

How Santos's presence had stopped her.

Santos.

"I must tell you something." She turned in his arms, staring into the corral. He turned beside her, one arm around her shoulders, one locked over the top of the corral. She felt his gaze on the side of her face.

"I'm listening."

"Remember I told you I was trying to escape Catorce?"

"Hmm."

"Well, I was going somewhere."

She felt his arm stiffen against her shoulders.

"I was going to Guanajuato."

"To the feria?"

"No."

"Somehow I didn't think it would be that simple."

She turned to look at him. His warm brown eyes were soft, sad. "Oh, Carson, I've wanted it for so very long."

He smiled. "I suppose I should be grateful it's an *it* you want and not a *him*."

She paused, considering his statement, finally understanding it. She spoke before she fully realized what she was saying. "You are the *him*. I want you to come, too. I thought about it all night. With us together, it would be wonderful. We would have a wonderful life."

"Doing what?"

She frowned.

He kissed her lips. "Besides the obvious, of course."

"We can find something."

He studied her, his expression changing from lustful to serious to playful. "Is this a proposal, ma'am?"

After the longest time, she grinned self-consciously. "I . . . well, Santos said—"

"That brother of yours is becoming a nuisance."

"I know, but he . . . I mean, you're his friend, and he doesn't want me to come between you. I don't want to, either. He said you . . . that you loved . . ."

Stricken by the shameless turn of the conversation, Aurelia diverted her attention to the corral, but Carson tipped her chin, bringing her face back to his.

"He told you I'm falling in love with you, is that it?"

She nodded.

"Well, he's right." Bending, he kissed her tenderly. "I think it's love. Since I've never experienced it before, I could be wrong." He kissed her again.

"You intoxicate me, angel. Your playfulness and enthusiasm, even your scheming—"

"You think I'm a child. Like Santos!"

He held her face, staring into her eyes, speaking softly but distinctly. "I *know* you are a woman."

Before she had a chance to complete the conversation, the second bell for breakfast rang. Carson kissed her again, soundly. He held her close, running his hands up her back, molding her curves to his.

"No telling when that birddoggin' brother of yours will leave us alone again," he commented when they turned toward the house.

"I know. He said I could have this one chance to tell you."

"To run me off, you mean?"

"No. He doesn't think I'm ready for marriage, that's all."

With a hand to her arm, he stopped her. "I'm not sure I am, myself. Marriage is a mighty big step. Too big to

156

take the first time the notion strikes." His eyes caressed her face, warming her, calming her. His next words kindled a spontaneous though unexpected sort of hope inside her. "I'm not trying to rush you, angel. But he isn't running me off, either."

"You are friends, and—" she protested.

"Let us worry about that. What is happening between you and me is no one else's business, not even your brother's." He planted one quick, deliciously wet peck on her lips. "We may have to play his game a while, though."

Breakfast went well, mostly, Aurelia suspected, because Santos believed she and Carson had settled the matter of their relationship.

They hadn't, and it nagged her the entire way to Catorce. That, and the visit from the Federales they received in the middle of breakfast that morning before they left the ranch.

The aplomb with which the two friends agreed to the Federales' insistence on escorting them to Catorce at first concerned, then excited her. Watching them together, she marveled at how congenial these two men were, at how well they worked together.

Santos introduced Carson as his friend from Texas, a Ranger who had come to spend some time helping him end his days as a bachelor in style.

The Federales had laughed at that, and though at first warily, they accepted Carson as one of their own. They were glad Aurelia had made it home safely, and other than a few cursory questions and a couple of raised eyebrows, they had not questioned her story of getting separated from her friends on their evening stroll, being accosted by the escaped prisoner, then set free. It was fortunate, they agreed, that she had been able to find her way home with little trouble.

By the time they rode into Real de Catorce two days later, Carson was joking and cutting up with the Federales as if he hadn't spent the previous several days avoiding the mere sight of them.

And true to his word, Carson played Santos's game, treating her with the same camaraderie as he did her brother. Well, she conceded, almost.

Around the campfire at night, she would suddenly find him staring at her, his eyes alight with warm passion. A couple of times she saw Santos's eyebrows shoot up, but his hackles did not rise. She supposed he thought she had ended the matter.

At night she slept on the ground between them. Close enough for protection and privacy from the Federales — who camped a discreet distance away on the other side of the fire — but not so close that there was any danger of chance contact.

During the daytime, she rode beside one or the other, occasionally between them, sharing their laughter and jokes as she had always done with Santos's friends. A sense of belonging settled inside her and left her feeling warm and secure and happier than she could ever remember being.

Even when Santos teased her about her fondness for trail living. When she asked where he had gotten such a notion, he slapped Carson on the back and hee-hawed.

That was the only occasion on the entire trip when the two men showed the slightest bit of hostility toward each other. And then it was Carson who shrugged off Santos's hand and turned abruptly away.

The night before they reached Catorce, Santos and Carson advised her of their plan.

"When we get home, you will have to stay indoors," Santos told her. "We have decided not to let anyone know you turned up safe. We don't want Nuncio Quiroz coming after you."

Aurelia watched Carson's jaw clench at that. "We will stick with the story your friends concocted," he added. "For the time being, no one is to know who I am."

"You mean who you were," Aurelia laughed. "You *are* Santos's friend, the Texas Ranger. You *were* a train robber."

His gaze held hers, his wry grin teasing. "You were the robber of trains, ang . . . ah . . . Aurelia."

Santos cleared his throat. "We won't even tell Mamá and Papá the truth right now. It will be enough for them that we have brought you home unharmed. The difficulties at the mine are coming from someplace high in the company. Papá might accidentally trust the wrong person."

When they advised the Federales of their plan to take Aurelia secretly into town, the soldiers were not convinced the sham was necessary.

Santos convinced them by saying they didn't want her to come to any undue harm until the escapee was caught. Then he called on their sense of pride, saying, "If the Catorce police discover the hostage is no longer in danger, they might slacken their efforts to catch the prisoner. You know how lax locals sometimes tend to be."

None of the three trusted the Federales to keep their mouths shut. But it was Carson who hit on the one thing that might do it. "The señorita's reputation is at stake here, señores. If word leaks out that she spent time with that criminal . . . well, you understand."

They nodded solemnly, giving Aurelia a tip of the hat,

even though to all appearances she was one of the men. Dressed in breeches, shirt, and sombrero, she reluctantly slipped a heavy serape over her shoulders before they entered the tunnel.

It was Carson she worried about being recognized when they exited the tunnel and rode into the high-mountain city. Their horses' hooves clattered along the twisting bricked streets, past the two-story Casa de Moneda, where she thought of Enrique Villasur for almost the first time since she'd tricked him into revealing the arrangements for moving the prisoner.

She watched Carson scan the streets from side to side with wide eyes. Even though he had seen Catorce through the eyes of a prisoner, today he viewed the opulent surroundings from a different perspective.

"So this is what you were trying to escape."

"It may look grand," she insisted, "but living here is like being in prison."

He shook his head. "If this is a prison, I don't think I'm ready to see Guanajuato."

The Federales parted company with them at the jail. Aurelia ducked her head and Carson held his breath until they were a good block up the street.

Around them the mountains rose as a backdrop for a stage play. Santos took the lead, turning his mount this way then that, rising and twisting with the streets, ever higher and higher.

Vines trailed down whitewashed walls from wrought iron balconies. Potted plants graced the unobtrusive entrances to various villas. Water splashed gaily from fountains at almost every intersection. The festive scene enveloped Aurelia, not with a joyous sense of homecoming, but with a pall of doom. Here she was, right back where she had started from. She felt like a captive being returned to prison.

Drawing rein at the side of the Mazón mansion, Santos dismounted to open the wide double gates that led into the stable yard.

Once inside the bricked yard, she turned to find Carson sitting his mount under the arched portal, shaking his head in dismay. "Come on, we're home," she called.

With a sigh, he spurred his horse past Santos. When he spoke, his voice was heavy with accusation. "I may change my mind about believing you, partner."

"How's that?" Santos asked.

"This here's mighty high cotton for an ol' country boy from Texas."

Before she had a chance to decipher his meaning, the gates swung closed behind them, and family members engulfed them from all sides.

Even Pia and Zita were there, since Santos had sent a vaquero ahead to alert the family to their arrival, with the specific request that Aurelia's two closest friends be present, but no one else outside the immediate family.

In a rare show of affection, her father hugged her, giving her a brief inspection before turning his attention to Santos.

Her mother wrapped her in her arms. Her tears, the first Aurelia could ever recall seeing on that usually placid face, brought moisture to her own eyes, deluging her with a great wave of remorse. "I'm sorry, Mamá. I didn't mean to worry you."

Her mother held her back, took both cheeks in her hands, kissed her, then looked her over from head to foot. "You are safe. I prayed to Santa Cecilia every day for your safe return."

161

"We all did, Relie."

Glancing toward the voice, Aurelia saw Enrique, his face a picture of stoic endurance.

"Enrique has been our strength," her mother said. "Our tower of strength."

Suddenly, the clatter and clamor surrounded Aurelia, resounding in her ears, deafening her. She smiled feebly, nodded her thanks, then looked around.

She found Carson's eyes on her. The pandemonium subsided. He stood to the back of the stable yard beside her father and Santos. Pia hovered near.

"Carson," she called, "come meet Mamá."

His eyes left hers, settling on the man beside her.

"Let me make the introductions." Santos dragged his friend by the arm. "Mamá, this is Carson Jarrett, my best man. Funny how he turned up early. He was a big help to me, searching for Relie and all."

Aurelia's eyes never left Carson, whose attention had turned on her mother. He waited until she offered her hand, then took it with well-mannered grace.

"Señora Mazón. I apologize for intruding at such a time."

Pia hugged Aurelia from one side. "Isn't it wonderful that he came early? Now I have one less thing to worry about."

Zita hugged her from the other side. "We were so worried about you, Relie." Her eyes didn't look worried, though. Aurelia watched her friend's gaze fasten on Carson.

"Isn't it exciting?" Zita babbled. "The best man is already here. It puts me in the wedding spirit."

Aurelia sighed. At least neither Pia nor Zita recognized Carson. Maybe that meant no one else would.

162

"I'm sorry you didn't arrive earlier," Enrique was saying at her shoulder. "We just finished lunch, and I must leave now before siesta begins." Raising his hand in a hesitant manner, he touched her cheek with his knuckles, then quickly drew his hand away. "You are all right, aren't you? That man didn't . . . I mean, he didn't harm you?"

She stared at him, aghast. With the greatest of difficulty, she restrained herself from turning to Carson to see if he had heard, to see if he was watching.

To reach for him. To hold to him.

Enrique's question brought back their glorious days on the trail . . . her first days with Carson. How dare this outsider speak of them with such innuendos? How dare he speak of them at all?

After Enrique took his leave, she allowed Zita to draw her through the back entrance into the marble-floored hallway of the Mazón mansion. "Don't be angry with Enrique, Relie. He has been worried about you. I mean, dreadfully worried. His bride-to-be abducted . . ."

Aurelia only half listened to her friend's chatter. Ahead of them she watched Pia and Santos, saw their struggle to keep from touching each other, felt their urgency, their desire. Where was Carson?

Turning, she saw him lounging against the arched doorway, boots crossed at the ankles, staring after her.

His eyes were warm but somehow lifeless.

"Come on," she called. "If we want lunch, we have to eat before the servants retire for siesta."

He grinned. Not the wry, provocative grin she had come to expect, the one that fired her spirit, but a dismal, what-the-hell sort of shrug from a man she did not know.

Even Santos appeared uncomfortable, she noticed

163

over lunch. The family sat around the table, watching the three of them eat, talking. Aurelia could tell Pia longed for Santos's attention, some of it, anyhow, but he concentrated on explaining the events that had transpired since Aurelia's *kidnapping* — the version they had agreed to earlier.

Carson sat quietly at the far end of the table, eating, adding to the conversation when Santos asked a direct question, but otherwise ignoring everyone.

Including Aurelia herself. Her ire began to rise. No wonder she hated Catorce. It had the most dreadful effect on everyone.

Then her mother announced siesta.

"I have invited Pia and Zita to stay over for siesta, Relie. I knew the three of you would want to visit while you rest."

Dutifully, they rose from the table. Santos stopped them.

"Remember," he cautioned, "no one outside this room is to know about Relie's return. Papá and I will inform the servants. We want to draw the train robber out of hiding if we can. And we certainly don't want to set her up as his target."

Agreements were mumbled.

Aurelia caught Carson's eye the moment he started to speak. He hesitated, then spoke.

"I hope you told that to the feller she's engaged to marry."

Even though his words indicated concern for her welfare, his voice carried an alarming tone of indifference.

"I'm not engaged to marry anyone," she retorted.

"He means Enrique, dear," her mother chided.

Carson's eyes held hers. She glared at him, feeling

moisture brim. "I am not engaged to Enrique," she spat, then turned on her heel and raced from the room.

"You must tell us all about it."

"You look all right, but are you?"

"How did you get away from that criminal?"

"What was he like?"

Aurelia stood behind the screen in one corner of her bedroom, stripping off her soiled traveling clothes. Her friends' babble settled over her rattled nerves, soothing her with its familiarity. Finally, submerged in the steaming sitz tub, she called to them, teasing.

"He was wild."

She heard Pia gasp.

"Wild and wicked."

"Tell us," Zita demanded.

"If you want to," Pia added.

"Tell us," Zita repeated. "What did he do?"

"How did you get away from him?"

Aurelia laughed. "I figured you would want to talk about other men. Santos, for instance, or that handsome Texas Ranger who will be best man."

"*Best man.*" Zita's voice swooned over the screen. "Carson Jarrett certainly fits that description."

Not until she had dried and buffed her body, then showered it with rose-scented talc and wrapped herself in a heavy cotton dressing gown did Aurelia consider telling them the truth.

The jesting had come naturally. Yet, once begun, she wasn't sure she wanted to share her time with Carson with anyone. Not even with her two closest friends.

By the time Aurelia finished her bath, Pia and Zita had removed their day dresses and donned wrappers for siesta. The three girls settled into Aurelia's soft feather mattress, propping themselves on several pillows each.

Aurelia studied first one, then the other.

"I know that look, Relie," Zita warned. "You are hatching another scheme."

"Please don't —" Pia began.

Aurelia laughed. "What would you give to know a secret?"

The girls' eyes popped — Zita's with delight, Pia's with guarded understanding.

"Since you are both involved, I suppose you are entitled to know the truth. But you can't tell a soul. Not anyone. Not even Mamá and Papá can know until Santos gives the word."

Zita nodded eagerly, while Pia continued to smile as if she knew what was going on.

Aurelia glanced from one friend to the other. "Carson Jarrett is the prisoner."

Chapter Nine

By the time the girls dressed for dinner that evening, Zita was still agog with the notion that the prisoner they had helped escape death by hanging was none other than Santos's friend, his best man, and a Texas Ranger, at that.

"Santos hoped that's who he was," Pia admitted. "Wouldn't it have been dreadful if we had let them hang him?"

Aurelia blanched.

"Why didn't he tell the authorities who he was?" Zita questioned.

"I don't understand all of it," Aurelia hedged, determined not to reveal that part of her promise which involved the problems at the mine. "It was some silly bet he and Santos concocted while they were herding cattle in Texas."

She had chosen a pink brocade gown with an off-shoulder treatment of tulle for dinner. Now she worked her hair into a twist, which she secured with golden combs.

There was more to the story than the mine difficulties that she hadn't told them. They didn't know, for instance, that Carson was falling in love with her.

And they certainly did not know how she had tricked him into making love to her in the cave.

Nor had she told them the lengths to which Nuncio Quiroz had gone in the tunnel chapel. At dinner, she began to regret leaving out one of those pertinent facts.

Doña Bella had prepared the elegant comedor of the Mazón mansion to reflect the family's thanksgiving for the safe return of their daughter. The pale pink silk-covered walls glowed from the reflection of new candles in the three brass chandeliers. The black marble mantel was topped by white candles, masses of red roses, and the carved figurines of several of the family's patron saints: the Virgin of Guadalupe, San Francisco de Asís, Santa Bárbara, and Aurelia's own saint, Santa Cecilia, on whose day, the twenty-fifth of August, Aurelia Cecilia Mazón had been born.

White candles, red roses, and gleaming brass adorned the length of the linen-covered dining table, which when fully extended could seat twenty-four diners. Tonight a couple of leaves had been removed, allowing ample room for the ten diners but no more.

Those ten diners, however, soon became too many to Aurelia's mind—a fact that had nothing to do with Santos's objection that Doña Bella had invited Padre Bucareli and Sister Inéz from the convent school.

"Padre Bucareli spent a fortune on white candles," Doña Bella told her son. "And Sister Inéz said a novena. They are entitled to know their prayers were answered."

"If the wrong people discover Relie's presence in Catorce, we may need more than prayers to keep her alive," Santos had retorted. But his objections had fallen on deaf ears.

Then there was Enrique, whom Doña Bella seated beside Aurelia. Of course Enrique had been present when they arrived today. And Enrique had been warned to keep his mouth shut. How well Aurelia recalled that. Carson's accusation that she was betrothed to Enrique still rang in her ears, along with the fact that he did not appear to have believed her denial.

Grimly, she knew her mother's seating arrangement would only strengthen the notion.

Doña Bella did love a balanced table. And since a private dinner was one of the few times señoritas were allowed to sit beside caballeros, no one usually objected.

That, in itself, was not Aurelia's objection tonight.

She did, however, object to being seated at one end of the table beside Enrique, who tried his best to monopolize her attention, while Carson was paired with an obviously enthralled Zita at the other end.

Aurelia could deliberately look down the length of the table at Carson — that is, if she wanted to call attention to herself. But since the few times she tried Zita had been falling all over him, Aurelia soon gave up.

Besides, Carson had not looked her way one time that she noticed. If only she had mentioned to Zita that he was falling in love with her, perhaps her friend wouldn't have made such a fool of herself.

Aurelia regretted her omission.

Zita did look beautiful. In a bronze silk *Mousseline de Soie,* she appeared much more mature and fashionable than Aurelia had ever seen her. They had all grown up, she thought. All three of them.

Was it Pia's approaching marriage?

Or the ordeal in the chapel?

She chanced a peek at Carson. How handsome he

169

looked in crisp white shirt and black cropped jacket. Handsome enough to cause a girl to want to grow up.

Talk centered around the ordeal she had been through, the difficulties they faced in keeping her safe from the escaped prisoner.

"Our local police will want to question you," her father was saying.

"I will not allow such a thing," her mother retorted from the far end of the table.

"At best they will insist on coming here to interrogate her. She can help them get a handle on the whereabouts of this fellow."

"For the time being, Papá," Santos objected, "we must not let them know Relie is here. No one in Catorce, beyond those of us at this table, must learn of her return."

Aurelia ate her *sopa de pechuga pollo,* absently scooping a piece of chicken from the soup while trying to concentrate on her own situation. Being a prisoner in Catorce had been bad enough. Now it seemed she was to be held prisoner in her own home.

Santos, she discovered, had considered her situation. "Since I'm taking bulls to Guanajuato for the feria, why not let Relie come along? She can stay with Tío Luís and Tía Guadalupe."

Aurelia caught herself in time to stem an overwhelming urge to resort to childish begging. In spite of her determination not to do so, she glanced down the table. Carson looked up at the same time and held her gaze. But where they had once warmed her with their softness, his eyes were now as cold as silver ore.

"Fine idea," her father responded to Santos's suggestion. "If Relie agrees. Before her ordeal with that criminal, she had decided against the trip."

"Por favor, Papá," she pleaded. Was she to be her own undoing? she wondered. Must she continually get herself out of messes of her own making? "I want very much to go to Guanajuato."

Her eyes held Carson's as she spoke. She felt her breath catch at the need welling inside her. What was he thinking? Why did he not smile? Abruptly, his attention returned to his plate.

When would she find a chance to talk to him? And how, in this household that suddenly seemed bent on keeping them apart?

"You would have to return in time to have your final fitting for the wedding," Doña Bella objected.

"Can't I do that before we leave?" She watched her mother consider the idea.

"I suppose we could arrange for Señora Velez to stop by again tomorrow," Doña Bella replied at length.

"Again?" Aurelia questioned.

"She dropped the gown off yesterday. Said it might lift our spirits to see it, help us hold onto the hope you would return safely in time for Santos's wedding." Her mother's hand pressed against her heart. "Praise Saint Cecilia, you did."

Aurelia smiled weakly, picking at her meal, waiting for her mother to work her way through the situation.

No one else spoke, and finally Doña Bella changed the subject, a tactic Aurelia knew meant she had agreed, reluctantly, and did not wish to discuss it further. "The color of Relie's gown is divine, Pia. You chose well. That shade of yellow will be glorious in the cathedral."

"I'm sure the color will be lovely on Relie, too," Enrique offered quite unexpectedly.

She turned startled eyes to him.

171

"Yellow should become you," he added, as though once spoken, the observation needed amplifying.

Suddenly, she recalled those same words.

Spoken not three days ago.

By Carson.

She looked up.

He was staring at her. His eyes were soft again. Warm again. They fired her spirit.

"I guarantee it, señor." He spoke softly, this time holding her attention with his wry grin, his dancing eyes. "Yellow definitely becomes Aurelia."

The next thing she heard was Santos clearing his throat.

But before Santos could speak, Carson added, "Although I must say, pink adds a touch of much needed color to her cheeks, since her ordeal with the train robber."

"Much needed color?" she retorted, but her mouth was dry, and her words sounded hoarse. From the corner of her eye, she saw Zita clap a napkin to her mouth.

Enrique's voice babbled from near her right shoulder. "Why, Relie, you're blushing. I mean . . . ah . . . pink does add color to your cheeks."

Santos's voice boomed from the other end of the table, and for once she welcomed his interference.

"You say Quiroz has not missed a day at the mine since the prisoner escaped?"

"Not a lick," Don Domingo replied.

"Well, what did he say for himself? How did he explain letting such a thing happen?"

"Enrique here talked to him," Don Domingo answered. "Tell him, *hijo.*"

While Aurelia grimaced at her father addressing

172

Enrique as *son*, Enrique launched a lengthy explanation of how he had interrogated Nuncio Quiroz.

She picked at her food, knowing she shouldn't worry but tense nonetheless, lest her charade be discovered. She certainly had not expected Nuncio Quiroz to admit his attempt to rape her. But if he implicated her at all, surely such a sordid fact would emerge. Fortunately, it seemed his job as mine superintendent was important to him, important enough that he had returned to work for her own father directly after that dastardly assault.

Listening to Enrique's voice drone on beside her, she began to wonder how he would react were she to suddenly blurt out the truth. What would he say if he heard how Nuncio Quiroz had attacked her in the darkened chapel?

Her fantasies came to an abrupt halt at the reverse of such a tale — the story of how Carson Jarrett had come into her life.

"Jarrett and I have laid our plans for tomorrow," Santos was telling their father. "First thing in the morning, we are going to the mine and have a talk with —"

"Con permiso," Carson interrupted. "With your permission, Santos, considering what we have heard tonight, maybe we should rethink our approach."

With the discussion turned to more normal things like train robberies and lost shipments of silver, Aurelia began to relax. She ate the main course, chicken in mole sauce, drank the deep red wine, and was grateful that Carson kept his attention on mining and off her.

As long as he kept it off Zita as well. With dessert, a rich almond and rice pudding, she began to reproach herself for such a disloyal thought. Surely this meal would end soon.

173

But if she had expected tensions to decrease with the end of dinner, she would have been disappointed. At her mother's signal the party adjourned to the drawing room, where Enrique stood possessively beside her chair. Directly in front of her, standing to one side of the black marble fireplace, Carson swirled a brandy, his long bronze fingers curled seductively around the voluptuous glass. Zita twittered at his side.

Zita, who had never shown the slightest interest in boys. She skipped directly to men, Aurelia thought.

Would this evening never end? In a far corner of the room Santos and Pia engaged in quiet conversation, and with Zita monopolizing Carson, the family was left to quiz Aurelia at length about her ordeal.

She was sorry, dreadfully sorry, to have worried them, but their questions were tiresome, especially since they bore no relation to the truth, but rather to a fantasy hatched in the immature brains of her two friends, the sort of fantasy she had trained them to concoct.

In all, the entire evening had been tiresome — Enrique babbling in one ear, Zita twittering to Carson in the other. And her mother — if Aurelia heard her mother praise Saint Cecilia one more time, she vowed she would scream.

Immediately, she repented. Remorse returned. She was the one to blame for worrying her family by such irresponsible acts as robbing a train and releasing a prisoner. Surely there had to have been another way. She recalled expressing the same sentiment before they left the ranch.

Her eyes shot to Carson. No. There had been no other way. The idea he had insinuated at the ranch came to mind, the idea he had stopped short of expressing in front of Santos. At the time she had not understood the way he shook his head, the look in his eyes, when she stated that surely there had been another way to save him from hanging for her crime.

Now she understood.

Seeing him now, handsome and courting Zita, she understood exactly what had been in his mind. As in a puzzle, the pieces fit neatly together. If every little piece had not fallen exactly as it had, everything would have been different. Nothing would have been the same.

If she hadn't robbed those trains, the Federales would not have been looking for a train robber. And if Santos hadn't asked Carson to come early, he wouldn't have been in the vicinity to have been captured.

Which, in turn, led to her meeting him, which led to her helping him escape.

Even Nuncio Quiroz played a vital role in this drama. If she had not believed Nuncio Quiroz had raped her, she would never have tricked Carson into making love to her. And if he hadn't made love to her . . .

He wouldn't have fallen in love with her.

Without those four days alone in the wilderness, he would never have known her.

Suddenly, Santos's teasing about her taking to trail life popped into her mind. She smiled. She had handled herself admirably out there, and Carson had been along to see it. Otherwise, he would have known her only as she would be at the wedding — a maid of honor in a yellow dress who lived in a mansion in an opulent city from which she was desperate to escape.

Enrique's words filtered through her overworked brain. "Relie, I was asking whether you might like to come to the Casa de Moneda tomorrow."

She frowned up at him. "No, I don't think so. I mean, I can't very well be seen at the mint, since no one is supposed to know I am in town."

"They say you are good at disguises."

"They?"

"Sister Inéz and the other nuns from the convent school." He laughed. "They have been talking of nothing else since the . . . ah . . . the abduction. You know how it is. When you think you have lost someone, you remember all their . . . ah . . . their . . ."

She tilted her chin, defiant. *"Outrageous schemes?* Is that what the town has been talking about, Enrique, while I was off fighting for my life? My outrageous schemes?"

Before she could stop him, he took her hand in his. "Relie, don't misunderstand. I didn't mean . . . ah . . ."

She wriggled her fingers from his grasp. "How fortunate that I lived such an outrageous youth. It furnished the town with entertainment while I was being abducted by some . . . by some . . ."

Quite without intending to, she looked up to find Carson watching her, that wry grin tipping his lips. Quickly, she looked away, feeling a blush creep up her neck. He had heard the whole thing. Damn him, he had listened to every word of her childish babble.

Enrique reached for her hand again. "I'm sorry, Relie. I didn't mean to offend you. Your disguises —"

"Disguises are for children, Enrique. Surely you know I am not a child."

He gaped a moment, then found his voice. "Of course. Of course, I know that, Relie. My feelings should have been clear at the mint the day . . . that dreadful day when you . . . when you disappeared."

Her head spun, and she knew if he babbled one more

176

sentence in her ear she would scream. As gracefully as she could manage, she rose to her feet. "It has been a dreadfully long day, Enrique. Would you excuse me? I feel I must retire."

"Certainly." He hastened to take her arm. "Time I was going, too. Have to be at the mint bright and early."

Her parents rose then, her mother saying how she knew the travelers were spent from their journey. Enrique had barely left when Serphino announced that the carriage for Pia and Zita was ready.

That taken care of, Doña Bella wished everyone a good night, and she and Don Domingo ascended the marble staircase.

Suddenly, everyone was talking at once. Aurelia watched Pia confer with Santos, then Pia and Zita hugged her good-bye. She couldn't help noticing the dreamy look in Zita's eyes.

Behind her, she heard Santos and Carson.

"Come with me to take the girls home?" Santos invited under his breath.

"I'm not your birddog, partner," she heard Carson reply.

"What?"

"Hell, man, this is your first night back. You don't want me tagging along."

She heard Santos grunt, then felt Carson step around her, brushing her elbow. With his back to her, he spoke to Zita, then proceeded to usher the girl into the foyer. Aurelia watched, stunned.

Santos followed them, disappearing down the hallway.

Pia was saying something about tomorrow.

"No," Aurelia answered absently. "No, I don't think we will leave for Guanajuato tomorrow."

She could see neither Carson's nor Zita's face, only their bobbing heads. First Carson's, as though he were instructing her. Then Zita's.

Santos returned, clapping his hands, taking Pia's arm. Behind him trailed Lucinda, who slipped unnoticed into a chair just inside the drawing room. Or she would have gone unnoticed had Aurelia not been staring so blatantly into the foyer.

Before escorting the girls out the door, Santos bent to speak to Lucinda, then to Carson, who chuckled and turned back to the drawing room.

The door closed behind them. Carson stood in the black marble foyer, staring at her as if he awaited an invitation to enter.

Carson stood stock-still in the black marble foyer, staring at the vision before him. He heard the outside door close, the clatter of hooves and carriage wheels on the bricked drive. But all he saw was Aurelia.

She looked every inch an angel with her head held high, her shoulders back, her gown regal. She stood still as death, as though waiting for him to take her in his arms and love her. Her eyes bore into his, searching, questioning.

But the search would serve no purpose, and the questions had no answers. He considered going straight to his room. Considered it, all the while knowing he could do no such thing. As hopeless as this relationship was, he could not deny himself the simple luxury of her presence.

It was as though he were starving and only the touch of her could feed him. As though he were thirsty and only her lips could quench that thirst . . .

As hopeless as things were between them.

The hacienda had merely amazed him. But this place, why, this place reminded him of passages his brother Benjamin used to read from the Good Book about mansions in heaven. He never even imagined such a place existed. And it wasn't enough for her.

She wanted to escape, called it a prison. God, what was Guanajuato like? The cities of gold that explorer had searched for so long ago? Had the Mazóns found the Seven Cities of Cibolo? And were they her kingdom?

Here he had thought his only worry in coming to Mexico would be making it through Santos's wedding ceremony. How he had dreaded it, knowing he was never comfortable in fancy places. Now he knew the weeks leading up to that wedding ceremony stood to be the most miserable time of his life.

He watched Aurelia step to the sideboard, watched her pour brandy into two fresh glasses. She carried them across the room while he still watched her. She was beautiful tonight. Stunning.

But he recalled how she had looked on the trail when he thought her no more than a peasant girl. She had been beautiful then, too. Beautiful to look at, to touch, to love.

She seated herself in one side of a contraption he had heard about but never before seen. It resembled two chairs connected at the arms on one side, with each turned away from the other, one chair facing one way, the other backwards. A courting couch, folks called it, designed to keep passions in check. When his already raced out of control just looking at her.

Without a word, she lifted one of the glasses to her lips and extended the other to him.

He glanced briefly at the chaperon sitting as though

oblivious to their presence. Looking back, he watched a grin spread across Aurelia's face.

In three steps he crossed the room and took the offered glass, his fingers closing around hers. The sensation rocked him, as he had known it would.

Seated with his back to the chaperon, he stared into Aurelia's eyes and she into his. He took a sip of the fiery liquid. It felt cold compared to the heat rising in his body.

She touched her glass to his, tilting her chin in that provocative way she had. "Much needed color?"

He clinked his glass against hers. "Fighting for your life?"

Her eyes held steady, still questioning, almost demanding now. God, how he wanted to respond.

He tipped his head toward Lucinda. "Any chance she will fall asleep?"

Aurelia laughed softly. "Not the slightest." Her black eyes danced. "If I could think of something for her to pray for, she might turn her attention to heaven."

Carson studied her. A deep sadness, like a loss, welled inside him. "I can think of something to pray for." Glancing quickly away, he took a large swallow of brandy.

"What were you and Zita discussing so seriously in the foyer?" she asked.

He looked back in time to see her lips tremble against the rim of her glass. "My plans," he replied.

"Your plans for what?"

He shrugged. "For the future, what else?"

"That was quick. I could tell she was enamored, but—"

"She's a pretty girl. She will make some lucky man a fine catch."

He watched her stare into the depths of her brandy snifter, swirl the liquid, silent.

180

"And you are a beautiful woman, Aurelia."

Slowly, she looked up from her glass, her bow-shaped lips slightly parted, beckoning.

"You will make some lucky man a fine catch, too."

He watched his words settle in, watched the questions form.

"But not me, angel."

"Why not?" she whispered.

He held her troubled gaze, silent.

"What reason did you give Zita?" she asked.

"The reasons are a great deal different for the two of you. Worlds apart." As we are, he thought. Even though Zita's blood was likely as rich as Aurelia's, it did not stir his. Would never stir his. He doubted if any woman's blood would ever stir his in such a manner again.

"That doesn't answer my question," she persisted.

"I told her my plans were already made."

She smiled. "What about me? You said? . . ." She tilted her chin again, waiting for his answer.

He held her gaze. Did she think he had forgotten? Did she think he could ever forget? She was his. A part of her would always belong to him.

"That was before—" he scanned the opulent room, "before all this."

"What does this have to do with it? I hate this place. It's a prison."

Growing up, he had heard this girl or that referred to as having been spoiled. He figured the term meant they were selfish, thoughtless, indulged.

Aurelia was none of those things. She was kind and compassionate and loving. But she was spoiled. All this, and she still wasn't satisfied. He could never provide her with even this grand a life-style. If she wasn't satisfied

181

now—here—how could she ever be satisfied with the meager life he could provide? How could he ask her to be?

"Compared to where I grew up, this is heaven." He laughed, striving to lighten the somber mood that had enveloped him since he caught sight of this family's lifestyle. "Angel."

"You can call me Relie," she snapped. "Everyone else does."

In spite of the chaperon, he reached for her hand. It was cold. But so was his own.

"When are you going to learn? I'm not everyone else."

"Oh." Her fingers trembled inside his grasp. "You make no sense. First you say you love me. Then you say you don't. Why don't you make up your mind?"

Releasing her hand, he held his glass in both palms and stared into its empty depths. "You are the one confused," he said. "But you'll straighten things out in your mind, once you get these crazy notions out of your head. Right now I don't think you know what you want. At least, not what you want from life in the long haul. But that's okay. You have time."

"I am not a child, Carson."

He looked at her again, wanting to kiss her more than ever. "I never said you were."

"Well, you did say you were falling in love with me."

He sighed. "Love and common sense are not always the same thing, angel."

Santos fidgeted on the seat beside Pia. These carriages never afforded enough legroom, he thought, especially not when the opposite seat was taken by a dueña cloaked in black, but definitely not blinded or deafened by the fact.

"You've been distracted all night, Santos," Pia told him. "Is it the mine?"

"No, the difficulties at the mine will work out now that Jarrett's here."

"I'm glad he came early. Why, to think . . ." She glanced at Tía Victoria, her mother's aunt who served as her dueña, then continued. "Think what a handsome best man he will be."

Santos grunted.

They had delivered Zita and now pulled up to the Leal mansion.

"You are worried about something," she challenged. "You don't even seem glad Carson arrived."

"I'm glad. I may end up sorry I asked him to come early, though."

"Why? You two are great friends."

"That's the trouble."

"You aren't making sense."

He sighed heavily. "Didn't you see the way they reacted to each other?"

"Who? Zita and Carson?"

"No, Pia. My . . . ah . . . your other friend," he finished, recalling in time that Aurelia's presence in Catorce was supposed to remain a secret from all but a select few.

Pia didn't answer until the carriage had rocked to a stop and Tía Victoria alighted.

"Relie?" she whispered as Santos handed her down.

He nodded. "Didn't you see the two of them?"

Pia shook her head.

"She didn't tell you?"

"Tell me what?"

183

"About the days—and nights—they spent alone together before they reached the ranch."

Pia's hand flew to her breast. "No," she whispered. "I mean, yes, but she didn't . . . I mean, she didn't tell me *anything* . . ."

Tía Victoria turned to frown at the straggling couple. They started for the house, keeping several paces between them and the dueña. "What happened between them, Santos?"

"They say nothing."

"Then why are you worried?"

"He's falling in love with her. He told me so."

"Santos, how wonderful."

"Wonderful? Disastrous is more like it."

"Don't be ridiculous. Of course it's wonderful. Just what she needed. A way to escape Catorce."

"It would never work."

"Now, Santos, don't make decisions for other people."

"They are not other people. She's my sister and he's my best friend. For a while, anyway. Until she breaks his heart."

"She won't."

"How do you know? They are different, I tell you, Pia. Different."

"So are we."

He stopped at the steps, conscious of the dark figure watching them from the shadow of the portal. "We are different in a . . . in a different way."

"You aren't making sense, you know that? Besides, we've spent the whole evening talking about other people." She faced him with her back to the dueña. Now she looked up, speaking in a whisper. "The last time we were together, you promised me something."

184

He stared at her, comprehension gradually dawning. "That's what I'm talking about, Pia. It was Relie who put you up to such a thing. If she can advise a friend to . . . to do something like that, what do you think she would do herself, given all those days and nights alone?"

"Santos Mazón! How dare you talk that way about your sister!"

He sighed, exasperated.

"Relie is a perfectly sensible girl," Pia chided, "no matter what kind of schemes she cooks up. She is modest and moral. And I will not have you say otherwise."

"I suppose you're right."

"They can work out their own problems. It's us you should be thinking about. Our wedding is little more than a month off, and you didn't even find a way to steal a kiss tonight."

He shook his head, suddenly sorry he had neglected her. "I admit I've been worried about how to handle Relie, but that will change as soon as I get her to Guanajuato, where she can't work her way any further under Jarrett's ornery hide."

Chapter Ten

Aurelia awoke the following morning, her mind wrestling with the new problem Carson had posed the evening before: his rejection. She snuggled into the comforter, wishing it was the hard rock floor of the cave behind the waterfall.

Carson loved her. She was sure of that. She hadn't been quite so certain during dinner from the way he carried on with Zita, but later after everyone left, he practically admitted he loved her.

So how could she persuade him to admit it to himself? For one thing, she would have to get him alone, and with Santos dogging their every step, that in itself would be a challenge. She had hoped to see him after everyone else retired, but when Santos returned from seeing Pia home, he immediately shooed her off to bed, saying he and Carson had plans to lay.

She sighed, knowing without having to be told the plans they had made for her: the entire day inside this house. She wished she knew how soon they would leave for Guanajuato. Once there, Carson would realize how much he loved her. She knew he would, only . . .

A noise sounded in the hallway outside her door, so natural in its occurrence she hardly noticed. Then she bolted from the bed. One of the maids had left a tray with orange juice, coffee, and pan dulces beside her door; she would leave a similar tray outside the door of every occupied bedchamber in the house. Aurelia crossed the room, opened the door, and picked up her tray.

She knew how she would do it. She knew exactly how she would see Carson alone.

Hurrying back inside, she rummaged through her wardrobe, finally pulling out the perfect disguise.

Not five minutes later, she tiptoed down the hall, checked right and left, then picked up the tray beside his door and knocked softly.

At his response, she answered, "Coffee, señor."

Hurry, she whispered, listening to sounds of stirring inside the room, tensed against the anticipated approach of someone from either end of the hallway.

The key turned in the lock; a face peeked around the door, followed by a bare arm. Head bowed, she handed him the tray, then before he could close the door, she slid inside. Behind her, she felt for the key and turned it in the lock.

Her heart was pounding. When she looked up, he was studying her with that wry grin on his lips.

She watched him slip the tray onto a bureau top, after which he reached over and tugged the white maid's cap from her head.

"Disguises are for children, Enrique," he mimicked, taking in her black skirt, white apron and blouse.

187

"Disguises are for when a girl is desperate for a kiss." The whispered plea trembled from her lips.

Before she finished speaking, his lips were on hers. His arms came around her and she clung to him, feeling his skin bare and hot beneath her hands.

As always, his arms brought her a sense of peace. Peace combined with a stirring of anticipation. Now that she knew where a kiss could lead, the expectation grew rapidly inside her. Her body fairly glowed with the want of him. She felt as though she had been doused with a splash of the brandy they had shared the night before.

His heart throbbed against her in a rhythm she knew echoed her own. His lips stroked and caressed hers until she felt faint and rested her head on the door for support.

The action dislodged his lips and he kissed her nose, then looked into her eyes. "I swore off you."

"No, you promised we would make love again."

When he didn't immediately kiss her, she lifted her lips and kissed him. He responded quickly, stroking and caressing, delving and probing until her heart pounded as fast as it had when as a child she had raced up and down the hills of Catorce.

His hair was tangled from sleep, and his chest was bare. Her hands roamed freely, tracing the edge of his long johns. When her fingers slipped beneath the band, he moaned, lifted his lips, and winked.

"You mean to hold me to it, don't you?" He cupped her face, kissed her, then let his hands slip down her neck, across her chest, drawing the blouse along with them.

It was the same type of garment she had worn in the cave, a simple length of white cloth gathered in a ruffle about her neck. When he wriggled it down across her arms, exposing her breasts, his hands stopped. His fingers clamped like a vise around her forearms.

She watched him stare at her, suddenly wanting him so badly she could hardly stand it. She grasped his head, pulling his face to her breast. When his lips covered her nipple, she inhaled deeply, drawing him closer.

His hands slipped to her waist, over her hips. He crumpled her skirt in his hands and beneath it clutched her bare buttocks in his palms. He pulled her to him, groaning.

"When you set out to seduce a man, angel, you don't stop halfway."

She grinned, nodding, too weak to answer. Against her abdomen, she felt the full force of his own desire. She pressed herself against him.

"Not this morning, though. There isn't time." His voice rasped from his throat. One hand slipped around her hips, between her legs.

She stared at him, trembling, wanting him so badly.

"Don't look at me like that," he whispered. "Santos is coming. We're going to the mine."

"When?"

"Early." His fingers slipped inside her, moving in a steady simulation of her pulsating heart, only slower, ever so much slower. She moved against him in agony.

"Slow, angel."

"Love me, Carson," she begged. "Please love me."

He kissed her, then spoke with their lips almost

189

touching. His eyes held hers, echoing the begging he saw on her face.

"I do, angel. That's the hell of it. I do love you."

He withdrew his fingers, lowered her skirt, lifted her blouse, studiously putting her back together while she stood scarcely breathing.

It was what she had wanted—his profession of love. What she had come to hear. Yet it wasn't enough. It wasn't nearly enough.

"I want you to make love to me," she whispered.

She watched his throat quiver when he inhaled. "I want it, too. As badly as you, believe me." He grinned then, glancing down inadvertently at his protruding long johns. She followed his gaze.

"With Santos taking his brotherly responsibilities so seriously, that's enough evidence to get me shot."

"No," she objected.

He kissed her again while she clung to him, pressing her body shamelessly against his. Her physical yearning had grown so intense, she had trouble thinking clearly.

A knock at the door rasped through her senses.

Very gently, Carson eased Aurelia away from the door and turned her around, glancing toward the wardrobe.

"Jarrett," Santos's voice called. The doorknob rattled.

She shook her head. Brushing him a kiss, she headed for the door that led to an adjoining bedroom.

"Coming," Carson returned. He struggled into his pants, watching Aurelia close the door behind her. Only then did he unlock the door leading to the hallway.

190

He ran a hand through his hair, turned to button his breeches.

Santos stepped into the room.

Carson watched him inspect the premises—the untouched tray, the bed, then Carson himself. His eyes riveted on Carson's crotch. Carson shrugged.

"Sonofabitch, can't a man even dream in this house?"

"That had better have come from dreaming." Santos flipped the covers back, then opened the wardrobe door.

Carson downed the orange juice, watching his friend with an easy grin. "Know what I like about our friendship?" He slipped into a clean white shirt. "Trust," he answered himself. "Complete and total, out-and-out trust."

Santos crossed the room, opened the door to the other bedroom, stepped inside, looked around, then returned.

"Sorry, Jarrett. You know how it is."

"Can't say that I do, partner. But you're free to watch over me. Likely you'll keep me from making the biggest mistake of my life."

"That's the way I see it, compadre."

They rode the same horses to the mine as they had ridden into town the day before. Carson stroked the mane of the dappled gray Andalusian.

"Think there's any chance I could get Sunfisher back from the Federales or whoever has charge of him?"

"You mean that pet horse of yours?" Santos questioned.

Carson grinned. "Yeah."

"What's that you told Relie about being anxious to ride our horses?" Santos teased.

"No offense, but when a man's been afoot four days out in those mountains, he isn't all that particular. If we have trouble ahead, I'd as soon face it on my own mount."

"I'll give it some thought," Santos agreed.

"Don't go telling her," Carson requested. "Wouldn't want her to think I wasn't grateful."

Santos pierced his friend with a friendly warning. "Long as that's all you want her to think—that you are grateful for the loan of a horse."

They rode in companionable silence, and by the time they approached the Mina Mazón, Carson figured he had worked through the trials of the morning. Lordy, how he had wanted to make love to Aurelia. Still did, for that matter. Wanted it more than he could recall wanting anything before in his life.

But he was not going to fall for another of her wiles. Not that he thought Aurelia insincere. She wanted him to love her, the same way she wanted to escape Catorce.

And if he had learned anything, it was that Aurelia Mazón was a girl who always got what she wanted. By one scheme or another.

Not that she was deceitful. She wasn't. Nor had he been. When he told her she was a woman, he meant it. She was a woman in ways that would haunt him to the grave.

But she was a child, too. She wanted him to love her. Yet she had never said a thing about loving him in return.

Not that she realized what she was doing. He was certain she wasn't deliberately leading him on. And therein lay the enigma that was Aurelia Mazón. Loving and generous and fanciful. Beautiful and courageous and daring. Would he lose his soul to this ethereal creature before the month was out?

Even her protective brother likely wouldn't be able to prevent that. He shrugged, figuring it might be well worth the risk, as long as he didn't endanger Aurelia's soul, too.

Santos might posture as her protector, but he, Carson Jarrett, was. She belonged to him. He would love and protect her as long as he was here, then he would leave.

She would follow her dreams to a life of high society, and he would return to chasing bandits and outlaws. And in the long cold nights under the stars, her memory would keep him warm — her memory and the sure knowledge that she belonged to him. Wherever she might be, whatever she might be doing, whomever she might marry, she belonged to him.

They hitched their mounts and headed for the mine. "Depending on what we find down here," Santos told him, "I figure Relie and I will pull out first thing in the morning."

Carson missed a step, caught up, then calmed himself before replying. "Pull out for where?"

"Guanajuato. You heard me say I have to take some bulls to the feria."

"Oh. Right."

"While I'm gone you can nose around, try to figure out what's going on." Santos eyed his friend skeptically.

"Don't figure you'll mind staying behind, since you seem to have hit it off with a certain female."

"She's *a certain female* now?"

"You and Zita."

Carson stared at him, wondering how this friend could be so smart about some things and so damned ignorant about others.

Santos continued. "Zita's a nice girl. Our families have known each other a long time. I'm sure her father will give you permission to call. I'll speak to him."

Carson put a hand on Santos's shoulder, stopping him in mid stride. "Let's get something straight right now."

Santos looked down at Carson.

"I speak for myself."

Santos cocked his head.

"No one, not even you, speaks for me. Not where women are concerned."

"I only thought to—"

"No one, damnit. I mean it. I'm riding out of here at the end of the month." He shrugged off the pall that statement cast over him. "Figure any woman I meet between now and then will be just that—a woman, an acquaintance."

Santos grinned. "Sure. I understand. A charmer like yourself can't go leaving broken hearts strung across two countries."

Carson nodded, and the two men continued to the mine entrance, where Santos introduced Carson to the guard.

They were handed hard hats, which Carson inspected before replacing his Stetson with it. It looked like an oversized cap that had been soaked in oil.

"You probably have a woman pining for you back in Texas, anyhow," Santos mused.

Carson put the hat on his head and patted it, considering his friend's unmistakable effort to keep him away from his sister. "Bunches of 'em, partner." He followed Santos into the mine office.

His first sight of Nuncio Quiroz shot white-hot rage spiraling through him with the shock of a bolt of lightning. He turned his head and studied a map tacked to the wall, forcing himself to concentrate on the tunnels and shaft of the Mina Mazón until he could bring his anger under control. He must not let the man know he recognized him. He must not.

Aurelia's life depended on Quiroz not recognizing him as the prisoner he had allowed to escape for a tryst in the chapel.

He must not give himself away. Yet, all he wanted to do, all he could think of, was to kill this varmint with his bare hands.

Quiroz wasn't an ugly man, yet to Carson he resembled no one more than the devil himself. Almost as large as Santos, he towered above Carson by half a foot. His muscles were obviously earned with a single-jack hammer and a double-jack.

Santos introduced Carson to Quiroz as he had to others — his friend from Texas who would serve as best man at his wedding, adding, "He came early to learn something about mining."

"You a miner?" Quiroz questioned. His eyes roamed Carson in a manner that suggested he found him familiar.

"No," Carson replied.

"He wants to become one," Santos said.

"It's hard work, mining."

Carson shrugged, not trusting his voice.

"The business end," Santos explained. "He wants to learn the business end. He will need experience working the mine, too, but he is mainly interested in how we conduct our business."

Quiroz turned his head, aimed at a spittoon, and spat tobacco in that direction. Mostly, he missed.

Carson noticed his teeth, stained and rotted. The idea of that mouth on Aurelia's . . .

Furiously, he turned away, gripping his emotions.

"Since we're here," Santos was saying, "we might as well look around."

Quiroz stepped aside for them to pass. Once inside the tunnel and away from the man, Carson's anger eased off, but he still had trouble concentrating on the mine tour.

Always good-natured and outgoing, Santos greeted the men they met in the tunnel the same way he had greeted those they encountered outside: with handshakes, slaps on the back, words of encouragement. His genuine interest showed clearly in the questions he asked each man about his work, how the mine was doing, about his family.

At a fork in the tunnel, Santos led the way down the truncated branch. "This blue stuff is the silver," he pointed out. "The vein is rich in this direction. We look for it to be a real bonanza when we open it up."

"Why aren't you mining it now?" Carson asked, while visions of what he would like to do to Quiroz's face danced in his brain.

"We're saving it. The vein running off the main tunnel provides more ore than Casa de Moneda can handle at the moment."

Santos introduced Carson at each stop, explaining his interest in mining, and the miners agreed to help all they could.

Afterwards they toured the yard—patios, Santos called them—where the noises were thunderous.

"Off over there," Santos shouted above the din, "is where we bring the stuff that's rich enough to be sorted by hand."

Carson followed his friend's pointing arm to an area where boys no older than ten or twelve squatted on haunches, working over mountains of broken rock with short-handled picks.

"And here," Santos continued to walk through the various yards, greeting each worker by name, as before, "this is the grinding patio—for ore that is harder to get to."

The area toward which Santos pointed this time contained huge rock crushers, which were only partially visible through the thick dust raised by the crushing of rock hauled to the yard by stoop-backed workers pushing wheelbarrows.

Following Santos fifty meters to the other side of the mine property, Carson stopped beside a rail fence that separated the walkways from a stone-paved patio where a couple of hundred mules tromped.

"They are mixing the amalgam," Santos explained. "Ore mud with copperas and quicksilver."

Carson pointed toward a row of railcars sitting on a

track in the distance. "Those the cars you use to haul it to the mint?"

Santos nodded. "Not this stuff, though." He indicated an area to the rear of the complex, where smoke rose in thick billows along a line a good fifty meters in length. "Those are the furnace beds. After the amalgam is purified in those beds, we cast it into bars over there." He pointed through the smoke to a row of low flat-roofed buildings, which were barely visible through the haze.

"So it's the bars that have been disappearing on the way to the mint?" Carson reasoned.

Santos nodded. "You can see how isolated we are up here. Thefts were common when we hauled bars to Potosí by rail. That's the reason the mint was supposed to have put a stop to our thefts."

Carson turned a full circle, inspecting the view. Real de Catorce sat on top of a mountain surrounded by deep arroyos, beyond which were more mountains. Rugged, difficult terrain. "The bars they are stealing now would have to be carried out by pack mules."

"Which everyone in town would notice," Santos added, leading the way back to the mine office.

"Catorce means fourteen," Carson mused. "Fourteen what?"

"Depends on who tells the tale," Santos laughed. "Some say the town is named for the fourteen hills surrounding us, others say fourteen soldiers were ambushed by Indians, still others argue it was fourteen thieves."

Carson laughed. "Maybe it's thieves and one of them is still around."

"In that case, you're hunting a ghost, compadre. The town was named a good three hundred years ago."

When they reached the office, Nuncio Quiroz was leaving for lunch.

"Go ahead," Santos told him. "We'll lock up. I want to make some notes for Jarrett."

For the first time that morning Quiroz hesitated before answering. He agreed, of course. What choice did he have? Santos was the owner's son, would likely be his boss one day — saying the surly superintendent survived that long, Carson thought.

Leaving his hard hat on a peg, Quiroz turned at the door. Again he examined Carson with a harsh perusal. "Have we met before today, señor?"

Carson returned his stare, knowing he had best keep a steady eye. This man might look inept, but he was likely shrewd as the day was long. "Not to my knowledge," Carson replied in clipped tones.

He watched the man disappear beyond the mine entrance. Forcing his attention back to the difficulties at hand, he peered over Santos's shoulder at the open ledger. "What do you know about Enrique Villasur?"

Santos glanced up. "He's president of the mint."

"I know that. And I know your father has him picked out for Aurelia. Whether she'll have him is another matter. But what do you know about the man? Is he from Catorce?"

"No." Santos scanned a page, then turned to the next. "That isn't Relie's objection. Don't worry about her, Jarrett."

"It isn't Aurelia I'm worried about. It's your mine. How long has Enrique been with the company?"

199

Santos shrugged. "Couple of years. Since right before we opened the mint. He came highly recommended by Tío Luís."

"Your uncle in Guanajuato?"

Santos looked up from the books again. "I hope this thing you have for Relie won't interfere with your investigation."

"This *thing*, as you call it, is irrelevant to the investigation. I never mix work and . . . ah . . . friendship. You know me better than that."

"*Sí*, but I have never watched you fall in love before."

"Then stop watching. It's making you cantankerous."

"You're the cantankerous one, Jarrett. Your problem with Enrique is jealousy, pure and simple. Don't let it bother you. She isn't going to marry him."

"I know that. Answer my damned question. Does Enrique look like the president of a mint?"

"Looks have nothing to do with it."

"Does he sound like one?"

Santos snapped the books closed and rose. Ushering his friend out the door, he locked it with a key he took from his pocket, then handed to Carson. "You might need this. But don't tell anyone you have it."

Carson turned the key over in his hand.

"Enrique sounds like a moonstruck calf," Santos admitted. "Even mint presidents fall in love." He grinned down at his friend. "That affliction is not limited to Texas Rangers."

"Speaking of love, partner, appears to me you've been neglecting yours."

"So she tells me."

Their return to the house was prolonged by Santos's

penchant for greeting every man, woman, and child they met on the street.

"Never knew you for the politician," Carson mused. "You would have made a good president for Casa de Moneda."

"Me? No way."

"You were the obvious choice," Carson countered. "You know the business inside and out, the townsfolk apparently trust you, not to mention the most convincing reason of all: As the owner's son, you are the heir."

Santos shook his head. "Someone has to run the ranch; that's the business I know."

"I see your point. Enrique likely knows next to nothing about ranching."

"Enrique again?"

"He's president of the mint. If he marries Aurelia, after your father is gone, he will likely inherit his position at the mine."

"It will be a partnership."

Carson agreed. "But by virtue of living in Catorce, the man will have control."

Santos laughed. "Thought you would have learned by now that I'm good at keeping my eye on people."

Carson laughed.

"So that's what you see in Relie," Santos teased after a while. "The Mina Mazón."

Carson turned serious. "I knew her before she had a centavo, partner. Wish to hell she still didn't."

"She ought to have her backside whipped for hiding that fact from you."

They took lunch on the patio, with the fountain burbling in the background and streamers of bougainvil-

201

lea dripping in fuchsia cascades from the balcony above—a romantic setting lost on the two of them, since the rest of the family had retired for siesta.

Along with their lunch the maid brought messages for both men, which they promptly read.

"Mine's from Pia," Santos said. "Appears she has found a way to capture my attention."

Carson glanced up from his telegram, his eyes vacant.

"We have an appointment with Padre Bucareli at the cathedral in half an hour," Santos explained.

"During siesta?"

Santos shrugged, grinning. "Guess Pia figured on the nuns being asleep."

"Enjoy yourself," Carson muttered, his attention riveted to the telegram in his hand.

Santos studied his friend. "Bad news?"

"Yeah. My brother, the one who was missing when I came down here, has been found. Dead."

"Benjamin?"

Carson nodded, fighting back tears.

"I'm sorry. If you need to go back to Texas, I can handle the difficulties at the mine."

Carson shook his head, indicating the telegram. "This is from Kale. He's taking care of things. The others are on their way to the ranch. He promised to let me know what comes of it."

They finished the meal in silence, then Santos scraped back his chair. "Hate to leave you at such a time, compadre. I won't be long."

"Don't rush back on my account," Carson told him. In an effort to shake off his rising sense of loss, he added, "You can trust me today, partner."

Santos slapped him on the back. *"Bueno.* Like I told Pia, your word is good as gold. Besides, Relie is occupied. Seems this is the only time Señora Velez had available to fit that gown."

After Santos left, Carson turned to the message behind the telegram.

Third floor, double doors at end of hallway.

Santos arrived at Pia's house to find her pacing back and forth in the front courtyard. She was attired in a proper riding habit; her horse was saddled and ready.

The moment he started to help her mount, Señora Leal came hurrying out the front door. "I am trusting you, Santos. Ride at a proper distance. With just over a month before the wedding, we cannot have a scandal."

"¡Mamá!"

"Sí, señora," Santos responded gravely. "I promise to remain conscious of Pia's reputation."

The señora watched, hawk-eyed, while he assisted Pia onto the sidesaddle. "Padre Bucareli must have lost his senses," she fussed. "A conference this time of day. Whoever heard of such a thing? A conference at the cathedral during siesta."

When they were out of earshot, Pia laughed. "Mamá decided it would be safer for us to travel horseback. More discreet than in a carriage like last time. One of her friends must have said something."

The idea of the town talking about Pia disturbed Santos as much as did the thought of those same wags

203

gossiping about Relie. Of the two, of course, his sister was the one more likely to deserve any tales the town might come up with. Relie was entirely too much like he had been in his early days for him to have any peace of mind about her.

On the way to the cathedral, he discussed his and Carson's earlier conversation.

"What do you think about Enrique?"

"Relie won't marry him. One way or another, she will get out of it."

Santos laughed. "I don't doubt that. But what do you think of him as a man?"

Pia turned to him with such affection that a familiar warmth began to spread through his body. "Remember what your mamá said," he teased.

She laughed. "You are a man, Santos. Enrique is . . . well, he seems more like a . . . like a pretender."

"Papá sets store by him."

"Enrique is good at persuading people of his importance. But he doesn't seem sincere. And he isn't a leader." She sighed. "You would have made a better mint president."

"You are prejudiced."

She beamed at him.

"Someone has to run the ranch, Pia. Like I told Jarrett, I can't see Enrique running the ranch."

She laughed. "Certainly not. But what will happen to him when Relie marries someone else?"

Santos shrugged. "He will still run the mint, I suppose. Papá would want that. I can see Jarrett's point, though. Don't need to tell you, the idea of Enrique in charge of things gave me pause."

"I wouldn't mind if we had to move back to Catorce," she told him. "I have never felt the way Relie does. She sees these mountains as walls, and you know Relie, when she comes to a wall, she has to climb it or break it down."

Suddenly, his thoughts returned to the situation between Aurelia and Carson. "She's heading for trouble."

"You can't fault her for the way she is, Santos. She is exactly like you."

"Don't you think that's what has me worried?"

"I know. But you don't understand her reasons for wanting to live in Guanajuato. She wants freedom, all right, but a different kind of freedom than you think. She doesn't want freedom to run wild."

"Robbing trains isn't running wild?"

Pia sighed. "It was a stupid thing to do. We all agree on that now. But at the time . . . Don't you see? Relie wants the freedom to make her own choices, to determine the course of her own life. Is that so wrong?"

He shrugged, his jaws set.

"I would probably have reacted the same way if I hadn't been able to choose for myself."

Dismounting in front of the cathedral, he helped Pia down, then hitched their mounts to the rail.

"Are you saying you chose me?" he teased.

"I certainly did."

"Here I was thinking it was all my idea."

"It was, Santos," she assured him with a coy smile. "But perhaps it took a little scheming to give you the initial idea."

He shook his head in amazement, reached to open the carved door of the cathedral, and she stopped him.

"No." Without further explanation, Pia drew Santos around the side of the cathedral along a path between the building and the graveyard.

"Where are we going?"

She skipped.

He tugged her hand, bringing her to a stop. "Where is the padre meeting us?"

She pursed her lips, her face coloring. "He isn't."

"He isn't?"

"Oh, Santos, don't be angry. I had to get you away. We haven't had any time to ourselves. I thought—"

"You lied to your mother?"

"A small one."

"A small one," he repeated. "It won't seem so small when Padre Bucareli tells her there was no meeting."

Her eyes widened briefly, then she composed herself. "I considered that. But like she said, we have little more than a month left until the wedding. How much damage can we do my reputation in that short a time?"

Santos let out a low whistle. "A hell of a lot, that's how much."

"You wouldn't back out, though," she insisted. "You would marry me anyway, no matter how soiled my reputation."

"Women," he wailed while she led him past the graves and behind a privacy hedge to a small place in the back of the garden he was sure the nuns had no idea they had left secluded. At the moment, he prayed they didn't know about this place.

"Here I've been hoping some of your good sense would rub off on Relie, and now I find the opposite has happened. You've become as outrageous a schemer as she is."

When they were finally out of sight of errant eyes, Pia stopped and looked up at him with such a sober expression that he melted. Taking her in his arms, Santos felt her respond immediately, felt her small arms encircle him, felt her body, encased in layers of protective clothing, snuggle next to his—a slender body he found all the more seductive for its lack of experience.

"You don't appreciate my schemes?"

With awkward hands, he untied the ribbon on her bonnet and tossed it aside. "You know I do." He kissed her. "But you women will be the ruin of us poor unsuspecting hombres yet. We have to get up before daybreak to keep up with you."

After another glance over his shoulder, he lifted her in his arms and carried her to a log that was large enough for him to sit on, but not for the two of them side by side.

He sat with her on his lap, cradled her to him, and held her tight a moment, thinking how glad he would be when she was his wife. How whole he would feel. How complete. Lifting her face, he kissed her gently. "I'm a lucky man, Pia. In a month, I will be even luckier. You will be my wife."

She placed a quick, chaste kiss on his lips. Resting her elbows on his shoulders, she played her fingers through his unruly hair.

Often he wondered how he had ever won the devotion of such a gentle woman. She had changed his life. She had made him a better man than he ever would have been without her. He wanted to protect her and cherish her. Once a hell-raiser with the best of them, all he wanted now was to take Pia to the ranch and love her. He wanted to sit with her at breakfast and walk with her at dusk. He wanted to rock with her in the twilight and . . .

Suddenly, he wanted more—so much more. He kissed her with such passion her head swayed with the fervor of it. At length, she lifted her face to catch her breath.

"I knew you wouldn't stay angry," she whispered against his lips.

He kissed her again. "I would have come without being tricked."

She scrunched her face, considering, tracing the outline of his eyebrows with wispy strokes of her fingers. "You would probably have brought Carson Jarrett along, though. You've been so caught up in keeping him and Relie apart, you have forgotten about us."

"Never, little one," he mumbled between kisses. But the reminder of Relie and Carson renewed his determination to resist Pia, a determination he was finding difficult to maintain with her in his arms.

She tasted so sweet, like roses and honey, and he had always been fond of sweetness. He ran his hand up and down her back. Even corseted as she was, he knew she would be soft and firm underneath. Thoughts of such a combination began to play havoc with his willpower. Without intending to, he slipped a hand between them and cupped a small, firm breast in his palm. It seemed to fit in its entirety, a fact that intrigued him.

When his kisses deepened, she responded with

enough fervor to expunge a bit more of his determination. Before he realized it, Santos had unbuttoned her jacket. Drawing their lips apart, he stared at the gaping bodice, then back to her face. Even though her cheeks were stained with great blotches of red, she squared her shoulders, creating an even wider gap between the edges of her riding habit and the silky white chemise beneath it.

His heart felt lodged in his throat, where it threatened to choke him. Great God in heaven, how was he supposed to resist her?

He watched her cheeks flame, saw her eyes beg, and contrary to all his noble intentions, Santos slipped one hand inside and clasped a small breast in his palm. She felt exactly as he had imagined she would—firm and soft and pliant, even with the silky chemise and the hard bones of her corset intruding. The only thing he felt was her softness, her firmness, the heat of her breast against his hand, and the aroused tip of her nipple.

Desire ripped through his determination. His thumb traced the rigid tip; his tongue, dry from wanting her, clung to his lips.

Terrified, Pia watched the hunger in Santos's eyes, felt the sensuously devastating touch of his hand on her breast. His eyes held hers, wide and black. What was he thinking? Was she too small? Was he repelled by her less than abundant figure? She had heard maids laugh about how men loved full-bosomed women. Was he disappointed?

He watched questions form in her eyes, questions that restored enough of his determination to enable him to withdraw his hand. Clumsily, he began to button her bodice.

"Don't . . ." she whispered.

He inhaled raggedly. "I may not be as strong a man as it takes to resist you."

Suddenly, she became desperate to prove to him that although she was small, she was still a woman; although her figure was less than abundant, she could still give him pleasure. She kissed him urgently, feeling herself flush with the forwardness of it. "Don't resist," she begged.

He took her lips greedily, exploring, plunging, consuming, being himself consumed by unquenchable yearnings for this woman. Damn his little sister's scheming brain. Damn friendships and brotherly love. With difficulty, he drew back, willing his heart to slow. "This isn't the place, little one," he whispered, his breath ragged. "Or the time."

"We can find a place. You said—"

He shook his head. "We can wait another month."

"You said after Relie was safe . . ." Her words trailed off, and she ducked her head to keep from looking him in the eye.

"I remember what I said." His voice, though husky, was gentle. "Things have changed."

Abruptly, she raised stricken eyes.

"No," he corrected quickly, "not between us. It's this thing with Relie and Jarrett. Worrying over them made me realize—"

"They have nothing to do with us."

"I know, but . . . well, I've given it a lot of thought, and I think we should wait until after we are married."

Embarrassed beyond belief at having her boldness rejected in broad open daylight, Pia slid to the ground. "It's time we were getting back."

Santos jumped up and pulled her to him. He held her tightly against his chest in a sheltering, protective embrace. "I'm sorry, Pia. Please don't think I don't want to. I do. I'm desperate to make love to you. I want it more than anything, except . . ."

"Except what?"

He took a long time before answering. "I promised to make it worth waiting for. I will. You'll see."

Still too embarrassed to express herself coherently, she buried her face in his broad chest.

"Look at me," he whispered, tipping her chin. "You are more important to me than Relie or Jarrett or anyone else on this earth. Worrying about them has made me realize how much I love you. This gift you offer . . . It isn't an act to be accomplished out here behind the hedge and forgotten. I want it to be a gift from me to you, too, something we can treasure all our lives."

Rising on tiptoe, she kissed his mouth. "I'll think of a place, then. I will tell you where when I come to your house for the fitting."

"What fitting?"

"Señora Velez wants me to be present when she fits Relie's gown. She knows how finicky I am, and—"

"I thought that's what Relie was doing right now."

Pia's eyes widened.

Santos glanced around the secluded glen. His eyes returned to hers. "You planned this to—"

"To give us time together."

"To give them time together." He pulled her along the

path toward their horses. "I should have known you weren't responsible for this . . . this scheme to seduce me."

"It isn't like that, Santos. Please don't be angry. Please." She dug the heels of her riding boots into the soft earth. "You've gone mad where they are concerned."

He stopped, looking down at her, confused. What had his outrageous sister done to his sweet Pia? "Maybe," he acknowledged. "But maybe not."

"Santos Mazón, you listen to me. I'm tired of you playing nursemaid to two grown people. And . . . and I'm tired of being neglected."

Her words needled his guilty conscience. "I didn't mean to neglect you, little one. I love you."

She stood her ground. "I know that. But I still don't like it."

"You shouldn't." He led her toward their horses. "Once this wedding is over, you will never have cause to accuse me of such again."

"Once Carson Jarrett is safely back across the Río Bravo, you mean."

"First things first," he managed. "In the morning, Relie and I are leaving for Guanajuato. That should cool their romance down a bit."

Pia cocked her head, glancing up at him through squinted eyes. "And ours as well."

Chapter Eleven

Third floor, double doors at end of hallway.

After seeing Santos safely on his way to meet Pia, Carson followed the directions on the unsigned message, promising himself with every step that he would meet Aurelia, talk with her, look at her, and leave her untouched.

The double doors opened into a great white ballroom with gold-leaf moldings, gilt-framed mirrors, and a good half-dozen golden medallions on the ceiling with a crystal chandelier hanging from each of them.

He let out a low whistle. Here he had thought ballrooms were found only in hotels. Showed how lacking was his storehouse of knowledge — one more fact to add to the lengthening list of reasons he should avoid becoming involved with the lady who lived in this gold and white prison. One more fact to strengthen his resolve.

But there in the center of this great empty room stood Aurelia, swathed in yellow lace. Her glossy black hair swirled in tantalizing disarray about her shoulders.

There stood Aurelia, and all his good intentions fled as before a fluttering of angel wings.

He crossed the room on unsteady legs, savoring the sight of her, recording it for later when she was no longer beside him.

"My sister said it's bad luck to be seen in your wedding gown before the wedding," he murmured.

She laughed, reaching her arms toward him. "It's my gown. Pia's wedding."

He wrapped her in his arms, pulling her tightly against his body and holding her there. He felt her heart beat against him, her gypsy heart so wonderfully alive and full of mischief and fun.

"The messenger who delivered the telegram told us about your brother," she said. "Do you want to talk about it?"

He kissed her then, thinking all he needed was her sweetness. All he needed was to kiss her and hold her, to feel her against him one more time before Santos took her to Guanajuato.

"Yes," he surprised himself by answering.

She led him across the great room and down a hallway off which opened several doors. They entered the first room, a cubicle of some sort. Without speaking a word, she discarded the yellow lace.

"Where is Señora Velez?" he questioned, suddenly worried.

She laughed. "She can't come until after siesta, silly."

He leaned a shoulder against the door and watched her slip off the slender gown of silk, hang it on a special hanger, then remove the undergarments and arrange them in a box that lay beside it.

She turned to him, wearing nothing except the loveliness she had been born in, scooped up an armload of clothing, and led him out the door and down the narrow passageway into the very last room, locking the door behind them.

She tossed her clothing to a chair, then pulled him by his hand to the bed, where she began to undress him. Once he was disrobed, she slipped onto the bed and pulled him down beside her.

He wrapped his arms about her, and she held him tight. "Tell me about your brother," she whispered.

For the next hour they talked. He told her about his brothers, all five of them, and his two sisters.

"Delta is about your age. She's the youngest."

"They live all over the country?"

"Benjamin encouraged us to seek our fortunes." He grunted derisively. "Some fortune, I guess. Rangering."

"Do you enjoy being a Ranger?"

He nodded.

"Then it's your fortune."

He smiled, thinking of this place, of Rancho Mazón, of the mine and the mint. Little she knew of fortunes, a girl who had never known anything else. Before he was finished, he had told her everything—how his pa had run off when they were kids; how his ma had pined so long she'd lost her mind; how Benjamin had raised them all, giving up any hope of a life for himself.

"That's the sad part, I guess. He had been married only about a year. Ellie was her name. Real nice girl, even though she was raised up in a house of painted ladies."

"Painted ladies?"

He laughed. "I forgot, you are sheltered. Have you ever heard of a whorehouse?"

"Of course."

"Same thing."

"She was . . . a *puta?*" Aurelia shuddered when she said the word, recalling how Nuncio Quiroz had called her that.

"No. She was an orphan. The madam who ran the house took her in, raised her proper, considering the surroundings."

"And Benjamin married her."

Carson nodded. "I had a wire from her not long before I left to come down here. She said Benjamin had turned up missing. I sent word to Kale—"

"Another brother?"

"The black sheep in the family," he told her. "But there's good in him. Someday maybe he'll come across the right woman and she can bring it out."

"They sound fascinating."

"They aren't high-toned."

"High-toned?"

He glanced around. "Likely none of them has ever been inside a house this fancy."

"So?"

He studied her nose. Close up like this it looked pug, but it wasn't really. "So, our worlds are far, far apart."

Nuzzling her body close to his, she kissed him gently. "No, they aren't. Can't you feel anything?"

He tightened his hold on her.

She pulled back. "Will you cry over him?"

He shrugged.

"Sometimes it helps to cry."

He kissed the pert little nose she so often flaunted at the civilized world. "I'll keep that in mind. Might come in handy one day soon."

His lips closed over hers then. He snugged her to him, running his hand the length of her, feeling his flesh burn at the touch of her.

Would he cry? he wondered. When he left her, would he cry? Quite possibly it would be the saddest leave-taking in his life — as definite and as final as Benjamin's death.

He drew a determined breath. He would grieve over the two of them together — later. This was not the time for grieving. His hand found her breast. This was a time for loving. If her brother had his way, it would be the last time they ever spent together.

She wriggled against him, anxious, overanxious. All morning she had schemed, trying to come up with the right time to meet him, the right place to love him. A time and a place where they would not be disturbed for as long as they wanted.

That it had to be today, she knew. Since this morning, she had wanted nothing else, had thought of nothing else. What about him was so addictive? She had thought she wanted to hear him say he loved her.

Then he had said it, and it hadn't been enough.

She knew she wanted him to make love to her.

Surely one more time would satisfy this craving inside her.

His hand skimmed her body, leaving in its wake fiery streaks, like lightning. His lips followed, igniting her pores like sparklers at a fiesta. Had it been dark inside the small room she was sure she would have radiated as much light as a star.

But it wasn't dark. It was light — light enough for her to see his glorious body. Unlike hers, his body was divided into sections, some obviously darkened by the sun, some lighter, almost white. She touched her lips to his brown neck, then bowed her head and touched them to his furry chest. Moving, she nipped at white flesh at the side of him.

He flinched.

"Did I hurt you?"

He grinned. His fingers began their magical exploration inside her. "Does this hurt you?"

"No." She inhaled a quivering intake of air. "No, never."

"Never," he whispered, covering her mouth, kissing her deeply, passionately.

She pulled him closer, wriggling herself beneath him.

He laughed. "I'm glad to see you're as ready as I am, angel. Your morning visit left me barely able to get through the day."

When he had positioned himself above her, he leaned on his elbows. "Remember what I told you? This won't hurt like before."

She pulled his shoulders toward her. "I know."

"You know?" he mimicked. "If you knew all you think you do," he spoke slowly, entering her with great tenderness, "we wouldn't be in the fix we are in."

She hadn't known. She told him that afterwards. After he had taken her to heights of glory, after they had soared with the eagles, after the stars had exploded in her head, she told him.

"I never dreamed it could be so wonderful."

The lovemaking had spent him so that he could but drop to her chest. He rolled to his side, waiting for the room to stop spinning, waiting for his breath to return.

Finally, he rose on an elbow and stared down into her awe-filled face.

"It was that good, huh?"

"You know it was."

"Hmm. I know something else, too: You are a lady who loves to live on the edge, who loves a chase."

"A chase?"

He hugged her to him, loving her for what she was, desperately wishing things could be different between them. "I keep asking myself why you are chasing me."

"What a dreadful thing to say. I'm not chasing you."

He lifted an eyebrow. "No? Think about it. From that first kiss when you arranged to get close to me while I was shaving—"

"I was keeping you from cutting your own throat."

"Hmm. And what humanitarian purpose did you have in mind when you lured me to your bed in the cave?"

"Well . . ." She felt her face flush. How she wished she had never hurt his feelings like that. "I apologized."

He kissed her tenderly. "So you did. Is that why you proposed marriage to me at the ranch? To salve my bruised ego?"

"Of course not," she pouted.

"Now, last night in the drawing room," he continued, running down the list, "that could have been a simple case of flirting, the result of finding the target of your fancy fancied by another."

"I was not—"

"But this morning disguised as a maid? And the message to meet you here hidden among our other messages? A girl chasing a feller, pure and simple."

Her eyes were wide.

"Don't think I'm not flattered. Fact is, I haven't been chased with such determination in some time."

"In some time? Who else—?"

He silenced her with a kiss, then continued. "What if the maid had gotten those messages mixed up? Or handed the whole batch to Santos?"

"She wouldn't have."

"No? I thought for a while you might be reacting to an overly protective brother, determined to prove to him that you could get your way."

"Carson, how could you think that?"

"How could I not?" He kissed her flushed face. A residue of lovemaking lingered, but he suspected most of the redness now came from rising indignation. "I've changed my mind this afternoon, though," he continued. "I think it's the danger you love."

"Danger?"

"You are noted for your schemes, angel. You take pride in them, and in your ability to stay one step ahead of everyone around you."

"You make me sound like a criminal."

He laughed. "We aren't talking about the train robberies, only about the way you are attempting to rob me of my sanity."

She flinched.

"Admit it," he teased. "Part of the thrill this afternoon was seeing how close we could come to being discovered by Santos without actually getting caught. How long do you suppose it will take him to find us?"

"He won't. I enlisted Pia's aid. She has taken him to the cathedral."

"The conference with Padre? . . ."

She pressed her lips together, shaking her head slowly.

"That message was a fake?"

She nodded, unable to keep a pleased look from her face.

"The padre didn't ask them to meet him?"

She shook her head.

Carson began to scramble from the bed. "Then Santos should be returning about now."

"No, Pia will keep him in the garden. Don't you think they want some time alone?"

"Not when he discovers the trick. He isn't about to give us time to—" He stopped suddenly, as his love for her washed over him, leaving his breath short. "—for ourselves," he finished.

"Santos won't realize why Pia tricked him. He thinks Señora Velez is here to fit my gown."

"So he told me," Carson agreed. He recalled the rest of Santos's conversation—that he would not leave Carson alone for long . . . alone to mourn the death of his brother; and that he trusted him with his sister. Trust. *Your word is good as gold.*

Carson reached for his clothes. "I don't doubt your ability to hatch and carry out a scheme, angel. But I'm not ready to hang my chances of living on Santos Mazón's ignorance, either. Or on your quest to live on the edge."

221

She pulled him back to her, holding their bodies close. "You make it sound childish. I thought you loved me. You couldn't love me . . . like this . . . if I were a child."

He buried his face in her hair, felt her womanly curves soft and provocative against his flesh. Finally, when he was able to muster a more detached approach to the situation, he drew her back and studied her face.

"Not only children seek danger, Aurelia. The Texas Ranger corps is full of men who thrive on the thrill of danger."

Her face brightened. "That's what we have in common, isn't it? We both love to live on the edge."

Before he could stop himself, he whispered, "We have nothing in common."

But she would not hear of it, launching into her plans for them in Guanajuato. "You will love the *charriada*. You'll be good at it, too. You may even win. Do you know what the winners receive? The tradition began long ago in Spain with the knights. Even very poor knights came away from tournaments owning all sorts of things: valuable arms, saddles, armor, even horses. Every time they won an event, they got to choose their prize from among their opponent's possessions."

He grinned, savoring her enthusiasm, loving her unrequited optimism. It would take her a long time to be hurt by any man. By that time, maybe she would be old and gray and happily married with a passel of children.

He let her babble on about Guanajuato, not telling her that because her brother possessed an unusually level head, he would not be going to the fair with her. Let her plan; she did so enjoy scheming.

And he did so enjoy her schemes.

"I know what you should choose," she continued as though he were already the winner. "Don Rodrigo Fraga will enter. He always does. The Fraga Stables raise the most sought-after Arabians in Mexico, and Rodrigo always brings a string of them to ride in various parades and events. That's what you should choose. You can start a herd of purebred Arabians."

Finally, he snuggled her still-babbling face into the lee of his shoulder and held her firmly in place. He was a practical man by virtue of necessity. In his family even the women were practical, not given to dreaming. He had never known a dreamer before, and he didn't know what to make of her.

Except to love her. Even if nothing could come of that love, he would cherish her unbounded visions, for they had begun to nudge the firm edges of his own practicality, and he liked the sense of freedom that seeped into the cracks.

Carson squinched his eyes closed, holding her tight. Perhaps that way he could etch every small detail of this moment into his mind forever. For he had no doubt that was the only place it would be allowed to remain true and alive past today.

Returning to the mansion, Santos found Carson in the patio strumming a pensive tune on a guitar.

"Been playing long?" Santos queried.

Although his tone was casual, Carson saw fire smoldering behind the coal-black pupils of Santos's eyes.

"Nigh onto all my life," he replied, strumming his thumb across the strings to produce a discordant chord.

"You know what I mean."

Before he could answer, Aurelia swished into the patio.

"Serenade me . . ." Her words trailed off at the startled expression on Carson's face. Turning in the direction of his gaze, she saw Santos, a grim set to his mouth. "Oh, *Papá* Santos," she quipped, sarcasm evident in both her tone and her pert curtsy.

"I thought you were having your gown fitted," Santos accused.

"I was waiting for Pia . . ."

Behind them a loud knock sounded at the front door of the mansion. Serphino shuffled to open it.

". . . and for Señora Velez, who seems to have just arrived."

Santos's gaze traveled from Aurelia to Carson, then back to Aurelia. "What have you two been up to?"

"Coming, señora," Aurelia called into the foyer. "Packing," she told Santos. "When do we leave for Guanajuato?"

"In the morning."

Excitement welled inside her. She turned to Carson. "You're going to love it."

"I won't be going," he answered, his attention riveted on the guitar he now plucked with great concentration.

Her spirits plummeted. "What do you mean?"

"He has work to do here," Santos told her.

Ignoring him, Aurelia crossed to Carson. When he

224

4 BESTSELLING HISTORICAL ROMANCES BY YOUR FAVORITE AUTHORS CAN BE YOURS, FREE!

Kensington Choice, our newest book club now brings you historical romances by your favorite bestselling authors including Janelle Taylor, Shannon Drake, Rosanne Bittner, Jo Beverley, and Georgina Gentry, just to name a few! Each book is filled with passion, adventure and the excitement of bygone times!

To introduce you to this great new club which is part of Zebra Home Subscription Service, we'd like to send you your first 4 bestselling historical romances, absolutely free! And once you get these 4 free books to savor at home, we'll rush you the next 4 brand-new books at the lowest prices available, as soon as they are published.

The way the club works is that after your initial FREE shipment, you will get our 4 newest bestselling historical romances delivered to your doorstep each month at the preferred subscriber's rate of only $4.20 per book, a savings of up to $7.16 per month (since these titles sell in bookstores for $4.99-$5.99)! All books are sent on a 10-day free examination basis and there is no minimum number of books to buy. (And no charge for shipping.) Plus as a regular subscriber, you'll receive our FREE monthly newsletter, *Zebra/Pinnacle Romance News*, which features author profiles, contests, subscriber benefits, book previews and more!

So start today by returning the FREE BOOK CERTIFICATE provided. We'll send you 4 FREE BOOKS with no further obligation: A FREE gift offering you hours of reading pleasure with no obligation...how can you lose?

*We have 4 FREE BOOKS for you
as your introduction to
KENSINGTON CHOICE!
To get your FREE BOOKS, worth
up to $23.96, mail the card below.*

FREE BOOK CERTIFICATE

Yes! Please send me 4 Kensington Choice (the best of Zebra and Pinnacle Books) Historical Romances without cost or obligation (worth up to $23.96). As a Kensington Choice subscriber, I will then receive 4 brand-new romances to preview each month for 10 days FREE. I can return any books I decide not to keep and owe nothing. The publisher's prices for Kensington Choice romances range from $4.99-$5.99, but as a preferred subscriber I will get these books for only $4.20 per book or $16.80 for all four titles. There is no minimum number of books to buy and I may cancel my subscription at any time, plus there is no additional charge for postage and handling. No matter what I decide to do, my first 4 books are mine to keep, absolutely FREE!

KF0896

Name _____

Address _____ Apt. _____

City _____ State _____ Zip _____

Telephone (___) _____

Signature _____

(If under 18, parent or guardian must sign)

Subscription subject to acceptance. Terms and prices subject to change.

KENSINGTON CHOICE
Zebra Home Subscription Service, Inc.
120 Brighton Road
P.O.Box 5214
Clifton, NJ 07015-5214

AFFIX
STAMP
HERE

didn't look up, she grabbed the neck of the guitar, stilling the strings.

He lifted his eyes to hers, silent.

"You must come to Guanajuato."

He glanced down at the guitar, at her hand there. "Like Santos said, there is work to be done here. You know that."

She nodded, grim. "But the *charriada?*" Tears welled in her eyes. "What about the *charriada?*"

He shrugged, staring at her hand.

She turned to her brother, who stood his ground.

"It's only a month before the wedding, Relie," Santos argued. "We have to get the mine difficulties settled so Jarrett can go home."

"Home?" She swung back to Carson, who still refused to meet her gaze.

He plucked a few notes.

"Relie," her mother called from the foyer, "Pia and Zita have arrived. You mustn't keep Señora Velez waiting."

Aurelia glared from one obstinate man to the other. She spoke to Carson in slow anguished tones. "If you don't come to Guanajuato, how? . . ." Desperation grew inside her. She turned to Santos. "If he doesn't come for the *charriada* — "

"We'll work it out later, Aurelia," Carson interrupted. "Go get your fitting over. And remind Señora Velez that she is not to tell a soul that you are back in town."

By the time Aurelia arrived at the sewing room adjoining the ballroom, tears brimmed in her eyes. Furiously, she wiped them away, then dried her face on her skirt so no one would know.

Pia and Zita waited with an impatient Señora Velez in the cubicle where Aurelia had removed the yellow lace earlier. The vision of undressing in this room under Carson's heated gaze brought more tears to the verge of spilling. She blinked them back.

But it didn't take tears for Pia and Zita to realize something was wrong. The girls immediately launched into a coded explanation.

"I'm sorry, Relie," Pia finished, after she had related the mishap at the cathedral. "I didn't intend to let it slip."

"It doesn't matter." She sighed heavily, and Señora Velez admonished her to hold still and breathe normally.

"That's difficult to do," she retorted, "with my brother determined to ruin my life."

"He means well, Relie," Pia defended Santos.

"Well, he should keep his well-meant intentions to himself. I tell you, he brings out the worst in me. Two minutes around him, and I'm acting like a child. Even in front of Carson . . ."

She glanced at Zita, her words trailing off.

"Don't mind me," Zita laughed. "Pia filled me in. As if I couldn't tell by looking."

"Tell what?" Aurelia gasped.

Zita laughed. "That you are head over heels in love, that's what."

"Me?"

Zita rolled her eyes, and Pia sighed.

Aurelia shook her head. When she spoke, her voice echoed the amazement she felt inside. "Maybe I am falling in love. I'm so confused." She paused to blink back tears. "That's why the Guanajuato trip is so important. I must see how he reacts to Guanajuato. If he could enter the *charriada* and win—"

"Relie!" Zita stopped her. "Don't tell me you are playing games with that man. He's in love with you. Whether you care anything about him or not, he's too nice a person, too trusting—"

"You sound like Santos," Aurelia snapped.

"We know you wouldn't intentionally lead him on, Relie," Pia added, "but if you aren't certain how you feel—"

"Are you certain, Pia? Is anyone ever certain? I'm so confused I don't know what to think. All I know is I'm different than I was before . . . before I met him. When I'm with him everything is wonderful, and when we're apart I feel desperate and lonely and . . . I guess it's the security he gave me after . . ." She stopped, conscious of Señora Velez's presence.

"Security, my foot," Zita replied.

"He's probably right," Aurelia said. "Maybe it is the danger I seek, living on the edge."

"Whatever you decide to call it," Pia informed her, "it sounds like love to me."

"Don't worry, Relie," Zita added. "Carson Jarrett is a man who knows how to handle any situation."

"If he wants to," she sighed, feeling more unprecedented tears well in her eyes. "He acts like all he wants is to get away from me."

"Here, here." Señora Velez stuffed a handkerchief into Aurelia's hand. "Don't be crying on this lace. It came all the way from Spain, and we don't have time to send for more."

Aurelia blew her nose into the handkerchief. "What I need is to get him away from Santos."

Her friends laughed.

"You will find a way," Zita assured her.

"You've always been able to solve your problems," Pia encouraged.

Aurelia laughed then. For some reason she felt much better than when she had left the patio, as though a heavy weight had been lifted from her shoulders. The girls were right. She could find a solution; she just had to set her mind to it.

The dressmaker finished, and by the time Aurelia redressed, the first bell to dinner had sounded.

"And I have to sit beside Enrique."

"Don't worry about me," Zita whispered when they neared the drawing room where the men had assembled. "But you could find me a handsome charro in Guanajuato."

"That's a promise," Aurelia replied.

Inside the drawing room Carson, Santos, and Enrique were engaged in a serious discussion of some sort. Seeing the women, Enrique immediately separated himself from the group.

"Relie dear, how lovely you look. A brandy?"

She nodded, not trusting her voice. Her gaze went straight to Carson's warm brown eyes and tears brimmed in hers.

The moment Enrique turned to pour her brandy, Carson was by her side. With his back to the others in the room, he lifted her fingers to his lips, squeezed them when they trembled in his hand, then, as briefly, turned her loose. "You're doing fine, angel."

"I can't . . ."

"Consider it another disguise," he whispered. "You'll make it."

"I don't want to." She twisted her linen handkerchief in her hands, striving to keep from reaching for Carson. If only she could touch him, she knew her trembling would still. Her brain was filled with one thought: She must tell him she loved him.

It had occurred to her during the fitting upstairs that he might not know. He should, of course, after all they had been through together, but she had never told him. Now she longed to. It was all she could think about.

That and Guanajuato.

When Enrique returned, Carson remained at her side, drawing Zita and the others into the broader circle. "I may come down to the mint for a tour in the next few days," he told Enrique.

"Heard you were planning to take up mining. You interested in starting a mint, too?"

Carson grinned. "I doubt my government would allow such a project. No, I'm just the curious sort. Thought since I will be around until the wedding, I should grab the chance to see a mint in action."

Enrique sipped the brandy, then swished the liquid in his mouth, pondering the situation.

"Of course, if it's trouble—" Carson began.

"It's no trouble, Jarrett," Santos spoke up. "As a guest of the family, you are welcome at Casa de Moneda. Enrique will be proud to show you anything you want to see. Isn't that right, Enrique?"

"By all means," Enrique mumbled. "Be sure to send

word ahead, so I will be present to personally conduct your tour."

"Even the books," Santos suggested. "Might find it interesting to see how a mint sets up business."

Enrique frowned. "No different than any other business." He took another swig of brandy. "But if you are interested, sure. Let me know ahead of time, so I can free myself to show you around."

Enrique turned his attention to Aurelia then, and Zita seized the moment to maneuver Carson across the room.

"I want you to know something," she half whispered. "Relie promised to find me a charro in Guanajuato."

Carson cocked an eyebrow. "You don't need Aurelia's help, Zita. You are perfectly capable of finding your own charro or anyone else you take a fancy to."

She smiled. "Thank you for being so kind."

"I am not kind, I'm right."

"I know." A shy blush crept up her cheeks. "I would never have thought such a thing if it hadn't been for you."

"Me?" He stared at her a moment, then understood. "Why, ma'am, if I had a hand in convincing you of your true beauty and worth, why, my trip will have been well worthwhile."

She laughed, her composure regained. "Your trip will be worthwhile for yourself, too."

He frowned.

"I'm on your side."

"I appreciate that. It helps to have one ally in this bunch."

"You have two—Pia and me."

"Yes, ma'am, my case is definitely lookin' up." But as he ushered her in to dinner, he wondered whether that was good or bad. After this afternoon he knew one thing: It would be harder now than before to leave here without Aurelia.

Glancing around the opulent room, he added something else to the list. It would be damned hard for him to make a life for himself in a place like this. He wouldn't even entertain such a notion, except for her.

They took the same places at dinner that they had the evening before. Tonight, however, Padre Bucareli and Sister Inéz were not present, so Carson and Zita sat directly opposite Aurelia and Enrique.

Aurelia concentrated on her plate and, for the most part, picked at her food. Zita and Pia were right. She had always been able to find a solution to her problems. Yet, try as she might, she couldn't decide how to persuade Santos to allow Carson to come with them to Guanajuato.

By the time dessert arrived she had almost given up, thinking she would have to bluntly tell Santos the truth—that she had no intention of going to Guanajuato or anywhere else without Carson.

Then Santos opened the subject.

"Relie and I will be leaving for Guanajuato in the morning."

She leaned down the table, smiling sweetly at her brother. "And Carson."

He shot her a warning with his eyes. "No, Relie. Jarrett is staying here."

She turned her attention to Carson, continuing to

speak to her brother. "He wants to enter the *charriada,* Santos. Surely you won't keep him from it."

Carson shook his head. "Santos is right. I need to stay here."

"He can enter rodeos in Texas." Santos spoke as though the subject were closed. "He wants to learn something about mining while he has the chance."

"Rodeos and *charriadas* are vastly different," she objected, still staring at Carson, begging for help.

At length he grinned. "Are you doubting my ability to compete with your charros, señorita? Is that what this is all about? You want to pit me against those magnificent horsemen to show me up?"

Her eyes danced. "No, señor. But you must be afraid to enter, else a few days in a dusty old mine wouldn't stop you."

The table dropped into silence at her unpardonable accusation. Carson held her gaze with one so intense she trembled. Not from fear. There was no anger in his eyes. Only recognition. For before she finished speaking, he had rolled his eyes around the opulent room, then settled them back on her.

She knew what he feared. She could read his expression as clearly as if it had been printed in the newspaper. She feared it herself.

But she feared losing him more, much more than she feared the unknown destination toward which they were propelling themselves at breakneck speed.

Animated gibberish erupted from either side of them.

"Hear now, daughter," Don Domingo admonished. "Jarrett is a guest of your brother."

232

"She didn't mean to say *afraid*," Doña Bella hurried to assure Carson.

"Relie!" Pia and Zita sighed from either side of the table.

"The *charriada* isn't for ten days yet," Santos admitted through clenched teeth. "Perhaps Jarrett can follow us later."

Carson spoke quietly into the melee, straight to her challenging eyes. "Well, angel, since you put it that way, guess I'll have to show up and set the record straight. Otherwise I would disgrace the whole corps of Texas Rangers."

Enrique remained a silent observer until the very end, when one word swished from his lips. *"Angel?"*

Chapter Twelve

Santos, Aurelia, and Aurelia's maid, María, arrived in Guanajuato on the opening day of the feria, having left Pepe in charge of the herd of brave black bulls at the Plaza de Toros, the bullring. They were eager to arrive at the home of their relatives by early afternoon.

Even though more than ten days had passed since they left Catorce, Aurelia could still think of little besides her last meeting with Carson the evening before their departure.

Oh, he had been present to wish them a safe trip the morning they left, but there had been no chance to exchange more than a few desperate looks and for her to issue a second warning for him to be careful of Nuncio Quiroz.

For a while the evening before, she had despaired of stealing a single moment alone with him. In the end, that was about all she was allowed. After Santos left to escort Pia and Zita to their homes, Don Domingo remained in the drawing room with Carson, discussing mine activities. He insisted that Aurelia retire, and finally she had done so.

At that point she had not given up hope of seeing Carson later, but no sooner had her father prepared to retire than Santos returned. The two friends sat in the patio well into the night, drinking cerveza and strumming guitars.

Aurelia huddled in an alcove on the second-floor landing, scrunching behind a marble pillar where she would be out of sight of passersby. Surely Carson knew she would attempt to see him.

Surely he wanted to kiss her good night.

She discovered the answer to the last concern when Santos excused himself to fetch more cerveza. Since they had already been drinking an hour or so, Aurelia decided her brother might take the opportunity to do more than bring more beer, so she tiptoed down the stairs and called to Carson from a darkened corner beneath the massive staircase.

He crossed the floor, reaching her in two paces. Taking her in his arms, he settled into the shadows and kissed her with eager lips. His arms tightened around her, molded her to him, weakening her with the want of him.

Clad only in a flowing white cotton nightgown and matching wrapper, her body fairly cried for his. At the feel of her near-nude body, he groaned.

She snuggled closer. "I'm sorry for calling you a coward at dinner."

He chuckled against her. "You hit the nail on the head. I'm plumb scared to death of what we're getting ourselves into."

"I am, too," she admitted. "But I'm more afraid of being away from you."

He kissed her in acknowledgment, delving deeply into her sweetness, exciting her and himself to limits he knew were futile here in the patio. He drew back.

"Will you truly come to Guanajuato?" she whispered.

He kissed her face, one cheek then the other, one eye then the other, nestling his lips among the scattered strands of hair across her forehead. "After I discover what's going on at the mine — what game Nuncio Quiroz is playing and who else has a hand in it."

At Quiroz's name, she tensed. "Please be careful."

"I will."

"Promise you won't fight him just to . . . just because of me."

He hugged her more tightly to him, recalling the anger that had welled inside him at the sight of the man. "I won't, angel. But it will be the hardest damned thing I've ever done."

"You have to do it." She traced her fingers over his face. "For me. I want you in Guanajuato alive and well."

He chuckled. "To compete against your fearsome charros?"

"To be with me. You can't deny me this."

He stiffened at the truth in her statement. "No, I can't. That's what has me worried."

"Worried?"

"When the time comes, how will I ever say no to you?"

Suddenly, bootsteps sounded in the hallway beyond

the patio. Carson kissed Aurelia once more, then turned her toward the darkened staircase, sending her off with a swat to her bottom.

When she reached the landing, she realized she hadn't told him the one thing she had waited so long to say. That she loved him. Perhaps she should sit a while longer and catch him after Santos went to bed.

"Where've you been?" she heard Santos question.

Carson laughed. "One of these days I'm going to take offense to this obsession you have about your sister and me."

"I know it's foolish," Santos admitted with a sigh. "Pia lectured me proper about the same thing this afternoon. But damnit, Jarrett, you don't know the half of what she's capable of doing."

"I'll have to admit, Aurelia is proficient in a number of areas," he teased.

"What's that supposed to mean?"

"Nothing. I like to rile you, that's all."

Santos's voice turned from quarrelsome to somber. "Would you believe me if I told you that my sweet, innocent-looking little sister advised Pia to seduce me before the wedding?"

Aurelia felt her face flush in the darkness. Below her, Carson let out a whoop of laughter loud enough to wake the household.

"So, what's the problem with that?" he questioned. "Makes a hell of a lot of sense."

"Nothing's the matter with it, except it occurred to me that if she would advise her best friend to do such a thing, she might consider it for herself, too."

They resumed strumming guitars. Aurelia leaned

her head against the pillar, waiting with held breath for Carson's response. Pleasant sounds of water splashing in the fountain merged with the sometimes gay, sometimes plaintive notes of the music.

When at length Carson replied, she heard no jesting in his voice.

"I think we've ridden this dead horse long enough, partner. Do you figure I'd be callous enough to make love to your sister and then admit it to you — or to anybody, for that matter? If I ever took Aurelia to bed, it would be between the two of us, private, special, and with . . . with . . ." He hedged so long she began to wonder what he was going to say. Then he said it. ". . . with a lot of love between us."

She heard the guitars strum again, first one, then the other, as though they were playing a duel, dancing around each other, tilting, maneuvering for position.

"Hell, Santos," Carson continued, "I figure I may have to fight that damned Quiroz over her one of these days. I don't want to have to whip you, too."

Finally, Santos laughed, not heartily at first, but a sick kind of laugh that gained strength the longer he tried. "That'll be a cold day in hell. But I worry about her, Jarrett. Can't help it. She's my kid sister, after all."

"You're right to worry about her. I would, too. I will while she's off with those damned charros in Guanajuato. But you're wrong about one thing. She's no kid anymore. She's a woman. A beautiful, strong, passionate woman. Like I told her, she will make some lucky man a good catch one day."

"Not you?" Santos quizzed.

"Not likely."

Aurelia went to bed on that, pondering it into the night. He did love her, she assured herself, she knew he loved her. But he still thought of them as being different. That's what it was. That's all it was. She was sure of it. But how was she ever going to change his mind?

Santos and Aurelia arrived in Guanajuato with three hours to spare before the first event of the feria season, a performance of Bizet's *Carmen,* a fairly new opera that was all the rage in Spain these days, their aunt assured them.

Aurelia had to pinch herself several times while she dressed in a gold faille gown with an off-the-shoulder neckline and daring décolletage. The skirt draped in graceful folds around her hips, then extended to an embroidered train that was lined with black velvet. The gold pumps were tight and uncomfortable after her long hours in the saddle wearing made-to-measure boots.

But she could endure a little discomfort, she told herself, anticipating the excitement that would soon build inside her.

With the help of María, Aurelia did her hair up in curls, finishing just as Tía Guadalupe peeked in to tell her it was time to leave for the Teatro Juárez.

"My dear, you will turn every head in the house tonight. Why, Doña Masania won't have a chance. You will receive all her curtain calls."

Aurelia tugged on the long white gloves and picked up her black velvet pocket, inside of which Mamá had placed a lace handkerchief and a pair of opera glasses.

The latter had belonged to the young Bella Lopez. At last her daughter had arrived in the city and could use them herself.

"Hurry, dear, we must not be more than fashionably late this evening. Since we are sitting in the governor's box, he and his lady have the honor of arriving last. Once Tío is elected governor, we can make our own grand entrances."

The Reinaldo house was even more elegant than the Mazón mansion, with uniformed servants scurrying to every beck and call, and liveried doormen and footmen.

City living, Aurelia sighed to herself. Real city living. And here she was, about to be launched into society at long last.

Tío Luís and Santos awaited them in the foyer, and Aurelia fairly beamed at seeing her brother in his evening clothes.

"Santos! How elegant you look in black silk."

He stared at her as though he were looking at a stranger, his lips pursed, his eyes solemn. He leaned forward and planted a kiss on her forehead. "Little Relie, I'm afraid Jarrett was right. You are a woman, beautiful and . . ." The word he refused to say died on his lips.

She smiled, warmed by the mere recollection of Carson's statement. Deliberately, she straightened her sleeves, drawing attention to the deep décolletage of the gown.

Santos heaved a heavy sigh. "You are sure to win every heart at the theater."

Tío Luís turned to allow the servant to whisk specks

of lint, dust, and other invisible objects from his black silk cape. "Then they will be broken, these hearts she wins, will they not, my dear? Since your heart belongs to Enrique."

She started to protest, but Tío Luís handed the servant his cigar to extinguish and they got on their way. In the excitement that followed, she forgot her uncle's assumption.

The Teatro Juárez glittered like a giant jewel in the night sky. Arriving carriages deposited their prestigious occupants in front of what Tío Luís described as a French-Moorish facade. Two tiers of marble stairs led to the entrance, which was guarded by a dozen graceful columns, each with its own ornate lamppost. Overhead, six enormous bronze statues stood atop the building, guardians of the muses, she heard someone explain. By that time, Tío Luís and Tía Guadalupe were well past the stage of playing tour guide.

"Tío certainly acts the part of a politician," Santos whispered in her ear. Together, brother and sister hung back, watching their aunt and uncle greet every person they passed.

Aurelia studied her aunt, chin aloft, head bobbing in a regal fashion. "What a grand manner Tía Guadalupe has."

"Looks like she's trying to keep her tiara from slipping."

"Santos, for shame!" But Aurelia was hardpressed to keep from giggling.

"Enjoying yourself?" Santos questioned.

"I'm enjoying the show."

"The spectacle," he replied. They followed their relatives up a red carpeted staircase to the front of the theater, where a uniformed guard checked the guest list, then admitted them to the governor's box with a deep bow.

"*Carmen* cannot possibly be more entertaining than all this," she told him. Once inside the box, however, the grandeur of the building took away all thoughts of her pretentious relatives.

Five tiers of seats swept around the auditorium, each one fronted by ornate railings and glowing lanterns. Every surface reflected light in burnished shades of gold and red and green. It was a fairy-tale land that came close to blurring the vision with its splendor.

Her perusal was interrupted by a jab in the ribs from Tía Guadalupe. "The governor, my dear. We must rise."

Governor Benevides and his wife entered to a fanfare of applause from their invited guests.

Aurelia watched the governor and Tío Luís embrace. "What Tía Guadalupe said must be true," she whispered to Santos. "About the governor choosing Tío Luís to be his successor."

"Lucky for Tío the governor is so popular," Santos added. "Although Tío seems more agreeable tonight than I remembered him."

Studying the gentlemen and ladies who followed the governor and his wife, Aurelia knew they were the elite of Guanajuato society. She had arrived.

Like her mother before her, she was being introduced. The next step would be the City of Mexico. She waited expectantly for the opera to begin and for her excitement to mount.

Several members of the governor's entourage were single men, who upon discovering Santos to be Aurelia's brother instead of a suitor, immediately launched suits of their own.

She smiled sweetly, laughed gaily, and compared each and every one of them to Carson Jarrett.

Was José as witty?

Did Juan speak as softly?

Would Jorge be as adept in the wilderness?

None were as handsome.

None had as bright a smile. None of their eyes were as warm. And none of them fired her blood or even came close to it.

So when Tío Luís leaned forward to tell a young swain, "Look but do not fall in love, young man. She is taken by the president of Casa de Moneda Mazón," Aurelia was able to reply, "Do not worry, Tío, I won't forget I am spoken for."

At the first lull, she whispered to Santos. "Do you think he might come tonight?"

"Who?"

Before she could respond, she saw the answer dawn in his eyes. He studied her with a wistfulness she did not understand. "When Jarrett says something, Relie, you can bank on it. He told you he would be here in time for the *charriada,* and he will be."

The orchestra began the overture. Patrons scurried to take their seats. A bright face appeared over her right shoulder.

"Allow me to introduce myself, Señorita Mazón. I am Antonio Suarez. Tomorrow I will fight one of your family's famous bulls at the Fiesta Brava.

I will dedicate him to you."

She felt herself smile. She heard her voice thank him. The curtain rose; the crowd applauded.

And all the while Santos's words etched themselves deeper and deeper into her heart. *When Jarrett says something. you can bank on it.* But the only words she could recall him speaking were the ones he had spoken in the patio the night before she left Catorce, when he told her brother it wasn't likely he would marry her. And that was one thing she did not want to bank on.

After four days of crawling through tunnels and poring over records, Carson was sure of only one thing: He would never be able to spend his life below ground. A man had to be plumb feebleminded—or crazed by gold fever—to work below ground day in and day out. Arising before sunrise and not crawling back out of the bowels of the earth until dark, he never felt sunshine or smelled flowers, never saw the morning dew with the sun glinting off the grass, never heard birds sing.

And these men did not work for riches, but merely because they knew no other way to make a living.

Some living, he was reminded day after day. By the time they arrived home at night, they were too tired to make love and too aware of the dangers facing them the next day to get drunk. Some life. A wonder there were so many children running around the miners' village.

The sight of these children had instilled a new fear inside Carson. Every time he saw a child run through the streets, he thought of Aurelia and wondered what kind of fools they had been, taking such a chance with her future. What if she had conceived his child? The idea needled him continually, sometimes with a depressing sense of guilt, other times with a swelling of pleasure.

The latter was always tempered by what a child would mean to Aurelia. She wasn't ready to become a wife, much less a mother. But the more he thought about it, the more certain he became that the fact was all too possible.

Aurelia a mother? The mother of his child? He thought of her every waking hour and dreamed about her at night. Aurelia, his guardian angel. Once again, he had failed to take care of her.

He didn't speak her name. He was afraid to, afraid of what he might say, how his voice might sound. He recalled teasing friends about being lovesick. Well, now he knew what that term meant.

And it was no joking matter.

The more he considered it, the more he was sure some of their outlandish teasing had shown itself for what it was. Was that why Don Domingo seemed determined to prove to him that his daughter was unavailable?

As if he had not emphasized the point enough before she left, after Aurelia and Santos departed for Guanajuato, Don Domingo pursued Enrique Villasur's case at every opportunity. He began the first morning after their departure, when he insisted on personally escorting Carson to the mine.

"In case that son of mine didn't make clear that you are to be shown around. Wouldn't want the guard refusing you access, would we? You coming all this way to learn the mining business."

Carson had not questioned Santos's reasons for wanting to keep his mission secret from everyone except themselves and Aurelia, including his own father. He had supposed the man might be given to verbosity.

And indeed the elder Mazón was a talker. But he stuck mainly to one topic: the virtues of Enrique Villasur. Don Domingo had nothing else on his mind, causing Carson to decide that it might not be himself who was jealous of Enrique so much as Santos.

Don Domingo went further than merely referring to Enrique as *hijo;* he treated the man like a son. To all appearances, Santos had been banished to the ranch, while Enrique was being groomed to take his place, not only in Catorce but in his father's favor.

"The Villasurs are old friends of the family?" Carson slipped the question into one of Don Domingo's discourses on his mint president.

Don Domingo laughed broadly. "No, no. We have never met the folks. Their blood is too rich for us." Then as if reconsidering, he grasped his lapels with two pudgy fists and puffed up his chest. "Or it was."

"You mean before the . . . ah . . . the betrothal?" Carson asked, wondering how anyone's blood could be richer than Don Domingo's. It must be royal purple.

"After Relie marries their son, they cannot very well look down their noses at the Mazóns, can they, boy? We will be family then. And I might add, they will be the poor relations."

"You mean the Villasurs are on hard times?"

"No, no. Not hard times. They are Castilian. Old Spanish. Never did have much in the way of money. Name and prestige, that's what they are worth. They are the ones who spoke up for me, convinced President Díaz to give me the mint."

"In exchange for the presidency for their son?" Carson ventured, trying to keep any trace of disapproval from his voice.

"More or less. Of course, I was free to choose."

"Of course," Carson replied. Like Aurelia was free to choose where she lived, whom she married.

After that, Carson considered he had learned two valuable lessons since Aurelia left: He could never live or work beneath the ground; and in Catorce he would not be allowed to live or work above ground, either. Certainly not as Aurelia's husband.

Coming on the heels of that revelation, Carson's first meeting with Nuncio Quiroz since Santos's introduction came off better than he had expected. The man virtually ignored him the first few days, having immediately turned his care over to a man they called Beto, his second in command, an infinitely more congenial man.

But Beto had not assaulted Aurelia, a fact that Carson admitted made a big difference in the way he felt about the man. The uneasy feeling of being recognized by Quiroz the day Santos introduced the two of them lingered and grew as time went on. Sooner or later, Quiroz was bound to put things together.

An enthusiastic miner, Beto readily showed Carson every aspect of the mining business, even though he spoke so rapidly that Jarrett had to occasionally ask him to repeat himself.

"Despacio, por favor," Carson would say. After which

the man would obligingly slow down his rapid-fire speech.

Although it had nothing to do with Beto's detailed instructions, a couple of days after Aurelia and Santos's departure, Carson began spending more time in the mine office. He even started taking lunch there. Not that he found inaccuracies in the records. He didn't know enough about mining to be sure, but the records looked in order, professional.

What kept him at the mine was one of the same things that would keep him from marrying Aurelia: Enrique Villasur. The man had become so constant a guest at the Mazón mansion that Carson would not have been surprised any day to return and find Enrique settled in permanently.

It was easier, he told himself, to fix a lunch in the kitchen and spend the time in the office. That was the only time of the day he could be sure of not being bothered, anyway, the only time he had to peruse the books without anyone around. Siesta was observed with a devoutness that bordered on holiness. And it was so for him, for siesta always reminded him of Aurelia and the last time they made love.

He wondered what she was doing. Wondered whom she was meeting, with whom she was dancing, whether the charros were handsome and dashing. He knew they would set their sombreros for Aurelia.

She was beautiful and exciting and as unpredictable as a blue norther. And yes, as he had told Santos, she was strong and passionate.

And that's what might have gotten her in trouble. Both of them. If she carried his child . . .

What if she carried his child? She hadn't even thought of such a thing, he knew. Neither had he. They had been careless and irresponsible.

He had exercised no control. He wasn't sure he was capable of such a thing where Aurelia was concerned. And if she carried his child, he would be hardpressed to be sorry, except for the misery and heartbreak it would cause her.

What would he find in Guanajuato? Was he to be a father? If not, he vowed to exercise control for both of them. In a city full of people, he knew there would be little time for privacy, and with Santos around to bird-dog them, they wouldn't be able to find privacy if they looked.

The day before he was to leave for Guanajuato, Carson was so consumed by thoughts of Aurelia when he entered the mine office that he acknowledged the presence of Enrique with a simple *"Buenas días,"* before he stopped to consider why the man was seated at the desk entering data in a ledger book.

"I keep these records, Jarrett. Did no one bother to tell you?"

Carson shook his head, while his mind raced to put facts together. "Fair enough," he responded. "Perhaps you can explain the process to me."

"Nothing to it," Enrique replied, somewhat more cordial than usual. After thirty minutes, Carson had to agree.

"Nothing to it, long as you know what you are doing. Where did you learn all this stuff?"

Enrique rocked back in the barrel-shaped office chair and twined his fingers behind his head. "Here and there. A couple of years at university, most of it by hard work in Mina Pizarro up in the Andes."

Carson raised his eyebrows, recognizing the field by name. "Don Domingo failed to mention that you come with prestige of your own. No need to rest on your family's laurels."

"My family's laurels?"

Carson grinned. "No need for modesty, Villasur. Any family with connections to the country's president shouldn't neglect to use them."

For a moment Enrique appeared not to comprehend, then he had the decency to blush, raising him a notch in Carson's estimation. If the man's family had bought him a position at the mint and marriage to the owner's daughter, he did not readily acknowledge the fact.

Especially not to a man he considered a rival, Carson discovered when Enrique spoke again.

"What exactly is between you and Relie?"

Now it was Carson's turn to color. Try as he might to stem it, he felt heat rush up his neck. "Santos calls it a *thing.*"

"I am not familiar with such a term."

"No need to be alarmed," Carson assured him. "Not much chance it will interfere with your plans."

Enrique eyed him with growing hostility, even though the physical difference between the two men would suggest to any able-minded soul that a fight would be considerably one-sided, against the mint president.

"She is to be betrothed to me."

"So I've been told."

"We are to be married soon after Santos and Pia."

"Does the lady know?"

"She did," Enrique challenged, "before you came to town calling her pet names."

Carson's eyes flashed. One more day and he would be out of this place. No sense rising to the fight now. Especially not a fight that was as unmatched and as unnecessary as this one. His fight with Enrique Villasur would be won or lost between himself and Aurelia.

Enrique did not appear to understand that fact. "In our country, familiarity with a woman who is not your wife is forbidden."

What about with a woman who will be the mother of your child? Carson immediately rebuked himself for not putting that notion behind him. But the fact that he was unable to stop thinking about it gave him further cause for concern. The image of Aurelia carrying his child had become so vividly etched in his brain that he knew it must be true.

And if it was?

"I wouldn't worry too much, Villasur. A man faces a lot of problems in life, and you would be surprised how unimportant some of them can make a little thing like a pet name."

But it wasn't unimportant. His name for Aurelia held a great deal of importance — for both of them. She was his guardian angel.

And he would be hers. Regardless of the consequences to either of them.

"Ultimately, it's the lady's choice, anyhow," he added.

"Not in this country," Enrique informed him. "She will marry me whether she wants to or not. Her father and I have decided for her. It is up to you whether she does so willingly or whether she begins her marriage to me with regrets."

Carson stared hard at the man. All he could think to reply was that Aurelia belonged to him. Regardless of whom she married, she belonged to him. She had belonged to him since that day in the cave. She would always belong to him.

Without a further word, he took his Stetson off the peg, crammed it on his head, and walked out into the bright sunshine, letting it warm the chill that always settled over him in the mine.

A chill made all the more unbearable by the fact that what Enrique Villasur had said could well become reality.

Chapter Thirteen

By the time Aurelia descended the staircase for breakfast the morning following the opera, she was determined to set Tío Luís straight on the topic of her relationship with Enrique Villasur.

The house was so quiet she thought for a moment she was the only person awake. But Santos had mentioned going to check on the bulls early, and she wanted to accompany him. So, even though she had not managed to get much sleep the night before, she arose at dawn and dressed in one of her riding habits.

She found Santos and Tío Luís on the patio having breakfast. Her uncle did not disguise his surprise.

"My dear, you should be abed getting your beauty rest."

She laughed, sliding into an elaborate gold-leafed iron chair next to Santos. A maid scurried to serve her coffee and orange juice. "Shame on you, Tío, for suggesting I need beauty sleep."

"My apologies, Relie. I should perhaps have used another term. We don't want to wear you out. Can't send

253

you home to Enrique haggard from your visit to the city, now, can we?"

Carefully, she replaced the porcelain cup in its matching saucer. "I'm not going home to Enrique, Tío."

A frown creased his forehead. *"¿Qué dice?"*

"I said," she rephrased, "I am not betrothed to Enrique."

Luís Reinaldo stared into the center of the table, obviously considering his niece's statement. Finally, he smiled at her. Waving a rolled tortilla in the air as though it were his ever-present cigar, he dismissed the subject with, "The formalities have not been taken care of; a mere technicality."

"They won't be."

Luís's black eyes studied her from beneath heavy lids. "What does that mean?"

"That I do not intend to—"

"That we decided to wait until after my wedding to announce Relie's engagement, Tío," Santos interjected.

"I won't—"

Santos kicked her under the table. Aurelia turned to dispute him, but relented at the bullheaded expression on his face.

When the maid set a plate of fresh fruit before her, she eyed it skeptically, then glanced at the food Santos and Tío Luís were eating—eggs, sausages, and beefsteak covered with salsa. "Bring me what they are having, please," Aurelia told the maid.

When Tío Luís cleared his throat, she looked up to see him shake his head at the maid.

"Your aunt insists on a light breakfast," he explained. "You ladies must watch your waistlines, you know."

For one instant she was certain she would not be able to

control her fury. But Santos nudged her boot with his own, and she picked up her fork and speared a piece of pineapple. In spite of Santos, however, she reached for a hot roll, smearing it with two pats of butter and a dollop of marmalade so large it ran off the sides of the pastry. And she didn't even like marmalade.

By forcing her mind to other thoughts, Aurelia was able to calm her inner rage. The other thoughts, as always, centered on Carson Jarrett.

"Is there a chance he will arrive in time for the corrida?" she asked Santos.

He grinned. "Do you think to make him jealous when Antonio dedicates his bull to you?"

"No, I—"

"Who?" Tío Luís inquired. "Enrique is coming for the bullfights? *¡Bravo!*"

"Not Enrique," Aurelia replied. "Carson Jarrett."

"Jarrett? Never heard the name. Who is he?"

"He is—"

"The best man for my wedding, Tío," Santos interrupted. "Jarrett is from Texas, and we are anxious to show him some of our customs during his visit."

"Arriving a bit early for the wedding, isn't he?"

Aurelia would have supplied the information that Carson was already in Catorce and that because of this handsome, virile Texas Ranger, Enrique Villasur would never have a chance at her heart—or at her hand.

She would have told this pompous uncle all these things, but she didn't because Santos kicked her again. She frowned at him, confused, wondering why he suddenly considered it a breach of etiquette to set their host straight where her own life was concerned?

No sooner had she wondered this, however, than he

confused her further by reopening the topic he refused to let her discuss.

"Tell me something about Enrique Villasur, Tío."

Tío Luís's eyes darted to Aurelia, then returned to his plate. He settled back, cupping his coffee cup in both hands, bringing it to just beneath his nose as though to inhale the aroma. The better angle from which to study them, Aurelia decided.

"What can I tell you that you have not already learned? The young man is making an exemplary president for your father's mint."

"Papá certainly thinks so," Santos agreed. "But I was out of the country when he was hired. I am curious how it all came about."

"Out of the country, sí," their uncle observed. "Spending time in Texas with that cattle-raising outfit."

Aurelia picked at her fruit, listening and fuming. He might as well have said *wasting time*, for the message was clear from his enunciation. Could Santos not hear the man's pomposity?

"When I left for Texas," Santos continued, "it was you, Uncle, who would head up the mint."

"True. Your papá expected me to take charge of the venture." Setting his cup aside, Luís studiously tugged at first one pristine cuff, then the other, arranging them to an exact length below his black jacket.

"But I never intended to do so," he explained. "I have too many obligations of my own. And with the governorship opening . . ." He shrugged expansively. "However, since Domingo looked to me for help, I was obliged to find him a president for his mint."

"Enrique Villasur," Santos added.

Suddenly, Luís clapped his hands twice, summoning a

256

servant, who appeared with a walking cane, a pair of white gloves, and a top hat.

Aurelia watched her uncle outfit himself, donning first the gloves, smoothing them on while he supplied his niece and nephew with Enrique's qualifications in a tone that suggested the matter was closed.

"Domingo must surely have related the man's impeccable credentials: son of an influential family in the City of Mexico, educated at the University of Madrid, a brilliant financial mind."

Taking his cane and hat in gloved hands, Luís dismissed the servant with a flip of his chin, then clapped his polished boot heels together and nodded toward Aurelia.

"You see, my dear, there is no finer catch in all of Mexico."

It was on the tip of her tongue to tell him she wasn't interested in the finest catch in Mexico, but Santos's hand settled on her shoulder, stilling her angry retort.

They took a carriage to the corrals, since Tía Guadalupe had arisen in time to insist on it, saying she would hear of no such thing as Aurelia riding a horse through the streets of town.

"She probably stays in bed until he leaves the house every morning," Aurelia spat after she and Santos started on their way in one of the Reinaldo coaches.

Santos laughed. "Can't say as I blame her."

"Why wouldn't you let me tell him how I feel about Enrique?"

Santos studied her in a strange manner. When he answered, she knew he was evading the issue. "Let's not rock the boat just yet, Relie."

The streets were already crowded with people, and the carriage made its way slowly.

257

"Look at us. The first day of the feria," Aurelia sighed, "and how did we begin? By fussing about that damned Enrique."

Santos stared at her across the way. "Look at you," he countered. "Here, you have been clamoring to get to Guanajuato . . ." He paused, then restarted with, "After the shenanigans you pulled, it would be considered a bit more than clamoring—"

She grimaced, turning her face to the window.

"—and you aren't even enjoying yourself," he finished. "What's wrong, Relie? Isn't it what you expected? Can't see how it could be much more glamorous."

"Oh, it couldn't be," she responded. "Wasn't the opera house splendid?"

He nodded. "If you like that sort of thing."

"And Tía Guadalupe's house is grander than I imagined."

Again he agreed. "Then what's the matter?"

"I don't know."

She stared out the window, watching the people, studying the city she had dreamed of living in, of escaping to. Beyond the hustle and bustle the mountains rose, but not nearly so high as at Catorce. Here you didn't feel hemmed in by them. But for some reason, things were not at all like in her dreams.

"It can't be for lack of swains," Santos was saying. "Why, you were swamped last night, and think what a good time you can have today without Tío along to watch over Enrique's interests."

The carriage drew to a halt before the entrance to the corrals. "I will wait at the corner, señor," the driver informed Santos.

"No, thank you, we can find our way to the parade."

"The señora instructed me to drive you."

"No need," Santos replied. "I can escort my sister. She will be safe with me."

The driver perused the size of the man. "Very well, señor."

Santos nudged Aurelia. "Do you want to come with me to check on the bulls or go straight to the stables?"

"The stables. I want to be sure Jorge is taking care of the bay." She rested a restraining hand on Santos's sleeve. "He will arrive in time, won't he?"

Santos frowned, but at the same time his lips curled in what could only be called a conspiratorial grin. "You take care of his horse, Relie. I promise you Jarrett will be here in time for the *charriada* tomorrow."

The stables consisted of several long buildings built of brick. Inside, in addition to numerous stalls for the competitors' horses, were areas filled with tack, where the grooms not only kept their supplies but where they slept as well.

She went immediately to find Jorge, who led her to their horses, talking all the way.

Unlike herself, he was taken with life in Guanajuato.

"Have a good time," she encouraged, "but be sure these horses are exercised. Especially the bay."

Aurelia examined the horses one by one, all dozen of them, rubbing their muzzles, patting their necks, giving them each a thorough going-over with her eyes.

At the stall where the bay was stabled, she opened the gate and stepped inside, inspecting the animal not only with her eyes but by touch. She ran a hand over his withers, along his back, then stooped to examine each leg, feeling the knee joint. She lifted each hoof, checking not only the shoe but the pastern and fetlock.

"He is in fine shape, señorita," Jorge informed her.

"See that he stays that way," she told him. "Señor Jarrett will need all the help he can get. He has never entered a *charriada* before, and we certainly don't want to handicap him more than he already will be."

"*Sí, señorita.*"

"*Hola,* Relie! What are you doing on your hands and knees in the stall? Could it be you are planning to help Santos beat me at the *paso de la muerte* this year?"

The voice was hearty, jovial, and full of welcome.

Aurelia stood, slapped hay from her hands, then brushed her split riding skirt. "*Hola,* Rodrigo." After issuing last minute instructions to the groom, she slid out the gate and closed it behind her, facing the handsome Don Rodrigo Fraga with hands perched on her hips.

"Are you prepared to lose?" she asked gaily.

"Lose? To Santos? Never. Unless it would assure me a date with you."

"Then you may as well not enter," she told him. "Unless you are ready to lose al-Tareg. You did bring him, I hope?"

The young man laughed. "So it is my horses you are interested in? I should have known." Leading the way down the aisle as they talked, he stopped before the stall of a white Arabian stallion.

Aurelia stroked the horse's nose, looking him over. "Magnificent."

"You wouldn't care to repeat that about his master, would you?"

She eyed Don Rodrigo up and down, her eyes dancing. "Maybe."

"Maybe? This is the first year you haven't said no. I am making progress, no?"

260

"Perhaps. Then again, perhaps it is too late," she parried.

His face fell. "Is it true? You are to marry that city slicker who is running your father's mint?"

"Never," she replied. "Not in a million years."

"That isn't what we hear," chimed in Juan Martinez, another of Santos's charro friends. She had known these charros since childhood, had ridden horses with them, and lately had evaded them as swains. How many times had Pia questioned her on that?

"Why not give Rodrigo a chance, Relie? Or Juan? Or Salvador?"

Why not? she had wondered. What was wrong with her that she couldn't see beyond friendship with these handsome charros?

Now she knew the answer to that question. She had been waiting for someone special. For Carson Jarrett.

By the time Santos found her, Aurelia was surrounded by a half-dozen charros, laughing gaily, teasing them about the *charriada,* assuring them they had no chance to win this year, that the Mazóns were bringing a surprise contestant.

Santos led her away with a chuckle. "Here I've been giving Jarrett hell, and I find you flirting with every eligible male in Guanajuato. Guess you couldn't be too sweet on him, else you wouldn't be able to see these other swains."

"Or," she suggested, "I may be so secure in my relationship with Carson that I feel safe flirting with all these inconsequential males."

Santos had been pulling her at a rapid pace toward the plaza where the parade was to begin. At her statement, he stopped to stare hopelessly into her enraptured face.

261

"Great God, Relie, you are going to be the death of me yet."

"Stop mothering me, Santos. Carson and I are well beyond the point of you being able to change things between us."

Aurelia saw his jaws tighten. She knew immediately what he was thinking. "I love him, Santos."

He stared hard into her eyes. "Be sure, Relie."

Her breath came short just thinking about Carson. "I am sure." She clamped a closed fist over her heart. "I miss him so much it hurts — right here."

He inhaled deep drafts of air, then pulled her along, more slowly this time. "I feel guilty, you know. If I hadn't invited him to come down — "

"You had no control over what happened," she insisted. "I'm responsible for everything. If I hadn't robbed that train, he wouldn't have gotten arrested, and I wouldn't have had to help him escape, and we wouldn't have spent those days alone in the wilderness getting to know each other, and — "

"Stop!"

They halted in the middle of the crowded street while Santos began to laugh. He laughed so hard, tears formed in his eyes. Aurelia laughed, too, with people jostling them on both sides.

Finally, he pulled her to his side. Sheltering her in the crook of his immense arm, he led her toward the cathedral where the parade was to begin.

"If it wasn't so personal," he said, still laughing in spurts, "it would be funny. *How did your sister meet her beau? Oh, she robbed a train and he got arrested for it and she had to rescue him and . . .*" His words were lost in new gales of laughter.

"It is funny, even now. Isn't it?"

"*Sí.*" Stopping on a corner, he gazed deeply into her eyes, serious again. "But it isn't going to be funny long. Not when you try to keep him here in Guanajuato. He wouldn't make it here, Relie. He isn't cut out for this kind of life. It would break his spirit. Like we break riding stock. And it's his spirit you love. I know, because that's what I love about Jarrett, too. He's wild and free, and if you love him, you will leave him that way."

They stood on the street corner, arm in arm, oblivious to the crowd, the parade forgotten.

"I will never hurt him, Santos. I promise you that." Standing on tiptoe, she kissed his cheek. Then she grinned. "I'm the one who saved his life, remember? I'm his guardian angel."

Carson figured he should have known he couldn't get out of Catorce without fighting Nuncio Quiroz. If he had thought long and hard about it, he would have known better than to go by the mine that morning.

The signs had all been there. Yet, a page in one of the ledgers had needled him during the night — in and among his dreams of Aurelia — and he didn't want to leave town without checking out the figures.

Since it was Sunday, he took along his key, figuring he would have to let himself into the office. That was the first clue. Or it should have been.

The office door was open. Not only unlocked, but ajar, as if someone had stepped out for a minute.

No one would go off and leave the mine office unlocked all day on Sunday. Inside, he tossed his Stetson to the peg and began rifling through the ledger, looking for the entry that had aroused his suspicion.

Thoroughly engrossed in his search, Jarrett wasn't aware of Quiroz's presence until the big man loomed over him. "Thought you were heading out of town."

Every muscle in Carson's body tensed. It wasn't that he was afraid of the man, not exactly, he assured himself. But he didn't want anything to interfere with his trip to Guanajuato. He had promised Aurelia . . .

"Going to meet your sugar?"

Carson's mind switched instantly from meeting Aurelia to whipping this sonofabitch. With the ease of a cat about to spring, he straightened his back. "My plans are just that, mine."

"Involve that feisty little daughter of Mazón's though, don't they, your plans?"

Carson eyed his adversary, searching for a weak spot, all the while cautioning himself to stay cool, not to think about Aurelia, not to think about what the man was saying, not to remember all that Aurelia had told him.

All she had cried over.

All she had lost to this bastard.

"What's your connection to her, anyhow?" Quiroz questioned.

Carson studied the man. His jaws were solid, like steel traps. His arms were barrels filled with muscles, honed to the strength of cables by his long years handling a double-jack. His swing would be nearly as wide, his reach almost as far as Santos's. Carson strove to recall every detail of the one time he had tangled with his friend.

The one fight in his entire life he had lost.

And they had been friends.

"Bet you can't wait to get hold of them tit—"

"You asked my connection, Quiroz. I'll tell you. She's a lady whose honor I am prepared to defend with my life."

On the last word he struck, hard and low, aiming for the gut.

Quiroz emitted a huff, merely a gust of air. "Fool" was all he said before he returned the slug.

Carson sidestepped that one and found himself on the other side of the office chair, which he slung into the path of the oncoming madman.

It caused him to stumble, but contrary to Carson's hopes, Quiroz was quick on his feet, light for a man his size. And his reach was as long as Carson had feared. His first blow struck Carson just below the chin.

Only the fact that Carson saw it coming saved a broken jaw, for he averted his head, deflecting the blow, causing it to plow into the side of his neck before the force of it carried him backwards into a table stacked with ledgers.

Quickly, he sidestepped, regained his position, and struck again, hammering now at the big man's body, knowing he would cause no harm, figuring only to slow him down, to use up time.

Time surely would be on his side. Surely he had more wind than this big bag of lard.

Quiroz landed a devastating blow to Carson's left temple, toppling him. He scrambled to find his footing, rethought his last statement. A big bag of muscle, he corrected. Definitely muscle, not lard.

He had trained his mind long ago, and now it came in handy. If he thought about the fight, he would be lost before he began. No man in his right mind could keep his composure fighting an opponent so overmatched.

So he wouldn't think about it. He would hit and hit and hit.

And hit. Jarrett pummeled his opponent, and Quiroz battered him back. That was the hell of it. If he was doing any damage, he couldn't tell by the way the man kept coming on.

Then he landed a powerful punch to Quiroz's right eye, staggering him backward. The man fell across the table, losing his footing.

Carson closed in, steering clear of the man's flailing legs—they were as big as mesquite trunks, he thought. Grappling with the downed man, he bashed him in the head, in the chest, aiming for his heart, hoping to keep him down.

But the man was as agile as he was powerful. After absorbing no more than a handful of punches, he tore loose from Carson's hold and slung him against the far desk, then bounded after him.

Gaining his footing once more, Carson feinted right, veered left, and Quiroz's punch landed with a thud on the oak desktop, smashing it to splinters.

That was the last blow the man missed. After that, Carson decided he had best hope for a pleasant funeral. That was about all he could see in the cards.

Then without warning, Quiroz turned him loose, dropping him to the floor, and stepped back.

Through a haze of sweat and blood, Carson could tell someone else had entered the room.

"Have you lost your mind?"

"He had it coming."

"Get out. Cool off. I don't want to see you around here until Monday morning. Do you understand?"

Seconds passed in silence. At length he heard a grunt, followed by heavy footsteps stomping out the door.

Carson shook off the hand that grabbed his shirt. He swiped at his eyes with the back of his other arm, then peered into the face of Enrique Villasur.

266

Enrique offered his hand. Carson considered it, refused it, and stumbled to his feet under his own steam.

"Lucky I happened by."

"Happened by?" Carson growled. His sarcasm was not lost on Enrique, he could tell at once.

"What's that supposed to mean?"

"It's Sunday morning. Mass. Or do you only attend when Aurelia is around so you can impress her?"

Enrique wanted to hit him. Carson watched the man consider it. Likely he looked an easy target at the moment. He started to suggest to Enrique that if he was ever going to hit him, this was his chance.

He held his tongue.

"I could ask you the same thing," Enrique replied.

"I never pretended to attend Mass."

"Not that. What are you doing in the mine on Sunday morning? How did you get in?"

"The door was unlocked," he said. "Like I was expected." Once the statement left his mouth, Carson became convinced of its validity. "I was expected. And what's more, Quiroz knows about Aurelia. He knows she was in town. He knows that . . ." Pausing, he reconsidered telling Enrique any more than he needed to know. "He knows I am on my way to Guanajuato and that she is there."

Enrique frowned, obviously studying the situation. "Someone let it slip."

Carson glowered through the bloody sweat that blurred his vision. "Who, damnit?"

Enrique paused but a moment before he replied, "The servants. I warned Don Domingo he could not trust them."

"There isn't a servant in that house stupid enough to

267

gossip about Aurelia, especially not since Don Domingo threatened to fire anyone who spoke of her return, and Santos promised to throw them out of town."

Enrique shrugged. "That seamstress."

Carson considered the dressmaker. It would be easy enough to check out.

"Pia or Zita?" Enrique suggested.

"Not on your life."

"Looks like it was your life, Jarrett."

"Not quite."

Enrique perused him.

"Don't go getting your hopes up; he won't get me next time, either."

Enrique smiled. "Perhaps I will happen by again, señor, should you find yourself in another such difficulty."

"If I find myself in another such difficulty, Villasur, I'll come looking for you."

"Me?"

"You. It couldn't have been you who let the cat out of the bag?"

"The what?"

"You know damned well what I mean."

Enrique clenched his fists. Carson wanted to taunt him into striking him, but he didn't have the strength. Possibly he wouldn't have the strength to fight the citified dandy, either, he mused.

"May I suggest that it was yourself who let the word out?" Enrique said. "Her name may have slipped unaware from your lips."

Carson stared at him, disbelieving the man's stupidity. His anger rose, nonetheless. "Listen close and get this straight: Aurelia's name has never slipped *unaware* from my lips, and it never will."

"I thought . . ."

"Take my advice, Villasur: Start thinking. Where Aurelia is concerned, you had best think long and hard before you let anything slip from your lips, whether carelessly or with purpose. Now, get out of here, before I catch my breath and give you the whipping I should have given Quiroz."

Chapter Fourteen

"Let's skip the parade," Aurelia suggested when Santos drew her to a halt at a corner where the Cathedral of San Diego met the Teatro Juárez. The streets and even the Jardín de la Unión were so crowded she wondered how anyone would be able to see the parade.

"What's the matter, Relie? You getting uptown like Tía? Can't associate with the peóns?"

"You know better than that. And Tía isn't uptown, either. Tío Luís is the snob in the family."

Santos laughed. "Tío is definitely a snob. But the parade will be fun."

"If we are able to see it for all these people," she countered. "Besides, Carson may have arrived."

Santos relented. "I don't like crowds myself," he admitted, after he found a livery and hired a hack to take them to the Reinaldo residence.

Tía Guadalupe met them in the foyer. Her voice betrayed her agitation. "You have a guest, Santos. Some Norteamericano. Disreputable sort of hombre; looks like he belongs in the stables."

Santos frowned at his aunt's remarks. "Jarrett?"

270

"That sounds like the name. I had Lupe show him to the side patio." She glanced around the opulent foyer, a look of concern creasing her usually placid forehead. "You don't think he would steal—"

"Tía! Carson Jarrett is—"

Santos interrupted Aurelia with a hand to her shoulder. "Jarrett is my compadre, Tía. He came to Mexico for my wedding."

Aurelia would not be stilled. "Mamá welcomed him to our home. He has been our guest for several weeks." Tearing away from Santos's hold, she rushed toward the side patio. Behind her she heard Tía call, "Stop, Relie. That man isn't the sort you should—"

"Tía," Santos interrupted, "Carson Jarrett is my best friend. If he is not welcome here and at every event we are to attend with you, then we will all leave."

"Bella!" Tía Guadalupe hissed behind Aurelia. "What has gotten into my sister, raising her children in such a manner?"

All thoughts of Tía Guadalupe fled when Aurelia reached the patio. She stopped short at the sight of him—at the beloved sight of him.

"You came." Tears formed in her eyes. Tears of happiness. In his eyes she saw the reflection of her own desperate longing. She started across the patio.

A bell sounded in the distance, followed by Tía Guadalupe's voice. "Dinnertime, children. I will set another place."

Santos came up behind her. "Jarrett! You old leather pounder! You made it!" He shook hands with Carson, while his eyes teased Aurelia. "Didn't I tell you he would come?"

271

How she reached him, she wasn't sure, her legs trembled so badly. Suddenly, however, her hands touched his, gripped his, and she wished they were far away from brothers and uptown aunts.

Carson lifted her fingers to his lips while his eyes studied her unabashedly.

"She's got you staked out for the *charriada,* compadre."

Aurelia heard the welcome in her brother's voice, noticed the smile on Santos's face. Resigned, yet genuine.

"How's that?" Carson still stared at Aurelia, taking in her black riding skirt and cropped jacket, her crisp white shirt, adorned with a silver and onyx brooch at the properly high collar.

Her hair was swept into a coil at her nape, and on her head a flat-brimmed black hat tipped at ever-so-slight an angle. Proper, elegant.

He felt her pulse beat against his hand, faster with his prolonged perusal. Lordy, how he had missed her. His eyes fastened on her belly—taut, flat. For how long?

She blushed at his scrutiny. "Where did you get those clothes?" She scanned his denim trousers and leather vest, the bandanna around his neck. "All you need is a star for everyone to recognize you as a Texas Ranger."

Carson's eyes strayed to Santos, then returned to her. "He didn't tell you?"

"Tell me what?"

"Our birddog here managed to get hold of the train robber's belongings before you left Catorce."

Aurelia beamed at Santos, suddenly loving him more than ever. "He isn't half bad . . . sometimes."

When Carson winked at her, his swollen eye twitched. Suddenly, she noticed the bruises on his jaw, the gash above his right eye. "What happened?" She tried to lift her hands to stroke his face, but he held them tightly in his.

He shrugged in answer, grinning that wry grin she had missed so dreadfully.

Santos frowned. "Quiroz?"

Carson nodded.

"Did you find answers?"

"Only more questions."

Then it was over. A second dinner bell sounded and Tía Guadalupe called them to the table, admonishing them to take their places. Santos introduced his guest to their hosts.

They dined in the elegance of the Reinaldo comedor, on roast quail and fresh fruit prepared by Tía Guadalupe's Madrid-trained chef.

"Wonder if he attended the same school as Enrique?" Santos mused over dessert.

Aurelia was delighted, but Tío Luís clearly did not appreciate Santos's flippancy regarding his protégé. "Enrique is possessed of a magnificent financial mind."

In the silence that ensued, Tía Guadalupe excused the table. "We ladies need time to change for the corrida. We are to sit in the governor's box again," she explained to Carson as they rose from the table. "Aurelia will be honored by the torero."

When Santos scraped back his chair, Carson glanced across at Aurelia, an amused expression on his face. The seating arrangement had put them on the same side of the table yet separated by Santos, so until now

273

they could not even look at each other without being obvious about it.

"It's nothing," she told him. Her eyes savored his nearness. She pressed her lips together to keep them from trembling at his hungry perusal.

Santos suddenly threw a brotherly arm about her shoulder, drawing her around to stand between himself and Carson. Her body—her clothing leastways—touched Carson's.

Although propriety demanded he step away from such contact, he did not. He didn't reach for her hand, either, but she saw him grip his fingers into fists.

"Nothing to it," Tío Luís echoed Aurelia's assessment of the honor the torero intended to bestow on her at the corrida. "A token extended to a guest of the governor, nothing more. Enrique will be honored, though."

Carson's eyebrows lifted a notch and a frown flitted across his brow. Under his breath, he spoke to Santos. "Is there someplace we can talk in private?"

"Sí."

Although Aurelia intended to remain below while her aunt changed clothes, she found herself being hustled to her room, where she remained only long enough to re-pin loose strands of hair, dab her shiny nose with cornstarch, and spray a spritz of rosewater over herself. Carrying her hat in her hand, she hurried back downstairs, telling herself that even if Carson hadn't arrived she would not have changed costumes. Nothing could be more appropriate for a corrida than what she had on, no matter whose box they were seated in.

If she had entertained doubts about her attire, they

274

would have fled the moment she stepped inside the shadowy drawing room and watched Carson's eyes roam her body. His eyes caressed her face, then dropped to her waist, lingering over her stomach, reminding her of the way he had stared at her earlier.

Her cheeks flushed, and although she intended to cross the room sedately, chin held high, showing him what a mature, sophisticated lady she could be, her feet simply would not comply.

She practically flew to him, her boots stumbling across the Persian carpet. In spite of Santos, who stood with his elbow propped carelessly on the mantel, his eyes taking in her every movement, she threw her arms around Carson and felt his come around her. She buried her face in his chest, holding on for dear life, as though to prevent his leaving her ever again.

She didn't say a word. She at least had control over her mouth. And she knew she couldn't kiss him. So she kept her face pinned to his chest, inhaling his wonderfully familiar scent, feeling his heart throb against her.

His arm rose to her shoulder and he gently drew her back, staring into her upturned face, devouring her with his eyes. Searching for something, questioning.

"Hey, don't mind me," Santos said at last. "I'm only her brother."

Carson's eyes crinkled when he smiled. He turned Aurelia against his side, his arm draped across her shoulders. She reached to hold his hand, rubbing the calluses on his palm with her thumb.

"How did you bring him around?" he asked her.

"She didn't bring me around," Santos responded. "I'm still not convinced this thing is good for either one of you, but she persuaded me to mind my own business—for the time being."

Carson laughed. "Fair enough."

His voice was husky and she snuggled to his side, too content with his presence to need conversation, too aroused by the want of him to trust her voice.

Finally, Santos bounced to attention, clapped his hands together, rubbing them a bit self-consciously, then cleared his throat. "Guess I'll run along. Need to . . . ah . . . freshen up, as the ladies say, before the corrida."

"By the way," Carson's voice stopped him at the door. "Pia sends her love."

Santos turned in the doorway, grinning at them. "Seeing you two together makes me miss her all the more." He left then, drawing the elaborately carved doors closed behind him.

Aurelia's heart beat faster at the prospect of being alone with Carson at last. She felt his hand slip to her back, splay against her jacket.

But his eyes held questions.

"Are you all right?" he managed.

"Now that you have come, I am. I missed you so."

"Me, too," he murmured. But instead of kissing her as she expected, he questioned again, "You are sure you . . . ah? . . ."

"Carson, you are one to ask. Of course, I'm all right." Her fingers trembled against the bruises on his face. "You are the one who had a fight. Was it bad? Did he—?"

276

"Come back to the drawing room, Santos," Tío Luís's voice boomed outside the door.

Startled, Aurelia froze in place, but Carson reacted. Pushing her to the settee, he stepped backwards, propping an elbow in the same spot where Santos had previously leaned. He stared intently at the gold-leaf carvings on the mantel.

"What are you two doing in here without the lamps lit?" Tío Luís strode across the enormous room, looking left, then right. "Where is that maid of yours, Relie?"

Instead of answering, Aurelia straightened the ties on her hat, then crossed to the mirror that hung above the mantel. Standing as close to Carson as she dared, she adjusted her hat on her head, concentrating on the exact angle, on the tautness of the tie beneath her chin.

Satisfied, she swiveled to face her uncle, smiling with the greatest of difficulty. "How is this, Tío? Do you think your dear Enrique would approve?"

My dear? . . ." Luís huffed a moment. "I am certain he would not approve of you spending time in a dark room with this . . . with another man. Such behavior is grounds for—"

"Come now, time to be going." Tía Guadalupe burst into the room, scattering the scent of gardenias in her wake, her fashionable gown sweeping the floor. "We mustn't be late. The governor's honor, you remember." She halted abruptly in front of Aurelia, perusing her attire.

"You didn't change." Her tone expressed such a depth of disbelief that Aurelia stopped just short of consoling her.

277

By the time they arrived at the Plaza de Toros, Aurelia had been properly chastised, which left her feeling no guilt whatsoever. Her happiness could not be diminished.

Enhanced, given the chance to be alone with Carson, but definitely not diminished since he had arrived. Santos, however, was outraged by their aunt's harangue.

That fact became apparent as soon as Tía Guadalupe issued their seat assignments in the governor's box. While the Reinaldos settled themselves, Santos took charge, maneuvering himself into the chair their aunt had indicated for Aurelia, leaving his sister to sit between himself and Carson.

"Tía will make us move," Aurelia worried.

"She won't make a scene with the governor present," Santos whispered.

Aurelia could have hugged him. She could have hugged both of these beloved men. How she longed to hug one of them.

"Looks like we're making headway," Carson whispered.

"I'm sorry about . . ." Before she could finish, the paseo began.

"Have you ever seen a corrida?" she asked him when the procession of brilliantly attired men entered the arena.

"Never from the shady side," he answered, his voice teasing, tantalizing. "Nor seated beside the guest of honor. Tell me, which one of those handsome men is your hero?"

She turned gleeful eyes on him. "The most handsome one of all, of course. The one sitting beside me."

His eyes held hers, then curiously darted to her stomach. What was his fascination? . . . She felt a flush rise up her neck. It wasn't her stomach. How foolish. She squirmed, trying to still her jangled nerves.

Santos leaned forward and a discussion ensued between the two friends about the Mazón bulls.

She listened more to the sound of Carson's voice than to his words. The words she wanted to hear would come later, much later. When or where she had not determined . . . yet.

Santos sat back in his chair when the procession stopped before their box. The toreros, three of them, removed their small caplike *montillas* from their heads and lifted them toward the governor in salute. Behind the men their cuadrillas stretched to the center of the arena — three banderilleros and two picadors each. The entire assemblage glittered beneath the afternoon sun. Each man's satin *traje de luces* was fashioned from a different color and decorated, both jacket and trousers, with an array of brilliantly colored sequins.

"I recognize him," Carson mumbled.

"How?" she questioned quietly, watching the majestic procedure.

"The one in the middle."

"Antonio Suarez, the junior torero," she acknowledged. "How did you know?"

"By the way he's looking at you."

She laughed, a soft challenge. "How's that?"

"The same way I do."

Her eyes flew to his. "He is not."

279

He nodded, grinning that wry grin of his, his attention riveted on Antonio Suarez, resplendent in his blue and gold suit of lights. "That's a look you only recognize when you feel it, too."

"Then it's the way I look at you," she whispered.

The paseo ended, the bugles blared another flourish, and as soon as the arena cleared, the toril gates opened and an enormous black bull charged into the ring. For the next couple of hours, Carson watched the unfolding drama of the bullfight with renewed interest.

The action rose steadily from the first simple passes to the intricate capework, during which the torero tested the bull, learning his disposition, his weaknesses, his strengths.

It reminded Carson of the way his relationship with Aurelia had begun—their meeting in the jailhouse, the way she had charged into his life, taking control, leaving him amused, confused, then totally mystified.

He identified with the heaving bull when with a flick of his wrist, the torero left him standing stupefied in the center of the arena, turning his back on the once-raging animal and walking out of the arena as if taking an afternoon stroll.

Music played, the crowd went wild, and the picadors entered the ring on fine horses, carrying long-handled lances. Carson gathered his wits.

"Do you provide the horses?" he asked Santos, leaning across Aurelia, brushing her breast with his shoulder.

"No, I don't risk my horses in this manner," Santos replied frankly. "We supply horses only for the *charriadas*."

"We brought the bay for you to ride in the *charriada* tomorrow," Aurelia added.

He exchanged a knowing smile with Santos, then sat back. "Thanks."

"How do you like the corrida so far?" she whispered.

He grinned. "I suppose I should be grateful you didn't shame me into performing here instead of at the *charriada*."

She laughed, gaily, happily. "I would never do such a thing. You mean too much to me."

"We'll see how much I mean to you tomorrow," he teased, "when I don't perform up to your expectations."

The banderilleros came next, one at a time, slim and graceful, possessing great control and much courage. When the bull lunged, the banderillero leaned far over the deadly horns to expertly place two barbs, which were decorated with multicolored paper ribbons.

The banderilleros, too, reminded him of Aurelia, of her grace and beauty. Her love of life had worked magic on him, old leather pounder that he had always been.

"What do you think of the Mazón bulls?" Santos asked.

He leaned across Aurelia again, showering her breast with tender yearnings once more. "Your bulls are very brave."

Santos watched the ring intently. "They have brave mothers."

She felt Carson tense against her.

"How's that?" he questioned.

"It is well known that a bull's courage comes from his mother," Santos explained, his attention riveted on the

281

bull's every move. "We use only the bravest Mazón cows for breeding."

Carson turned stricken eyes to Aurelia. She saw his questions, his seriousness.

"What?" She laughed, uneasy for some reason under his strange scrutiny.

Silently, he gazed into her eyes, questioning like before, then turned back to the arena.

When time came for the *brandis,* Antonio approached the governor's box. He held forth his *montilla,* toasting Aurelia by calling her name.

"La señorita Aurelia Mazón."

The governor nodded approval. Antonio stepped three paces sideways, as gracefully as he had danced around the bull, she thought, and bowed deeply in salute. Before he performed the customary toss of the hat, however, he held forth his glistening sword, and she caught her breath.

She had completely forgotten his intention to seek a favor. She should have carried a scarf. Striving to disguise her unforgivable lapse, she glanced to Carson for help.

His raised eyebrows said it all. He had no idea what she wanted. She spied his neckerchief. That would do.

It must do. Reaching quickly, she untied the knot, while he sat as though mesmerized. Removing it from around his neck, she leaned forward and tied the Texas bandanna to the hilt of the torero's sword.

"Buenas suerte," she whispered, blowing Antonio a good-luck kiss from the palm of her hand.

His startled expression melted into a broad smile. He bowed again, then turned his back and tossed his *montilla* over his head, straight into her waiting hands. The band played and the crowd roared its approval.

Carson eyed the fancy black hat that lay clutched in Aurelia's hands. "Some exchange," he whispered. "What the hell am I supposed to do with that?"

"He warned me last night he would ask for a favor, but I forgot."

"A favor? Last night?"

She laughed. "Something to tie on his sword for good luck."

His eyebrows remained raised, questioning.

"If I thought it would make you jealous," she teased, "I would lie. But the truth is, I was sitting in the governor's box at the opera with Tío Luís expounding Enrique's virtues in one ear and Santos breathing down my neck on the other side."

Carson laughed at that and they turned their attention to the arena, where Antonio had begun a breathtaking series of seven right-hand passes that, before he finished, had them all on their feet, holding their collective breath in one instant, shouting *"¡Olé!"* in the next.

"Seven *derechazos*," Santos shouted. "Seven! What a fight! What a bull!"

"What a torero," Carson added. But as he watched the finale, seeing Antonio standing poised and courageous in front of the raging bull, inciting him for one last charge with the brilliant maneuvering of his red *muleta*, held low now, directing the bull's head downward in order that the sword might find the exact spot for an instant kill, he saw only himself and Aurelia.

Aurelia, carrying his child. Aurelia, who had teased

and flirted and led him on. Aurelia, who had excited his passions and taught him to love. Now in the moment of truth, their roles were reversed, and he was the one who had thrust the perfectly honed sword into her life. He was the one responsible, in the final analysis.

Drained by the drama they had witnessed, by the courage and honor played out before them, the Reinaldo party filed from the Plaza de Toros in silence. Carson's fingers tipped Aurelia's waist, bringing a measure of life back to his energy-sapped body.

Tía Guadalupe declined to visit the Patio de Caballos, where they would return Antonio's *montilla*. When Tío Luís declared that he, too, would forgo congratulating the young torero in order to accompany his wife home, Aurelia exhaled a sigh of relief.

Her aunt, however, did not leave without a stern aside to Santos to watch Relie around that Norteamericano.

"You must return in time to dress for the ball," she added to Aurelia.

"This social life would soon take its toll on an old cowpuncher like myself," Carson commented when the Reinaldos were out of sight.

Santos studied his sister. "That's what I told Relie."

Ushered into the dressing room by Antonio's aide, the three of them entered reverently, subdued in the presence of a man who had faced death with such grace and courage only moments before.

Aurelia introduced Carson, and Antonio thanked him for the use of his bandanna, saying how it must have been lucky for him. When he extended it to him, Carson refused.

"I would be honored for you to keep it. Your performance is one I will long remember."

"*Gracias.*" Antonio glanced from Carson to Aurelia with a gleam in his eyes. "And the woman by your side, my friend, you will long remember her as well?"

"I guarantee it."

"So be it, then. But I will request a dance or two tonight at the *baile.*"

"At the lady's pleasure," Carson agreed with a pleasant smile.

Back at the house, Aurelia further annoyed Tía Guadalupe by refusing to eat a bite, by rushing through her bath, and by returning downstairs ready to leave for the ball without María to attend her as dueña.

María had been sent on a hasty mission, although Aurelia dared not reveal as much to her aunt. After helping Aurelia comb her hair into a nest of small curls on top of her head, she had sent the girl off with a shopping list.

"Señorita," María had wailed, "your aunt will not like this. Neither will your uncle. We are not in Catorce, where you can run about at will."

"Never mind, María," Aurelia had chided. "There is no other way. Be careful that no one becomes suspicious."

"What if the shops are closed?"

"Then borrow the clothing from one of the household maids, but don't tell them who it is for. Do you understand?"

"*Sí, señorita, pero —*"

"Wait until everyone leaves for the ball, then slip into

285

Señor Jarrett's room and leave the package on his bed. Do not let anyone see you. Do you understand?"

"Sí, pero —"

"But nothing!" Aurelia returned. "Just do as I say." She caught up her red taffeta cape and swished from the room, arriving at the top of the staircase only to catch her breath at the sight below.

Carson and Santos stood in the foyer — waiting for her, she knew — attired for the ball. The beloved figure who turned to watch her descend the steps took her by such surprise that she grasped the banister to keep from tripping.

"Where did you find those clothes?" She gaped at Carson's black evening costume. Much like the suit Santos wore, it was cut to the customary Spanish tailoring — snug trousers, cropped jacket, string tie. He looked as if he had been born to the highest strata of society.

He grinned self-consciously. "Your mother advised me what to bring."

"You look wonderful."

His perusal of her attire sent fiery tingles running down Aurelia's spine. He scanned her slowly, from the curls atop her head, across her tawny shoulders and the mounds of bosom rising above the deep décolletage of her dress — cut in the fashion of the gold gown she had worn to the opera, off-the-shoulder with a fitted bodice — to the full skirt that belled gracefully from her nipped waist, all in the deepest blood-red.

Carson offered his hand. "My common vocabulary can't come close to describing you tonight, angel."

She placed trembling fingers inside his hand, feeling

his warmth radiate up her arm. "I'm yours, that's all that needs to be said."

But when she stepped into the foyer, Tía Guadalupe emerged with a lot more to say.

First she questioned where Aurelia's jewels were. Receiving a negative answer, she sent a maid to fetch some of her own.

Then she asked if María was ready.

"María isn't coming," Aurelia answered.

"She must."

"She can't. She is . . . ah . . . indisposed."

Tía Guadalupe stewed, her fashionable green gown swaying to the rhythm of her discontent. "Unthinkable, unthinkable. Bella always was too provincial for her own good. I should have taken you long ago, while there was still time."

Carson had stepped aside when the lady approached, but at her belligerence he moved toward Aurelia. Santos cleared his throat.

The maid rushed back into the room, handing their aunt a brocaded jewel case into which Guadalupe dipped manicured fingers.

"Here we go." She approached Aurelia with a string of rubies in hand.

"They're enormous," Aurelia murmured. The rubies clanged against her collarbone when her aunt tried to fasten them around her neck.

Aurelia's eyes went to Carson's. Her hands flew to the necklace. "No, Tía, I couldn't."

"They are a perfect match for that gown, Relie."

"Thank you, but no." Aurelia tugged on the necklace, pulling the ends loose from her aunt. "I prefer

287

not to wear them. Thank you."

"This isn't some country dance, dear. It is a *baile de etiqueta*. You cannot attend a dress ball without jewels."

Aurelia almost laughed at her aunt's tone. She could just as well have been telling Aurelia she couldn't attend the ball without bloomers. Without warning, the morning she'd sneaked into Carson's room wearing neither bloomers nor any other kind of underclothing popped into her mind.

She blushed.

Carson grinned. He couldn't have guessed her thoughts, she knew that, but his presence gave her courage. "Thank you, Tía." She returned the handful of rubies to her aunt. "I don't like things . . . of this nature . . . around my neck."

Guadalupe shook her perfectly coiffed head. When Tío Luís joined them, advising that they must hurry to be ahead of the governor, Guadalupe was still in a stew about the jewels.

"Whoever heard of a girl not wanting to wear jewels? It is Bella's fault. I should have taken you over your father's objections. I could have made something of you."

Inside the carriage Aurelia burst into laughter, and after a stunned moment, Santos and Carson joined her.

They were obliged to take two carriages, since Guadalupe would not hear of arriving with crushed gowns. A fact that made instantly clear their aunt's concern over Aurelia's missing dueña.

"I assure you, Tía," Santos had said, "I have provided Aurelia with that service since she grew to wom-

288

anhood and needed such protection. Most gentlemen find me a formidable dueño."

Aurelia was still laughing when the carriage pulled away. "She could have made something of me." She wiped tears from her eyes.

"I didn't find that amusing," Carson observed.

"Neither did I," Santos said. "Not only was she maligning you, but Mamá as well."

Aurelia strove to bring her laughter under control. "Wouldn't you love to see her face if she ever discovered what I have made of myself?" She squeezed Carson's hand. "Can't you see both of them if they knew I was a robber of trains?"

The ball went well from Carson's point of view, considering how he had dreaded the ordeal. Not that he minded dancing. At least he would be able to hold Aurelia in his arms, something he had anticipated all day. But he had never been comfortable in situations where everything from a man's looks, to his attire, to his manners, was constantly under scrutiny.

Besides the fact that the one problem foremost in his mind remained unresolved. He hadn't found a moment to talk privately with Aurelia, and he knew that until he did, he would not relax anywhere.

She was the loveliest woman at the ball, but that didn't surprise him. Nor did it surprise him to have every single man in the room vie for her favor.

It did surprise him a little, though, that he wasn't jealous. Not even when he lounged against one of the three dozen ornate pillars that held up the ceiling of the giant ballroom and watched her flirt and dance.

"She's the best dancer of the lot," Santos mused from his side.

"Hmm," Carson agreed. "Seems we find ourselves in the same boat tonight, partner."

"*Sí,*" Santos answered. "Fish out of water, both of us."

"Unlike that feller she's dancing with at the moment. Don . . . who did she say?"

"Don Rodrigo Fraga," Santos supplied. "He will be your major competition tomorrow."

"The feller with the Arabians?"

"How did you know that?"

Carson sipped the champagne punch, wishing it was redeye and that he was in a bar back in Texas . . .

No, he wished it was Aurelia's lips and he was somewhere wrapped in her arms and nothing else.

"She told me about him before we left Catorce."

"Didn't know she was interested in Rodrigo. True, he has been after her the last couple of years. But she's never shown much interest."

"It's his horses she's interested in, Santos. She said when I beat him tomorrow, I am to choose some stallion named al-Tareg and a couple or three mares as my prize. She figures I can start a herd that way."

Santos watched his sister a moment longer. She let Rodrigo twirl her about the floor, her blood-red skirt swaying gracefully with each step, revealing a glimpse of red slipper, a glimpse of trim ankle.

"You were right about her," he told Carson. "She's all woman, sensual and passionate. The only thing hidden from view tonight is that brain inside her pretty head. But from what you just said, I can tell it has been working overtime."

290

Carson laughed. "Is that unusual?"

"Afraid not, compadre. You had best get on out there and grab hold of her. She's about to take you for the ride of your life."

Carson was still grinning when he cut in on Don Rodrigo, a gallant, much-too-handsome fellow, who relinquished his partner with a bow. "Until we meet in the arena tomorrow, Señor Jarrett."

They finished the dance without either of them uttering a single word. She savored his hand on her back, his grip on her hand. His strange questioning gaze pierced directly through her eyes to her erratically beating heart.

"What are you thinking?" she asked when they began the next dance, a waltz.

He twirled her expertly about the floor. Expertly, but silently.

"You dance with much elegance, señor," she affected.

"Thank you, ma'am. The credit's due my partner."

She laughed, then caught her breath suddenly, following his gaze downward. Between them. "Tell me what you are thinking."

He glanced up, self-conscious that his mind had wandered to that same old thing. This was a ball. A party. And he held the prettiest girl in the room in his arms. *Perk up, Jarrett,* he chided.

"Tell me what's worrying you," she insisted.

He shrugged, twirling her again. "Later. In private."

"No," she answered. "When we get time to ourselves, I don't want it spoiled by serious things. Whatever is on your mind is serious, isn't it?"

He nodded.

"Then get it over with."

He grinned, but the mirth did not reach his eyes. Worry knit itself into a tight ball in the pit of her stomach.

He danced her away from the crowd, toward a corner of the floor that, although not deserted, lent a measure of privacy. He didn't want the crowd to see her expression when he asked her the question that had troubled him since he first thought of it back in Catorce.

"What?" she prompted.

Carson cleared his throat. His mouth felt as if it were full of tumbleweeds, but he managed to talk around them, blurting out his question in one gasp. "Are you carrying my child?"

"What?"

"Are you with child?" He whispered it this time, bringing his lips as close to her ear as he dared here in the brightly lit ballroom.

Her feet stumbled; she stepped on his boot.

"No," she managed.

His fingers gripped her hand. "I don't believe you."

She stared at him, dumbfounded. "I never even considered such a thing."

"Neither did I until after you left Catorce. I've worried about it ever since."

Tears rushed to her eyes. She wanted to hug him, to hold him near. "Well, you can stop worrying."

"You aren't?"

She shook her head.

"Are you sure?"

She nodded.

"Absolutely sure?"

The way he emphasized the words, Aurelia knew exactly what he meant. She pursed her lips, felt her face flush. "Is there nothing about us women you men don't know?"

He laughed, albeit halfheartedly. "A lot, angel. Tell me the truth."

"I am not carrying your child, Carson Jarrett."

Deep inside he began to relax. The pace of the waltz had picked up and he twirled her about the room, reentering the mainstream, sidestepping a couple here, another there.

With the worry gone, a strange sort of letdown seeped into the vacuum. "Good," he whispered at length

"You're glad?"

"Hmm." He shrugged. "Aren't you?"

The next dance was slower and they moved about the floor as though they floated on a pillow of silence, each sifting through the previous conversation, letting new emotions, new ideas, settle into place.

At length he laughed. "So this is it?"

Startled from her reverie, Aurelia's eyes flew to his. "This is what?"

"Guanajuato. Where you have always wanted to live."

They made their way smoothly around the floor. The music supplied a gentle backdrop to their raging emotions.

"I don't want it anymore."

"Oh?" He maneuvered them away from a helplessly awkward couple.

"Right now all I want is to kiss you."

His eyes answered for him, because for a moment he was afraid that if he moved his lips to speak, he would find them on hers.

"To kiss me?" he questioned after a while. "Only to kiss me?"

She shook her head, grinning. "More than that. Much more than that."

"I thought so." His gaze left hers to sweep the room. "You want it all."

"Not all of this. Just all of you."

They danced without speaking again. Holding her became a chore. Holding her, but being allowed to do nothing else. Unable even to hold her close. He longed to feel her against him. His body began to ache.

"That probably isn't entirely true," he challenged. "If you had all of me but nothing else, you would want all of this. You only think you could give it up because you have it."

She laughed. "You talk in riddles, and nothing you say is true."

"You think you know what you want, don't you?"

"I know I do."

"It would mean taking an awful chance to find out. The odds aren't good."

"I can see you haven't changed your way of thinking." She lifted her chin, grinning in her familiar conspiratorial fashion. "But I am prepared to prove my point. When you return to your room tonight, you will find a package on your bed."

He squeezed her waist. "A package filled with what, angel? You?"

Her eyes held his, teasing yet serious. "Before dawn tomorrow," she instructed, "dress in the clothes you will find in that package and meet me outside the servants' entrance to the mansion. I intend to show you the real me."

His amusement turned to wonder. "Why do I always underestimate you?" Then he thought of the consequences. "Your relatives will have our hides, mine most of all."

"Don't you trust me? I'm the one who rescued you from death by hanging. Remember?"

His eyes danced upon her glorious face. "Only to snare me in a trap of angel wings."

She laughed, absorbing the warmth in his eyes, the love in his voice.

"How will you be dressed?" he teased. "Will I recognize the real you?"

Aurelia laughed again. "I guarantee it."

Chapter Fifteen

Back at the Reinaldo mansion, Aurelia let María help her remove her blood-red gown.

"Did you get the items I sent you for?" she asked, tossing her corset and petticoats over the carved screen.

"Sí, señorita."

Pulling an embroidered cotton gown over her head, she slipped into its matching wrapper. How she wanted to go to Carson tonight. But it would never do for her aunt or uncle to discover her in his room. No telling what they would do to Carson. No telling what they would tell her parents.

And her own parents were looking better by the hour.

"You delivered the clothing to Señor Jarrett's room?"

"Sí, señorita."

Sitting at the dressing table, she unpinned her hair and let María brush it the obligatory one hundred strokes, although she was hardpressed to sit still that long tonight. "Did you get the directions I asked for?"

"Sí." Digging into her apron, the maid pulled out a crumpled piece of paper.

Aurelia's mouth fell open. "This map has no words . . . no directions."

"The maid who drew it does not write, señorita." María shrugged. "Neither do I."

"How can I use such a map?"

"The cross is the Basilica." María patiently pointed to other markings on the paper. "This skull is where the dead look alive, and these arches lead to the tunnel on the outskirts of town."

Aurelia followed María's moving finger. "This is the road we take?"

"Sí, señorita." Aurelia studied the map, while María began to brush her hair once more. "I do not like it, this thing you are planning."

"A picnic? What is wrong with a picnic?"

"We are not in Catorce. You should not take so many chances."

Aurelia laughed. "I have taken chances all my life, María."

A sudden rap at the door set her heart to racing. She glanced at her maid, wondering what the girl would think should she invite Carson in and send her out.

The knock came again. Stuffing the crude map into the bodice of her nightgown, she pulled open the door, only to find Santos lounging against the opposite wall.

"What are you doing here?" she demanded.

"Expecting someone else?"

"Certainly not. What do you want?"

He grinned. "Sorry to have caused you unnecessary . . . ah . . . excitement."

"What do you want?" she repeated.

"May I come in?"

She stood aside.

He spoke to María. "Run along now. Relie can tuck herself in."

"Come back in the morning, María," Aurelia instructed. "Early, like I told you. And don't be late."

Sitting down, she began to brush her own hair. In the looking glass, she watched Santos survey the room. Finally, she tossed her hairbrush at him. "Why don't you check under the bed?"

He grimaced.

Por Santa Cecilia! Give me strength to endure a meddlesome brother."

He chuckled, sinking to the settee. "I didn't expect to find him here."

"I should hope not. He has enough sense not to come to my room in a place like this, even if I wanted him to."

"That's the problem, Relie."

"What?"

"He would come if you wanted him to. He will do anything you ask."

Aurelia turned back to the dressing table to hide her distress.

"Couldn't you tell how uncomfortable he was tonight?"

A flush crept up her neck. "That was a matter between the two of us, Santos. We worked it out."

"What about the horses?"

"What horses?"

"Don't close me out on this, Relie. I feel responsible

enough as it is. What are you up to with Rodrigo's Arabians?"

"I'm not up to anything with Rodrigo's Arabians. It was a whim, a game."

"A game? What if Jarrett should win? What do you expect him to do then? Where is he supposed to run this herd of Arabians if he wins them?"

She took her brush from his extended hand and began to apply long, slow strokes to her hair. "At Rancho Mazón?"

"Rancho Mazón? You hate the ranch."

"I do not." Her hand stilled. "How can you say what I like and what I hate?" She stroked her hair idly, wondering whether she herself knew what she wanted. The only thing she knew for certain was that she hated being separated from Carson—for ten days, for one day, for a moment.

"I told you, the *charriada* is a game," she continued. "Carson knows that. He also knows his chances of winning are practically nonexistent. The *charriada* is for fun. Are we not allowed to have fun?"

"You're playing with a man's life."

She glared at his reflection in the looking glass. "What do you want me to do?"

"I don't know, but I have to think of something before this thing goes any further."

"You can start by calling *this thing* what it is—love. Admit it. I am in love with Carson Jarrett, your best friend. And he is in love with me."

"I know that. Everyone can see it. You mope around for ten days, then he comes to town and you light up like candles on a Christmas altar. So does he. I felt the heat tonight just standing beside him, watching him watch you from across the room. I see no way out now, short of one of you getting hurt."

With a heavy sigh, she crossed the room and sat beside him on the settee. "We are in love, Santos. That means we're going to be happy, not hurt."

"You can't ask him to live in Guanajuato," Santos insisted. He ruffled her carefully brushed hair, reminding her of when they were kids. She brushed his hand away, but playfully. "And living in Guanajuato has been your dream, Relie. It's all you have ever wanted."

"I don't want it anymore."

He stared at her, his uncertainty clear.

"I don't," she insisted. "All I want is to live with Carson. Even if that means moving to Texas, living out under the stars." She shrugged. "Or wherever he takes me."

He chuckled at that thought, then turned serious again. "Your life is at stake, too. Before you marry someone, you need to consider whether you would be happy with that kind of person, whether you could make him happy."

"I—"

He held up his hand. "Don't tell me you would be happy living in the wilderness. I know better. Somehow I will have to work this out."

"No, Santos. You stay out of it. I know you mean well, but Carson and I can solve our own problems."

"That's what Pia told me. She said all you wanted was the freedom to choose for yourself, to make your own decisions; that Guanajuato wasn't all that important to you."

300

"She's right," Aurelia admitted. "I didn't realize it until I came here, but she is right. We could even live in Catorce."

"Catorce?"

"Papá expects my husband to run the mint and eventually the mine."

He shrugged, noncommittal.

"Carson Jarrett could run either one of them better than Enrique."

"You hate Catorce."

"No, I hate being forced to live there. And being forced to marry Enrique." She laughed, hugging her arms about her. "Even Mamá's suggestion that Papá would build me a villa next to theirs doesn't sound so bad anymore."

Santos's eyebrows lifted a notch higher. "Jarrett wouldn't cotton to having your papá build him a house."

"A minor detail, Santos." She hugged him. "We can build our own house in Catorce. Don't you understand? I love him. He loves me. We will find a solution to everything."

"If you say so, Relie." At the door, he kissed her forehead. "You've convinced me that you love him, not that things will work out worth a damn."

"Please don't spoil our happiness. We're going to have a wonderful life, all of us — you and Pia and Carson and me."

"Even if he takes you to Texas?"

She nodded. "His family sounds fascinating."

Her last statement stopped him short. "*Fascinating* isn't exactly the word, Relie. They are good, solid people, but tough as nails. I've met most of them, and they are folks to ride the river with. You have never known people like that."

"I know one of them, and I've fallen in love with him. I will love his family, too."

The only hitch in her plan the following morning was that Santos had sent María off to bed before Aurelia could ask her to pack a lunch for them.

It was still dark when she tiptoed down the stairs and into the kitchen, garbed in her disguise. The cook had already lighted the fires and was busy with the day's baking.

As luck would have it, when Aurelia began rummaging through the larder for food, the cook assumed she was one of the maids sent to fetch for the masters.

So Aurelia rose to the occasion, saying how a guest asked her to prepare a basket of food to carry to the corral this morning. The cook supplied a clean cotton sack and freshly cooked tortillas, and she showed Aurelia where to find some cheeses and peppered beef.

A while later, when Carson tripped through the kitchen, the cook had become a bit wiser.

"Shoo! Be off with you. We are civilized folk. We don't feed beggars."

After she slammed the door behind him, he glanced up and down the narrow alley, finally spying a serving girl giggling at the end of the house.

Carson strode toward her with purpose.

"Where exactly do you expect me to go in this getup?" He held the ballooning white britches to either side while he spoke, and her giggles turned to hysterics.

"And these sandals. Do you know I haven't worn anything but boots since I learned how to stand on my own two feet?"

Gaining a measure of composure, she surveyed his costume. "María chose well." In the white shirt and pants, he would blend into the feria crowd, especially with the woolen poncho. The stiff-brimmed straw sombrero covered his head and most of his face. "Your disguise would be ruined if you wore Texas boots."

He grinned then, scanning her own costume. His hands followed his eyes down her shoulders, fingering the tie on the white blouse, then across her breasts, taking special notice of the corset stays beneath, and onto her waist, where they stopped. He grasped her there, his hands splayed across her stomach. She watched the humor die on his face.

"Would it have been so terrible?" she whispered.

His eyes found hers. "I don't want it to happen that way for you."

"But it would have been our baby."

He nodded. "I hadn't realized how strongly I would feel about that until last night, when you said it wasn't true."

"You were disappointed?"

"Hmm."

"So was I."

His lips had barely touched hers, when the back door burst open and the cook shouted after them. "Away with you before I call the master. We don't allow carrying on around here."

Carson grabbed her hand. "The adventures you get us involved in, angel!" He pulled her around the corner, up a street, and down another hill.

"First things first," he whispered. Stopping behind a wall that had no outside windows or doors, he pulled her into his arms and covered her lips with his own, kissing her until they were both gasping for breath.

"Every day without you has been hell," he murmured into her lips, "but yesterday was worst of all, being so close and hardly getting to touch you."

She held him, not wanting to ever let him go, responding in kind to his deep, delving kisses, to his passionate embrace, to his roving hands.

Finally, he drew back. "I'm not near finished, but considering the time and place . . ."

"I know. I have a lovely day planned for us."

He followed her down the winding streets, unconvinced this scheme of hers, pleasant though it appeared to be, could end in less than disaster. "What will they do when they discover us gone?"

"They won't."

He tugged on her arm, waiting for an explanation.

"María will tell Tía that I am ill . . . that she has given me manzanilla tea and I will sleep until evening."

"What if your aunt decides to check on you?"

"You know Tía Guadalupe. How much time do you think she will spend tending to an ill relative? Besides, María will keep the door locked."

"What about me?"

"If they question your absence, Santos will offer some excuse."

"He knows?"

"No, but . . ." A grin somewhere between contrition and pride bowed her lips.

"He knows *you.*" Carson sighed, wondering again what price they would pay for the simple pleasure of being together.

The premonition passed quickly though, as she led him on a tour of the quaint, romantic city. Their first stop was the market, where farmers had come to town with all manner of fruits and vegetables, nuts and meats, even clothing and jewelry.

Carson bought her a lacy black shawl to drape about her shoulders. "Completes your gypsy costume," he said.

She dragged him to a stall where they sold shoes made of strips of leather woven basket-style. "They will cover your white feet better than those sandals María picked out."

He tried a pair. "They fit better, too, but I still feel naked without my boots."

He spied a stall that sold earrings and insisted on buying her a pair made of silver wires so intricately entwined they resembled lace. When he started to pay for them, something else caught his eye.

"Try it on," he suggested, slipping a gold band on her third finger, left hand. It didn't fit, but with the vendor's help, they found one that did.

"I don't need this," she insisted when they walked away from the market. But he noticed how she held her hand out to admire the new ring.

"When I kiss you in public today, I want people to think we are without manners, not that you are a loose woman."

Aurelia laughed gaily. "I don't care what people think. We won't see anyone we know all day long."

"It doesn't matter whether they know your name or not. I don't want them looking at you and thinking that."

The next place he kissed her was in the Alley of the Kiss, where they stood on opposite sides of the narrow street, leaned together, and kissed.

"The lovers who lived in these houses were kept apart by their cruel families," she told him. "According to the story, their only contact was when they leaned across the alley from those balconies up there and kissed."

He pulled her back to his side of the street, held her tight a moment, then released her.

"Your family is dead set on you marrying Enrique." They ambled up one street and down the next.

"Mamá isn't so bad about it."

He agreed.

"Nor Santos anymore."

He chuckled. "I never expected him to come between me and true love, but he sure as hell tried to for a while there."

"I straightened him out."

He pulled her to a bench in the narrow little square she called Plaza de la Paz.

"How did you do that?" he asked. "What did you tell him?"

She ran a gentle hand over his cheek, cupping his jaw. How she loved this man. "I told him I don't want to live in Guanajuato."

At his frown, she related Santos's visit the evening before. "He was concerned that you might relent and

306

try to live in Guanajuato to please me. So I told him the same thing I told you at the ball: I don't want to live here."

Carson shook his head, marveling at the interference of this friend, at the accuracy with which he had judged the situation. "Are you sure?"

She nodded.

"How sure?"

Without hesitating, she leaned closer and kissed him soundly on the lips. He quickly pulled her hands from his face and dislodged their lips. "Not here, angel."

"You asked me; I wanted to show you."

He tugged her to her feet, glancing about the plaza.

"That's the opera house." She pointed across the street to the grand building. "Do you want to go inside?"

"No, I want to show you something." With that, he guided her to the fountain in the center of the plaza, where he seated her on its narrow edge.

After speaking with a musician nearby, he took the guitar the man offered, slipped the strap over his neck and, with a foot propped on the fountain rim, proceeded to serenade her.

Her eyes danced.

*"Oh, I came from up in Texas
With my guitar on my knee,
To serenade Aurelia
And to win her love for me."*

She clapped her hands, holding them to her lips. "You're courting me."

"Why not?" he laughed. "You've been so busy chasing me, you didn't notice when I caught you."

"When I saw her in that jailhouse,
Where she came to set me free."
I knew she was an angel
Who would steal my heart from me."

Her eyes lit up. She pursed her lips between her teeth, listening to him sing and strum the guitar.

"You also asked me to serenade you, remember?"

She nodded, recalling how she had burst into the patio in Catorce. "I could have died when I saw Santos standing there."

He laughed. "Actually, I figured I might be the one to expire . . . by his hands."

He stuffed a bill between the strings of the instrument and handed it back to the man he had borrowed it from. "What next, guide?"

Moving to a park bench, she pulled out the crumpled map and studied it. He sat beside her, amused. The sun felt warm, the flowers smelled sweet. Around them the crowd milled, laughing, talking, enjoying the holiday.

"We could eat that lunch you swiped from the kitchen," he suggested.

"Not here. We need to go there." She showed him the map, pointing to their destination.

He whistled low between his teeth. "Glad you're the guide and not me." After glancing up and down the street, he clapped his hands to his knees and stood up, pulling her to her feet. "Let's get on with it, then. My feet are ready to find their boots."

"We can't walk," she told him. "We have to hire a carriage."

"You think a driver can decipher that map?"

"Not a carriage and a driver." She held up the sack of food. "We don't want a driver on our picnic."

His eyebrows lifted; his grin teased. His brown gaze caressed her face, lingering on her lips, dipping further. "A picnic? Right clever of you, ma'am."

A couple of blocks away they found a livery, where he hired a hack and followed her directions out of town.

"Reckon this picnic will get me out of the *charriada?*"

"Do you want out?"

"Truth known, I'm looking forward to beating the spurs off those damned cocky charros."

She laughed.

"Especially that Don Whatshisname Fraga."

"Carson, you didn't think I was serious, did you? About beating him? About the horses?"

"Weren"t you?"

"Well, it was an idea," she admitted. "But it has nothing to do with . . . I mean, if you should lose, it wouldn't . . . What I mean is . . ."

Reaching over, he rested a hand on her knee, squeezing her thigh. "Shhh, angel. I know it has nothing to do with us. It's competition, fun. But it never hurts to dream a little."

"In that case," she admitted, "we need to return before siesta is over."

He winked. "I'm not all that anxious to hurry through this picnic you went to so much trouble to arrange . . ." He glanced away, surveying the country on either side. ". . . especially since we're fixin' to leave the city behind."

She told him where to turn off the main road, follow-

309

ing a double-rutted trail into the foothills. They rode in silence for a while, each relishing the anticipation that spread like wildfire between them, traveling through their thighs where they touched, their shoulders.

She recalled how Santos had accused her of moping around all week. Right now, she bubbled with life and dreams.

"I worried about the authorities recognizing you in Catorce," she said.

"No need. The haircut and shave did the trick. Of course, I didn't traipse into headquarters to test 'em out."

"I heard you tell Santos you think we have real trouble at the mine."

He nodded.

"With Nuncio Quiroz?"

They both tensed at the name. He shifted the reins to one hand and put his free arm around her, drawing her near. "More people are involved than Quiroz."

"Who?"

"Wish to hell I knew. I couldn't find anything wrong with the books or in the mine, either. But that fight . . . well, someone tipped Quiroz off that I would go to the mine before I left town."

"How do you know?"

"He was waiting for me."

"Who could it have been?"

He shrugged. "Figure whoever it was meant business, though. And they aren't finished. I must have come close to something, close enough to scare them."

"I'm frightened for you."

"I'll be okay. Fightin' bad men is my job. It's you I'm

worried about. Quiroz taunted me about you, openly, like he wants us to worry about what he'll do or say."

Aurelia snuggled against him, then recognized the trees in the distance. "There's the place," she said. "See those trees by that stream?"

He pulled the mare off the road. "I've been thinking about something," he told her. "Didn't you say your aunt and uncle are coming to Catorce for the wedding?"

She nodded.

"I want you to stay here and ride up with them. Let Santos and me go back and settle the ruckus."

She stiffened on the seat beside him. "I will do no such thing."

He laughed. "They say a man generally gets what he wishes for." He shook his head. "Somewhere back in time, I must have wished for a headstrong woman."

"Carson, you can't mean that."

"What? That you're headstrong or that you belong to me?"

"That you want me to stay here."

"No, angel, I don't mean that at all." He had drawn rein beneath a stand of poplar trees. "But it's for your own good."

Carson helped her off the wagon seat, then removed his sombrero and pulled the poncho over his head. He handed them both to her. "Spread the poncho under that tree while I water the mare." He cocked an eyebrow. "That is why you made me wear this heavy thing on such a hot day, isn't it? So we would have a . . . ah . . . a tablecloth?"

While he led the mare to the river, she did as he suggested. Actually, she hadn't thought of the poncho in that light, but it was certainly a good idea. After she spread it on the ground, she reached beneath her skirts, removing her petticoat and bloomers, then adroitly unlaced her corset, hiding the lot of them beneath one corner of the poncho.

He returned to find her leaning against the trunk of the tree, her knees pulled up with her skirt tugged down over them. Mostly.

He settled himself lazily, facing her and grinning. One hand slipped beneath her skirt, cupping her bare calf in a hot palm. He rubbed idly back and forth, still grinning.

"I think I've said it before, but it bears repeating. When you set out to seduce a man, you don't stop halfway."

Her heart pounded against her ribs. She held out her arms, and he came into them.

"Now, kiss me like you did in our cave behind the waterfall," she whispered.

"I'll do my damnedest, angel."

Serenaded by nature—the wind rustling through silvery leaves above them, the stream gurgling by at their feet, birds and crickets singing in off-key but not discordant harmony—he kissed her.

The soft mounds of her breasts nuzzled into his chest; her back already felt warm to his hand, even through her thin blouse. Fumbling from haste he had trouble controlling, Carson untied her blouse and drew it over her shoulders, exposing her breasts, while she wriggled her arms free.

Then she tugged and pulled at his shirt, helping him

312

discard it as well. When they came together again, he held her close and still, savoring this lovely free spirit who was unlike any human he had ever known or even imagined.

Would he ever learn not to underestimate her schemes? He supposed not, not being given to such things himself. Likely she would always be one step ahead of him in that department. It didn't really matter. He liked surprises as much as the next man. Aurelia's best of all.

The thought of surprises, however, called to mind the terror he had lived with the past ten days.

"Are you sure about this?" His husky voice betrayed the passion rising inside him.

She bumped her head on his chin in an effort to look in his eyes. "Why would you ask such a thing?"

"Since we discussed the consequences . . ." He tried to sound matter-of-fact but knew he didn't succeed. His hand shifted from her bare back to her belly, which was still covered by the coarse black skirt.

"You said you were disappointed," she whispered.

"I was, but . . . I don't want it to happen like this."

She nipped tender kisses onto his face. "We know the consequences." She hugged him tighter, nuzzling her breasts into his furry chest. "And we know the wonder of it all. What is so wrong with that?"

"Nothing, as long as we are prepared to . . ."

She ran her hand along his back, his side, slipping her fingers beneath the waistband of his loose white trousers, eliciting a shudder.

"That didn't hurt," he hurried to assure her, calling to mind the last time they made love. She was right, of course. Now that they knew the wonder, now that they were here in each other's arms, how could they stop?

Even if they wanted to. But that didn't mean he had to jeopardize her future, take all her choices away.

His hand slipped beneath her skirt, bunching it around her waist, where the fabric from both garments formed a roll between them. He wouldn't remove her clothing, he told himself, running his hands along the outside of her thigh, then traveling inside, feeling her legs open to his quest. He wouldn't remove her clothing, not here in the wilds where they could be discovered.

And he would make sure she did not conceive his child. His heart tolled like a heavy church bell, reverberating against his ribs. When he slipped his fingers inside her, a tremor passed through her body, radiating to his. She threw back her head and his lips slid from hers, leaving a trail of wetness across her chest to her breast.

Again a tremor passed through her body to his. Her hips lifted suggestively against the sensual cadence of his hand.

Her fingers splayed around his head, grasping chunks of his hair. "Love me, Carson. Please love me."

Without completely removing them, he tugged and pulled his breeches over his knees, all the while staring into her begging eyes. *God help him, he did love her so much.*

He entered her as slowly as he could manage under the circumstances, letting her liquid heat fire his already intense desire. He watched her lips part and quiver; that Comanche bow had just released another arrow, and her aim was perfect. His heart trembled with love for her. When she moved her hips against him, he felt the velvet of her core close around him, inviting him, welcoming him.

Suddenly, all he wanted was to plant his seeds here inside her, where his child could grow surrounded by her love, nourished by her romantic, fun-loving nature, protected by her fierce independence. He wanted it. God, how he wanted it.

"No," he whispered, stilling her hips with his hands. "Don't move." He feathered kisses across her face. "Let it happen, angel. Be still and let it happen."

He concentrated on her face, her gloriously begging eyes. He kissed them closed, then moved across her cheek, tracing the outline of her ear with his tongue, swirling inside it, feeling her tremble beneath him.

"Let it happen, angel." He moved his lips to hers. Suddenly, his kisses turned wild, plunging deep again and again.

Beneath him he felt her pumping heart. Her ragged breath escaped in heated gasps against his mouth. She closed her lips over his tongue and suckled it in an impassioned rhythm that set her hips to moving.

Again he stilled them, gripping his own rampant passions with the greatest of difficulty. "Just let it happen," he mumbled, his lips to her ear, his fingers to her breast. "Let it happen. Feel me inside you. Feel the throbbing. The hot and wonderful throbbing. Let it happen, angel."

And then it did. He felt her tighten around him, squeezing him as though to squeeze the seeds of life from his body into hers. Her arms trembled against his back, before falling slack.

"Carson, I love you," she whispered.

In that instant he withdrew himself. Her eyes flew open. She reached between them, clasped her hand around his throbbing flesh, wet now from her own passion, felt his release spray like teardrops into the palm of her hand.

"Why? . . ." she whispered. Her eyes begged him.

Still trembling from the exertion, Carson fell to his side and clasped her tightly against his chest, rocking her back and forth.

She struggled to look in his face. "Why?"

"I can't let you . . ."

"But I love you."

He stared long into her imploring eyes. Her words, intense, begged him to believe her.

"I love you. You've known it all along, haven't you?"

He held his breath, staring at her, loving her.

"I do, Carson. I love you. I wanted to tell you back in Catorce, but we never had a chance after I realized it. You should have made me tell you that morning I made you tell me."

In spite of it all, he grinned. "Run that by me one more time."

"The morning I came to your room disguised as a maid. That's why I came, to make you tell me you love me."

He traced her lips with an index finger. "You didn't make me tell you I love you. No woman can make a man say that. Not so he means it."

"Now we have plenty of time," she said. "I can tell

you every day, a hundred times a day, for the rest of our lives."

He stilled her delightfully scheming lips by burying them in the lee of his shoulder. What had he gotten himself into? What had he gotten her into? He had nothing to give a girl like Aurelia. And she had everything to lose. But how did he think he could ever live without her?

"When did you change your mind about us?" she asked at length. When he didn't answer, she pulled her head away from his shoulder and looked into his troubled eyes. "You haven't?" The words whispered like an ill wind from her lips. Anguish filled her heart.

He trailed his fingers across her forehead, brushed strands of hair from her face. "I have never felt as empty and lost as I did after you left Catorce," he admitted. His warm brown eyes caressed her face. "But that didn't convince me we could make a life together. We are so different . . ."

"No—"

"Shh, angel. It's true. You were raised in mansions with servants at your beck and call. I haven't even had a home since I grew to manhood. We cannot deny the problems that will create for us."

Her spirits fell at his words. "You haven't changed your mind."

He kissed her so tenderly it brought tears to her eyes. "I can never leave you, Aurelia. I guess that hit me when I realized you could be carrying my child. You belong to me. Your children will be my children, too. I love you. I can never, never leave you."

She took his face in her hands and brought his lips to

317

hers. She kissed him as tenderly as he had kissed her. "We will work everything out, Carson, beginning with this: I am not staying in Guanajuato without you."

He argued with her about that most of the way back to her relatives' mansion. Afterwards, he realized that as in a lot of other things, Aurelia Mazón had been one step ahead of him.

Chapter Sixteen

Unwittingly, of course. When she vowed not to stay in Guanajuato without him, she had no way of knowing the uproar their day together had caused. They entered the mansion through the kitchen, only to have the cook announce their arrival to Tío Luís and Santos, who waited for them on the patio.

"So much for returning before siesta ends," Aurelia whispered.

Her uncle overheard. "Siesta? How could we rest with you cavorting around town like a . . . like a? . . ." His eyes swept her rumpled peasant attire, then fastened on Carson. "Like some loose woman with this Norteamericano." He spat the last word as if it were vile.

Carson bit back a caustic reply. "I apologize for causing you concern, señor. Aurelia has come to no harm."

"That had better be the case." Luís clamped his cigar between his teeth, once again scanning her costume with a menacing frown. "How dare you cheapen yourself like some . . . some common . . ."

Carson stepped toe to toe with the choleric man. "Be careful of the words you choose, señor."

Santos placed a restraining hand on Carson's shoulder. "Easy, compadre."

"We were only enjoying the feria," Aurelia hastened to say.

"The feria?" Again the livid man scorched the two late arrivers with both his eyes and his tongue. "That is not the way it looks."

Aurelia straightened to her full height. "I don't care how it looks, Tío. We—"

"Run along, Relie." Santos nudged her toward the staircase. "Change for the *charriada*."

"The *charriada*?" Luís questioned.

After another insistent nod from Santos, Aurelia turned toward the staircase with her uncle calling after her.

"Over my dead body will I allow you to ruin your good name this way. You will not go to the *charriada*."

Aurelia gritted her teeth to keep from responding.

Santos released Carson's shoulder. "You, too, compadre. Get into your riding clothes. I will wait down here with Tío."

Luís was swiping his flushed forehead with a white linen handkerchief. He waved it toward Aurelia. "Thank heavens your aunt is dressing for dinner. If she saw you like this . . ."

"She won't," Aurelia assured him, hurrying now. The thought of Tía Guadalupe's reaction to her rumpled disguise made her even more eager to dress and be gone from this house.

Luís continued to rage. "If Enrique were to hear of your behavior . . ."

His words brought Aurelia to a halt halfway up the grand staircase. She swirled to face her uncle by marriage. "Enrique! Find someone else to marry your precious Enrique, Tío." Her voice echoed through the suddenly still air in the foyer below.

"Someone else?" The question dropped like a stone from Luís's mouth. "Someone else to marry Enrique?" He stomped toward the staircase.

Carson reached for him. Santos shouldered his friend aside grabbing hold of the livid Luís. "Calm down, Uncle. Relie, go ahead. You, too, Jarrett. Now."

"You are betrothed to Enrique," Luís shouted.

"I am not."

Reaching Aurelia, Carson nudged her up a step, while Luís roared below them.

"You will be."

"I will not."

"Yes, you will."

Carson nudged her again, wanting instead to sweep her in his arms and carry her bodily up the stairs. Around them the air buzzed with tension. It reminded him of being inside that infernal mine—always expecting an explosion to go off.

"No, I won't." Aurelia was insisting.

"I will not stand by and let you do this again," Luís vowed. "You almost threw everything away in that chapel, but . . . but . . ." He sputtered, then regained momentum. "Domingo promised you to Enrique. He promised me . . ."

Somewhere along the way, Carson stopped hearing

the argument and started listening to the words, and the words became terrifying.

"Your precious Enrique," Aurelia mimicked. "You think the sun rises and sets with him. Well, it doesn't. Not my sun, in any case —"

Carson grabbed her around the waist, stopping her words in mid sentence. He looked down at Santos. "Five minutes. Will you be ready to hit the trail?"

Santos nodded.

With giant leaps, Carson bounded up the stairs. He deposited Aurelia beside the door to her bedchamber. "Get dressed. When you return downstairs, apologize to your uncle."

"Are you mad? I will do no such thing."

"Angel," his voice held a warning. "I will explain later, but for now trust me. You must make peace with him." He planted a quick kiss on her quivering lips.

"How can I apologize for something I —?"

He chuckled. "Use your training. Pretend you are disguised as a dutiful niece."

"You think it's necessary?"

"I know it is," he insisted. "Have María wait in your room. Tell her to pack and be ready to leave for Catorce before sunup."

She tilted her chin.

"I will explain," he repeated, wondering exactly what there was to explain. The pieces to the puzzle still didn't fit, but at last they were beginning to fall into place.

In less than five minutes, he had removed the peasant clothing, replacing it with his own breeches, shirt, vest, and boots. Those boots had never felt so good.

322

Heading for the stairs, Carson removed his Texas Ranger badge from the inner lining of his vest and pinned it on the outside with trembling fingers. His mind whirred with images of ledger books, of the highly touted virtues of Enrique Villasur.

At the landing, he almost collided with Aurelia. Her costume surprised him enough to take his mind off their troubles for a moment. Instead of the riding skirt he had expected, she wore a red cotton dress, tiered in ruffles and bedecked with multicolored ribbons.

They could hear Luís Reinaldo still raving below. "What do you mean you are taking her back to Catorce in the morning? She is supposed to stay in Guanajuato and ride up for the wedding with her aunt and me."

Carson guided her down the staircase, his fingers pressed lightly to her waist. "Don't argue with him," he whispered. "Apologize and let's get out of here."

Seeing her uncle's still-livid face, she faltered. But Carson had a hand to her back, gently forcing her along, quieting her anger with the sense of reassurance she always felt with him beside her.

Crossing the floor, she took Tío Luís's hand, startling him into momentary silence. "I'm sorry, Tío. You know how I have always had to fight a willful tongue." She swallowed back the urge to spit in his face. "And actions," she added. "I didn't mean a bit of what I said. I was just angry not to have my way."

He stared hard, his eyes searching hers.

Carson nudged her in the small of the back. "Papá always did spoil me," she added. "You said so yourself."

"Guadalupe was right," he responded. "Domingo should have let you come to us long ago."

323

"We must run along." She tiptoed to plant a kiss on his damp cheek. "I promise not to bring dishonor to you, especially not at such an important time."

His eyebrows came together.

"It will be good for your bid for the governor's office, don't you think? For some of the family to be seen at the *charriada?*"

Luís eyed Carson, who had stepped away from her, standing now near the outside door.

Santos motioned them toward the door. "I sent a servant for a carriage." He turned back to his uncle. "Don't worry, Tío. No one can question Aurelia's right to go anywhere in the world with me." Taking her by the shoulders, he guided her through the door. "I am an expert at keeping her out of trouble."

A single "Hurrumph" resounded behind them as they headed for the carriage that stood ready to depart at the curb. The Reinaldo driver held the door.

Aurelia climbed into the coach and sat trembling like a poplar leaf.

Carson took the seat opposite her. When the carriage pulled away, he sank elbows to knees and buried his face in his hands.

She watched his arms tremble. The muscles across his back were so taut they also quivered.

"Don't worry," she told him. "The day was worth every flutter of Tío's double chin."

He groaned into his hands, then looked up, meeting her eyes. "Hmm." His eyes found the little gold ring hanging from a red ribbon around her neck. He grimaced.

"First Quiroz, now your uncle. One of these days I'm

going to be in a position to kill the man who slanders you."

"I don't want you to fight for my honor," she whispered. Taking his hands in her own, she held them against her knees. "Tell me what happened in there that caused you to take charge so magnificently."

"What was it all about?" Santos echoed.

Carson leaned back against the seat. Slipping his hands from Aurelia's, he stared into the depths of her eyes. "Your uncle mentioned the episode in the chapel. Did he mean either of the two times you told me about?"

"There were only two."

"Then how did he know?"

The only sound inside the carriage was that of Santos and Aurelia gasping, almost in unison.

"Papá?" Santos whispered.

Aurelia shook her head. "The three of us and Pia and Zita are the only ones who know."

"Besides the boys," Carson reminded her.

"Kino and Joaquín would not have told. They couldn't have, anyway. They didn't know about—"

"—Quiroz," Santos finished. "Quiroz damned sure knew. What does it mean? What did you find out in Catorce?"

"I'm not sure," Carson told them. "Reinaldo mentioned your father promising him something . . . What?"

"Me," Aurelia sighed. "Although I'm beginning to feel more like he sold me."

Carson's eyes caressed her face. "Don't worry, angel. That deal is off." Then he added, "Something is happening at the mine that doesn't add up, but I hadn't suspected Reinaldo."

"You suspected Enrique, though?" Santos questioned.

He nodded.

"Couldn't be the green-eyed monster acting up?"

Carson chuckled, still looking at Aurelia. "Me? Jealous of that lily-livered, egg-sucking coyote? Never."

At the corral, both Santos and Aurelia tried to dissuade Carson from entering.

"We could head on to Catorce tonight," Santos told him.

"No, we can't rock the boat right now. We have to spend the night with your relatives. At least, the two of you do."

"What about you?" Aurelia objected.

He chucked her under the chin. "I'll bed down here with ol' Sunfisher. He's likely homesick for me, anyhow."

"Sunfisher?" she questioned.

"You think it's that serious?" Santos asked.

"Until we find out for sure, we had best assume it is." He turned to Aurelia. "I want María to sleep in your room tonight. Tell her we are leaving bright and early. And be sure you lock your door."

"Hey, remember me?" Santos pointed a finger to his own chest. "I'm her brother. I can take care of her."

Carson grinned, but his words were serious. "I know, otherwise I wouldn't let her return to that house. But hey, we're here for a rodeo, and you haven't met Sunfisher." His pace picked up when they neared the stall.

"Sunfisher?" Aurelia skipped to keep up with the two long-legged men. "Your horse?"

"I told you Santos got my belongings back from the jailer. That included Sunfisher."

"Don't enter the *charriada* for me," she pleaded.

He patted the nose of the great line-backed dun mustang, favoring Aurelia with a wry grin. "Come meet Sunfisher, angel."

When she approached, he instructed his horse, "Say hello to my guardian angel, Sunfisher."

The horse tossed his head up and down three times.

Delighted, Aurelia stroked her hand along his muzzle. "Hello, Sunfisher." She kissed his nose, then turned to Carson.

"Don't do this for me. You haven't practiced, and you are still steaming from that fight with Tío Luís."

"Maybe it'll put a little steam in my performance," he suggested. "As for practice, ol' Sunfisher and I have bulldogged a few steers and saddled our share of broncs, haven't we, feller?"

Again Sunfisher nodded his head.

Aurelia laughed. Carson stood beside her so serious and proud she wanted to kiss him. Since she couldn't, she kissed his horse again.

While Carson buckled on his chaps, Santos saw to saddling Sunfisher. Aurelia hovered nearby, nervous. Up and down the aisle, charros donned the same sort of clothing—with a number of differences.

The rowels on the charros' spurs were larger than Carson's, the brims of their sombreros were wider than his Stetson, the legs of their *calzoneras* were tighter, after they buttoned down the belled bottoms, than his den-

327

ims.

They wore tight-fitting jackets instead of loose vests, and their *chaparreras,* as well as their saddles and tack, were more elaborately adorned with silver than his own smaller Texas saddle and bat-winged chaps.

"All in all," Carson told Aurelia, "I should have the advantage. Muscle and bone and not much else."

She scrutinized his costume, then looked to the handsomely suited fellows she had pitted him against. Before he knew what she was up to, she took the ring from around her neck and tied it around his.

"I gave your bandanna to Antonio yesterday," she reminded him.

He fingered the little gold ring and looked at her, his eyes caressing, teasing. "This ain't apt to keep much dust outta my face."

"Be careful," she told him, serious.

By the time he climbed aboard Sunfisher, he had already begun to discover that things were done a little differently south of the Río Bravo. Much like courting a woman, a rodeo down here followed circumspect rules.

"Their spurs may jingle louder than mine," he told Aurelia, "but otherwise, a cowpuncher is a cowpuncher and a rodeo is a rodeo, no matter what you call it."

Santos slapped him on the back. "Ride easy, compadre."

"Can't do otherwise." He polished his badge with the palm of his hand. "Ranger honor, and all that."

Don Rodrigo Fraga took charge of the visitor, while Santos and Aurelia found places as close to the front of the arena as they could.

The show began much as the bullfight had the day before with what Carson called a grand entry.

"The paseo," Don Rodrigo told him, leading the way into the ring.

Aurelia clasped her hands in her lap to keep from wringing them. "I wish we had the governor's box today," she told Santos, "so we could sit on the front row. But I don't suppose the governor comes to events like this."

"Don't know why he wouldn't," Santos responded. "He looked like a down-to-earth sort of hombre. It's our relatives who wouldn't stoop to attend a *charriada*."

Aurelia watched the fifty or so performers ride single file around the inside of the ring. The judges took their places in the middle, ready to signal the start of the first event.

"There he is." Standing in place, she waved her handkerchief to Carson when he passed. "He can't find us," she whispered. He rode straight and tall in the saddle, his Stetson dwarfed by the large brims of the sombreros that surrounded him.

"How will he keep his hat on?" she worried.

"Texans don't tie a strap under their bottom lip like we do," Santos told her.

"Won't his hat fly off?"

"I've ridden many a mile with him, Relie, and I have yet to see the man lose his hat."

She settled down when the first event began, the *cala de caballo*. Each horseman entered the arena at full gallop, bringing his mount to a halt inside a rectangle drawn on the ground with chalk. As soon as the animal stopped, the rider turned him in a circle within the rectangle, first to the left, then to the right. The event was finished by the rider backing his horse out of the arena.

"His horse isn't trained for these events," she worried. "He should have ridden the bay."

Santos teased her when Carson scored the highest possible number of points. Several charros scored as high, however.

"After the way you goaded him into performing," Santos teased, "I expected you to show a little more faith in the man."

"But he has never done this before."

"He has worked cattle most of his grown life, Relie. A man uses the same skills in the *cala de caballo* as he does in cutting cattle out of a herd from daylight to dark."

Carson located them before the next event got under way. He lifted his hat and she stood again, waving in return.

Neither he nor Rodrigo participated in the following events, and word finally reached Aurelia and Santos of a one-on-one contest, a *mano a mano* between Don Rodrigo Fraga and Carson Jarrett of Texas. Her heart flipped.

"Why did he do that?"

Santos laughed. "First you goad him into entering, then you whet his appetite with the prospect of winning Rodrigo's Arabian horses, now you want him to withdraw?"

"Not withdraw, just . . . well . . . He isn't doing this for me, Santos, no matter what you think."

"I know that. He's doing it for himself. Watch him, Relie. He's enjoying the hell out of it."

While Santos spoke a steer burst from a gate, and Carson spurred Sunfisher after it. Riding alongside the animal, he suddenly hefted himself from the saddle and dropped his body onto the steer, throwing his right arm around the animal's neck and grabbing its nose with his right hand. With his left hand on the steer's left horn, he plunged himself downward, twisting the animal's neck, bringing it to ground.

By that time, no more than ten seconds, Aurelia had wrung her handkerchief into a wrinkled scrap of linen.

Santos patted her hands. "It's all right, Relie. That's called bulldogging."

"It looks dangerous."

"How else do you propose to get an animal down to brand its ornery hide?" he questioned. "Besides, I wouldn't consider bulldogging half as dangerous as robbing trains."

That shut her up for a while, but she still gripped the handkerchief in wet hands.

Don Rodrigo took the next steer, but he didn't look nearly as proficient as Carson, a fact that lifted Aurelia's spirits considerably.

When the second event of the *mano a mano* was announced, a roar went up. The *coleadero* was always a favorite of the crowd, but today she sensed they tasted blood.

The blood of a Texan.

Don Rodrigo went first, as Carson had done with the bulldogging, to show the technique. The bull charged from the chute into the arena, with Rodrigo pressing his mount close behind. When he came close

331

enough, he reached over and grabbed the animal's tail, jerking it hard, pulling.

She knew the intention: to wrap the end of the bull's tail around the pommel of the saddle, while at the same time turning his horse in such a manner as to throw the bull off balance and roll him over. Don Rodrigo performed the event with grace and skill.

The next bull belonged to Carson, and it was all Aurelia could do to watch. Her hands trembled; she raised them partway to her eyes and ended up with her knuckles in her mouth.

Carson caught hold of the bull's tail. Santos cheered. Carson pulled. The crowd roared. The section of tail Carson held suddenly came off in his hand, and he toppled sideways in the saddle.

Aurelia covered her eyes with her hands.

Santos pulled her hands away. "Watch him, Relie. He won't fall off that horse."

"But? . . ."

"Carson Jarrett is as good a horseman as any charro out there. Do you think I would have let you goad him the way you did if I hadn't known it would be a great contest?"

"But the tail? . . ."

Santos shrugged. "The breaks. Bulls' tails come off like that all the time, you know that. No reflection on Jarrett."

The crowd was on its feet, cheering. She stood on wobbly legs.

"They know it, too," Santos was saying, clapping loudly for his friend. "He's game; they respect him."

By the final pair of events in this duel of charro versus cowboy, Aurelia found her knees weak and her heart tired. She knew what the final event always was.

"They wouldn't? . . ."

"Why not? It's as much a part of range work as the other events."

Across the arena she watched Carson and Don Rodrigo twirl their lassos, limbering their roping arms.

Don Rodrigo went first, again obviously to show Carson the technique. Afoot, he walked to the center of the ring, twirling his rawhide *reata* in flourishes to either side of his body, above his head, even stepping through the loop. Three riders entered the arena, driving a wild horse in front of them around the edge of the ring.

After a couple of passes, Don Rodrigo stepped to within ten feet of the arena fence, directly in front of the section where Aurelia sat. He glanced up, saluting her with his sombrero without dropping the loop of his twirling *reata*. Then he turned to face the oncoming wild horse. Suddenly, he jumped through the loop and immediately afterwards tossed the loop to the ground in front of the running horse, who stepped into it with his hind legs.

Don Rodrigo expertly jerked his *reata* to tighten the noose, twirled his body, dug in his heels, and dropped the surprised horse to the ground.

The hushed crowd came to its feet once more. Don Rodrigo bowed to Aurelia, sweeping the ground with his sombrero.

Then it was Carson's turn.

"He can't."

"He'll manage," Santos assured her.

Instead of walking to the center of the arena on foot, Carson rode Sunfisher. And instead of stopping there, he headed straight across the ring, guiding his horse at a leisurely gait, sitting tall and straight in the saddle. His left hand rested lightly on his thigh; in his right hand he held the reins in a loose grip. He drew up in front of the section where she sat.

Tipping his Stetson with a flick of his forefinger, he lifted the reins, and without further prompting, Sunfisher buckled his front legs at the knees to kneel before her. Carson stared into her eyes, still sitting tall and straight, that familiar wry grin tipping his lips.

Her hands flew to her heart, which gave warning of stopping altogether. All she could do was smile back.

"A trick horse," she muttered.

"That sonofabitch," Santos mused, nodding his head in appreciation. "He's become a regular Bill-show cowboy."

"A what?"

"Buffalo Bill, the Western showman. Truth is, Jarrett's been working with that horse since it was a colt. Not much else to do in a Ranger camp after you clean your rifle. And you can clean your rifle only so many times."

With as much grace as he had entered the ring, Carson turned Sunfisher back to the center, shook out his lariat, and nodded to the men who held the chute closed.

The same three riders burst forth, driving another wild horse. Carson sat Sunfisher in the center of the ring, casually twirling the rope in a loop beside him. He turned his mount by degrees, watching the bronc hug the arena wall. After the second pass, he nudged Sunfisher. They approached the wall, with Carson still twirling his horsehair lariat in an offhand fashion.

The end came like lightning. The bronc approached. Carson twirled the lariat above his head. The bronc drew even. Carson tossed the lariat.

Not at the animal's head but at its feet, drawing up suddenly, tightening the loop, wrapping the rope around the small pommel of his Texas saddle.

Sunfisher dug in his hooves, much as Don Rodrigo had dug in his heels before him. The bronc tumbled, stunned, surprised, but otherwise unharmed, to the ground, all four feet caught in the loop.

Again the crowd jumped to its feet.

Aurelia ran down the aisle, leaned over the fence.

Dismounting, Carson released the bronc and watched it bound to the far end of the arena, while he coiled the lariat. After remounting, he trotted Sunfisher up to the fence beside her.

His warm eyes teasing, he leaned forward, grasped her about the waist, and pulled her over the fence and onto the saddle in front of him. Her red skirt fanned like a blanket of roses on the winner of a horse race.

He hadn't won it all, of course.

The judges ruled it a tie. And Carson considered himself lucky to have been given that much, since he came away with only the tail of the bull.

Back in the corral, he apologized to Santos. "Hope you didn't mind. I know a lady isn't supposed to be made a spectacle of, but . . . well . . ." He winked at Aurelia where she stood rubbing down Sunfisher's lathered back. "I had to show I won the girl."

Santos laughed. "Under the circumstances I figure she got off light, seein' how she goaded you into this."

The music had already started behind the corral in a large outdoor arena, where dancing would go on well into the night.

"The *jarabe tapatío*," Santos informed Carson. "The national dance of charro country."

Carson watched Aurelia dance about the stall. "Wondered why she came dressed like that."

Out back the charros had laid their camps in and among a vast grove of liveoak trees. Smoke from their fires wafted through the autumn air, redolent with the aroma of roasting cabrito. Jugs of tequila circulated freely.

Don Rodrigo materialized again, taking charge of Carson, who was the hero of the day, dragging them from camp to camp, where they were obliged to eat plates of succulent cabrito rolled in flour tortillas and wash it down with tequila produced on first one rancho then the next, as group after group toasted Carson and the Texas Rangers and Don Rodrigo and the charros.

When the dancing began, Carson was the first to admit that the flashing steps of the *jarabe* were a little much for him after the other events of the day.

Aurelia led him in the steps, but his eyes were drawn to her swishing skirts and glimpses of her shapely calves, and his thoughts roamed to the picnic by the river and the feel of her calf in his hand.

And to so much more.

He gamely tried to learn the dance, though, after watching Don Rodrigo spirit her about the packed-earth floor, and he promised he would brush up on his technique by Santos and Pia's wedding.

As he told them earlier he would, Carson spent the night at the stables, while Santos and Aurelia returned to the Reinaldo mansion, arriving at a late enough hour to avoid an encounter with their relatives.

They tarried only long enough the following morning for Aurelia to once again apologize to her uncle for her unacceptable behavior, at Carson's instructions.

The morning sun found them on the road to Catorce. They stopped by the stables for Carson and their horses, then by the Plaza de Toros to pick up their vaqueros and those of the Mazón bulls that had not met their fate in the blood and sand the day before.

"Can't use them for fighting after they have been exposed to men on foot," Santos told Carson, "but they make good breeding stock, since we cull all except the best long before they reach this age."

It took four days and three nights to reach Catorce. They passed through the outer fringes of the Mazón range on the way. Santos and Carson talked of Rangering and cowboying, and Carson learned many things about the raising of fighting bulls and fine working horses.

"So you didn't win Rodrigo's Arabians?" Santos mused around the campfire the third night out.

"Nope."

"Kind of hate that," Santos continued. "I know Relie was sure countin' on it."

"I was not," she objected, wondering why Santos pursued a subject she had already explained to him.

"I bought a few head off him, though," Carson revealed.

"You what?" she asked.

"I bought a few head of those Arabian horses. A stallion and three mares."

"Where are they?" she demanded, startled.

"Didn't have the money on me," he commented. "I'll wire Austin for it when we get back to Catorce, then after we get ol' Santos married off, I figure to ride down and pick 'em up."

"The money?" she questioned.

He laughed. "You know, the stuff your papá coins at his mint."

"But where would you get that kind of money?" No sooner had the words left her mouth than she saw a frown crease his forehead.

"I didn't rob a train." His jesting tone turned serious. "I may look like nothing more than a footloose cowpoke who hauls all his worldly possessions in his saddlebags like a turtle in his shell, but that isn't sayin' I don't have a dime to my name."

"I didn't mean it that way."

"Rangers make decent pay, Relie," Santos explained. "They don't get rich, but if they save their money instead of squandering it on women and such, it adds up. Oftentimes they save enough to buy a good-sized piece of land, build up ranches, herds of cattle, that sort of thing."

"I never did," Carson stated simply. "Always intended to, but I never found a place that tickled my fancy enough to cure the itch in my feet. My gold's in the bank down in Austin."

"I didn't mean I thought you were . . ."

"Down-and-out?" he questioned. "Don't much blame

338

you, seein' how you found me in jail and all." He scratched his three-day growth of beard, eyeing her in a teasing manner. "Speakin' of which, I sure could use a shave."

She had been cleaning the skillet, packing the utensils they used for supper when he said the last. Their gazes locked; remembrance ran hot between them, bringing a flush to her cheeks.

In defense, she threw the dish towel at him. It wasn't what she wanted to do, of course. They both knew that. But again they crawled into separate bedrolls.

That night she dreamed of horses. Arabian horses. Herds of them roaming the Texas prairie. And of Carson and herself and their children.

How many children? She awoke while counting.

Chapter Seventeen

They rode into Catorce with the problem at Mina Mazón foremost on their minds — that and Aurelia's safety, which worried Carson most of all.

"Until we nail down the difficulty," he told them after they emerged from the tunnel onto the brick-lined main street of Real de Catorce, "I think we had best keep everything we have learned between the three of us."

"You mean everything we have not learned," Santos corrected.

"Hmm." Carson exchanged glances with Aurelia. "And everything we have planned . . . and not planned."

"Carson — ?"

Before she could object further, he explained. "We can't afford to rock the boat. Your parents wouldn't believe any of this right now, anyway. Wait until we have proof."

"That makes sense, Relie."

"In the meantime, it's best if — I can't believe I'm telling you this — it will help if you keep up appearances with Enrique."

Her chin went up. "No."

"If we call their hand too soon, they may go into hiding," he argued.

"How long?"

He shrugged.

Her eyes pierced him. "Tía Guadalupe is determined to announce my betrothal to Enrique at Santos and Pia's wedding reception."

Carson held her gaze steady. "We'll solve the mine difficulties before them."

"The place to start is at the mine," Santos suggested.

Carson shuddered. "That place gives me the all-overs." He glanced sheepishly at Santos. "No offense, partner, but I don't see how a man stands working inside a mine day in, day out."

At Santos's amused expression, he hurried to explain. "That doesn't mean I don't intend to go through with this thing. I'm ready to put it behind us."

When Santos continued to stare past him, Carson turned to see Aurelia gripping the pommel of her saddle.

"What is it, angel? Are you all right?"

She nodded. Loose strands of hair fell around her face. Confused, he reached to brush them back.

"Is it what I said? I didn't mean to offend you. I mean, about your father's mine and . . ."

"She's all right," Santos interrupted.

Carson turned to find Santos's eyes dancing with amusement.

"Don't worry about her," Santos repeated. "She just discovered she may have to accept my help after all."

Aurelia shot him a spiteful glance that further confused Carson. "Don't listen to my brother," she replied dismally.

When they reached the gates leading into the Mazón

stable yard, Santos again broached the subject of the mine.

"Think we should ride over there after we drop Relie off? Since we're mounted and all?"

"No!" The word erupted in chorus from Carson and Aurelia.

"Hey!" Santos held up both hands. "Don't jump on me. What did I do?"

"You cannot go to the mine before you see Pia," Aurelia informed him.

"She's right," Carson added. "For a man about to get himself hitched, you don't act very anxious to . . . ah. . ."

"I get the message, compadre. No need to draw me a picture."

Carson and Aurelia laughed, and when they drew their mounts to a stop inside the stable yard, Carson came around and lifted her from the saddle.

His hands, warm and sensuous, spanned her waist, bringing a surge of memories and dreams.

She lifted her lips to the brush of his own, savoring the brief contact, desiring so much more, filled with alarm at what lay ahead for them.

Not in the distant future, however. Their future would work itself out once the difficulties at the mine were settled. She knew that. Even if Carson decided against running the mint and mine.

Through the years, she, Pia, and Zita had often held deep though unschooled discourses on the meaning of dreams and whether they were forecasters of one's future.

Aurelia recalled her dream about the horses and herself and Carson and their children on the Texas prairie. She wouldn't mind that. With Carson beside her, not even the Texas prairie would be lonesome.

Thoroughly chastised by his longtime partner and his sister, Santos considered himself fortunate that they gave him a chance to grab a bite to eat before hurrying him off to see his fiancée.

"It isn't that I'm not eager to see her," he assured Aurelia. "But when I get headed in one direction on a difficulty, I like to finish the thing."

Aurelia hugged him. "I understand you, Santos. Pia does, too. But you have to consider her before anything else now."

He laughed. "My little sister, teaching me about love."

"Who better?" she challenged. "I'm an expert."

"As of when?"

She smiled sweetly, kissed him on the cheek, and sent him on his way. "Tell her I'm home, and since I am no longer quarantined, I will be over to see her."

To which she promptly received another lecture from Carson.

"I won't have you running around town alone. If you want to go somewhere, ask Santos or me. We will take you."

She tilted her chin in mock defiance. "Or Enrique?"

Pia must have seen him ride up, Santos suspected, for no sooner had he tied his horse at the hitching rail and approached the entrance to the Leal mansion, than the outside gates burst open and she leaped into his arms.

Lifting her off her feet in one swoop, he held her close and kissed her eagerly. Her warm body wriggled against his, enticing, exciting him.

Suddenly, he felt the fool for Relie and Carson having

to prod him to come to Pia. He set her gingerly on her feet, held her face in his hands, and let the light in her eyes infuse him with happiness. It was a light he recognized.

"I don't know how I made it through these last days without you, little one."

In response she pulled his lips to hers, and once more he enfolded her in his arms. Her lips were small, delicate, and the eagerness with which she responded set his body aflame.

Suddenly, a voice called from inside the courtyard. "Pia, who is there?"

Quickly, he released her. Pia frowned and he mimicked it. "It's Santos, Mamá."

"Santos." Señora Leal burst through the gate. "What a relief that you have returned. When will the charros arrive? In time for rehearsal next week, I hope. What about that young man from Texas . . . what is his name? Has he returned as well?"

"Mamá," Pia scolded. "Do not drive him away before the wedding."

Santos laughed good-naturedly. "Everything is taken care of, señora. The charros will begin arriving tomorrow and our family from Guanajuato by the end of the week. Jarrett, my friend from Texas, returned with Relie and me."

"Oh, praise the Holy Mother, Relie has returned, too. I have been so worried. Pia, have you told him about the *charriada?*"

Without waiting for her daughter to reply, the señora rushed ahead. "We have decided on a dinner and baile instead of the *charriada*. Decorators are coming from Potosí to turn our ballroom into a—"

344

"Mamá, it is to be a surprise," Pia interrupted. "Surely we can let Santos catch his breath before we overwhelm him with wedding preparations."

Señora Leal stared from one to the other, as though Pia's suggestion were unheard of. "I suppose —"

Pia interrupted again. "If you don't object, we will walk a while in the garden."

Señora Leal's expression resembled a dervish, Santos thought. He wondered at the chaos inside her head. At Pia's request, her eyes narrowed on Santos.

"If you promise not to cause a stir."

In your garden? he wondered. "Certainly, señora."

"I shall never live down that little scheme involving Padre Bucareli. He called no conference."

Santos's eyes widened. He remembered all too well the day Padre Bucareli called no conference. "I am sorry, señora."

"Go ahead." She shooed them off. "Walk in the garden a bit, then Pia must help me with wedding preparations."

"So Relie returned," Pia mused after they reached the edge of the hillside behind the Leal compound.

"Relie, Jarrett, and I arrived not an hour ago."

"How is she? Did she hate coming back?"

Santos squeezed her hand, which lay in the crook of his arm. His body stirred at the touch of it. "She didn't mind returning at all. I doubt we could have forced her to stay behind, even without . . ." His words drifted off. "She's fine, although she might expire from finding herself head over heels in love."

"In love? With Carson Jarrett?"

He nodded.

"Then it's true," Pia mused. "Oh, I'm delighted. I know you don't think they are right for each other, but —"

"I've changed my mind. Reluctantly, I admit. But seeing them together . . ." He shook his head at the image, then looked lovingly into Pia's eyes. "They are like us," he whispered. "The looks they exchange, the light that fires their eyes every time one or the other enters the room. I tell you Pia, watching them together left me weak with wanting you."

She giggled, snuggled closer to him, then cast a wistful glance toward the house.

"Relie has changed, too," he went on. "She's different . . . more mature." He recalled the harrowing afternoon when he was forced to wait with Tío Luís for the two of them to return. "In some respects," he added.

"She probably isn't much different than she was a month ago, or two months. You see her in a different light now — as a woman, not just your little sister."

"You could be right." He told her about the episode in Guanajuato. "That wasn't responsible thinking on either of their parts."

"Oh, Santos, don't you understand how desperate they were?"

When he looked into her uplifted face, flushed with wanting him, he almost gave in and kissed her right there in her own backyard. "Sí." He cleared his voice to get past the huskiness. "Never more than at this moment."

Santos arrived back at his own house in a querulous mood. "What do you mean Jarrett went ahead to the mine?"

He had found Aurelia in the library with their mother, who was engaged in balancing the household books.

"I tried to persuade him to wait for you," Aurelia ad-

346

mitted. "But he said not to worry, that the mine is full of people."

Doña Bella glanced up from the desk. "Why shouldn't it be full of people? This is a workday."

"No reason," Santos assured her. "I wanted to accompany him. . . ."

"Señor Jarrett is perfectly capable of taking care of himself, although Relie doesn't seem to agree. I have never seen such carrying on. As if the man couldn't find his way to the mine, when he spent a week or more working there before he left for Guanajuato."

"I'll go fetch him, Mamá," Santos mumbled, kissing her cheek. "We won't return in time for luncheon, but we'll be here for dinner."

"I should hope so. Enrique and the girls will be here."

When Aurelia shot him a signal of distress, he chuckled, then kissed her on the cheek, too. "Ready for some help with your life, little sister?"

At her grimace, he turned sober. "Careful, Relie," he whispered with his mouth close to her cheek. "Trust him." He winked. "Trust both of us."

"What was that all about?" Doña Bella questioned after her son left for the mine. "If I didn't know better, I would suspect you two of being up to your old childhood pranks. What are you quarreling about?"

Aurelia laughed. "Nothing, Mamá. You know how fond Santos is of taunting me when he thinks I might need his help to get out of a . . . difficulty."

"What kind of difficulty, dear?"

"Nothing," she repeated. Crossing to her mother's side, she peered over her shoulder, watching Doña Bella add a column of figures. "You kept books for the mine before Enrique came, didn't you?"

"For years, dear."

"Would you teach me?"

Doña Bella laughed in a placating sort of way. "Whatever for, Relie? You won't need such skills. Enrique will continue to keep the books after you are married. He has a brilliant financial mind, you know."

Aurelia groaned before she could stop herself.

Doña Bella eyed her daughter. "What does that mean?"

"I'm a little tired of hearing Enrique's virtues expounded. Tío Luís spoke of nothing else."

"He is fond of the young man, isn't he?"

Aurelia grimaced. *Por Santa Cecilia! Let this ordeal be over soon.* Suddenly, she leaned down and touched her lips to her mother's cheek.

"What was that for?" Doña Bella asked, surprised. "You haven't been one to show affection for years."

"Maybe I have changed," Aurelia mused.

Doña Bella studied her a moment. "It's Pia's wedding. A best friend marrying does things to a girl. Sentimental things."

Aurelia shook her head. "I learned something in Guanajuato."

"What, dear?"

"That I owe you an apology. I haven't appreciated you like I should have."

Flustered, Doña Bella started to object.

"It's true," Aurelia went on. "I wanted to be like Tía Guadalupe, because she lives such a glamorous life — always going to parties and wearing the latest European fashions."

She gazed into her mother's startled eyes. "I missed the meaning of your life, Mamá . . . all the good you do here in Catorce. The way you help the miners' families, the way you work at the church and with the convent school. I should have been patterning myself after you. You are the kind of mother I want to be to my children."

At the sight of moisture brimming in Doña Bella's eyes, Aurelia threw her arms around her neck, a thing she hadn't done since she was a child.

Finally, Doña Bella withdrew a handkerchief from her sleeve and dabbed her eyes. "Are you saying your stay in Guanajuato was not all you expected?"

"I've changed my mind about wanting to live there."

"Oh, child, your Papá was right. He knew you wouldn't mind living in Catorce."

"It isn't the place I live that will determine my happiness," Aurelia agreed. "Only I can do that. And my husband."

Doña Bella fairly glowed. "Enrique will be so happy."

Aurelia turned away, careful this time not to betray herself to her mother. How she wished she could tell her the truth. But she had promised.

"We should have sent you to Guanajuato long ago, then it would have all been settled."

"No, Mamá. I could not have learned the truth any earlier."

Carson didn't know what to expect at the mine. He wasn't even sure why he felt the urge to go ahead without waiting for Santos. He told himself that Santos might not return from seeing Pia before the mine closed for the day, but he knew better. Santos was as anxious as he and Aurelia to have this matter settled.

If he had feared Nuncio Quiroz, his worries would

have been for naught, he discovered upon entering the mine office, for the only trouble Quiroz offered was a hard look. And it was hard, no doubt about that. But the man went about his business, leaving Carson to himself in the office.

By the time Santos arrived, he had succeeded only in confirming a fact he had already known: Without more information than they presently possessed, they weren't going to learn very much.

"We need something to compare these figures with. Dates and facts that aren't in the ledgers, when the goods were discovered missing, things like that."

Santos pulled up a chair and studied the neatly entered figures. "His penmanship is without peer."

Carson chuckled. "His penmanship is without peer? Where in hell did you learn such gibberish?"

"From those books you Rangers carry in your saddlebags, compadre. Shakespeare, Donne, Pope. You think I didn't learn anything on the frontier except how to herd longhorns and catch badmen?"

"It's the badmen we're after now, case you forgot." Carson eyed his friend from top to toe. "That little gal got to you, huh?"

Santos grinned. "*Sí.* Don't know why I needed you and Relie to tell me how the cow ate the cabbage."

Carson nodded sagely.

"Especially not after I spent the last week watching the two of you moon over each other like a pair of lovesick calves."

"That bad, huh?"

"*Sí.* Reckon you'll be able to hide it from the family until we settle this matter?"

"Aurelia can; she's good at disguises. I'm not sure

350

about myself." Carson shrugged, grinning. "Hell, I've never been in love before."

"It becomes you, compadre," Santos teased.

"And yourself, partner. Now, let's get to work."

Santos glanced out the office door. "Seen our friend Quiroz?"

"Once, when I first arrived. He's made himself scarce since then."

"Good. Then he won't see us carry these ledgers out of here."

"What do you figure to do? Burn 'em?"

"Mamá kept these books for years. Maybe she can tell us what we are overlooking." He scooped up the ledgers. "Come on before we get caught stealing from our own mine."

"Your mine, partner. It's none of my own."

Santos grinned. "So you think. Remember back on the road when you spouted off about how much you hate this mine?"

"I didn't say I *hate* it."

"Might as well have," Santos replied in a jovial tone. "You saw Relie's reaction?"

Carson felt something turn sour inside him. "So?"

"So you spoiled her plans for your future."

"Back up a minute. My future?"

"None other. She has the two of you living here in Catorce, you running the mint and mine."

For a moment Carson felt as if the wind had been knocked from his lungs. He walked out of the mine beside Santos, his mind awhirl with nothing but air. No pictures. No thoughts. No solutions.

Santos slapped him on the shoulder. "Cheer up, compadre. All is not lost."

"No? I thought you were on our side?"

"I am."

"Then why is it you always seem happiest when things sour between us?"

True to Santos's word, he and Carson did not return by lunchtime, and Aurelia was forced to endure the entire meal with Enrique fawning over her return, her father despairing over the disappearance of Santos when his son knew he demanded an immediate report on the showing of their bulls in Guanajuato, and Doña Bella bouncing around like a school girl, eager to tell the news that her daughter had explicitly forbade her to reveal, namely that Relie would be content to live in Catorce.

It was the embellishment Aurelia did not want to hear, their expectation that she would live here with Enrique Villasur, which she had no intention of doing.

Fortunately, siesta called. Enrique bid her adiós, saying he would see her at dinner. Her mother and father retired to their chamber, leaving Aurelia alone. Suddenly, she could bear it no longer. She must see Pia and share some — not all, certainly — of her newfound happiness.

She felt herself blush, thinking how naive she had been in urging Pia to seduce Santos. She must apologize for the boldness of it, the gall. Now that she knew what a private, beautiful experience it was to love a man, she was ashamed she had taken it so lightly.

Draping a shawl about her head, she slipped out the door. The Leal mansion was a kilometer or so from her own, but she took her time. Since no one would be out during siesta, she felt safe, knowing she could enjoy the walk in solitude. For the first time she could remember, she looked to the hills with wonder instead of repugnance, with anticipation instead of dread.

By the time she had gone a mere three blocks, she found herself breathing hard. The streets were no more steep here than in Guanajuato, but the air was thinner.

She hugged herself for the pure joy of being home in Catorce, of being alive today, of Carson's being here, of Pia's approaching marriage.

No matter that Carson didn't want to work at the mine. There was always the mint. Or even Texas. She laughed aloud, lifting her face to the blue, blue sky, inhaling deep drafts of cool mountain air.

She wondered what the Texas prairies were like. Santos had come home saying the weather was hot as Hades. She laughed again. It would be hot, all right. With her and Carson in the same country, the temperature was bound to rise.

Then rounding a corner, her reveries stopped short. Her joyous homecoming fell, shattered like a looking glass smashed viciously against a wall.

Her heart pounded.

She fought the chest to which she was pressed.

Dug her head into it.

Kicked her feet.

She bit the arm of Nuncio Quiroz. Jumping away, he stuffed a rolled piece of cloth inside her mouth, then shook her shoulders until her shawl fell to the street. "Make a sound and you are dead."

The words seemed unreal, dreamlike, far away.

"Turn me loose." Her demand died in the foul-tasting fabric inside her mouth. She struggled to free herself, to kick at him. But his superior strength held her easily.

He leered lasciviously at her, his eyes lingering on her breasts until she shuddered with the remembrance of his vile mouth upon them.

"Remember how it felt, Miss Uppity-Uppity? Wet and hot? Next time I will show you a few more tricks."

She tried to scream, felt as if she were choking. Bile rushed to her throat.

"But not today," he continued. "Today I must disappoint you. All you get today is a warning. Tell anybody about that chapel, so much as a hint, mind you, and you are good as dead. You and that brother of yours and his Ranger friend. All three of you. Dead."

He threw her against the building, then released her with all but his eyes. She stared at him, seeing nothing. Her eyelids felt as though they had been propped opened. The cool mountain air dried her eyeballs. They stung.

Her brain felt dead.

Dead.

"Hear me?"

She tried to nod, but even her neck felt paralyzed.

"Don't think we won't do it. There are a lot of ways to kill folks in these mountains. Nobody would ever be the wiser."

She knew he was right. She tried to think.

"And you, *puta*. You will belong to me." Again his eyes traveled her body, resting on her breasts. Suddenly, he grabbed her arms, holding both wrists in one hand while he ran the other over her gown, across her breasts, her belly, and down, cupping his palm against her in a despicable manner, then returning to her breasts, one of which he pinched until she finally managed to squeeze

354

her eyes closed. Her scream was trapped behind the filthy rag stuffed in her mouth.

Then he was gone.

For a moment all she could do was lean against the wall and tremble. When her legs sagged and she began to slide down the wall, she caught herself. By fierce determination, she straightened her back, edging upwards against the rough plaster wall until she stood erect.

For a moment she couldn't open her eyes. Panic gripped her. How would she get home if she couldn't see?

She made it, of course. She forced her eyelids open and made it all the way home and to her bedchamber without seeing another person. Fiercely, she stripped the clothing from her body, wrapped herself in a heavy robe, and fell onto the bed, where she lay until the first bell for dinner sounded.

By the time Aurelia descended the stairs, she had composed herself. Bathed and gowned in yellow faille, she steeled herself behind an outer wall of serenity. She knew what she must do.

She must never tell anyone about her encounter with Nuncio Quiroz. If she did, she could well get either Santos or Carson or both of them killed. It was over, she told herself. She would not go out alone again until the matter was solved. She would take care.

And she would keep her frightening experience a secret.

But when she reached the bottom step and saw Carson sitting on the edge of the fountain, a guitar across his thigh, her resolve faltered. All she wanted was to rush across the foyer and throw herself into his comforting embrace.

To feel his arms around her, holding her tight, loving

her, protecting her. She stiffened at that last thought. She must protect him.

He came to her, offering his hand, singing softly. *"I knew she was an angel who would steal my heart from me."*

Tears brimmed suddenly. Memories flooded her brain. Warm memories, of meeting him in the jailhouse, of him serenading her in the plaza in Guanajuato.

Cold memories, of the first time he had called her angel and of her reply, that she was no angel.

And of the reason she had said it.

As things turned out, it hadn't been true then.

Por Santa Cecilia! It must never become true.

Chapter Eighteen

Through the busy days that followed, Aurelia smothered her horrible secret beneath houseguests and parties and preparations for Pia and Santos's wedding.

The day after their return to Catorce, family members began arriving. Soon the Mazón mansion overflowed with guests. Santos and his attendants—eleven charros and one Texas Ranger—moved to quarters at the rear of the compound, leaving the bedrooms inside the mansion for aunts, uncles, and cousins, all of whom Aurelia wanted to meet Carson.

But although several charros could be found in the house at any given time during the day, strumming guitars and generally enjoying themselves, Carson made himself scarce.

Even at meals, when she was forced to sit beside Enrique and respond graciously to his prattle, Carson remained outside, where he ate at one of the many tables set along the porches to accommodate the overflow of guests.

That he was staying out of sight of the Reinaldos who

arrived a week before the wedding, she knew. She also knew she had never felt quite so lonely as during those hectic days when no matter how busy her hands, no matter how occupied her time by family and friends, no matter how the ever-present Enrique tried to engage her attention, she longed for a glimpse of Carson, for a brief touch of his hand, for the brush of his lips against her own. Finally, she cornered Santos.

"Tell him to at least come to the comedor for breakfast," she insisted.

He shook his head. "It's best this way, Relie. Let everyone think you are going along with their plans for you and Enrique. Direct their attention while Jarrett and I wrap things up. It won't be long now."

She sighed. "Tía Guadalupe has been pressing to have the engagement announced at your rehearsal dance."

Santos squeezed her shoulder. "We won't let that happen. Don't worry."

"I told her it wouldn't be fair to you and Pia. She seemed to understand."

As the days passed, Aurelia lived for the wedding rehearsal. She would see Carson there. She would touch him. Since they were maid of honor and best man, they would stand together, walk up the long aisle arm in arm. And he would dance with her afterwards at the baile. Surely he would dance with her.

The morning of the rehearsal, she awoke with her stomach aquiver, knowing that this day she would be with him, for however brief a time. Even when she ran into Tía Guadalupe on the stairs going down to breakfast, her spirits did not dim.

"You are up early," Aurelia teased.

"To speak with you, dear. We have plans to lay. Bella

and Domingo agree that the announcement will be made tonight."

"But —?"

"I know how you feel, Relie. You are thoughtful to consider your brother, to be sure, but it isn't fair to your uncle and me. Think about it. We want to be present for the announcement. You cannot expect us to travel all this way again in such a short time."

"It doesn't have to be a short time, Tía."

Guadalupe hugged an arm around Aurelia's stiffened shoulders, guiding her downstairs to the comedor, which was vacant of diners except for Don Domingo and Luís Reinaldo.

Before Aurelia could but mumble *"Buenas días,"* Tío Luís rose from his chair, drew one for her, and her aunt deposited her in it.

"We have a little something for you, dear," Tía Guadalupe said.

While the two of them perched over her like hawks, her uncle by marriage handed her a jewel case that felt cold and looked familiar.

"Open it, dear. Open it," her aunt urged.

Aurelia stared across the table at her father, her signal of distress either unnoticed or unacknowledged.

"Where is Mamá?" she asked him.

"She is busy, Relie." Don Domingo indicated the jewel box. "Open the gift. Your aunt and uncle are eager to see you open it."

Her hands gripped the box so tightly Tío Luís finally tugged it from her grasp, whereupon Tía Guadalupe opened it herself, setting it in the center of Aurelia's silver service plate. A gray brocade box. Lined with black velvet.

Upon which gleamed the abominable red rubies from Guanajuato.

"These belong to you," Aurelia objected, striving to sound polite for her father's sake.

"They are yours now, Relie," Tío Luís purred, no sign of the belligerence she knew lay hidden beneath all that sugar.

"Your betrothal gift," her aunt added.

Gift? She felt sick. These rubies were not a gift. She recalled with growing trepidation the scene in Guanajuato when she refused to wear them.

These rubies were no gift. They were a bribe . . . a warning for her to cease her resistance, for her to meekly accept the future they had laid out for her.

She wanted to scream, *I will not marry your precious Enrique.*

She wanted to cry.

She clasped cold fingers over her mouth. "Where is Mamá?"

"You must wear that ruby-red dress tonight, dear."

Blood-red, she thought.

Her voice rose. "Where is my mother?"

"In the library with Santos," her father said. "She will be along directly."

Before either of her relatives could speak, she scooped the rubies in her hand, scraped back her chair, and raced to the library.

Seated at the desk at the far end of the room, her mother studied a set of ledger books. Santos stood over her left shoulder. Carson stood to the other side.

They glanced up at her entrance. She pursed her lips, striving to keep whatever wits she still possessed inside her brain. Quickly, she closed the double doors behind her, felt for the key, found it, and turned it in the lock.

She stood frozen against the door, her eyes pleading with Carson. Suddenly, he was there. Crossing the room, he stopped in front of her. His hands, his warm, loving hands, grasped her trembling shoulders.

She fell into his arms.

She heard her mother's voice. "Relie, what — ?"

Then Santos's voice. "Bring her over here, Jarrett."

With his strong arm supporting her, Carson walked her the length of the library, halting across the desk from her mother, who had now risen and watched the procession with a deepening frown.

Aurelia threw the rubies to the desk. They landed in a heap on top of the ledger book. Her mother stared, startled. Santos gaped.

Carson swore beneath his breath. "From Guanajuato?"

"You sold your daughter for these?" she demanded.

Tears streamed from her eyes. Her breath came short; she felt faint. Suddenly, she was in Carson's arms, clutching him about the waist, her face buried in his chest, sobbing her heart out. His hand smoothed her hair, patted her head. His voice soothed.

"What is going on?" Doña Bella demanded.

Santos's voice rumbled behind Aurelia, but all she could think was that she had found Carson. She drew her head back. "We can leave. We won't let them do this. We can leave now."

"Shh," he murmured. "Of course we won't let them do it."

"But, Relie, you . . ." her mother began, then stopped. "You said you wouldn't mind living in Catorce. Why do you object to the announcement tonight?"

"Sit her down, Jarrett," Santos instructed. He turned to his mother. "She isn't going to marry Enrique. As soon as we get these books figured out, she and Jarrett plan on getting married." He looked at them where they sat side by side on the settee. Carson dried Aurelia's tears with his handkerchief. "They may live in Catorce; then again, they may not."

Doña Bella sank to her chair. "I don't understand anything you said."

"We need to keep things quiet until we figure out what's happening at the mine," Santos went on. He glanced at Carson. "Looks like we have about all the pieces, don't you think?"

"We have guesses, no proof," Carson answered.

Doña Bella stared aghast from her son to her daughter and their guest. At length, she started to rise. "I am going for your father."

Santos gently pushed her back to her chair. "No, Mamá. Not yet."

"But you can't think—?"

"Like Jarrett says, we have no proof."

"Proof of what?" she demanded, clearly aggravated now.

"That Tío Luís has been stealing from the mine."

Doña Bella turned pale. "You are right about that. Domingo certainly would never believe such a thing. Neither do I."

"That's what they mean, Mamá." Aurelia leaned back on the settee. Carson had moved to a more acceptable distance, but she still clutched his hands in both of hers. "You can't go to Papá until we have proof. He would tell Tío Luís and Enrique and—"

"Enrique?" Her mother's eyes widened.

362

"You discovered the discrepancies between the ore that was mined and the ore that was minted," Santos told her.

"Errors in recording, not discrepancies. You know better than to question such things," Doña Bella defended. "All ore does not test—"

"This did. We have the assay reports."

"But how could Enrique have managed something so despicable? He didn't even work at the mine. A theft cannot be accomplished with books alone."

"They had a man at the mine. Nuncio Quiroz. Likely, he was involved in the mine's problems even before Tío Luís sent Enrique."

At Quiroz's name, Aurelia tensed in spite of herself. She gripped Carson's hand so tightly he responded.

"It's all right," he soothed. "You won't have to see him."

She felt new tears roll from her eyes; she squinched her lids together.

"If you persist," Doña Bella worried aloud, "the wedding will be ruined, and the rehearsal as well."

"No," Santos told her. "With what we know now, there's a possibility we can wrap things up by tomorrow."

"Tomorrow is your wedding, Santos." Doña Bella's voice quivered.

"Mamá," he soothed in a lighthearted tone, "you know the groom is not allowed to see his bride on the wedding day. I'll have the whole day free."

Doña Bella shook her head as if to rid it of such preposterous thoughts. Then she clutched it in her hands. "You must be wrong. You must be. Not Guadalupe's husband. Not Enrique."

"What we need is a way to call their hand," Santos was saying. "If we could discover where they hid the ore and coins in transit, we could—"

"I know where," Aurelia said suddenly.

All eyes turned to her.

"In the chapel. That's what he meant."

"What who meant?" Carson asked.

"Nuncio Quiroz."

His hands tightened around hers. "Don't think about that man. You won't ever have to see him again."

She stared into his distraught face. His warm brown eyes, so full of love, soothed her. She had fully intended to keep her meeting with Nuncio Quiroz a secret for life, but before she realized it, she had blurted out the entire story.

By the time she finished, tears again streamed from her eyes. She wiped at them fiercely, her hands meeting Carson's as he, too, attempted to stem the flow with a wet handkerchief and callused fingers.

"Relie, we told you not to go out alone," Santos accused.

"It's all right," Carson soothed. "It's over. He won't bother you again."

Fear flooded her senses. She stilled Carson's hands with her own, holding them to her face while her eyes pleaded with him. "You won't go after him?"

Their gazes locked. Messages of fear and sensuality created an aura around them, shutting out everyone else in the room. "Not until this is over, angel. Then I plan to whip him within an inch of his life."

"And I'll be right behind you," Santos vowed.

"Children!" Doña Bella raised her voice above the others. "I demand an explanation." She stared hard at Aurelia and Carson, missing not a thing. "For everything."

They told her, for the most part, about the holdup, the breakout, the abduction — which was not an abduction but a measure to save Aurelia from the clutches of Nuncio Quiroz — by the prisoner who was none other than Carson himself.

"Relie? How could you?" Doña Bella propped her elbows on the desk and held her head in her hands.

Santos brought them each a glass of brandy, holding his mother's while she dabbed her face with a lace-edged handkerchief.

"So you see, you cannot tell Papá until we gather enough facts to prove the case against them," Santos was saying.

Doña Bella stared into the center of the room for ever so long. Finally, she heaved a great sigh. "All right. Here is what we will do. You two" — she indicated Santos and Carson — "may have today and tomorrow to gather your facts. After that, I will tell Domingo, whether you are ready for me to or not. And you must attend all wedding functions," she added, then turned to Aurelia. "You will remain beside me at all times, except when Pia needs you. And you will be escorted to and from this house."

Carson listened, amazed, unsure whether they had been chastised or issued marching orders from their general. He saw in a flash where Aurelia got her penchant for clandestine activities.

"As for the two of you . . ." When Doña Bella stared again at Aurelia and Carson, he thought her expression might have softened — a little. " . . . we will discuss that problem after we settle everything else."

"*Sí, Mamá,*" Aurelia whispered, bringing her hands, twined with one of Carson's, to her lips.

"Now for the plan?" Santos questioned.

"I will tell Guadalupe that we must hold off the betrothal announcement, that we simply cannot interfere with Pia's wedding," Doña Bella schemed. "After all, we must make a good beginning as in-laws. I will suggest we travel to Guanajuato after the wedding for the betrothal announcement."

"Brilliant," Santos beamed.

Carson smiled. By that time they would have taken care of Enrique and there would be no betrothal announcement.

"No," Aurelia objected. *"Excusame, Mamá.* Your plan is brilliant as Santos said, but we would stand a better chance of drawing them out by tomorrow if I tell Enrique tonight that I won't marry him."

For a long moment the library remained quiet, while they considered Aurelia's suggestion. Finally, Santos shook his head.

"No, Relie. You are thinking with your heart. We must—"

"She's right," Carson interrupted. "The key to this whole shebang is to make them angry enough that they make a mistake."

Aurelia agreed. "We learned in Guanajuato that nothing will make Tío Luís as angry as the thought that I might refuse to marry Enrique."

Doña Bella inhaled a heavy sigh. "You are saying Luís wants control of this business your father spent his lifetime building? Whatever for? He is a successful businessman himself."

"We don't know the answer to that, Mamá," Santos admitted. "He is a powerful businessman. Perhaps he wants the business for Enrique."

"What is Enrique to Don Luís?" Carson questioned.

The three Mazóns studied one another, then shrugged in turn.

"A financial wizard," Doña Bella repeated the oft-spoken phrase. "Luís found him for Domingo."

"He studied at the University in Madrid," Santos added.

"And learned his trade in the mines in Peru," Carson added. "Where did Don Luís meet him?"

"In the City of Mexico," Doña Bella replied. "Enrique is from a well-established family. They helped Domingo obtain permission to establish the mint."

"But you have never met them."

"No, Luís arranged . . ." Her words drifted off. "It cannot be true. Not Luís. He has everything he could need or want . . . money, power. Why, he is spoken of as the next governor of Potosí."

"Where does his money come from?" Carson asked.

The three Mazóns again exchanged anxious glances. Doña Bella cradled her head in her arms.

Santos spoke in hushed tones, his hand on his mother's head. "Now you understand why it is important that you not tell Papá until we find proof."

"*Sí, hijo,*" she replied. Carson recalled the way Don Domingo persisted in referring to Enrique Villasur as *son.*

Doña Bella regained her composure. "Run along now, both of you. Relie and I have work to do for the rehearsal and baile tonight."

Before he and Santos left the room, Carson approached the desk with Aurelia's hands still clutching his. "I know this is" — he glanced down at Aurelia, then back at the stricken woman — "unexpected, señora. As soon as we settle the mine trouble, I will speak to you and Don

Domingo about your daughter. Aurelia and I love each other. Like Santos said, we want to be married."

Aurelia stood beside her mother watching them leave, her heart in her throat. Doña Bella drew her to her side with a loving arm.

"So that is what changed your mind about Guanajuato?"

"Sí, Mamá."

Doña Bella inhaled heavily. "It cannot be, daughter. Your papá will never approve. He is not of our faith, this Texas Ranger."

In the end she wore the red dress to the rehearsal, with its matching stole draped high about her neck to hide the gaudy rubies. It also hid, she hoped, the two fears that grew insidiously inside her heart: the fear that Nuncio Quiroz would carry out his threat to harm Carson and Santos, and the new fear that her parents would find a way to destroy her relationship with this man whom she loved more with every passing day.

As dusk settled over the high mountain peaks, the entourage of wedding participants made their way from various points in Catorce to the cathedral. The brilliant red and gold of the sunset invigorated Aurelia, adding to the urgency she felt to get on with her mission for the evening: to tell Enrique that she did not intend to marry him.

When she stepped from the carriage in the blood-red gown, the vibrant sunset streamed across her dress, illuminating the red fabric in sprays of iridescent hues.

Outside the enormous double doors of the cathedral, the charros waited for the rehearsal to begin.

Carson stood among them, talking, laughing, his Stetson dwarfed by their sombreros, as it had been at the *charriada*. When she gathered up her skirts to climb the steps, his eyes traveled her length, sweeping her body as with the heated rays of the setting sun. She expected him to come to her, to offer his hand and escort her inside the cathedral.

Instead, he suddenly averted his gaze. Before she could reach the vestibule, he and Don Rodrigo Fraga disappeared inside.

"Hola, Relie." Enrique's voice pierced her reveries. The instant he took her elbow, her slippers ground to a halt, reminding her of a burro who, when prodded, often braced its legs and held its ground.

Inside the church, Enrique waited politely for her to dip her fingers in the Holy Water, then he did the same.

Her mother's words reverberated through her already-muddled brain. *He is not of our faith, this Texas Ranger.* Well, here was one who was of their faith and look what he had done — lied to her father and stolen from her family.

Her mother and Tía Guadalupe were fast on their heels. She could hear Tía Guadalupe whining about Santos. "He said he wanted only charros in the wedding. That Norteamericano certainly is not . . ."

"Relie, over here," Zita called.

Aurelia broke from Enrique's grasp and hurried toward Zita and the other bridesmaids, who were babbling in one corner of the vestibule while Pia's mother busily instructed them.

"You will go last, Relie. Just before Pia."

"Sí," Aurelia acknowledged.

"Do not forget to straighten Pia's train when she

reaches the altar," Señora Leal instructed. "And again before she comes back down the aisle."

Aurelia nodded, her eyes on Pia. "Are you excited?"

Pia held forth two shaking hands, which Aurelia immediately took in her own.

"This is only rehearsal, silly. Wait until tomorrow to be nervous."

The organ music sounded. The choir began to sing.

Aurelia glanced behind her. Thankfully, Enrique and the Reinaldos had entered the cathedral.

"What are they doing here?" Zita questioned.

"Birddogging me," Aurelia sighed.

"When will you tell him?" Pia questioned, rocking from foot to foot.

"Hurry, girls," Señora Leal called. "The processional."

One by one the bridesmaids began the long walk down the aisle of the grand cathedral.

Zita lifted an edge of Aurelia's stole, revealing the rubies. She cringed. "They *are* garish."

Aurelia craned her neck to see down the aisle. From the interior of the cathedral came the padre's voice, instructing the wedding party.

Then it was Zita's turn. "When are you going to tell Enrique?" she whispered just before she stepped off.

"Tonight," Aurelia called after her. "At the end of the dance."

Zita had time for no more than a wrinkled nose, but Pia scolded her from behind.

"Tell him at the beginning of the baile, Relie. Then you can dance all night with your handsome Ranger."

The padre signaled Aurelia and she stepped into the aisle, walked slowly toward the great golden altar. Tomorrow it would be banked with flowers.

Tomorrow the cathedral would be filled with people.

Tonight Carson stood at the end of the long aisle, wearing his black silk suit, standing as straight and as proud as if he were sitting in his saddle atop Sunfisher. He beckoned Aurelia with his eyes, and she could not tear hers away from him. She marched, step by halting step, praying she would not trip, so out of pace was the slow majestic music with her racing heart.

When she neared the end of the aisle the padre spoke to Carson, who stepped forward, offering his arm. She wanted to run to him, yet at the same time she savored the intense joy that suffused her as he slowly drew her to him with his eyes.

Reaching him, she slipped her hand in the crook of his elbow. Even through the layers of shirt and jacket, Aurelia felt warmed by the touch of him. How different from the way Enrique's touch had affected her outside the cathedral.

"Have you ever been inside a cathedral?" she whispered suddenly.

Carson's eyes held hers, warm, sensual, playful.

"I have now." He turned them toward the altar. She genuflected, he bowed, then they separated to make room for the bride and groom to stand between them.

She glanced at him once more before turning her full attention to Pia. Nothing could separate them now. Not this space. Not the church. Nothing. Neither Enrique, nor her parents, nor even time itself.

At the padre's instructions, she left Carson, walked with Rodrigo to the altar, and returned to Carson, all as if in a trance. She would tell Enrique tonight. She would tell him tonight, then she and Carson could plan their life together.

Their wonderful life together.

Suddenly, the rehearsal was over. Padre Bucareli's voice startled her out of her reveries with the instruction to see to Pia's train.

She stared at the carpeted floor, momentarily disoriented.

"Tomorrow, Relie," the padre prompted. "Tomorrow evening at the wedding, do not forget to help Pia around with her train."

Pia and Santos strode briskly up the long aisle, headed toward the cathedral doors, and Carson stepped into the space that had separated them.

The padre shooed them down the aisle. *"Andale,* Relie, take his arm."

Carson grinned. He offered his elbow.

She took it, her heart skipping to the faster beat of the recessional.

"I'm going to tell Enrique at the beginning of the baile."

He studied her, his eyes slicing through her loneliness and fear.

"Is that all right?" she asked.

"More than all right," he whispered in a husky voice. Before they reached the vestibule, he questioned. "Where?"

She shrugged. She had worried over the words she would say; she hadn't considered where she would say them. But thinking on it, she knew she could not reveal such a thing in the middle of the dance floor.

"Be sure you let Santos and me know where," Carson cautioned. "We don't want you alone with him."

"Hey, come on, you two," Santos called. He and Pia stood in the doorway of the cathedral, waiting for the charros to form an arch of sombreros for them to walk

372

under. Carson hurried to take his place; again his smaller Stetson was dwarfed by the sombreros.

The Reinaldos engulfed her. Although she was able to refuse their offer to ride in their carriage, she could not very well refuse Enrique's suggestion that he ride in the carriage with her and her parents.

Since the baile was to be held in the Mazón ballroom, they headed straight home. Doña Bella was in a rush to complete last minute details.

"Relie and I will walk in the patio, señora," Enrique suggested after they alighted from the carriage.

For a moment, Aurelia was afraid her mother had forgotten her promise under the weight of party preparations.

"No," Doña Bella finally said. "I need Relie's help, Enrique. Be a good soldier and help Domingo greet our guests."

As things turned out, she did not see Enrique again until the dancing began. The ballroom was filled with people seated around the perimeter in little gold chairs at small white-clothed tables, sipping champagne and indulging in the abundant supply of seafood Doña Bella had shipped in from Veracruz for the occasion.

But Aurelia remembered the room as it had been the day she sent for Carson. It had been empty then, except for the two of them, and instead of candles on the chandeliers, the room had been lighted by sunshine — and the glow of their love. Guests though they were, this crowd of people seemed an affront to the sanctity of her private place. She stared across the room at her aunt and uncle . . . some more than others, she thought.

Much to her chagrin, Tía Guadalupe and Tío Luís had taken a table of honor at the edge of the dance floor near the orchestra, at Papá's invitation, she knew.

During the long afternoon of waiting and worrying, Aurelia had begun to wonder how her father would take Luís Reinaldo's betrayal . . . and Enrique's. Did Papá suspect what they were up to? If not, he was certainly in for a big surprise.

The orchestra tuned its instruments. Don Domingo strode to the podium, from where he toasted the bride-to-be, setting off a series of toasts. The first dance was announced for members of the wedding party only, but Carson was nowhere to be seen.

Aurelia pursed her lips, searching the room for him, chagrined that he would miss the one dance during the entire evening when he was expected to be her partner. She turned away, straight into Enrique's arms.

"Allow me, since that Norteamericano does not know what is customary in our country."

Her brain whirred when he swept her onto the floor. Was this the time? Should she direct him to a corner and tell him now?

"I'm pleased you agreed to let Don Luís make the announcement tonight," he was saying.

She glared at him, then swept the room with her gaze, searching for Carson. Santos, of course, danced with Pia. Perhaps she should wait.

"My father will make the announcement," she replied. "As is *customary.*"

He babbled on, talking about the rubies, her gown, their plans.

Their plans? His plans. Tío Luís's plans.

The dance ended with her considering whether to take Enrique into a corner and break the news. Before she could decide, however, Santos and Pia approached.

"How about changing partners?" Santos asked Enrique, adding, "For one dance only. I should dance with my little sister once tonight."

He whirled her around the room. His grace filled her with pride. Brawn usually denoted a fighter, not a dancer.

"It's the years of fighting that taught me how to move like this," he enjoyed telling skeptics.

She squeezed his hand. "I'm so happy for you and Pia. You are perfect for each other."

His playful eyes turned serious. "Jarrett is on the balcony, back to the left behind those heavy wisteria vines."

Her pulse quickened.

"Take Enrique out there during the next dance. When you finish, stay on the balcony. Send him back inside alone. I'll stand by in here to see what happens."

Aurelia swallowed against a suddenly dry throat. "Stop and let me get a drink."

Santos took two glasses of champagne from a passing waiter. "You all right?"

She nodded, sipping. "What did you find out today?"

"Kino and Joaquín took us down in the chapel." He pursed his lips. "Relie, I can't believe you really went down there. . . ."

"Santos, please. Chastise me later. Right now, let's concentrate on getting out of this with our hides."

He squeezed her shoulders. "We will, Relie, and with a whole lot more." His voice suddenly lightened. He fingered the rubies. "But probably not with these."

She grimaced. "I can't wait to get rid of these gaudy things."

When the dance ended, Enrique returned Pia to Santos. The two men talked, about what she didn't know.

375

Her head swam with what she would tell Enrique, with what the consequences would be.

At the first strains of the next set, she caught his arm. "Would you escort me to the balcony?"

"Sure thing . . . ah? . . ." He glanced to Santos, questioning.

"Go ahead," Santos replied jovially. "I'll have my eyes on you."

Aurelia inhaled a quivering breath. Trust Santos to add levity to such a moment. Enrique held the door for her. The starlit night swallowed them up.

She crossed to the rail, glancing right, then left. Her gaze lingered half an instant on the wisteria before she drew her attention back to the situation at hand. Knowing Carson was nearby gave her courage.

"Those rubies are perfect —" Enrique babbled.

"I'm not going to marry you, Enrique."

"What?"

"You heard me."

"You don't mean that. Why, Don Luís said —"

"Tío Luís does not speak for me. I speak for myself. There will be no announcement tonight. There will no announcement — ever." She stopped, breathless.

"It's that damned Norteamericano," he spewed. "He has come between us."

"He has nothing to do with it. I don't want to marry you."

"But you said — ?"

"I never said I would."

"Your father — ?"

"My father does not speak for me, either."

"Relie! That's blasphemy."

She sighed. "I agree it is *un*customary. But that's how it

376

is. I . . . I think you should resign your position at the mint. Monday morning."

"Resign? Now wait a minute."

"You were hired to run the business — as my husband."

"That isn't true."

"It is," she repeated. "But even if it weren't, you have no reason to stay now. Papá wants control of the mint to stay in the family."

"That gringo?"

"I doubt it. Nevertheless, you should leave. Tío Luís can find you another position."

"You'll regret this, Relie."

Reaching behind her neck, she unhooked the clasp and handed him the ruby necklace. "Please return these to my aunt."

"Relie, you'll be sorry."

She sighed again. "Not as sorry as we both would be if I married you. Now, why don't you go back inside? Feel free to enjoy the baile for as long as you wish."

"Enjoy the baile? You fling my proposal of marriage in my face, expect me to resign my position at the mint, then tell me to enjoy myself." He juggled the rubies in his palm. "You won't get away with this, Aurelia Mazón. Don Luís will set you straight."

"Let me set you straight. Tío Luís does not control me or my family, regardless of what he or you might think. Now go, please, before you are the one who is sorry."

He stuffed the rubies in his pocket and stomped back inside the ballroom. Aurelia stood gripping the rail, until at length she felt Carson behind her.

He reached around her shoulders, removed her hands from the rail, and drew her back behind the wisteria vines.

"You did fine, angel." He pulled her tightly against him.

She buried her face in his silk jacket, while he ran a hand up and down her back, slipped it beneath the red stole, and massaged her through the boning and ribbing of her costume.

She squeezed her eyes tightly closed until the urge to cry subsided. She lifted her face to his. "I didn't know it would be so hard."

He feathered soft kisses across her face.

"He seemed so human," she continued. "Like it mattered to him."

Carson stopped, staring deeply into her eyes. "He'd be a damned fool if it didn't matter." Then his lips descended with purpose, and she gave herself up to his kiss.

How she had longed for his touch. Her arms went around him, drawing him near. Her lips opened to his search. "Does this mean we won't have to stay apart anymore?" she sighed.

"After tonight," he mumbled against her heated skin. "The parties are tonight, remember?"

"I will be at Pia's. Maybe later . . ."

He laughed, then gave her a big smacking kiss. "Santos's bachelor party is out of town at your father's lodge. I can't let him down."

From behind the vines they heard the balcony door open. Footsteps crossed to the railing. Carson drew her face to his chest, holding her head protectively in the palm of one hand.

"Hey, you two. We got a reaction."

At Santos's voice, they stepped from behind the vines.

"He made a beeline for Tío Luís, whispered something in his ear," Santos related. "Tío in turn spoke with

378

Tía Guadalupe, whose face froze in an expression of pure anguish. Then the three of them stormed from the ballroom."

Aurelia caught her hand to her breast. "You aren't going to follow them? Please don't . . ."

"Not tonight, angel. We promised your mother we wouldn't skip the wedding festivities."

"They can't do much without us finding out," Santos told her. "We hired Kino and Joaquín to watch Quiroz's house. All we can do now is wait for somebody to make a move."

"In the meantime, partner, you had best get back in there and dance with your bride-to-be." Carson squeezed Aurelia to his side. "And I intend to dance with mine."

At Carson's insistence, Santos slipped back inside the door to signal the all clear.

"I have enough strikes against me with your father as it is," Carson told them. "Don't need to be caught spoonin' on the balcony."

"Spoonin'?" Aurelia asked after he approached her inside the ballroom, requested a dance, and twirled her onto the dance floor.

"Say that again," he prompted. His warm brown eyes danced as merrily as his feet, causing her heart to skip at the sight of them.

"Spoonin'?" she asked.

"You sound every bit the Southern belle, ma'am."

Laughter bubbled from deep inside her. "I don't even know what it means."

"Spoonin' means courting." He twirled her in great circles around the room.

Her feet fairly flew, until one corner of her stole, which had wound itself around her body, slid unnoticed

379

to the floor. Her feet caught in it. She stumbled.

He caught her, juggled his own feet a bit, and found his footing. When he saw the stole dragging the floor, he ceremoniously unwrapped her and tossed it to an empty chair beside the dance floor. "That thing almost hog-tied us."

She laughed again for the sheer joy of it. Then in the next moment, her heart fluttered at the sensual gleam in his eye.

"I like you better without those damned rubies."

She wanted to squeeze him to her, she wanted to kiss him. She wanted it desperately. She wanted him desperately.

When they passed a door they both recognized, she nodded toward it, her eyes beckoning. "I'll meet you in our room at the end of the hall."

His feet missed a beat. He squeezed her hand. "You don't know how tempting that is."

"Yes, I do," she whispered.

"But since I'm courting *you* now, I will make the arrangements." He laughed. "And they will be designed to protect your good name."

She tilted her chin. "I liked my way better."

"So did I." His husky voice revealed his own impatience.

The baile ended early, since the big day lay ahead.

"Remember what we told you," Carson warned when they finished the last waltz. "Stay with the crowd. Not just one or two girls, but all dozen. Surely a dozen dizzy bridesmaids can quell any harebrained schemes you come up with."

"You don't think I take this seriously?"

His hand tightened on her waist, his eyes delved into

380

hers. "I know you do, angel. But I can hardly stand to go off and leave you unprotected."

She grinned. "Like you said, a dozen dizzy bridesmaids . . ."

Chapter Nineteen

Pia's wedding day dawned on a dozen sleepy bridesmaids and one very nervous bride. They were awakened by a maid who gently shook Pia.

"Señorita, your mamá says you must arise if you are
to finish the preparations."

Aurelia, who shared the bed with her friend, sat up
at the voice. She watched Pia run a small hand through
her disheveled hair.

"Did you sleep at all?" Aurelia questioned.

Pia's expression, a combination of awe, expectation,
and fear, bordered on hysteria.

"Not a lot." She began to vigorously pat her face,
pinch her cheeks. "Oh, Relie. We shouldn't have stayed
up so late. My eyes will be lost in dark circles. I won't
be able to see to walk down the aisle."

"Yes, you will." Aurelia jumped from the bed. "Stay
right there. I'll fix you up."

Pia moaned. "That usually means trouble."

"Not today. Today I promise to be good as gold." She
issued orders to the maids, who were busy setting out
juices and pan dulces for the roomful of sleeping girls.

Stepping over first one heap of clothing, then another, she returned to the bed bearing two glasses of orange juice. "Drink this. I sent the maid to fetch compresses for your eyes."

As soon as Pia sat up, Aurelia began fluffing pillows and stuffing them behind her. "Lean back now. Drink this and try to relax."

Pia obeyed, then reached for Aurelia's hand. "By the end of this day, we will be sisters."

Aurelia hugged her friend, hoping to hide her own fears, which had plagued her through the long, mostly sleepless night. Was Carson all right? Was Santos? Or had Nuncio Quiroz made good his threat?

Desperately, she forced these concerns to the back of her mind, alongside the worry that Papá might somehow destroy her relationship with Carson. Today was Pia's day. She must put aside her own worries and take care of Pia.

After a quick glance at the still-sleeping bridesmaids, Aurelia turned back to her friend. "Are you still frightened . . . about? . . ."

"Later, I probably will be," Pia admitted. "Right now I'm too worried about everything else to think about it."

Aurelia studied her a moment before dropping her eyes to her juice glass. She wanted to reassure Pia. She wanted to tell her not to be afraid . . . that it would be magical and wonderful. But she couldn't say all that without telling Pia about herself and Carson. And she could never discuss something that personal — never again — not even with her best friend.

Except now she had a new best friend. And soon Pia would, too. "Pia, I'm sorry I badgered you. I shouldn't

383

have interfered. It was none of my business, and I . . ."

"You were trying to help, Relie. And you did."

"No, your relationship with Santos is private." She swallowed, studying the bottom of her empty glass. "I didn't realize it, but . . . but I had no business discussing such a thing with you." She gazed into her friend's understanding eyes. "I've grown up a lot. I guess I really needed to."

Pia hugged her around the neck. "Oh, Relie, I'm so glad you have found someone to love."

The maid returned bearing the articles Aurelia had requested: a cold tea made of fresh Yerba Mansa leaves and several pieces of soft cotton wool.

"This feels good." Pia waved toward her sleepy bridesmaids. "You all need compresses. And the men, too, I suspect. They probably need a lot more than cold compresses after drinking Rodrigo's tequila."

For the thousandth time, Aurelia stifled her fears over what might have happened during the night. What had Tío Luís done? And Enrique? And if they had done something, had Santos and Carson been so inebriated on Rodrigo's tequila that they couldn't defend themselves?

The other girls roused gradually. They laughed and talked, teasing Pia, helping her pack for her wedding trip, the destination of which, even though they bedeviled her mercilessly, she refused to reveal.

The house was abuzz with servants and hired workmen who traipsed up and down the stairs, preparing the Leal ballroom for the dinner and baile that would follow the evening wedding.

Sometime around mid-morning, the maid announced a visitor.

"Don Rodrigo Fraga to see Señorita Zita Tapis."

While the other girls speculated on the budding romance, Aurelia had trouble keeping herself from rushing downstairs to quiz Rodrigo about Carson and Santos. Had anything happened during the night?

Zita returned before lunch, dreamy-eyed. "Carson told me I could catch a charro on my own," she told Aurelia. "I think he was right."

"Did Rodrigo mention Santos?" Pia asked. "He didn't drink too much tequila last night, did he?"

Zita shook her head. "None of them did. Relie saved the day."

Anxiety gripped Aurelia. "Me?"

"Your telling Enrique to get lost didn't set too well with your father. He and your uncle burst into the lodge before the groomsmen had time for more than a couple of drinks. So you needn't worry, Pia."

"And?" Aurelia prompted. "What did Papá do?"

Zita shrugged. "Rodrigo said he was angry, no doubt about it. Santos and Carson left with him. The charros have all returned to your house by now."

The plan had been for the girls to return to their homes before siesta. They would meet at the cathedral later in the afternoon, where they would dress together to avoid wrinkling their gowns.

Now Aurelia could hardly contain her eagerness to be on her way, but as she had promised, she waited for a carriage to come for her.

"Don't worry a minute about all this ruining your wedding, Pia. I will take care of everything. You get

385

some rest. I'll see you at the cathedral."

For all her assurances to Pia, however, Aurelia entered her own home with trepidation.

María took her satchel from Serphino. "Your mother wants to see you in the library, señorita."

Her mother? What about the others? Fear rushed through Aurelia's body like a house fire. Where were Carson and Santos?

The doorknob felt cold to her touch; she entered the dark-paneled room with her heart in her throat.

A whiff of cigar smoke struck her a nauseating blow. She looked immediately for Tío Luís, but saw only her mother and father, Carson, and Santos.

Carson and Santos.

Santos stood beside her father at the sideboard; Carson stood apart beside a wing-back chair. She studied him. He looked all right.

But he made no move to come to her, and when she started toward him, Santos intercepted her, guiding her to a chair nearer the desk. He set her down, then perched on the arm of the same chair. She struggled to rise, but he held her in place with a firm hand to her shoulder.

She glanced desperately toward Carson. "What happened? Are you two all right?"

He nodded, an almost imperceptible movement, but the warmth in his eyes reassured her.

Across the room Don Domingo poured a stiff glass of whiskey, downed it, and turned to Aurelia, scrutinizing her silently.

Santos spoke at her shoulder. "We're fine, Relie. Tío Luís, Tía Guadalupe, and Enrique left this morning."

"Left?" she whispered. Across the room, her mother sat with hands clasped in her lap. Her expression held neither anger nor sadness, merely a solemn resoluteness.

Aurelia turned her attention back to her father.

When he spoke, her mouth went dry at the anguish in his voice. "I should turn you over my lap, young lady, for pulling that foolish stunt. Robbing my own train. Twice."

She felt her face flush. It was not what she had expected, what she had feared, yet to be chastised in front of Carson was humiliating enough to make her wish her father had ranted and raved.

"But I suppose I have to thank you for calling their hand," Don Domingo continued. "Until you pulled off those stunts of yours, they were stealing from me and getting away with it. You worried them, Relie."

His tone changed while he spoke. Rebuke gave way, if not to approval, at least to an awareness of the role she had played in saving his business.

"That you did," he repeated. "You had them worried. They didn't want someone else cutting into their profits, stealing from the ore trains."

"They admitted it?" She listened, a bit dazed that while she had fretted the night away, the difficulties had been solved.

"No, Luís would never admit such a thing," her father was saying, "but he hightailed it out of here bright and early, taking along his . . . his protégé." His words drifted away, hanging heavy in the silent room. His hurt became obvious. More even than the loss of silver, he felt the loss of this man he had called *hijo*.

387

"I'm sorry about Enrique," she said.

He stared at her a long time. Finally, he excused them, saying, "Run along now, all of you. We don't need long faces on your brother's wedding day."

"Is it really over?" she asked Carson and Santos in the central patio.

"Looks like it," Santos said.

"How did you convince Papá?"

"Showed him the books and assay reports," Santos told her. "He was hard hit that he had turned his business over to Enrique so completely that he lost touch with the day-to-day working of it."

"What about . . . Nuncio Quiroz?"

"Your father sent him packing," Carson said. "That was the first thing he did after we convinced him of the setup. Said he'd had a hankerin' to do that for a long time, but he had never been able to come up with a good replacement or a good enough reason for letting a family man go."

"Family man." She clasped her arms across her chest to keep their trembling from showing. Carson didn't miss her distress, though.

He ran a palm over the top of her head, resting it on her shoulder. "We didn't tell your father about . . . about the way Quiroz treated you." He grinned, but his eyes remained serious. "Couldn't risk a killing on Santos's wedding day."

"I'm glad. I don't want anything to ruin the rest of this day." She stood on tiptoe and placed her lips gently against his. "Or the rest of our lives."

He responded with a tender but chaste kiss.

Santos cleared his throat. "We didn't tell him about

you and Jarrett, either."

Her face fell.

"It wasn't the time, angel," Carson whispered. Santos left, and Carson kissed her again, this time soundly.

"Are you going to be as understanding with me when I've been hurt as you were with your father back there?" His eyes probed hers, caressing, loving.

"What do you mean?"

"You said exactly what he needed to hear. Telling him you were sorry about Enrique."

"I didn't mean—"

"I know what you meant." He kissed her again. "Your father did, too. To discover that the man you handpicked to take over your business and marry your only daughter had been planted by your brother-in-law to steal from you is a hell of a thing."

With the mine problems settled, Aurelia no sooner touched the bed than she fell fast asleep, only to awaken an hour later with a new and terrifying thought.

The wedding would be over tonight. Carson would have no excuse for remaining in Catorce. They had made no plans.

And there was no chance to make them now, she discovered. When she hurried downstairs after siesta, Carson was nowhere to be found.

"I do not know, señorita," Serphino answered her frantic question. "He and Don Santos have gone out."

She considered going to her mother for help, but the moment she saw Doña Bella, concerned by the betrayal of her sister, harried over her last minute toilette, Aure-

389

lia knew she could not add any more weight to those sturdy shoulders.

By the time she arrived at the cathedral, she had forced all thoughts except of this joyous occasion from her mind. "Twelve dizzy bridesmaids . . ." she laughed, telling the girls what Carson had called them the evening before, ". . . and one beautiful bride."

"Oh, I am . . . aren't I?" Pia's sentence ended on a high note of near hysteria.

"I've never seen anyone so beautiful." Aurelia fluffed Pia's mantilla, gently draping it from the high crown of the comb downward, across Pia's satin-clad shoulder. "Don't go getting nervous," she consoled. "You need all your strength to drag this train down the aisle."

The wedding music began, even more majestic and full-bodied than at the rehearsal.

The procession got under way, with one attendant after the other strolling in stately elegance down the long aisle. Their multihued gowns glimmered beneath the light of hundreds of candles.

Zita's time came. Then Aurelia's. Her stomach was knotted with anxiety by the time she stepped off to the beat of the music.

The aisle seemed twice as long as the evening before. Ahead of her Santos stood near the first pew. She caught her breath at this handsome brother whose breadth and height would equal two average-sized men. Silver conchos gleamed across the broad chest of his fitted black charro jacket and down the length of his long-legged *calzoneras*.

When he winked at her, she relaxed a little. Then, as she drew nearer, he stepped ever so slightly aside and her eyes found Carson, although it took her a moment to recognize him. For one terrifying instant she thought a stranger stood in his place.

The stranger stepped toward her, his elbow crooked, his eyes strumming her senses, creating a magical music all their own.

"Definitely," he whispered when she came within range. "Yellow definitely becomes Aurelia."

She took his arm, an arm swathed in the same black as her brother. Across the chest of his tight-fitting charro jacket gleamed a row of conchos, and above them that wry smile that never failed to take her breath away.

He squeezed her hand against his arm. His eyes teased. "You wanted a charro, didn't you, angel?"

Her knees felt weak. He held her steady while they ascended three steps to the chancel. The nearness of him radiated a warmth that lulled her previous fears. His shoulder brushed her lace-covered arm, showering her with the familiar sense of peace she always felt at his side.

But high above them the crucifix taunted her with the knowledge that this man was an interloper. And from behind, she felt her mother's eyes accusing, condemning. *It cannot be. He is not of our faith, this Texas Ranger.*

"Are you all right?" Carson whispered just before Rodrigo took her arm and escorted her to the altar behind Pia and Santos, as they had rehearsed the evening before.

To the altar away from Carson. They knelt, Rodrigo and Aurelia, one to either side of the bride and groom.

391

They knelt before the altar where Carson — *not of our faith* — was not allowed to follow.

They had rehearsed it the evening before. But the evening before she had been consumed by the problem of telling Enrique she would not marry him. Hers and Carson's future had seemed secure — at least, more secure than it did at this moment when she knelt in a place he was not allowed to so much as set foot.

By the time the service was over and Rodrigo returned her to Carson, himself returning to escort Zita, Aurelia's head fairly spun. She clung to Carson fiercely.

"Hey," Carson whispered, seeing tears in her eyes. "I thought you approved of this wedding."

She tried to smile, but not until they stood outside in the arch of the sombreros did she manage to. Standing beside him, she tossed rice on Pia and Santos while he held the sombrero high above their heads. A sombrero, she noticed, not a Stetson.

The customary restrictions were relaxed a bit following the service, when the bridal party was allowed to ride to the Leal mansion without dueñas, two couples to a coach. Riding in the carriage with Zita and Rodrigo, Aurelia sat silently, squeezing Carson's hand, willing her anxieties to ease.

By the time they reached the reception she had gathered her wits, telling herself that as soon as Santos and Pia left, she would talk to Carson. Together they would work things out. Together.

Escorting her up the stairs to the ballroom of the mansion, he grinned. "If I didn't know better, I might think you had changed your mind about wanting a charro."

Gathering her skirts with one hand, she lifted her chin and matched his stride. "I told you in Guanajuato what I want. All I want is you."

Her voice was so plaintive he halted a moment to study her. "What's wrong with that, angel? Sounds pretty good to me."

She did not speak again until they stepped into the grand ballroom that had been decorated to resemble a Greek garden, complete with fountains, flowers, and tables to accommodate the two hundred guests.

"What will you do tomorrow?" she asked.

"Tomorrow?"

"When you no longer have a reason for staying in Catorce?"

He cocked an eyebrow. "You are my reason for staying in Catorce, Aurelia."

"But? . . ."

"What brought on all this worrying?" he questioned. "You don't think I am planning to run out on you?"

Her lips trembled when she started to speak and she pressed them together.

"Come on," he urged, "let's not ruin the party. You aren't about to get rid of me."

"No matter what?"

He studied her a moment longer, wondering what had happened to suddenly cause her to doubt him. It wasn't like Aurelia to doubt. "No matter what. Not tomorrow. Not ever."

She relaxed then and smiled. The rest of the evening he watched her closely, finding her subdued, wondering at the change in her.

Finally, he teased her out of her melancholy.

First by scrutinizing her gown. "Hmm, yellow definitely becomes you." He fingered her yellow mantilla. "But I liked that gown better in your ballroom."

She felt her cheeks flush under his sensual scrutiny.

"Do you suppose we could find a small room off here somewhere?" he continued.

When he rose to propose a toast to the bride and groom, her heart swelled. He did look handsome in the charro costume. But she preferred him as she knew him best, as a Texas Ranger—her Texas Ranger.

"To the luck of my friend Santos," Carson toasted. "They say every charro needs two things: a good horse and a good woman. Don Rodrigo supplied the horses, a wedding gift, and you, my friend, found a good woman all by yourself. Make her happy."

The crowd cheered. Everyone drank, and he slipped back to his chair. "Same as I intend to make my good woman happy," he whispered.

Her euphoria began to return at his words, at his teasing eyes . . . eyes that begged her to smile, to laugh with him. So he believed their problems had fled with Nuncio Quiroz and Tío Luís. Perhaps they had.

Another toast was given, this one from Don Domingo to his new daughter-in-law. A cheer arose from the charros. When Aurelia turned laughing eyes to Carson, he lifted his champagne glass to her lips and their eyes met across the rim, passing sensual promises through the bubbles.

Everything would work out, she assured herself. With him beside her, everything would work out.

When she left to help Pia dress, Aurelia learned others had been concerned about her dilemma, too.

"I'm so excited, Relie. Santos is telling Carson right now, but he let me tell you." Pia slipped her gown off as soon as Aurelia had the buttons undone, then began to wriggle out of the petticoats.

"We have decided to live in Catorce. Santos will run the mint for your father. And . . ." She paused, stepped into a robin's egg blue serge skirt, and held the band together while Aurelia fastened it from behind.

"Turn around," Aurelia instructed, half listening to Pia's excited babble, the rest of her brain filled with what she would tell her father, how she would convince him that Carson would be her husband, regardless of his faith, regardless of anything.

". . . and you and Carson can run the ranch."

Aurelia lifted startled eyes to Pia's.

"That is all right, isn't it?" Pia questioned. "I know you always said you didn't want to be stuck on the ranch, but—"

Aurelia pressed her lips together, her eyes wide, her heart pounding. "It's a perfect solution." She shrugged. "If Carson agrees."

Suddenly, she became leery. "Whose idea was it?"

"Why, ours, of course."

"What about Papá?

"Don't worry, Relie. It isn't like you." She set a prim blue hat atop her head. "Here, stick a pin in this from behind, will you?"

With numb fingers, Aurelia pinned the hat to Pia's curls. "What about Papá?" she asked again.

"Santos thinks he will be relieved to have both problems solved—the mint and mine here in Catorce, and the ranch."

Aurelia's mind raced back to her mother's warning. *It cannot be. It cannot be.*

"What's the matter, Relie?" Pia asked. "We thought you would be happy. Santos and I—"

Aurelia snapped out of her trance. Clasping her friend's hands in her own, she laughed. "I am happy, Pia. It's your wedding day. Today all my happiness is for you."

And indeed it was. Even when she returned to the ballroom to find her father and Carson in conversation, she refused to let her spirits fall. Her heart skipped a frantic beat at their serious expressions, but when her father slapped Carson on the back, she began to breathe again.

Later, the guests gathered in the courtyard to wave Santos and Pia on their way. Aurelia clutched the bridal bouquet in her arms and felt a tear roll down her cheek.

Carson took her arm. "Come on. Your father gave me permission to see you home."

She stared at him, astonished.

"Don't be too impressed. He and your mother will be right behind us."

"Did you think Relie acted strange tonight?" Pia questioned after she and Santos arrived at the lodge where they were to spend the next week in virtual seclusion, except for a couple of servants who lived in a cottage behind the main house.

The fire had been laid, but otherwise the lodge was

396

deserted. Pia had changed into a frothy white gown and dressing robe, and she sat brushing her hair.

"Women," Santos teased. "I will never understand you. Here we are on our honeymoon, and you want to talk about my sister."

"No, I don't," she answered. "She seemed strange, that's all. She wasn't as excited as I expected her to be about living at the ranch."

"They have a few problems to work out, Pia."

"Such as?"

Santos came up behind her. He took the brush from her hand and stroked the long black strands of her near waist-length hair. Holding her gaze in the looking glass, he ignored her question.

"Tonight when I saw you walk down that aisle with the candlelight burnishing off your satin gown and your eyes gazing right into mine, I thought you were the most beautiful sight in the whole world."

She shivered at his words.

"But now . . ." Laying the brush aside, he pulled her to her feet, turning her to face him. His big hands disappeared in the billowing fabric. ". . . now your beauty leaves me tongue-tied."

His lips descended at the same moment he folded her in his all-encompassing arms. She felt her heart begin to flutter. Frantically, she tried to recall all the things she had rehearsed in her mind—little things to keep her mind off the physical deed that loomed before her.

Stretching on tiptoe, she threw her arms around his neck while opening her lips to his kiss.

Suddenly, he drew back. "You're trembling, little one."

She shook her head to deny it, but her eyes remained wide open. She saw confusion in his eyes.

"Are you afraid?" Santos whispered.

Once again she tried to deny it, but once again she failed. With the most tender of motions, Santos gripped her shoulders and stood her back on her feet. His fingers found the ribbon at the neck of her robe and untied the bow. The frothy fabric fell instantly to the floor, leaving her standing before him in a sheer panel of white lace.

His eyes, wide and filled with passion, traveled her length, sweeping her with great streaks of heat. Although her fear remained strong she felt it begin to slacken beneath a growing sense of expectation.

"Don't be afraid, Pia." His husky voice added to her feeling of detachment. She felt her nipples tighten, and she flushed with the knowledge that he could see them through the sheer fabric of her gown.

Then it was gone, her gown. She felt it drift beneath his hands over her shoulders, down her arms, across her hips, to pool around her ankles. She stood before him, bare as the day she was born, and Pia knew she must surely glow like the sun at midday. Heat like molten liquid flowed through her veins; she felt it hot and moist between her legs, hot and moist and suddenly urgent.

"Say something, Pia." His eyes caressed her face before traveling her length again.

"I . . ." Her voice rasped from a dry throat. "No one has ever seen me unclothed before . . . not since I was . . ."

Santos's hands swept from her face down her neck to her breasts, which he cupped, one in each palm. She felt her nipples, rigid against his roughened palm.

"You are so fine, Pia," he mumbled. "So fine." His hands left her breasts, tracing her ribs, her waist, her hips. Suddenly, he scooped her in his arms and carried her to the bed. Still she trembled.

"Don't be frightened, little one. I promised you this would be worth waiting for. Now I will show you what I meant."

At the bed, he tore back the covers with one hand, depositing her in the center of the feather mattress. When she reached to cover herself with the sheet, he stopped her.

"Let me look at you."

She felt herself blush from the roots of her hair to the tips of her toes.

"Don't be embarrassed." While he spoke, he began removing his own clothing. "I'm your husband. I intend to look at you every day for the rest of our lives." He tossed his shirt aside, removing his boots, then his trousers. "Soon you will enjoy having me look at you."

Her eyes darted down his body, then quickly she averted her gaze. "And you will enjoy looking at me," he told her, "lunk that I am."

His body, large as a mountain, loomed over her, then settled beside her. He traced one hand down her face, across her chest, stopping to cup her taut little belly. "Even when you are big as a melon with my child," he mused, "I will love to look at you." His hand retreated to her breasts, which he fondled, one by one. "And when your breasts are heavy with

399

milk to feed our babes."

His rumbling, melodious voice lulled her into easiness; his sensuous handling caused her body to tingle. His hand left her breast and traveled downward again. This time he didn't stop until his fingers played in the triangle of black hair at the base of her abdomen. Pia flinched.

His lips lowered to hers, where he nipped gently between soft commands. "Relax, little one, relax. That's it. Relax."

Before she knew what had happened, his kisses became demanding, urgent, and she was responding, mesmerized by his gentle coaxing.

When he had slipped his fingers inside her secret moistness she didn't know, but suddenly they were there, stroking her, encouraging her, thrilling her. Then quite by surprise, Pia realized that passion had leaped to life inside her.

"You aren't a lunk, Santos." She spoke as though she had only now found her voice. "You are beautiful and I'm not afraid anymore." Twining her arms around his neck, she played her fingers in his hair. Her lips opened to his quest, and her hips lifted against his hand.

He squeezed her in the crook of his free arm, while his fingers spread and deepened inside her, awakening her passions, measuring and judging at the same time.

"I know what comes next," she whispered. "I'm ready . . ."

"We have all night, little one. I want it to be good for you."

"We have the rest of our lives," she responded. "Let's begin now."

Painstakingly, he arranged her on her back, then positioned himself above her. "You aren't afraid?"

She shook her head, feeling it sway from the passion that engulfed her. Why had she been so foolish? She pulled on his shoulders. "Come to me, Santos." At the same time, she lifted her hips to meet his.

When he entered her small, silky sheath, he knew he was the one who was frightened. She fit him like a glove, one that was two sizes too small. He moved with caution, slipping by increments into her moist interior.

Pia glowed now, not from embarrassment but from wonder. Standing before the altar beside Santos, hearing the padre pronounce them man and wife, had been the most wonderful moment in her life . . . until now. Feeling him move into her, become one with her, watching his face so full of love and passion, she knew this was indeed a moment to savor for all times. Then he stopped.

His face took on a pained expression.

"It doesn't hurt," she assured him.

"It will."

Her brain balked at his words. "No."

He nodded. "There's a barrier. Until it is broken —"

"Then break it. Now." Her words gasped on ragged breath. "Hurry, Santos, so we can enjoy this moment."

He watched her face, flushed now with innocent passion.

"Hurry, Santos," she whispered.

Suddenly, he dreaded what lay ahead. If she had been afraid before, how would she feel after he shattered her body with pain? His own physical demands became secondary, her welfare everything. He wanted

401

to hold her and love her and protect her.

But this damned barrier must be broken.

"Hurry, Santos," she urged.

So he thrust. Deep. And hard. Destroying her innocence and her youth in one great surge. Making her his forever.

When she tensed against the splintering pain that raced from her abdomen straight to her brain, Santos stopped. Lowering himself on his elbows, he nuzzled her face with his lips, soothing her with words, sprinkling kisses into her hair.

After a while the pain ceased, and a while after that she was able to convince him to resume their quest. The end came quickly. When she felt him stop, then finally fall to the side, drawing her with him, she was confused. Her face rested on his chest. She felt his heart race beneath her cheek.

"Why did you stop?" she asked.

With a limp hand, he fluffed her hair. "Ah, little one. The first time is not always good."

"It wasn't good?"

She felt his chest heave a few more times, then he shifted to an elbow. Cradling her head on his arm, he kissed her tenderly. "For me it was wonderful. Next time it will be wonderful for you, too."

"It was wonderful for me," she objected.

"Not like it can be."

"Then let's do it again."

He grinned. "Not so soon. Even if I was able, we should let you rest." As he spoke, his hand traced down her body. His fingers entered her once more, sending shafts of passion racing through her veins. His eyes bore into hers, conveying sensual messages of love and commitment and passion. "How does this feel?"

"Wonderful." Closing her eyes, she let the feeling swell inside her as he plied her to higher and higher peaks.

"This is a taste of how it will be," he was saying, while inside her great swells of passion rose and waned, rose and waned, spiraling ever higher and higher.

Suddenly, the fire he had ignited exploded into a great ball of brilliant light in her brain and spread quickly like lightning through her body. She shuddered in his arms.

He rocked her to him. "Next time that will happen while I'm inside you, and it will be even better."

"Then let's do it again as soon as you are ready." She snuggled into his embrace, where they both soon fell fast asleep.

"What about Relie?" she whispered sometime later, rousing him.

He grunted.

"Relie? What kind of problems must they work out?"

"The church," he mumbled. "Papá will likely give them trouble over the church."

Pia curled into the lee of his enormous body. She smiled. And to think she had been afraid of him.

She thought of Relie's apology for encouraging her to seduce Santos before the wedding. Had Relie been speaking from experience? Quite possibly.

If so, would she regret not saving something so special until her wedding night? Probably not, Pia decided. With the right person, the magic would be the same.

With the wrong person . . . A chill coursed through her body and she snuggled closer to Santos. The story Relie had related about Nuncio Quiroz filled her with anguish.

Santos gathered her into his encompassing embrace, bringing a catch to her throat as she realized that even asleep, he wanted her near.

With the wrong person, it would have been a nightmare.

"What were you and Papá discussing at the baile tonight?" Aurelia asked after she and Carson returned to the Mazón mansion.

Although her parents had gone straight to bed upon arriving home, she and Carson remained behind in the patio. Not that her parents approved, she knew, but they hadn't actually said as much. Nor had they awakened Lucinda to chaperon.

The first thing her mother had done when she stepped inside the patio was to remove her shoes. "I'm going straight upstairs," she said. "No nightcap for me."

She kissed Aurelia, who sat on the fountain's edge.

"You, too, dear. You must be as tired as I am after the week full of parties — and our other difficulties."

"*Sí Mamá.*" Aurelia watched her mother bid Carson good night. Although she neither offered her hand nor went so far as to touch his shoulder, Doña Bella did acknowledge his expertise on the dance floor.

"You made Santos a fine best man, Señor Jarrett. And thank you for that lovely turn about the floor."

"It was my pleasure, señora," Carson replied.

"*Buenas noches.*" Her father kissed her cheek, then

shook Carson's hand. "Good night, Jarrett. Thanks for your help."

Aurelia watched her parents climb the wide staircase, her mother's shoes dangling from two fingers. Suddenly, she thought of Tía Guadalupe, who never emerged from her chamber with so much as a hair out of place, much less barefoot.

"I have been such a fool all my life," she muttered.

"Not since I've known you," Carson said quietly.

From the landing, her father turned to look at them. Aurelia still sat on the edge of the fountain. Carson sat in a chair, a guitar resting across one *calzonera*-clad knee.

"Coming?" her father called.

"*Sí Papá.*" She watched her parents top the stairs, heard the door to their chamber close.

Carson rose, setting the guitar aside. "Guess we had best hit the hay."

Tears rushed suddenly to her eyes. Without replying, she dashed across the patio, not stopping until she reached the privacy of the drawing room, where she turned to wait for him.

He came into her arms, his lips meeting hers, hungrily acknowledging the yearnings that had built inside him. His arms drew her near, nearer, closer to his aching heart. He felt her heart throb against his chest, tasted her salty tears.

Finally, he pulled her face from his, dabbing her tears with his thumbs. "We can't get carried away, angel. Your father could return any second."

"Let's go someplace else, then," she begged. "Please."

He pulled her close, nestling her head to his chest,

rubbing his chin across the top of her head. "That might be foolish on both our parts, considering I haven't asked him for your hand yet."

Her heartbeat quickened. She wanted to cry, *Don't ask him. He will say no.*

With his hands to her shoulders, he guided her to the settee, where he deposited her, then turned to light a lamp on a side table.

She heard him find matches in the enamel box, heard him lift the chimney from the lamp, heard him strike the match. A small halo of golden light cast a shadow about her face.

When he sat beside her, his head blocked the light. He took her face gently in his hands and wiped away her tears with his thumbs. "What's got you runnin' scared?"

"What if he says no."

"Who?"

"Papá. What will you do if he refuses to give his permission?"

Suddenly, Carson felt the earth drop from beneath him, leaving him suspended above a vast black void. A heavy, sickening emptiness engulfed him at the thought of living without Aurelia. With great difficulty, he kept his hands from trembling on her face. Bending forward, he kissed it — her eyes, her cheeks, her lips. "You expect him to refuse, don't you?"

A sob rose in a choking tremble up from her chest. She nodded.

"Then the question is, what will *you* do?" he responded in grave tones.

"I will marry you anyway." She pulled her face from

his hands, burying her head in his shoulder. "Nobody can keep me from marrying you." His gentle hands stroking her head and back only intensified her sobs.

"Why will he refuse?" Carson enunciated his words carefully.

"The church. You don't . . . you can't be married there."

He heaved a heavy sigh.

"And anything else is . . ."

"I know, angel. Anything else is not considered a valid marriage."

Of all the problems he had anticipated coming between them, he had never thought of this one. Now he wondered why. A girl raised in a convent school, from a strict, religious home. Why hadn't he thought to expect this? And if he had expected it, what the hell could he have done about it, anyway?

With gentle hands he drew her shoulders back and again tried to dry her tears, this time with his lips. Their saltiness seemed to sting his very heart, bringing moisture to his own eyes.

"I know how important the church is to you and your family," he said at last. "But I also know how important you are to me. Whatever I have to do to marry you and make you happy, I will do."

"Do you mean? . . ."

He grinned. "It isn't like we don't believe in the same God. No matter what we call Him, you can't tell me He doesn't want us to be together."

For a moment she let the simple truth of his observation wash over her, dissolving her fears like a heaven-sent rain cleanses the earth, allowing her euphoria to return.

She threw her arms around his neck. "Oh, Carson, why did I doubt you?" Her lips found his.

"Beats me," he mumbled into her mouth, just before he sealed their lips, their loves, their very souls. But again he drew back, feeling the torturous plea of her body, the uncomfortable warning of his.

"But I will have a hard time convincing him if he throws me out of the house for seducing his daughter."

"I'll come to your room."

"No." Awkwardly, he turned her so her back rested against his chest. Lamplight played off the yellow satin and lace of her gown, casting her in a golden radiance. He wrapped his arms around her, pulling her close against him, clasping his palms over her breasts, feeling his body react as he did so.

He knew they should head upstairs, but he hadn't held her in so long. A few minutes more, he promised himself. A few minutes to hold her, to talk to her. To hear her voice and fill his senses with her.

She snuggled against him. "What do you think Pia and Santos are doing right now?"

He grunted. "Let's not think about that."

She wriggled against him, snuggling closer. "I hope it worked out."

"Worked out? What?"

"Their wedding night."

He chuckled. "Why shouldn't it work out?"

"Because she was frightened. You know, her being so small and all."

He tightened his grip on her breasts, kneading them sensuously through her layers of clothing. "Don't worry about it, angel."

"I can't help worrying. I want it to be good for her, like it was for me."

His hands stilled. "Like it *is* for you," he corrected. "It will be good for her. Santos will see to that."

"I hope so. It's . . ."

"Aurelia, I am in no condition to discuss someone else's wedding night. Trust me, just because a man has long legs and broad shoulders, it doesn't mean . . . ah . . . what I'm saying is . . ."

"You mean he — ?"

"Shh," he cautioned. "Santos will be able to handle the situation without our involvement." He stirred. "Maybe we should hit the sack."

"Not yet." She squeezed his arms, hugging them to her. "We can talk about something else. You choose the topic."

He relented. Her body felt so good against his. Too good. "How 'bout the letter I received from my sister Ginny today?" he suggested. "From the sound of things, I need to go see what the family is up to."

She struggled to turn in his arms.

"Hold still," he instructed softly. "Do you think I would head out for Texas without taking you along?"

She settled down again, and he chuckled. "Seems my brother Kale up and married Ellie."

"Ellie? Isn't she the new widow of your other brother? Benjamin, wasn't it?"

"Hmm, and Kale is — was — the biggest rounder of us all. How would you like a wedding trip to Texas?"

She struggled to turn around. *"Sí, Sí, Sí."*

"Hold still. Can't you see I'm courting you?"

"I liked my way better."

He chuckled again. "Maybe I'll surprise you before long."

After a few minutes of glorious silence, she recalled the question she had asked when they first returned. "Tell me what you and Papá were discussing so seriously."

He hesitated, then answered. "Nuncio Quiroz was seen at the mine late today."

"What happened?"

"Nothing yet." He fluffed a hand through her hair. She had removed the tall comb while they were still in the carriage, draping the mantilla about her neck. Now she was swathed in layers of lace. "Your father expects him to be gone tomorrow. Likely he returned to fetch personal things he left behind. He worked in that mine a long time."

"Close to twenty years," she responded, tightening her hold on Carson.

Rising then, he pulled her into his arms. "That's a sour note to go to bed on." He kissed her soundly, while holding her at bay. One more nuzzle from those aroused little nipples, and he knew he likely wouldn't be able to resist a taste—and one thing always seemed to lead to another.

"By the way," he told her when they reached the stairs, "Rodrigo and Zita want us to go riding with them after breakfast."

Her tired eyes lit up.

"A late breakfast." He kissed her one last time, then swatted her bottom. "Get some sleep now."

Chapter Twenty

Dawn had not yet broken over the ragged hills of Catorce when María shook Aurelia awake with a message that set her heart to racing.

The gray vellum notepaper embossed with a silver crested "M" had come from the downstairs library desk. She did not recognize the bold black scrawl, but her heart fluttered at Carson's signature.

He meant it. He said he would surprise her and he meant it. But she had not expected it so soon.

Meet me outside the kitchen, same as Guanajuato.

In the back of her wardrobe, Aurelia found the maid's costume she had worn to sneak into his room that morning so long ago. Quickly donning it, she had to stop twice to peer in the looking glass and pinch her cheeks. Where would he take her?

Never mind where. If he couldn't find a secluded place, she certainly could. She considered leaving her undergarments at home.

But what if she was stopped by one of the real maids? No, she would let him remove them this time — one by one. As long as he was quick about it. Her skin

411

tingled at the mere thought of lying in his arms again.

Aurelia slipped through the house without being seen, out the back door, around the corner.

Blood pounded in her temples, at the pulse point above her collarbone and low, deliciously low. Anticipation ran high.

Fear fell hard, like a boulder from the mountain peaks surrounding Catorce.

Like the hand Nuncio Quiroz clamped over her open mouth, lifting it only to stuff a filthy gag inside. Her inferior strength was no match for his brawn, although that did not stop her struggling until he bound her, hands and feet, then stuffed her inside a canvas bag, just like those used at the mine. She thought she might suffocate from the ore dust.

She thought how that might be the best thing for her.

Her body, which had wept with joy in anticipation of Carson's loving touch, now recoiled in parched, stiff fear of this demon's promise — a promise of torture and pain, of humiliation.

A promise he would keep this time, for bound and gagged as she was, she could offer no resistance other than in her heart.

By the time she was thrown unceremoniously onto a hard surface, her fear had grown so all-encompassing that she did not at first recognize the next voice she heard.

"Careful there."

Tío Luís? From long-standing habit, her spirits lifted at his familiar voice. Here was a savior, a member of her family. Then her head cleared, allowing harsh memories to rush in. Tío Luís was no friend.

"Remove that sack," he was instructing. "Careful now, careful. If she is marred, there will be questions."

Although she could see nothing, she knew the hands that obeyed her uncle belonged to Nuncio Quiroz. They were large. They were bold. They slithered up her legs, sliding her skirt before them, lifting the sack by degrees.

Never had she been so glad of anything as that she had worn undergarments, even though she knew these simple garments would not protect her from vicious men.

His hands struggled to work between her legs searching for the opening in the crotch of her bloomers, hindered by the bonds he himself had tied. She rocked her body back and forth, cringing at the touch of his hands, at her memories of his hands.

Suddenly, she heard a slap, as though someone had been backhanded, and Nuncio Quiroz's hands fell away from her. Aurelia crumpled to the floor with the sack still covering her upper body.

"What'd you go and do that for?" Quiroz demanded.

She visualized the difference in size between her uncle and the mine superintendent. No doubt who would win a physical struggle between the two men.

Evidently, this was not a physical struggle — for anyone except herself. The sack was jerked from her body.

She lay sprawled on the floor of a hut she recognized. Back of the fire pits, behind the mine, she thought.

"Don't look so surprised," Tío Luís barked into her face. "You have only yourself to blame."

If the gag in her mouth had not tasted so foul, she

413

would have been grateful for it. She had no desire to speak to this despicable man other than to demand he set her free, which she knew would be futile.

"Leave her with me," Quiroz argued. "Let me take care of her until time to leave."

Her heart beat so fast at the fear of finding herself alone with this beast that she thought she might expire before Nuncio Quiroz could get his hands on her again.

"Not on your life," Tío Luís barked. "She must remain unmarked."

"I wouldn't mark her so you could tell," Quiroz grumbled. His eyes held a promise she had no trouble interpreting.

She turned her face.

"No one saw you leaving the mansion?" her uncle demanded of Quiroz.

Squatting on his haunches nearby, Quiroz shook his head.

"How did you get the message inside the house?"

"That kid, the one from the village."

Tío Luís checked his gold pocket watch. "Figure we have three . . . four hours until the household awakens. Santos was the early riser and he's out of the way."

"If that Ranger hombre gives us trouble, he's mine," Quiroz said.

"Fine. Only wait until we get her away from here before you tackle him. Enrique will meet us in Matehuala. He is bringing a judge."

Luís smiled down at Aurelia, a self-satisfied smile full of malice. "Thought you got out of marrying him, did you? You didn't count on the determination of your old uncle."

Marry Enrique? She struggled to speak.

"Rest assured, I have my reasons," he told her. "Before I finish, you will be the only heir to this business. With your marriage to Enrique, it will all belong to me—the mine, the mint, the rancho."

Quiroz grunted from across the room.

"Other than what it costs to take care of . . . details."

Details? Her family? Mamá? Papá? Santos? Pia?

And Carson was to be left to Nuncio Quiroz.

Suddenly, she knew that if she had the choice, she would prefer Quiroz's manhandling, even her death at his hands, to what this uncle by marriage planned for her family.

But of course, she did not have a choice.

"Why don't you let me take her down to the chapel?" Quiroz suggested. "You could stop there for her. Here, they are sure to find her."

"That chapel is the first place they will look," Luís objected.

"She didn't tell anybody about the chapel." Quiroz's eyes mocked her with the knowledge of what he could have done in the tunnel chapel, with what he would do yet, given the chance. "She didn't have guts enough to tell about the chapel."

"I am not taking the chance," Luís replied.

Quiroz shrugged. "Fine by me, but the mine is the first place they'll look."

"She isn't in the mine."

"They won't stop until they tear this end of town apart."

415

"It will take a few hours yet for them to realize she is missing. Then it will take more time to get their bearings. I know Domingo. He will spend the morning worrying over what has happened to her before he settles on a way to find her. By that time, we will have the silver bars loaded and be gone."

"That Ranger hombre ain't so easy," Quiroz objected.

"He doesn't know our ways, either. I know what you are after, Quiroz, and you can have her if Enrique decides he doesn't want her."

Luís frowned down at Aurelia. "Hear that, Relie. You have a chance to save yourself. Enrique is smitten with you for some fool reason. I promised him the chance to try to make a good wife out of you. It is up to you whether you live peaceably with Enrique or—" he jerked his head toward Quiroz, "or get yourself thrown to him."

The morning sun accompanied by a brisk autumn breeze streamed through the bedroom windows Carson had opened the evening before. He stretched, limbering tight muscles. Lordy, he was getting soft, still in bed and here it was mid-morning. He bounced his palms on the side of the bed. Such a soft bed. If Aurelia were here beside him, he would be tempted to lie abed a while longer.

His body definitely liked that idea, so he rose in self-defense. He whistled while he shaved, knowing his high spirits came from their talk the evening before. He had worried over her not enjoying the wedding.

416

Then when he discovered her reasons, he had gone weak-kneed at the thought of losing her. But he hadn't lost her.

Nosiree. He surely had not. Rinsing his face, he patted his skin dry, then mopped up spills around the washbowl and pitcher. Here he was about to get himself hitched.

And Kale, too. The idea of it — two Jarretts bitin' the dust at near the same time! What was the world comin' to?

Downstairs, he was disappointed to find Aurelia still asleep, but she needed her rest. All the worrying she had done lately was enough to tire her out.

He grinned, taking his place at the empty table. The maid filled his coffee cup, brought him orange juice, then scurried off to fetch his breakfast.

She really beat all, Aurelia did, worrying over Santos and Pia that way. He had always known women were a bit like that, but lordy . . . His heart pumped extra hard, thinking about Aurelia and their future together.

When Don Domingo came to the table, Carson considered speaking to him about their situation then and there. He hesitated. Maybe he should wait until Santos returned. Likely he would need someone to back him up.

"What are your plans, Jarrett?" Don Domingo asked into his reveries.

"Well, sir . . . ah . . . your daughter and I agreed to go riding later this morning with Don Rodrigo and Señorita Tapis."

"Later?" Don Domingo questioned. "We had better

417

send someone to fetch that young lady, then."

"No, sir, let her sleep. She's been through a lot lately."

Don Domingo eyed him, moving a shoulder when the maid set his coffee and orange juice down, while never breaking eye contact. "You were a big help in our little difficulty, Jarrett. Glad Santos asked you in on it."

"Thank you, sir. I'm happy to have been here."

Doña Bella swished into the room. *"Buenas días, Señor Jarrett."*

"Good morning," Carson returned. He rose until she was seated then settled back down. It took a moment for her frown to register as one of disapproval.

"Where is Relie?" she questioned him.

"Still asleep, I suppose, señora."

Doña Bella's frown deepened. She held his gaze. "She returned to bed after your rendezvous?"

"¿Excusame?"

Her expression hardened. By way of reply, she handed a folded sheet of notepaper across the table.

He opened it, read the message, then reread it, while his coffee settled like hard rock ore in the bottom of his stomach. When he tried to speak, he had to clear his throat twice to make himself heard.

"I didn't write this. What does it mean?"

"You tell me. I found it on her bedside table when I looked in on her," Doña Bella informed him. "Her nightclothes were strewn across her empty bed."

Carson scraped back his chair, but when he rose, his legs trembled, and he grabbed the edge of the table for support. "The only thing I know about this message is that Aurelia is in trouble." He regained his balance, turning to her father. "Who delivered it? Find the person. Now."

While the Mazóns found and questioned María, Carson returned to his room, bounding up the stairs, throwing open the door, hoping she would not be lying nude in his bed, praying she would be. Next he checked the ballroom, the cubicle where she had dressed, each room down the hallway from it, staring finally, bleakly, into the one they had shared. The bed where they had loved lay empty, undisturbed.

He returned downstairs carrying his holsters and an extra cartridge belt. The Mazóns waited in the library.

"The message was delivered before dawn by some ragamuffin from the miners' village." Doña Bella's voice broke. Don Domingo patted her shoulders, his own sagging. He watched Carson belt on his holsters.

"What are you doing?"

"Going after her, señor." He heard his own voice quiver.

Don Domingo took a pistol from a drawer in the desk. "I will come with you. She is my daughter, after all."

Carson turned in the doorway, eyed the troubled man and, before he could stop himself, replied, "And she is to be my wife, soon as we find her."

If the words registered, Don Domingo did not betray the fact. He nodded toward a cabinet. "We should arm ourselves with carbines."

In the foyer they met Rodrigo and Zita and hurriedly apprised them of the situation.

Tears sprang to Zita's eyes. "This time it's real."

Carson's jaws clenched against his own fears. "We'll find her."

"I'll help," Rodrigo said. "My horse is saddled."

The three men rushed to the stable yard, where Carson and Don Domingo saddled their own mounts.

The women followed. "What can we do?" Doña Bella cried, wringing a linen handkerchief in a manner that reminded Carson so strongly of Aurelia that he had to look away.

Pray, he started to reply. He held his tongue. No need to suggest the obvious. "Can you find Kino and Joaquín, María's brothers?"

"I will send her after them." Doña Bella hurried back inside the mansion.

Carson stepped into his saddle, plunging the carbine into an attached scabbard. "I'll start at the mine. Someone should go to that chapel in the tunnel."

"Quiroz was last seen at the mine," Don Domingo replied. "That is where I am going."

"Where is the chapel?" Rodrigo questioned.

Suddenly, Zita reached for his pommel. "Help me up. I can show you."

Serphino threw open the stable yard gates and the three horses bounded into the street. The instant they parted ways, however, a train whistle rent the silence.

Don Domingo frowned. "What the hell?"

"What's the matter?" Carson asked.

"We have no departures today."

The three men exchanged glances.

"That train is the only sure way they have of getting her out of town," Carson said.

"Why would—?" Don Domingo began.

420

"There are no answers, señor," Carson cut in, "and we have no time for questions. Pray we guess right."

He turned to Rodrigo. "Ride for the tunnel. If you can make it to the chapel, fine; in any case, get close enough to stop the train . . . if I don't do it before you."

Rodrigo quirked an eyebrow, accepting the challenge. "If I beat you, do I win the girl this time?"

"Not on your life."

Rodrigo tightened his hold on Zita. "This time I wouldn't even try."

María ran from the house on her way to find Kino and Joaquín.

"Tell them to head for the other end of the tunnel," Carson called after her. "Tell them not to let the train get through."

Carson spurred his mount. "Go ahead to the mine, Don Domingo. We may be wrong. She may be there."

"Where are you going?"

"To catch a train," he shouted over his shoulder. Fears for Aurelia simmered like a boiling cauldron in the back of his brain, and he fought to keep them there.

Back behind his working mind. For to save her, he would need every whit of intelligence and common sense he had ever possessed. And a cool head, to boot.

He wove his mount in and out, up and down the narrow bricked streets of Catorce, cursing their slick surface, grateful for Sunfisher's surefootedness.

Smoke plumes from the engine stack seemed hopelessly far away but drew nearer and nearer as he raced to intercept the train. When it came in view, he studied the cars — an engine, a passenger car, and a caboose. Was Aurelia in one of them?

Sunfisher's hooves clattered against the brick streets. The train clacked along the track, smoke churning from its stack. Carson focused on the train one car at a time. First the engine. The engineer, a large man, stuck his head out the window, looking toward the tunnel.

A huge head, shaggy.

Quiroz.

Sweeping his gaze the length of the train, Carson saw another man inside the passenger car. A form, no more. In the caboose, nothing. No one.

Or so it seemed. The train could carry a hundred men, for all he could see from here.

Sunfisher galloped closer. Still they had not seen him.

Where was Aurelia? Was this a chase without meaning? Was she even now lying hurt and needing him somewhere else?

All doubts evaporated when the first shot ricocheted from bricks nearby. Carson shucked his carbine.

The man in the center car fired again.

Luís Reinaldo! The bastard. All they needed to complete the picture was Enrique.

All he needed, Carson corrected, was to find Aurelia safe and well. His blood boiled at the thought of what they might have done to her, at what they intended to do to her.

He drew closer. Another bullet. He dodged to the right, zigged to the left, all the time heading straight for the train.

And then he was there. The caboose whipped by and he turned Sunfisher in beside it. It gained; he pushed his horse.

Eyeing the window from where Reinaldo had fired, he saw no one. Quickly, he scanned the other windows. Nothing.

Reholstering the carbine, he unhooked his rope, limbered it, tossed a loop above his head, then zeroed in on the railing along the back of the caboose.

His loop caught.

"Take care of yourself, Sunfisher," he mumbled, hefting himself from the saddle, clinging, climbing, reaching.

He grabbed the rail, landed with a thwack against the steps, then scrambled aboard. After a glance inside, he flicked his rope free, tossed it off beside the rails, and unhooked the thongs holding his revolvers in place.

His heart throbbed with every turn of the wheels. He glanced into the caboose, found nothing, then climbed up the side of the racing train.

Gaining the top, he flattened himself, got his bearings, and glanced toward the tunnel, which they fast approached.

Rodrigo was there. Did he know about Reinaldo firing from the train? Carson watched Rodrigo climb aboard his horse. His rope was attached to something; he headed off at right angles to the tracks.

The rails. He was pulling the rails apart.

Carson moved. At the juncture between the caboose and the single car, he peered through the doorway, saw nothing, then dropped to his feet on the other side of the coupling.

He peered inside. Reinaldo was nowhere to be seen. But Aurelia was there.

He rushed to her side, his heart pounding. He kissed her face, her frightened eyes. "It's all right," he tried to say, but his mouth was too dry for the words to come out.

Tears leaked from the corners of her eyes and he kissed them away. Fumbling with haste, he removed the gag from her mouth. He braced his feet against the jolt they would receive when the engine hit the ripped-out section of track, fished his knife from his pocket, and cut her bonds.

"Where is Luís?" he asked.

She glanced toward the caboose. Her eyes pleaded with him. "Nuncio . . ."

"I know, angel. It'll be all right." Removing his second revolver, he handed it to her. "If one of them returns before I get back, shoot."

She nodded.

"Shoot to kill," he added. "Don't take a chance on them living to—" He bit back the hated words.

She inhaled quivering lungfuls of fresh air, although her mouth tasted so foul from the filthy gag the air did not seem the least bit clean.

Suddenly, a shot ripped the air. She flinched; Carson gathered her to him. "Shhh. It's Rodrigo. He's at the tunnel. Brace yourself. The train is fixin' to hit a section of ripped-out track. Hold on for dear life and don't climb out until I come for you."

Her smile was faint, but a smile nevertheless. He kissed her, then made for the front of the car. "Be careful," she called to him, her voice trembling.

He turned quickly, a feeble grin on his lips. "Don't shoot Rodrigo if he comes through that door."

424

Rodrigo, it turned out, had shot Reinaldo, toppling the would-be governor from the side of the engine where he had gone for safety.

Carson stared at the man's writhing body as the train passed. Only Quiroz remained a threat.

Carson crept forward. Hadn't he known that sooner or later it would come to this? Hadn't he dreaded it?

Didn't he still?

While he was deciding whether to hold his ground and wait for the train to hit or to go after the man now, the decision was taken from his hands.

With a mighty jolt, the train plunged into the missing section of track. Surging forward undirected, it rammed into the side of the tunnel with a force that rattled his teeth. Desperately, he fought to retain his balance, his sense of direction, watching all the while for Quiroz.

Then, suddenly, Quiroz jumped free of the listing engine. Recalling the superintendent's agility, Carson was on him in a flash. "I promised you something." Carson jerked the man to his feet before Quiroz caught his balance. "Remember? I promised to uphold her honor with my life."

He struck the man's jaw, heard it crunch, and jumped to the side when Quiroz flailed back. Then he struck again at the same place, hoping to add injury to insult . . . or at least a little pain to chase the first.

Quiroz had not slowed down since their fight in the mine. If anything, he fought more ferociously today — likely from finding himself with nothing to lose, everything to gain, Carson mused.

They grappled, while behind them the train rocked

to a stop. It did not topple to its side, but it came so close that Aurelia feared it would. As soon as she found her footing, she scrambled out the nearest door.

Where Carson was she had no idea, since she had been unable to see out the windows. The first person she saw was Rodrigo, who emitted a cheer at the sight of her, then raced to catch her when she crumpled to the ground.

He and Zita reached her at the same time.

"Where is Carson?" she mumbled.

"Gone after the engineer," Rodrigo told her.

"Quiroz." Aurelia struggled to get up.

Zita held her down, cradling her head in her lap. "Rodrigo will see about Carson, Relie. You lie still."

Rodrigo grinned. "Me see about Jarrett? That Ranger can handle himself." But he spoke from over his shoulder, already heading around the caboose where he saw Quiroz land a near-knockout blow to Carson's head, then take off running up the hill.

Rodrigo caught up to Carson, limbering his *reata* as he approached. Carson stood up. Together they watched the running, stumbling man.

"Want me to take him, or do you want to?" Rodrigo offered his rope.

Carson grinned, gasping for breath. "You loop him, I'll hog-tie him."

Both of which tasks were easier than hauling the man down the hill after they trussed him.

"By the saints, Jarrett, the man is solid muscle," Rodrigo quipped.

Carson rubbed his aching jaw. "No need to tell me."

Sunfisher had wandered up to the girls by the time

the two men returned, dragging their captive behind them.

Aurelia managed to stand, then fell into Carson's arms.

"Think they can hold each other up?" Rodrigo questioned Zita. "Or do they need our help?"

Carson grinned. "Get on out of here, both of you. We'll be along."

"What about our two friends?" Rodrigo nodded toward Luís Reinaldo and Nuncio Quiroz.

Carson's mouth tightened. "How 'bout we leave 'em here? Send the authorities to fetch 'em when we get around to it?"

"Suits me." With his arm around Zita, Rodrigo turned toward his horse. "Guess we can count you two out for that ride in the country this afternoon."

"No," Aurelia managed. "Wait for us."

Carson led her to his horse. "Say hello to the señorita, Sunfisher." He kissed Aurelia on the forehead, while he stroked one hand down the horse's nose. "I would ask him to bow to you, angel, but he's plumb tuckered after chasin' that train."

He helped her into the saddle, then climbed up behind her. For a moment they sat, letting the feel of each other settle their jangled senses.

"Where are Mamá and Papá?"

"Lordy, your father is still at the mine looking for you. We had best send someone to fetch him." The morning came back in a rush then. "I think I told him."

"Told him what?"

"That we are getting married. Soon as I found you, that's what I said." He chuckled.

Aurelia leaned against him, felt his arms tighten around her in a protective, wonderful embrace. "What did he say?"

"He didn't reply that I heard." Carson touched spurs to Sunfisher's flanks. "How 'bout we go get an answer while it's still fresh on his mind?"

Chapter Twenty-one

By the time Pia and Santos returned at the end of the week, all that was left to decide was the location of the wedding, for as Doña Bella confided to her new daughter-in-law, "Even if Carson was willing, a week is hardly enough time for a conversion."

"I know where we can have the wedding," Pia told the family, including Zita and Rodrigo, who had been persuaded to stay the week. "In the garden." She looked to her new husband. "Don't you agree, Santos? Wouldn't our garden be a perfect place for their wedding?"

"Our garden?" Doña Bella inquired. "We have no—"

"She means the garden behind the convent school," Santos explained, a gleam in his eyes the still-barely-single men in the group were quick to note.

Aurelia's euphoria had returned in increments during the week as they made wedding plans and wrapped up the mine difficulties.

Her father had not given his blessing to this union, her mother reminded her from time to time. Doña Bella's distressed tone every time she voiced Don

429

Domingo's objection caused Aurelia to wonder which of them had not accepted the marriage — her father or her mother.

"The church has been her life," Aurelia explained one afternoon when she and Carson sat in the patio. He strummed a guitar, while she sat on the fountain edge, studying him, thinking. "She never dreamed her only daughter would be living in sin or that her grandchildren would be born out of wedlock, which will be the case since our marriage cannot be consecrated by the priest."

His fingers stilled on the strings. For an indeterminable time, he stared at her, grim-faced. "What about you, angel? You never dreamed such, either."

"We won't be living in sin. Not in my mind."

"Nor in mine. But I wasn't raised in a convent school."

"Papá will come around," she assured him. "As soon as he stops worrying over Tío Luís's betrayal."

"I hope so. I don't want us to leave Catorce without his blessing."

"Neither do I," she admitted, "but if we have to, we will. I'm going to Texas with you, Carson. Don't think you can get away from here without me."

He grinned at that. "Don't think I would try."

The household was aflutter on the day of the bride and groom's return. Pia's parents had agreed that the couple should stay at the Mazón mansion so the girls could spend time together before Aurelia left.

Zita, too, became a permanent fixture, since Rodrigo decided to wait around to see how Santos was taking to married life.

430

"Thinking of taking the plunge yourself?" Carson had teased.

"Might as well. All my amigos are getting hitched. Won't have anyone left to carouse with." But the gleam in his eyes whenever Zita entered the room betrayed his real reason for considering the state of matrimony.

Siesta had just ended when Serphino alerted the household to the arrival of the bride and groom.

Everyone rushed to the stable yard.

"Don't ask her about it," Carson whispered to Aurelia.

"Do you think I would ask *that*?"

He chuckled. "When you get a notion in your head, I doubt there is anything you wouldn't ask."

In spite of the family standing nearby, she slipped an arm around his waist. "Not that," she whispered. "That's something I will never talk about."

"Never?"

"Never with anyone but you."

Their first glimpse of Pia and Santos reassured both of them. Carson grinned.

"Even if you wanted to ask," he whispered, "don't reckon there's a need."

His throaty voice brought a skip to her already-throbbing heart. The sight of Pia and Santos, so radiant and obviously pleased with themselves, filled her with happiness for them.

And with impatience to get on with her own life. She and Carson had not found a single opportunity to be alone—really alone—since Pia and Santos's wedding. Time was wasting.

That evening after dinner the entire family sat in the

431

patio beside the fountain, where Santos demanded to be brought up to date on the situation at the mine.

"Luís took me for a fool," Don Domingo stated flatly.

"You trusted a friend and brother-in-law," Carson told him in quiet tones. "You cannot fault yourself for that."

The older Mazón stared into the fountain a time before returning to his son's question. "He had been stealing from me from the beginning," he admitted. "Before we built the mint, Quiroz was taking ore out for him, hiding it in that chapel, then smuggling it to Guanajuato. They had a good thing going."

"So that is how he financed his high living?" Santos mused.

"And how he planned to finance his run for the governor's office," Don Domingo added. "He told me the story. I went up to the jail before they moved him to Potosí. He said he had to change his tactics after I started talking about establishing a mint. Since we would no longer ship ore, he would need a way to get to the coinage."

"That's where Enrique came in?" Santos asked.

Don Domingo's teeth clenched. He nodded, still unable to discuss the young man who had ingratiated himself to the Mazón family to the extent that Don Domingo had intended to give him his business. And his daughter.

"Anybody learn the true story behind Enrique?" Santos inquired.

"Like he told Carson," Aurelia answered, "he learned his trade in the mines in Peru. He never saw the University of Madrid. His family was not old Spanish, either. In fact, he was orphaned young. And now he is in jail. He will be branded a criminal for life."

"Where did Tío Luís find him?"

Aurelia shrugged. "Men like Tío Luís can always find other evil men to do their bidding."

"Stop calling that man *tío,*" Doña Bella instructed them. "Guadalupe petitioned for an annulment of her marriage when she learned the truth. My sister may be a social climber, but she was not involved in Luís's illegal schemes."

"So now it's over," Santos mused.

"*Sí,*" his father answered, "thanks to you for taking matters into your own hands." He turned serious eyes on Carson. "And to you, Jarrett. You saved my business and my daughter's life, at great risk to your own."

Carson squirmed under the scrutiny. "Rodrigo here played a part in the final scene."

"And to you, Don Rodrigo," Don Domingo added.

"So what does that mean, Papá?" Aurelia questioned.

He studied her with weary eyes, looking to Carson, then back to his daughter. His face was grim-set when he answered. "It means if you decide to go through with that thing up at the garden, I will be there."

Her heart pumped waves of happiness through her body, sending moisture to her eyes. "*Gracias, Papá.*"

Ignoring her, Don Domingo scraped back his chair. "Time for us to retire, Mamá. You children stay down here a while if you like. I will send Lucinda to keep watch."

Carson followed them to the staircase. "*Gracias, Don Domingo.* This means a lot to both of us."

433

"Do not thank me, Jarrett. I could see my choices—agree to it or lose her. I do not approve of the way you are going about it, but I will not stand in your way."

Carson nodded.

"About Rancho Mazón," the elder Mazón added. "Santos had the right idea. You are a man who gets things done. You will do a good job running the ranch."

Aurelia's eyes glistened when Carson returned to sit beside her. "Papá agreed," she whispered.

He nodded, still a bit dazed. "Conditionally—I think."

Santos broached the subject. "What have you decided about the ranch?"

"We'll give it a shot," Carson said. "First, we need to visit my family."

Santos laughed. "That may take a while, compadre, considering how they're strung out."

Carson laughed, too.

"We plan to return by early spring," Aurelia told them.

"By that time, our house here in Catorce will be finished," Pia said.

Santos nodded. "And you two can set up housekeeping at Rancho Mazón."

"Can't promise we will stay forever," Carson told him. "But it's a good place to get started."

Rodrigo spoke up. "Why don't I drive those Arabians to the ranch for you, Jarrett? Save you having to worry about them."

At that suggestion, all eyes focused on Rodrigo and Zita, who sat blushing beside him.

"And give you an excuse to come back this way?" Santos questioned.

"Suits me," Carson agreed. "Only Santos and I had best warn you about these girls."

The girls protested, but Santos and Carson persisted, ribbing Rodrigo, telling secrets — a few of them — while the girls fidgeted, blushed, and generally tried to hush them up.

"In other words," Santos finished, his hand massaging the back of Pia's neck in a way that made the other two men squirm, since they were still under the watchful eye of the dueña, "if you are not interested in a life filled with intrigue and chaos, you had best hightail it."

Rodrigo handled the insinuations in typical charro fashion, strutting a little more than the average man would have done. "I have kept my eyes open the last couple of weeks, and from the looks of things, you two can use an extra hand keeping these ladies in line."

The wedding was set for mid-morning two days hence. Since it would not be church sanctioned, there was some question about using the garden. In the end Padre Bucareli relented, with the provision that no one from the cathedral or convent attend. After all, Don Domingo always financed the feast of San Francisco and a number of other parish projects.

The alcalde agreed to perform the civil ceremony.

"Hope he doesn't recognize me," Carson quipped.

Aurelia laughed, too happy for anything to dampen her spirits. "If he does, we can spend our honeymoon in jail."

"Not on your life, angel. I promised you a surprise."

For her wedding gown, her mother insisted on a silver faille costume that had never been worn, but Aurelia objected. Searching her wardrobe, she pulled out an old gown, one of her favorites, designed of tissue taffeta with large bouffant sleeves and a wide skirt she always had trouble maneuvering down the staircase. It swished and crinkled when she walked.

And it was yellow.

"That skirt will not fit in the carriage," her mother objected.

"For the short ride to the garden it will, Mamá. I will wear riding clothes when we leave."

"I still think you should take one of our carriages on your wedding trip instead of riding horses," her mother fussed.

To no avail, of course, since traveling all the way to Texas in a carriage would present more problems than they bargained for, broken axles and such.

The sun was high by the time they reached the garden. Pia, Zita, and Doña Bella had all squeezed into the carriage at Aurelia's insistence.

"Please ride with me. I won't see any of you for months." But if she had thought to chatter on the way to the ceremony, she hadn't counted on a last minute case of jitters.

"It's natural," Pia consoled. "You know how nervous I was all day long. If only my wedding had been in the morning."

"You can still back out," her mother suggested.

Aurelia gripped her mother's cold, clammy hands in her own, which closely resembled them. "I have no doubts about Carson, Mamá. No doubts about anything. It's just . . ."

She paused, knowing her mother would never understand. Pia would. And from the looks of their developing relationship, Zita might someday.

But she doubted that her mother had ever experienced the depth of emotions she had known with Carson in the short time they had been together.

Thinking on it, her pulse quickened and her hands warmed. She would not see these three special women for several months, but it seemed even longer since she had lain in Carson's arms.

And he had said he had a surprise for her.

Anticipation warmed her cold feet and she skipped toward the garden, her bridesmaids rushing to catch up.

"Pia, the setting is perfect." Aurelia twirled in a circle as she viewed the fountain, the sundial where the alcalde would preside, the fruit trees glowing in red and gold autumn splendor against towering green pines. Jagged mountains rose around them as a backdrop to it all, lending a majesty not to be found inside any building, no matter how grand, no matter how sacred.

Then she saw Carson approach, flanked by Santos and Rodrigo. He wore the black charro suit from Santos's wedding, as did his attendants, their sombreros carried in their hands. Her father, similarly attired, kept pace.

At the sight, tears formed in her eyes, and by the time Carson reached her, they threatened to roll down her cheeks.

His eyes warmed her, caressed her, reassured her. Reaching into an inside pocket, he withdrew a handkerchief with which he dabbed her tears. "Figured I might need this," he whispered, before greeting her mother and the girls.

When she slipped her hand through his elbow, he fastened it there with his other hand, clasping her with a firm touch, steady and loving.

The civil ceremony was brief, ending when the alcalde advised Carson that he could kiss the bride.

"Wait a minute." Carson fished into another pocket. "We forgot something."

Her left hand trembled when he slipped the gold ring on her third finger. He grinned that wry grin of his. "Something a lady once gave me for luck."

She looked from the gold ring to his loving eyes. "Something a gentleman once gave me for love," she whispered.

"One of the few good things to come from Guanajuato." Carson eyed Rodrigo. "That, and a good friend."

He kissed her then, soundly but quickly, and they left the garden. Before he handed her into the carriage, however, Padre Bucareli and the nuns approached, hugging her in turn. They did not voice approval—in fact, they made no mention of the marriage—but she could tell they still loved her, and that sent Carson digging for his handkerchief again.

"Keep her out of mischief," the padre advised Carson with a twinkle in his eyes.

"I will try, padre," he answered.

It was harder to leave than she had expected. Even Santos blinked back tears when he hugged her goodbye.

"Couldn't send you off in better hands, Relie. Jarrett

will take care of you."

"Spring isn't far away," Pia added. "You can stay with us in our new house before you move to the ranch."

Doña Bella hugged her daughter silently, then buried her face in her handkerchief, while Don Domingo shook Carson's hand.

"Take care of her, Jarrett. She has been raised proper; might not take to wilderness living."

Santos laughed at that. "She'll do fine, Papá. You will see when they return."

Only Zita and Rodrigo remained dry-eyed, and Aurelia recognized the look all too well. They were as engrossed with each other as she and Carson had been at Pia and Santos's wedding.

"Don't get married until we return," she whispered in Zita's ear.

"Then hurry back," Zita urged.

They rode away, each pulling a pack mule, one laden with Aurelia's satchels and a trunk, the other with provisions Carson had insisted on seeing to personally.

She knew where they were going, although she did not intend to spoil his plans by letting on — to the lodge where Santos and Pia had spent their honeymoon. She had overheard Carson and Santos discussing it the evening before.

They entered the tunnel and rode past the chapel carved into the side of the mountain, the chapel that had caused so much heartache, the chapel where Carson had saved her from the clutches of Nuncio Quiroz.

"We could have had the wedding there, I suppose, if . . ." Her words drifted off. No use talking about things they could have done. They were set on a course of their own choosing, one she would not change for anything in the world.

"Maybe we can have our children christened there," he replied.

She let the darkness of the tunnel enclose them like a giant black womb, nourishing his words, her thoughts, their situation. They still had many things to work out in the days and months and years ahead. But they would do it. She did not for a moment doubt that.

Before they reached the cutoff to the lodge, he drew rein and studied a crumpled map that he had fished from his pocket.

"The cutoff is about a kilometer or so further," she supplied without remembering she had intended to feign surprise when they reached the lodge.

He glanced at her, that wry grin tipping his lips. "Oh? You know where we are headed?"

She lifted her chin, challenging him, unwilling to give herself away.

Finally, he returned the map to his pocket and pulled the reins toward a dim trail that led down a steep incline in the opposite direction from the lodge.

She sat her horse a minute.

"Come on. You led me across this country once," he told her. "Now it's my turn."

An hour of hard riding later, they crossed a creek and headed up the side of a mountain. He drew rein again, this time in a sparse grove of oak trees beside a cave carved into the cliff.

"It isn't what you would call a waterfall," he mused, indicating a creek that tumbled down the mountainside. "But with your imagination, I expect we'll never know the difference."

Dismounting, he swept his Stetson in a wide arc. "Your honeymoon suite, ma'am." He lifted her from the saddle and carried her inside. "Stay put, while I get things settled."

She laughed, both surprised and delighted. The cave was large enough to walk around in. And it was clean. She glanced to the corners. Not even any cobwebs.

"Kino and Joaquín did a good job cleaning the place," he acknowledged. He stowed their gear in one corner. "Santos agreed to add the time they spent out here to their tally sheet for repayment of the silver."

"I feel guilty about that," she mused. "It was all my fault."

He glanced up with a grin. "Santos will go easy on them, so don't you start regretting anything."

"I don't regret it. It was the only way for us to get together."

He chuckled. "The only sure way. All those days and nights with you . . . I knew if I didn't win the girl, I would sure as shootin' lose my soul trying."

By the time he finished, he had laid out a wedding feast of cold roast beef, tamales, and empanadas, some filled with meat, others with a sweet raisin sauce, along with a joggled bottle of champagne to toast their new life and a feather comforter for their marriage bed.

She clapped her hands to her lips, letting the thrill and excitement build to excruciating levels within her.

"What have I missed?" he asked, surveying his handiwork.

"It won't be the same, you know," she whispered.

He frowned.

"I mean, if you don't make your own weapons and kill our food."

Taking her hands gently in his, he transferred them from her lips to his, clasping them against his skin, staring deeply into her eyes. "By the time this journey is finished, you won't want to hear the word *squirrel* again."

She moved her hands to either side of his face, pulling him slowly toward her until their lips touched.

"I love my surprise," she whispered.

His lips met hers, caressing them with delicate, delicious, increasingly demanding strokes.

Fumbling then, he reached for the buttons on her riding jacket. His mouth closed over hers, delving into her sweetness. He found himself swimming in her passion.

She tried to help him remove her clothing, but he resisted. "I've never done this before, angel. You were always one step ahead of me, remember?"

But he let her help with his own garments, and at length they stood amid a pile of clothing. The late afternoon sun streaked great shafts of light into the mouth of the cave, highlighting their bodies.

He held her neck between his palms, kissing her lips, then her cheeks, traveling to her neck, where her pulse beat for him . . . for him alone.

He drew her back, perusing her sun-drenched body. "You are so beautiful. Your body looks like spun gold."

She studied his body, partitioned into segments of dark and light. "And you look like the Artist may have let His creativity run unchecked." She traced the lines around his neck where his shirt collar ended, found the

442

line on his arm where his sleeve had stopped, then fingered the white streak running across his forehead that marked the band of his Stetson.

"Hmm, He did sorta run amuck with me."

She kissed his neck, running her tongue along the collar line. "He knew what I liked best," she whispered when a quiver ran the length of his body.

His palms clasped her buttocks, and her own body trembled. He drew her close, holding her tightly.

His chest rumbled against her breasts. "Angel, angel, what you do to me." He stroked her thighs, pressing her close against him, and she felt his passion grow with each stroke—and hers along with it.

Suddenly, he lifted her off the floor and in two steps deposited her on top of the pallet, following her, entering her, thrusting deep . . . holding steady.

"Ah, angel, it has been too long."

Blood pounded at her neck and at points all over her body. Pounded and pumped, as Carson moved in an aggravatingly slow rhythm until suddenly the sun shafts burst into great balls of fire, blinding her, burning her, searing fire and life through her body.

She clung to his now-wet shoulders, waiting for the lightning to stop flashing through her brain, relishing the magnificence she had known but not known, expected but not expected.

"You surprised me again," she mumbled against his wet neck.

He chuckled. "Surprised myself. Next time we'll take it slow."

And they did, loving again as soon as he recovered. Afterwards, she snuggled against him, holding him tightly against herself. "Do you think we made our first baby?"

He sobered. "With the trip ahead of us, I hope not."

"You wouldn't be sorry, though, would you?"

His chin nuzzled the top of her head. "No. Not for one minute."

"Do you think that's the reason we feel this desperate need to —" she snuggled closer to him, "to do this?"

He drew her back and stared, grinning, into her smiling face. Her lips were parted. They quivered a bit, reminding him again of a Comanche bow that had just released an arrow. He knew exactly where that arrow had landed.

"Do you?" she prompted.

"Do I what?" he questioned, lost in the magical nonsense of this woman, his wife. *His wife.*

"Do you think we feel this desperate yearning to make love because we need to make babies?"

He laughed at that. "Partly, I suppose." He kissed her soundly. "Mostly I think it's because —" he kissed her again, a loud, smacking kiss, "because it's so damned much fun."

Later they sat side by side on a log and ate their wedding meal, Aurelia wrapped loosely in a sheet, Carson wearing only his breeches.

"So you prefer squirrel to Mazón beef," he teased.

"I prefer you," she answered.

They drank the champagne, all that didn't bubble out when he removed the cork.

"What a honeymoon," she laughed. "Champagne in a cave."

"It won't be all hardship," he promised. "In San An-

444

tone, we will stay a night at the Menger Hotel. You did bring your yellow dress . . . the one from our wedding?"

"*Sí*," she told him. "I stuffed it in a satchel, with Mamá insisting all the while that I would never need such a gown in Texas."

He chuckled, thinking of his family, wondering how she would take to them. "Never can tell what we'll find in Texas."

A wide grin bowed her lips. "And here?"

He kissed her. "Here we know exactly what we will find," he whispered. "Love. Enough love to see us through everything ahead, enough love to last a lifetime."

445

Author's Note

Real de Catorce and Guanajuato are two of my favorite places in Mexico. My husband and I first visited them in 1970 with two couples who fall under the classifications of both family and friends, Bobby Mae and Don Huss and Robert Henry and Marian Kidd. Real de Catorce is a virtual ghost town today, although a few people still live there. The remains of the once-opulent city are so vivid as to have remained clear and intriguing in my memory all these years. Guanajuato is a picture-book town, straight out of a fairy tale. Travelers, both the real and the armchair kind, as I often am, can find information on both places in travel books such as *Insight Guides*.

My major research source for Real de Catorce is a book I purchased on the 1970 trip, *El Real de Catorce* by Octaviano Cabrera Ipiña. A special thanks to friends, Raul and Blanca Macias, who, at great expense of time and effort, translated this book for me, in the process discovering that one of Raul's ancestors worked the silver mines in Catorce.

This is the second story in my "Jarrett Family Sagas." The first, *Sweet Autumn Surrender*, told the story of Kale and Ellie Jarrett, mentioned here. The next book will feature a younger sister to Carson and Kale, Delta Jarrett, in a story of passion, love, and intrigue that takes us from a Mississippi River showboat to the decks of a pirate ship and back again, from St. Louis, Missouri to the swampy bayous of Louisiana. Once again, I will explore places and cultures the reader may enjoy visiting later, either in person or through additional reading.